NOTHING MORE to TELL

BOOKS BY KAREN M. McMANUS

One of Us Is Lying

Two Can Keep a Secret

One of Us Is Next

The Cousins

You'll Be the Death of Me

Nothing More to Tell

NOTHING MORE to TELL

KAREN M. McMANUS

DELACORTE PRESS

Text copyright © 2022 by Karen M. McManus, LLC
Jacket photo © 2022 by Design Pics/Getty Images; additional figures © 2022 by iStock/Getty Images
Jacket lettering by Kerri Resnick
Jacket design by Alison Impey

All rights reserved. Published in the United States by Delacorte Press, an imprint of Random House Children's Books, a division of Penguin Random House LLC, New York.

Delacorte Press is a registered trademark and the colophon is a trademark of Penguin Random House LLC.

Visit us on the Web! GetUnderlined.com

Educators and librarians, for a variety of teaching tools, visit us at RHTeachersLibrarians.com

Library of Congress Cataloging-in-Publication Data is available upon request.
ISBN 978-0-593-17590-3 (trade) — ISBN 978-0-593-17592-7 (lib. bdg.) — ISBN 978-0-593-17591-0 (ebook) —
ISBN 978-0-593-57257-3 (international edition)

The text of this book is set in 12-point Adobe Garmond.
Interior design by Ken Crossland

Printed in the United States of America

10 9 8 7 6 5 4 3 2 1
First Edition

Random House Children's Books supports the First Amendment and celebrates the right to read.

For Ro and Allison

CHAPTER ONE

BRYNN

"Do you have a favorite crime?"

The girl sitting beside me in the spacious reception area asks the question so brightly, with such a wide smile, that I'm positive I must have misheard her. "A favorite *what*?" I ask.

"Crime," she says, still smiling.

Okay. Did not mishear. "In general, or—" I start cautiously.

"From the show," she says, a note of impatience creeping into her voice. Which is fair. I should have known what she meant, considering we're sitting in the middle of temporary office space for *Motive*.

I try to recover. "Oh, yeah, of course. Hard to pick. They're all so . . ." What's the right word here? "Compelling."

"I'm obsessed with the Story case," she says, and bam—she's off. I'm impressed by all the rich detail she remembers from a show that aired more than a year ago. She's obviously a *Motive* expert, whereas I'm a more recent convert to the true-crime

1

arm of journalism. Truth be told, I wasn't expecting to land an interview for this internship. My application was . . . unconventional, to say the least.

Desperate times and all that.

Less than two months ago, in October of my senior year, my life was fully on track. I was living in Chicago, editor in chief of the school paper, applying early decision to my dream school, Northwestern. Two of my best friends planned on staying local too, so we were already dreaming about getting an apartment together. And then: one disaster after the other. I was fired from the paper, wait-listed at Northwestern, and informed by my parents that Dad's job was transferring him back to company headquarters.

Which meant returning to my hometown of Sturgis, Massachusetts, and moving into the house my parents had been renting to my uncle Nick since we'd left. "It'll be a fresh start," Mom said, conveniently forgetting the part where I'd been desperate to leave four years ago.

Since then, I've been scrambling to find some kind of internship that might make Northwestern take a second look at me. My first half dozen rejections were all short, impersonal form letters. Nobody had the guts to say what they were really thinking: *Dear Ms. Gallagher, since your most-viewed article as editor of the school paper was a compilation of dick pics, you are not suitable for this position.*

To be clear, I neither took nor posted the dick pics. I'm just the loser who left the newspaper office door unlocked and forgot to log out of the main laptop. It doesn't really matter, though, because my name was in the byline that got screenshotted a thousand times and eventually ended up on BuzzFeed with the headline WINDY CITY SCHOOL SCANDAL: PRANK OR PORNOGRAPHY?

Both, obviously. After the seventh polite rejection, it occurred to me that when something like that is your number one result in a Google search, there's no point trying to hide it. So when I applied to *Motive,* I took a different tack.

The girl beside me is still talking, wrapping up an impressively in-depth analysis of the Story family saga. "Where do you go to school?" she asks. She's wearing a cute moto jacket over a graphic T-shirt and black jeans, and it comforts me that we're dressed somewhat alike. "I'm a sophomore at Emerson. Majoring in media arts with a minor in journalism, but I'm thinking about flipping those."

"I'm still in high school," I say.

"Really?" Her eyes pop. "Wow, I didn't realize this internship was even open to high school students."

"I was surprised too," I say.

Motive wasn't on the list of internships I'd compiled with my former guidance counselor's help; my fourteen-year-old sister, Ellie, and I came across it when we were combing through Boston.com. Until we did a Google search on *Motive,* I hadn't realized that the show's host, Carly Diaz, had temporarily relocated from New York to Boston last summer to be near a sick parent. *Motive* isn't a household name, exactly, but it's a buzzy, upstart true-crime show. Right now the show only airs on a small cable station, but there are rumors that it might get picked up by one of the big streamers soon.

The Boston.com article was headlined CARLY DIAZ MAKES AND BREAKS HER OWN RULES, accompanied by a photo of Carly in a bright pink trench coat, standing arms akimbo in the middle of Newbury Street. She didn't look like the kind of person who'd judge you for a public setback; she looked more like the kind of person who'd expect you to own it.

"So do you work for your school paper?" the girl asks.

Way to twist the knife, Emerson Girl. "Not currently, no."

"Really?" Her brow furrows. "Then how—"

"Brynn Gallagher?" the receptionist calls. "Carly will see you now."

"Carly?" Emerson Girl's eyes widen as I scramble to my feet. "Whoa. I didn't know she was doing the interviews herself."

"Here goes nothing," I say. Suddenly Emerson Girl and her endless questions feel like a safe harbor, and I smile at her like she's an old friend as I loop my messenger bag over my shoulder. "Wish me luck."

She gives me a thumbs-up. "You got this."

I follow the receptionist down a short, narrow hallway into a large conference room with floor-to-ceiling windows overlooking Back Bay. I can't focus on the view, though, because Carly Diaz gets up from her chair at the end of the table with a megawatt smile, extending her hand toward me. "Brynn, welcome," she says.

I'm so flustered that I almost say *You're welcome* in return but manage to catch myself just in time. "Thank you," I say, grasping her hand. "It's so nice to meet you." The phrase *larger than life* springs to mind, even though Carly would be tiny without her four-inch heels. But she radiates energy, like she's lit from within. Her dark hair is impossibly thick and shiny, her makeup is impeccable, and she's wearing such a simple yet elegant dress that it makes me want to throw out my entire wardrobe and start over.

"Please, have a seat," Carly says, settling back into her chair as the receptionist slips into the hallway. "Help yourself to a drink if you'd like."

Glass tumblers are in front of us, on either side of a pitcher that's filled to the brim with water and ice. I weigh my slight thirst against the strong possibility of spilling the pitcher's contents all over myself or, worse yet, the laptop beside Carly. "No thanks, I'm good."

Carly folds her hands in front of her, and I can't help but notice her rings. She's wearing one on almost every finger, all bold designs in rich gold. Her nails are glossy with dark red polish and perfectly shaped, but short. "All right," she says, smirking a little. "You know why you're here, right?"

"For an interview?" I ask hopefully.

"Sure." The smirk gets bigger. "We received almost five hundred resumes for this internship. Mostly local college and grad students, but a few willing to relocate for the opportunity." My heart sinks a little as she adds, "It's hard to stand out when there's that much competition, but I have to admit, I've never come across an application quite like yours. One of my producers, Lindzi, saw it first and forwarded it right away."

Carly presses a button on her laptop, angles the screen toward me, and—there it is. My email, all nine words of it. *Not my best work,* I wrote, underlined with a link to the BuzzFeed dick pic article. *Thank you for your consideration.*

My cheeks warm as Carly says, "You did some interesting things with that email. First, you made me laugh. Out loud, once I clicked the link. Then I actually went searching for articles you'd written, since you hadn't bothered to include any. I took fifteen minutes out of a very busy day to look you up."

She leans back in her chair, fingers steepled under her chin as her dark eyes bore into mine. "That's never happened before."

I want to smile, but I'm not entirely sure she's complimenting me. "I was hoping you'd appreciate the honesty," I hedge. "And the, um, brevity."

"Risky move," Carly says. "But bold, which I can respect. It's bullshit that you got fired for that, by the way. Any idea who posted the pics?"

"I know exactly who it was," I say, folding my arms tightly across my chest. I'd been working on a new story about rumored grade-fixing involving a few players in our state-champion basketball team. Their captain, a mouth-breather named Jason Pruitt, cornered me at my locker after English one day and said the only two words he'd ever spoken to me: *Back off.* I didn't, and a week later the dick pics happened, at almost exactly the same time that basketball practice ended. "But the guy denied it, and I couldn't prove it."

"I'm sorry," Carly says. "You deserved more support than that. And your work is excellent." I relax my rigid posture and almost smile, because this is all going a lot better than expected, but then she adds, "I wasn't planning on hiring a high school student, though."

"The job description didn't say you have to be in college," I point out.

"That was an oversight," Carly says.

I deflate, but only briefly. She wouldn't have brought me in if she weren't at least considering waiving that requirement. "I'll work twice as hard as any college student," I promise. "I can be in the office anytime I'm not in school, including nights

6

and weekends." *Because I have no life here,* I almost add, but Carly doesn't need that much context. "I know I'm not the most experienced person you're talking to, but I've been working toward becoming a journalist since I was in middle school. It's the only thing I've ever wanted to be."

"Why is that?" she asks.

Because it's the only thing I've ever been good at.

I'm from one of those families where people are effortlessly talented. Dad is a brilliant research scientist, Mom is an award-winning children's book illustrator, and Ellie is practically a musical prodigy on flute. All of them knew from birth, pretty much, what they wanted to do. I flailed around for most of my childhood trying to find my *thing*—the talent that would define me—while secretly worrying that I was another Uncle Nick. "He just doesn't know what he wants out of life," my dad would sigh every time his much younger half brother switched majors yet again. "He never has."

It seemed like the worst possible trait for a Gallagher, to not know what you want. As much as I love Uncle Nick, I didn't want to be the family slacker, part two. So it was a relief when I reached eighth grade and my English teacher singled me out for my writing. "You should work on the school paper," he suggested. I did, and for the first time, I found something that came naturally to me. It's been my identity ever since— "Brynn will be anchoring CNN one of these days," my parents like to say—and it was terrifying to lose that last fall. To see something that I'd worked so hard for, and been so proud of, turned into a joke.

I don't know how to explain that in an interview-friendly

sound bite, though. "Because you can make a real difference with every story, and give a voice to people who don't have one," I say instead.

"Well stated," Carly says politely. For the first time since we sat down, though, she looks a little bored, and I flush. I gave what I thought was a safe response, but that was probably a mistake with someone like Carly. She didn't bring me in here because my application was *safe.* "You do realize we're not the *New York Times,* though, right? True-crime reporting is a very specific niche, and if you aren't passionate about it—"

"I am, though." It's a risk to interrupt her, I know, but I can't let her dismiss me. The more I looked into *Motive,* the more I realized that it was exactly the kind of opportunity I needed—one where I could do more than just check a box on my college applications. "That's something I wanted to talk to you about. I've done all the things you mentioned in the job posting—social media, copyediting, fact-checking, et cetera. I have an actual resume I can show you, plus references. But also, if you're interested, I have a story idea."

"Oh?" Carly asks.

"Yeah." I dig into my messenger bag and pull out the manila folder I carefully assembled in preparation for this interview. "An unsolved murder from my hometown."

Carly raises her brows. "Are you pitching me right now? In the middle of an interview?"

I freeze with the folder half-open, unable to tell from her tone whether she's impressed, amused, or annoyed. "Yes," I admit. "Is that okay?"

"By all means," she says, lips quirking. "Go on."

Amused. Could be worse.

The clipping I'm looking for is right on top. It's a photo from the *Sturgis Times,* captioned *Saint Ambrose Students Brynn Gallagher and Noah Talbot Win Statewide Eighth-Grade Writing Competition.* My thirteen-year-old self is standing between two other people, smiling widely and holding up the Olympic-style medal around my neck.

"Aw, look at how cute you were," Carly says. "Congratulations."

"Thanks, but I didn't hang on to this because of the award. I kept it for him." I tap my finger on the man in the picture—young, handsome, and smiling. Even in two-dimensional photo form, he's brimming with energy. "This was my English teacher, William Larkin. It was his first year teaching at Saint Ambrose, and he was the one who insisted I enter the writing contest. He also got me started on the school paper."

My throat thickens as I hear Mr. Larkin's voice in my head, as clear today as it was four years ago. *You have a gift,* he said, and I don't think he realized how much those words meant to me. I never told him, which is something I'll always regret. "He was constantly trying to get students to live up to their potential," I say. "Or see it, if they didn't think they had any."

I look up to make sure I have Carly's full attention before adding, "Two months after this picture was taken, Mr. Larkin was dead. Bludgeoned with a rock in the woods behind Saint Ambrose. Three of my classmates found the body." This time, I tap the boy in the picture, who's wearing a medal identical to mine. "Including him."

CHAPTER TWO

BRYNN

I pause to let my words sink in, keeping my eyes on the photo of Mr. Larkin. He's wearing his signature lemon tie, its bright colors muted in the black-and-white photo. I asked him once why he liked it, and he told me it reminded him of his favorite motto: *When life hands you lemons, make lemon cake.* "That's not the saying," I told him, feeling a small thrill that I knew more than a teacher. "It's 'make lemon*ade.*'"

"Yeah, but I hate lemonade," he said with a shrug. "And I love cake."

Carly crosses her legs and taps the toe of her shoe against the table leg before reaching for her laptop. "You said this is unsolved?" she asks.

My pulse picks up at her show of interest. "For the most part, yeah."

Her eyebrows rise. "That's usually a yes-or-no question."

"Well, the theory is that a drifter killed him," I explain.

"There was a guy who'd started hanging around downtown a few weeks before Mr. Larkin died, swearing and yelling at people. Nobody knew who he was or what was going on with him. One day he came by Saint Ambrose and started screaming at kids during recess, so Mr. Larkin called the police and they arrested him. He spent a few days in jail, and Mr. Larkin died almost right after he got out." I smooth a wrinkled edge of the clipping. "The guy disappeared after that, so people think he killed Mr. Larkin in retaliation and took off."

"Well, that's a tidy resolution," Carly says. "You don't believe it?"

"I used to," I admit. When I was in eighth grade, it made the kind of sense I needed. The notion of a violent stranger passing through town was almost comforting, in an odd way, because it meant the danger was gone. And that the danger wasn't *us*—my town, my neighbors, the people I'd known for most of my life. I thought a lot about Mr. Larkin's death over the years, but somehow I never applied a journalistic lens until I binged a season of *Motive* to prepare for my interview. As I watched Carly methodically break down flimsy alibis and half-baked theories, all I could think was *Nobody ever did that for Mr. Larkin.*

And then it hit me, finally, that I could.

"But I've been thinking about it a lot since I moved back to Sturgis," I continue. "And it feels too . . . well, just what you said. Tidy."

"Indeed." Carly is quiet for a few beats while she taps her keyboard. "I don't see much media coverage on this. Just your local paper, and a couple of brief mentions in the *Boston Globe.* Latest story was in May, a few weeks after he died." She squints at the screen and reads, " 'Close-Knit School Rocked by Teacher's Death.' They didn't even call it a murder."

My friends and I rolled our eyes at *close-knit* back then, even though Saint Ambrose's motto is literally *Stronger Together.* Saint Ambrose runs from kindergarten through twelfth grade so that, theoretically, students can be *stronger together* right up until college.

Saint Ambrose is a strange kind of private school, though; it charges tens of thousands of dollars in tuition, but it's located in run-down, unglamorous Sturgis. Every smart local kid applies in the hopes of getting their tuition covered by scholarship, so they can avoid the low-ranked Sturgis school system. But it's not prestigious enough for people who have their pick of private schools, so the paying kids tend to be lackluster students. Which creates a have/have-not rift that not many students crossed when I was there.

In middle school, before Dad got the big promotion that sent us to Chicago, Ellie and I were scholarship students. Now we can afford the tuition, and my parents wouldn't hear of us going to Sturgis High instead. So we'll be heading back to Saint Ambrose in a few weeks. *Stronger together.*

"Yeah, it never got picked up anywhere else. I'm not sure why," I say.

Carly is still gazing at her screen. "Me either. This is true-crime catnip. Fancy prep school, handsome young teacher murdered, his body found by a trio of rich kids?" She taps the edge of the *Sturgis Times* photo. "Including your buddy—what's his name? Noah Talbot?"

"Tripp," I say. "He goes by 'Tripp.' And he's not rich." *Or my buddy.*

Carly blinks. "You're telling me a kid named Tripp Talbot isn't rich?"

"It's because he was the third Noah in his family," I explain. "His dad is Junior, and he's Tripp. You know, like 'triple'? He's a scholarship kid, like I used to be."

"What about the other kids?" Carly's eyes return to her screen as she scrolls. "I don't see any names here, although that's not surprising, given their ages at the time."

"Shane Delgado and Charlotte Holbrook," I say.

"Were they scholarship students too?"

"Definitely not. Shane was the richest kid at Saint Ambrose, probably," I say. In fourth grade, when we did family trees, Shane told us that his parents had adopted him from the foster system when he was a toddler. I used to try to imagine what that must have been like—going from a life of uncertainty to one of total luxury. Shane was so young, though, that he probably doesn't even remember. "And Charlotte was . . ."

I'm not sure how to best describe Charlotte. Wealthy, yes, and almost shockingly beautiful for a thirteen-year-old girl, but my strongest memory of Charlotte is of how infatuated she used to be with Shane, who never seemed to notice. That doesn't feel like the right kind of detail to share, though, so all I say is "Also rich."

"So what was their story?" Carly asks. "The three kids, I mean. Why were they in the woods that day?"

"They were collecting leaves for a science project," I say. "Tripp was Shane's partner, and Charlotte . . . Charlotte pretty much went wherever Shane was."

"Who was Charlotte's partner?" Carly asks.

"Me," I say.

"You?" Her eyes widen. "But you weren't with them?" I shake my head, and she asks, "Why not?"

"I was busy." My eyes stray to the photo, taking in Tripp's thirteen-year-old self: all skinny limbs, braces, and too-short blond hair. When I learned that I'd be moving back to Sturgis, curiosity got the better of me. I looked him up on social media, and was shocked to see he's had an epic glow-up since I saw him last. He's tall and broad-shouldered, and the hair that always used to be in a crew cut is longer and attractively tousled, framing bright blue eyes that were always his best feature. The braces are off, and his smile is wide and confident—no, *cocky*, I decided. Tripp Talbot got unfairly and undeservedly hot, and worst of all, he knows it. All of which I added to my list of reasons to dislike him.

"Too busy to do your homework?" Carly asks.

"I was finishing a story for the school paper," I say.

It's true; back then I was *always* finishing a story. The *Saint Ambrose Sentinel,* our middle-school paper, had become my life, and I worked there most afternoons. Still, I could've made time for the leaf-gathering excursion. But I didn't, because I knew Tripp would be there.

We used to be friends; in fact, between sixth and eighth grades, we were in and out of one another's houses so much that his dad used to joke about adopting me, and my parents made a habit of stocking up on Tripp's favorite snacks. We had all the same classes, and friendly competition for grades. Then, the day before Mr. Larkin died, Tripp loudly told me, in front of our entire gym class, to stop following him around and asking him to be my boyfriend. When I laughed, thinking he had to be joking, he called me a stalker.

Even now my skin crawls with remembered humiliation, how awful it felt to have my classmates snicker while Coach Ramirez tried to defuse the situation. And the worst thing was, I had no idea why Tripp had said that. I'd been at his house doing homework just the day before, and we'd gotten along fine. There was nothing I'd said or done that he could've misinterpreted. I hadn't so much as flirted with him, ever; the thought had never crossed my mind.

After Charlotte, Shane, and Tripp found Mr. Larkin, there was something strangely glamorous about the three of them—as though they'd aged a decade in the woods that day, and knew things the rest of us couldn't possibly understand. Tripp, who hadn't been at all friendly with Shane and Charlotte before, was absorbed into their group as though he'd always been there. I never spoke to him again; people used to roll their eyes if I so much as looked in his direction, like my alleged crush was even more pathetic now that he was a semi-celebrity. It was a relief, two months later, when my dad's transfer to Chicago went through and we moved away.

I'm not going into that level of detail with Carly, though. Nothing screams *I'm still in high school* louder than being mad at a boy for embarrassing you in gym class.

"Fascinating to think you were almost a murder witness, isn't it?" Carly says. She squints at her laptop. "This says there was no physical evidence left at the scene, beyond fingerprints from one of the boys picking up the murder weapon. Was that Tripp?"

"No, that was Shane."

She cocks an eyebrow. "Did people think he might've done it?"

"No," I say. I certainly didn't back then, and even though I haven't seen Shane since eighth grade, it's still hard to imagine. Not because Shane was rich and popular but because he always seemed so laid-back and, well, *uncomplicated*. "He was just a kid, and he got along great with Mr. Larkin. He had no reason to hurt him."

Carly just nods, like she's reserving judgment on that. "Did anyone?"

"Not that I ever heard."

Carly gestures at the laptop screen. "This article says your teacher had been looking into a recent theft at your school?"

"Yeah. Somebody stole an envelope full of money that had been raised for the eighth-grade class trip to New York. It was more than a thousand dollars," I say. That happened at the end of March, and I was excited to have actual news to report. Mr. Larkin was asked to lead the internal Saint Ambrose investigation, so I interviewed him almost daily. "The school searched our lockers after Mr. Larkin died, and they found the envelope in Charlotte's locker."

"Charlotte from the woods?" Carly asks, a note of incredulity creeping into her voice. "Let me see if I have this straight. One of the witnesses leaves his fingerprints on the murder weapon, another took the money your teacher was looking for, and—what? Nothing happens to either of them?" I nod, and she folds her arms. "Let me tell you something. Things would have been a lot different if kids of color had been involved."

"I know." I hadn't considered it at the time, but I did when I thought about the case during my *Motive* binge—the way that Tripp, Charlotte, and Shane had gotten to be *kids*. They weren't doubted, or scrutinized, or railroaded, even though nobody other than the three of them could corroborate their story. "But Charlotte said she didn't know how the envelope got there," I add.

I'd been hoping to interview her about it, but I never got the chance. After Mr. Larkin died, all extracurricular activities were put on hold for a few weeks, and when they started up again, our head of school, Mr. Griswell, told me I couldn't report on the theft anymore. "This school needs to heal," he said, and I was too shell-shocked over Mr. Larkin's murder to argue.

"Okay." Carly leans back in her chair and spins in a slow semicircle. "Congratulations, Brynn Gallagher, you have officially captured my interest."

I almost bounce in my seat. "So you'll cover Mr. Larkin?"

Carly puts up a hand. "Whoa, hold up. A lot more goes into that kind of decision than just—this." She waves a hand at my folder, and I flush, suddenly feeling naïve and out of my depth. Carly seems to notice, softening her tone as she adds, "But I like your instincts. This is absolutely the sort of case we'd consider. Plus, your portfolio is solid, and you don't let a few dick pics get you down. So, what the hell. Why not, right?"

She pauses, waiting for my response, but that's not quite enough information for me to go on. "Why not what?" I ask.

Carly stops spinning her chair. "That was me offering you the job."

"Really?" The word comes out like a squeak.

"Really," Carly confirms, and a surge of excitement—mixed with relief—buzzes through my veins. It's the first good news I've had in a long time, and the first sign that maybe, possibly, I haven't blown my entire future. Carly glances at a calendar on the whiteboard, where the month of December is so overbooked that it's impossible to read anything from where I'm sitting. "Are you in school right now or on break?"

"No. I mean, it's not break yet, but we only moved back last week, so my parents figured we could start classes with the new semester in January."

"Great. How about you come in around ten o'clock tomorrow morning, and we'll get you started with orientation?" I just nod, because I don't trust myself not to squeak again. Then she adds, "And by all means, write up what we discussed about your teacher, and I'll have one of our producers take a look when they have time. Can't hurt, right? And who knows." Carly closes her laptop and stands, signaling that my time is up, for now. "Maybe we'll get a story out of it."

CHAPTER THREE

TRIPP

I set the application down on the counter I just cleaned at Brightside Bakery and study the words at the top of the page. *The Kendrick Scholarship will be awarded to the most well-rounded student in the Saint Ambrose senior class, as chosen by school administrators.* I scan the rest of the document, but there's no definition of "well-rounded"—nothing about grades, financial need, or work experience.

"This is pointless," I say to the empty room. Well, mostly empty. The owner's dog, Al, a ridiculously fluffy Samoyed, thumps his tail at my words. "Don't be happy. We're not happy," I tell him, but he just drools in response. Happily.

I exhale in frustration as Brightside's owner, Regina Young, comes from the kitchen with a fresh tray of Pop-Tart cakes. They aren't much like the real thing except for their shape and size, and the rainbow sprinkles on top. Regina makes them from vanilla cake, cream cheese frosting, and her secret-recipe jam filling, which I would eat by the bowlful if she let me.

"Why aren't we happy?" she asks, setting the tray on the counter beside the cash register. Al leaps up at the sound of her voice and races for the counter, then sits quivering beside it in anticipation of a treat. Which he never gets. I wish I were that optimistic about anything in life.

I slide off my stool to help her load the cakes into the display case. Regina finished making this batch early, so we have time before people start lining up at four-thirty. I'm not the only one in Sturgis who's obsessed with these cakes. "That Kendrick Scholarship is a joke," I tell her.

She rolls her shoulders and adjusts the kerchief she uses to cover her short twists while she's baking, then steps back to give me access to the case door. "How so?"

The sweet, fruity smell of the cakes hits me full force, and my mouth waters. "It goes to the most 'well-rounded' student in the senior class," I say, lifting my fingers in air quotes before pulling a pair of plastic gloves from a box beneath the counter. "But they don't define it, so basically Grizz will just give the scholarship to whoever he likes best. Which means I'm screwed, since he hates me. There's no point in even trying." I start arranging the Pop Tart cakes in neat rows, making sure they're exactly one-quarter inch apart.

Regina leans against the counter. "You know what I like most about you, Tripp?"

"My passion for precise measurements?" I ask, squinting at the display.

"Your can-do attitude," she says dryly.

I grin despite my rapidly souring mood. "I only speak the truth."

"Go on, then. Keep talking," Regina says. "Get all that negativity out of your system. Then fill out the application, send it in, and hope for the best."

I make a face to hide the fact that I kind of like when she sounds like a mom. Well, not *my* mom. The last postcard I got from Lisa Marie Talbot, seven months ago, was of the casino in Las Vegas where she works. All it said on the back was *Full of craps!*

"I will," I grumble. "Eventually." Then I clamp my lips together before I can spew more complaints that Regina has already heard.

She can read my mind, though. As she changes the roll of paper in the cash register, she adds, "Offer stands, you know."

Every time I moan about the fact that whatever financial aid package I manage to scrape together for college probably won't cover room and board, Regina reminds me that she and her husband have a spare room, now that only two of their sons live at home. "I know it's still Sturgis," she said. "But if you need a change of pace, just say the word."

I got a similar offer from my friend Shane, except it was more along the lines of "Dude, let's just live in my parents' apartment in the South End when we graduate." When I took him seriously, though, and asked when we could move in, he remembered that it's rented out. "But the place in Madrid is free," he said. Like Spain and Massachusetts are interchangeable to someone who doesn't even have a passport.

Whatever. It's not as though I actually want to live with

Shane. But Regina . . . maybe. After years of just me and my dad, hell yeah I need a change of pace. But I was hoping my next step would involve a new town too.

When I first heard about the Kendrick Scholarship, I had hope. It's brand-new, funded through a grant from a rich alumnus, and it's for twenty-five thousand dollars *a year*. For four years. That would cover some state schools, and get me close to a full ride at UMass Amherst, which is where I'd really like to go. I told my guidance counselor it's because of their Exploratory Track program, so I could "consider potential majors based on my interests and aspirations." The real reason isn't admissions-essay-friendly, though: *because it's big enough, and far away enough, that I could maybe start to feel like a new person there.*

"What makes you think Mr. Griswell doesn't like you?" Regina asks, sidestepping Al to swipe a streak of dust off the display case front. All her kids went to Saint Ambrose, so she's familiar with Grizz's nickname, and still hyper-plugged into the PTA. Half the time she knows more about what's going on at school than I do.

"Because of the shelves."

"Oh, come on now." Regina plants her hands on her hips. "He cannot possibly hold a disagreement that happened with a former contractor years ago against that contractor's child."

"He can and he does," I say.

When I was younger, my dad used to occasionally do carpentry projects at Saint Ambrose. In eighth grade, Grizz asked him to make built-in bookshelves for his office, which my dad did. But when he finished and gave Grizz the bill, Grizz insisted he'd never agreed to that price and would only pay three-quarters of it. They argued for a few days, and when it was clear Grizz wouldn't budge, Dad made his move. He went into school over the weekend, dismantled the entire shelving system, and repainted the wall like he'd never been there. Except for the note he left for Grizz: *Changed my mind about taking the job.*

That's the thing about my father; he's Mr. Mellow until you push him too far, and then it's like a switch has been flipped. Grizz was lucky that all he got was some unbuilt shelves, but he didn't see it that way. He was beyond pissed, so there's no way he's handing Junior Talbot's kid a hundred thousand dollars for college.

"Okay, so maybe Mr. Griswell isn't your number one fan," Regina says. "But you know he's not the only decision-maker right? Ms. Kelso's got a big say. Maybe the biggest. And hmm, let me see." She taps her chin, pretending to be lost in thought. "Wasn't she just in here asking you for a favor the other day? A favor that you foolishly declined to provide?"

"No," I say.

"Oh, come on, Tripp."

"I'm not doing it."

"You're saying *no* to free college?"

"I'm saying *no* to that committee. It's too weird," I protest. Regina folds her arms and glares. "It would be weird for me to help make a memorial garden for someone I . . ." I pause, swallowing hard. "Someone I found."

I've spent years trying to forget that day in the woods with Mr. Larkin, although not for the reasons Regina might think. So I guess I can't blame her for believing that the Larkin Memorial Garden Committee is a good opportunity, and not a total fucking nightmare.

"It's not weird. It's respectful and helpful," Regina says. "And maybe healing." Her voice turns as gentle as Regina ever gets, which isn't much, but still. Points for effort. "You deserve to heal as much as anyone else, Tripp."

I don't answer her, because my throat might as well be filled with cement. I can handle a lot, but not Regina Young earnestly telling me what I deserve when she doesn't know shit about the things I've done. "Besides, you know damn well Ms. Kelso needs some muscle," she adds. "There's heavy work involved, and you Saint Ambrose boys aren't famous for filling up the volunteer committees." She steps back behind the counter and points a finger at me. "So stop whining and do it, or I'll fire your pasty ass."

"You're bluffing," I say, although I'm honestly not sure. And I'd hate to lose this job. Regina pays better than anyone else in Sturgis, and Brightside is kind of like a second home. One that's a lot cleaner and better-smelling than my first home.

The bell on the front door jingles, and a half dozen guys wearing yellow-and-blue-striped jerseys beneath their parkas tumble inside, laughing and shoving at one another. Fall lacrosse season might be over, but indoor league is still going strong. "What's good, T?" Shane calls in a booming voice, dropping his bag beside one of the large window tables. Then he gives my boss his most charming smile. "Hey, Regina. We'll take all the Pop-Tart cakes, please."

Regina shakes her head. "You get two apiece and that's it," she says as the other guys start grabbing napkins and drinks. "I'm not running out before my regulars get here."

Shane puts his hand over his chest like he's clutching a wound, shaking a strand of dark hair out of his eyes. My father

24

calls Shane "Ronaldo," after some European soccer star Dad claims he looks like. "How, after all this time, are we not considered regulars?" Shane demands.

"Two each," Regina repeats sternly, her mouth lifting slightly at one corner. Even though Shane is always on his best behavior around her, she can never decide whether to be amused or annoyed by him.

"One day," Shane sighs, flopping into a chair. "One glorious day, you'll let me have all the cake I want, and my life will be complete."

"Your life is too complete as it is," I say. He grins and flips me off.

Regina comes up beside me and tugs at my sleeve. "I need to get some muffins into the oven," she says. "Put Al in the back, would you?" Technically Al isn't supposed to be in the dining area, so even though nobody in Sturgis cares—including Regina's cop regulars—he always goes into the storage room once it gets crowded.

"Yes, ma'am," I say, with a salute that she ignores as she shoves the kitchen door open and lets it close behind her. I lure Al away with the promise of a cookie, which he falls for every time, and offer a bowl of water as a consolation prize. Then I get back behind the counter and ring up a giant order on a bunch of different bank cards.

As soon as I finish and everyone is sitting down to eat, the door jingles again, and a girl steps inside. "Playtime's over, Shaney," I hear one of the guys mutter. "Your wife is here."

Shane's grin only slips for a second before he calls out "Hey, babe" and accepts a kiss from Charlotte. "Want some cake?"

"No, I'll just get coffee," Charlotte says. She's wearing a

black coat with a lot of buttons and straps, and takes her time undoing them all before draping it over the back of an empty chair.

"Black with honey?" I ask as she approaches.

She rests her hip against the counter. "You know me well."

"You realize that's a weird combination, right? I've been working here almost two years, and you're the only person I've ever met who puts honey in their coffee."

Charlotte's lips curve into a smile. "I like to stand out."

She has no problem doing that. Charlotte is the kind of girl who's heard *You should be a model* her entire life. No awkward stage, ever, for Charlotte Holbrook. It's not like there's any one thing about her that's extraordinary. When Regina asked me to describe Shane's girlfriend, I said, "She's pretty. Brown hair, blue eyes, a little taller than you." Then Charlotte walked in, and Regina shook her head.

"Pretty," Regina muttered under her breath. "That girl is pretty like Mount Everest is high."

While I get Charlotte's coffee ready, she says, "Did you check the intranet today?"

"No. It's winter break," I remind her.

"I know, but class rosters went up, and I wanted to see who I'll be spending my final semester with." I just grunt, and she lightly swats my arm. "Some of us care about things like that, you know. Anyway, guess whose name I saw?"

"Whose?" I ask, uncapping a bottle of honey and squeezing it over Charlotte's cup.

"Brynn Gallagher." Charlotte's eyes drift toward Shane's table as he lets out a loud laugh, so she doesn't notice me almost drop the honey. I don't think Charlotte knows that Brynn and

I used to be friends; in all the years that Charlotte and I have hung out, we've discussed Brynn Gallagher exactly never.

"What?"

"Brynn Gallagher," Charlotte repeats, returning her attention to me. Then she frowns. "Tripp, that's too much."

Oh shit. It's honey overload in Charlotte's coffee. "Sorry," I say, dumping the whole thing out so I can start over. There's no point trying to convince her to accept the extra sweetness; Charlotte is rigid about her coffee-to-honey ratio. "Did you say 'Brynn Gallagher'?"

"I said it twice," Charlotte says, eyes narrowed as she watches my second attempt.

"That's weird," I say, aiming for a nonchalant tone. I don't need Charlotte wondering why I'm suddenly incapable of performing the simplest tasks. "Considering she doesn't live here anymore."

Charlotte lifts one shoulder in a shrug. "Maybe she moved back."

"Too bad for her," I say, handing over a perfect coffee. "There you go."

"Thank you, Tripp," Charlotte says, turning away without paying. She knows I'll put it on Shane's card. She heads back to the table but doesn't pick up her coat from the empty chair. Instead she just stands there with an expectant smile until one of the guys sitting next to Shane moves over so she can take his seat.

Charlotte doesn't give Shane an inch of space. She never has, since they became an official couple at the end of eighth grade. He used to be just as Velcro'd to her, but lately I see signs that all that togetherness might be starting to wear on him.

Like now, when his mouth tightens as Charlotte settles herself beside him. But then he relaxes into a welcoming smile, and I wonder if I'm imagining things.

It's not like I'd ever ask. Shane, Charlotte, and I have been friends for almost four years, but we're surface friends. We talk about school, or TikTok, or sports, or Charlotte's favorite subject, which is Shane-and-Charlotte. There's a much longer list of things we *don't* talk about, including the unspoken rule that we've lived by since eighth grade.

We never, ever talk about what happened in the woods that day.

TRIPP
FOUR YEARS AGO

I'm standing in the birch grove in the woods behind Saint Ambrose on Wednesday afternoon, music blaring through my earbuds as I watch my breath fog the air while I wait for Shane Delgado. It's not quite mid-April, one of those unseasonably cold days that feel like an extension of winter, and the trees aren't fully green yet. I'm not sure the timing is right to, as Ms. Singh put it, "Create a leaf collection showcasing the diversity of species in the area," but oh well. Nobody asked for my opinion.

My three-ring binder is thicker than I need for a twelve-leaf project, its plastic sleeves full of leaves I plucked from my backyard this morning. I figured I might as well get a head start, because I've been Shane's lab partner since January and I know for a fact that I'll end up doing all the work.

Shane is the type of Saint Ambrose kid who skates by because he doesn't have to worry about hanging on to a scholarship. He doesn't have to worry about anything. He's so relaxed, in fact, that he's known for taking the occasional nap in our class coatroom. Teachers even joke about it, in a way they never would if I were the one falling asleep whenever I felt like it.

I know it's pointless to be jealous of somebody like Shane, but today I am. Today I wish I were him—or anyone, really, except me.

CHAPTER FOUR

TRIPP

My interview after Mr. Larkin's murder was the first time I'd ever been inside a police station. We'd frantically called our parents—well, Shane's parents, even though they were at work in Boston, because everybody knew instinctively that my dad wasn't equipped to deal with the situation. The Delgados contacted the Sturgis Police, and we all met up in the Saint Ambrose parking lot so we could lead the officers to Mr. Larkin. Everything was a blur, so surreal that I barely remember it, until we were brought to the station to give our statements.

When my dad showed up, I was taken into a small room, away from Shane and Charlotte. I understood, even then, that the police needed to know if our stories matched up. I pushed the image of Mr. Larkin out of my mind and did my best to answer Officer Patz's questions. I thought back then that he was in his forties, like my dad, because most adults looked middle-aged to me. Especially ones with receding hairlines. I learned later that Officer Patz was just twenty-five then, the same age as Mr. Larkin.

"Why were you in the woods, Tripp?"

"Doing a leaf collection project for science class. We're supposed to identify twelve species and mount the leaves in our binders." I'd brought my binder with me to the station. Someone had taken it when I'd arrived and then, about half an hour later, given it back.

"Why were you with Shane and Charlotte?"

"Shane's my lab partner, and Charlotte is his friend."

"Why didn't they have binders like yours?"

Because they knew they could dump all the work on me and I'd do it. That was the truth, but I didn't say it, because Saint Ambrose scholarship kids are supposed to be grateful, not bitter. What I actually said was "They forgot."

"Where was Charlotte's partner?"

I couldn't get away from Brynn Gallagher; even when she didn't show up, she was there. "I don't know" is all I said, and he didn't push it.

"Did you, Shane, and Charlotte ever separate? Lose sight of one another?"

Before my mother left, she rarely talked to me like a parent. Lisa Marie left the basics of life, like how to brush my teeth or prepare a bowl of cereal, to my father. But sometimes she liked to ramble about things she found interesting when I was nearby. It was more like she was talking *near* me than *to* me, but I still soaked it up. More than once, she said, *"The world would be a better place if more people knew when to stop talking. Everyone says too much, all the time. Ask them a simple question, and they'll give you their entire life story. No one cares! Just say yes or no. It doesn't even matter which one is true."*

I rubbed the callus on my thumb with my forefinger and said, "No."

"Not even for a minute or two?"

"No."

"And how did you happen across Mr. Larkin?"

This was the important part, I knew, so I took a few seconds to organize my thoughts before answering. "We were near the edge of Shelton Park—you know, where people go to watch birds sometimes? There was this huge tree branch that had fallen, like it had been struck by lightning or something. Charlotte said it would be easy to find good leaves on it. So we walked toward it, and then we saw something white behind the branch. It was a sneaker."

"Did you know right away that it was a sneaker?"

"No, I thought maybe it was trash. A paper bag or something. But then we got closer—"

"How much closer?"

"I don't know. Close enough to tell it was a sneaker."

"Okay. And then what?"

"Then we saw Mr. Larkin."

We spent a lot of time on that part. It felt like hours, Officer Patz asking question after question about Mr. Larkin and the space around him. Did we know he was dead right away? Did we touch him? Did we see or hear anyone nearby?

"There was a rock next to him. It was big and sharp and— it had blood on it."

"How did you know it was blood?"

"It was red, and it . . . looked wet."

"Did you touch it?"

"Shane did. He picked the rock up and turned it over, and got blood all over his hands. Some got on his pants too."

"Did you think that was a good idea, to pick up the rock?"

A long pause, while I stared at four deep, even scratches on the table's surface and imagined they'd been put there by a demon claw. Some creature the Sturgis Police had tried to capture and hold but couldn't.

"I don't know. I guess I didn't really think about it at all."

"Anything else you want to tell me, Tripp?"

"No. There's nothing more to tell."

When we were finally done, Officer Patz thanked me and sent me home with my father. Dad heard later, through the grapevine, that all three of us had said exactly the same thing. Everyone was sympathetic about how traumatic the experience of finding the dead body of our teacher must have been, and our neighbors kept dropping off casseroles and desserts for me and Dad. They hadn't done anything like that four years before, when my mother had taken off. I guess it's not much of a tragedy when people choose to leave.

Then, less than a week later, I got called back to the police station.

"Tripp, are you aware that money was stolen from your school recently?"

Of course I was aware. The money had gone missing at the end of March, and it had caused an uproar at Saint Ambrose. It was practically the only thing Brynn had been writing about in the *Sentinel* for weeks.

"Yeah. It was for the eighth-grade field trip to New York."

"Do you know how much it was?"

"No. A lot, probably. Now the scholarship kids can't go, so nobody gets to." This had caused a lot of division in our class, between the paying kids and the scholarship kids. Saint Ambrose liked to pretend we were all the same, but everyone knew who was who.

"Did you know Mr. Larkin was heading up the school's investigation of that theft?"

"Yeah, sure."

"Tripp, I'm going to share some information with you that recently came to light. The money stolen from your school was found in Charlotte Holbrook's locker last Friday during a routine search at Saint Ambrose. What do you think about that?"

I could have told him that there was nothing *routine* about it. Saint Ambrose students had never been searched before, let alone by a Sturgis cop. But the class money had been missing for two weeks by then, and Grizz was on edge and looking for somebody to blame.

I doubt Grizz had wanted that person to be Charlotte Holbrook, though. I doubted she would get into any trouble at all. That seemed like the sort of thing Officer Patz could figure out for himself, though.

"I guess I'm surprised," I said.

"What surprises you?"

"That it was there. Did Charlotte take it?"

Officer Patz didn't like when I asked questions; or at least, he rarely answered them. "Are you and Charlotte friends, Tripp?"

"No." That was true, back then.

"Are you friends with Shane Delgado?"

"No." Also true.

I don't remember all the questions that followed, but at some point, Officer Patz shifted the conversation toward me. "We've spent some time talking to your classmates, Tripp. You seem to be pretty well-liked. Some kids told us you can be a little bit mean, though."

"Oh yeah? Who?"

I asked it offhand, like I had no idea what he was talking about, even though I was pretty sure he meant Brynn. My dad, who'd seemed half-asleep during most of the conversation, stirred to life and leaned forward, elbows on the table. "What does it matter?" he asked. "Kids not getting along isn't a crime."

"Of course not, Mr. Talbot. I'm just trying to get a better sense of who Tripp is."

"He's a good kid. A good, honest kid who's doing his best to help you."

I should've been grateful to him for saying that, but I wasn't. The only thing I wanted, right then, was for my father to shut up so we could leave.

It's past six when I get off work, so I text Dad after I say goodbye to Regina and close the bakery door behind me. *What's the dinner situation?*

Nonexistent, he writes back. *Couldn't make it to the store today.*

Should I pick up Chinese?

That'd be great. I'll pay you back.

He will, eventually.

I call Golden Palace and place our usual order: shrimp fried rice and beef with broccoli, which are by far the best items on the menu. The owners like to coat most of their proteins in batter and fry them to death. A couple of years ago, Shane's parents took a bunch of us to Chinatown for dim sum, and it was the first time I'd ever had authentic Chinese food. I must've eaten my weight in dumplings alone; I couldn't believe how good they were. I've resented Golden Palace ever since, but they're fast, cheap, and right down the street.

I walk past Ricci Hardware, and pause at Mo's Barber Shop when the door half opens. Someone's having no luck pushing it the rest of the way, so I grab the handle and tug. "Hey, Mr. S," I say as a small, white-haired man peers up at me with watery blue eyes.

"Excuse me?" he says uncertainly, and then his expression clears. "Oh, hello there, Noah." Mr. Solomon, who used to be the groundskeeper at Saint Ambrose before he retired, has never been a fan of nicknames. "I didn't recognize you at first. All you kids are so big now, my goodness. Practically adults."

"It happens," I say in a weird, hearty tone that's nothing like my usual voice. I don't know why old people bring that out in me. Especially Mr. Solomon, who's gotten kind of spacey lately. His left hand is clutching a red tackle box, but I know better than to ask him if he's going fishing. He's started using it like a portable bank, pulling a pile of crumpled bills from it whenever I see him at the grocery store or the pharmacy. It makes me sad in a way I can't explain, and I find myself asking, "How's your garden doing?"

Which is a pointless question in January, but he brightens

anyway. "It's seen better days, but I've made some improvements to the yard." Mr. Solomon lives on the line between Sturgis and Stafford, the much nicer town where Shane is from. When I was a kid, I used to imagine Mr. Solomon's place was a portal to a different dimension, because it looked like some kind of magical garden that didn't belong in New England. Climbing vines everywhere, fruit trees, and flowers as big as your head. "You should stop by and see it sometime. Catch up a little. I'll make us some tea."

"Sounds great," I say, hoping he knows as well as I do that it won't happen. "I gotta run, Mr. S. I'm picking up dinner. You got the door, there?"

I'm still holding it, because he hasn't moved, and a frown crosses his leathery face. "You're in my way," he says peevishly. I guess nostalgia time is over.

"Sorry," I say, stepping aside so he can shuffle past me with a side-eye. I know he's just a confused old guy, but it's stuff like this—that I can't go two feet in this town without feeling like somebody's judging me—that makes me so desperate to leave.

I get to Golden Palace well before the food is ready, so after I pay, I settle myself on the bench in the vestibule, barely registering that a man is already sitting at the other end, until he speaks.

"Well, if it isn't Tripp Talbot."

I just used up all my sociability being nice to Mr. Solomon, so my mood plummets even before I see who it is. "Oh, hey, Officer Patz."

He's bundled up in a down parka, scarf, and Patriots wool hat. Even though the hat is fully covering his head, I've seen

Officer Patz around town enough to know that he's embraced his receding hairline with a shaved head. "Picking up dinner?" he asks.

No, I just like this bench, I think. But I don't say it, because I'm not an idiot. "Yup. You too?"

"My wife loves this place," he says.

"Cool," I say, wondering briefly if I knew before now that Officer Patz is married. Then I decide I don't care, and turn back to my phone. But before I can pull up a game to keep me busy, Officer Patz speaks again.

"I hear Saint Ambrose is doing a memorial garden for your teacher. Mr. Larkin," he says. I just nod, noncommittal, and silence falls until he adds, "I still think about that case sometimes. You know, you were the first witness I ever interviewed for a murder investigation."

The first and last, probably. Sturgis has plenty of low-level crime, but there hasn't been another murder since Mr. Larkin. But that doesn't seem like the right response, so I just say "Oh yeah?" as politely as I can.

"It's a tricky thing, interviewing kids," he says, and I don't know what he wants from me. Am I supposed to apologize for having been thirteen? "Last kid I talked to, witness to a robbery, kept changing his story. First he said one thing; then he said another. Kept forgetting stuff, or leaving information out because he didn't think it was important."

There's a space heater chugging away in the corner that's making Golden Palace's vestibule way too warm. I push my hair off my forehead and say, "Sounds like he wasn't much of a witness."

Officer Patz must be overheating too, because he takes off his hat and folds it between his hands. "It's actually not uncommon with kids, I've learned. Children's memories are less developed than adult memories. Plus they're more suggestible, and less reliable. Not you, though. You were always very consistent in your statements."

"I have a good memory," I say, stealing a glance at the girl behind the counter. Where the hell is our food?

"Shane and Charlotte were lucky you were there," Officer Patz says. "In the woods, I mean. Things could've added up differently if those two had been alone when they found the body. Even when you're dealing with kids, if one of them leaves fingerprints and the other has stolen property in her possession—well, you'd have to keep asking questions."

"Order for Patz," the girl behind the counter calls.

He doesn't get up, so I say, "That's you."

Officer Patz acts like he didn't hear either of us. His gaze is trained on the wall across from us, and his brow is furrowed, as though he's lost in thought. I'd almost believe he was, if I didn't catch his eyes drifting toward my reflection in the window. "But you? You weren't friends with Shane or Charlotte. I interviewed every kid in your class, and they all said the same thing. Even the ones that didn't like you." *Fucking Brynn.* "You and Shane didn't get along as lab partners, and you and Charlotte had hardly talked before she tagged along on that assignment. There was no reason for you to lie for either of them."

"Right," I say, rubbing my thumb. I knew that memorial garden was going to be trouble, and here's proof; I can't even pick up shitty fake Chinese food in peace anymore. "Why would I?"

"Order for Patz," the counter girl repeats.

"Over here, thanks," Officer Patz calls, finally getting to his feet.

I relax my shoulders, thinking we're done, but before he goes any farther, he gives me one last, searching look. "That's the question that keeps me up at night. Why would you?"

Then he puts his hat back on and grabs his food off the counter. "Have a good evening, Tripp. Enjoy your dinner."

CHAPTER FIVE

BRYNN

"Did you miss the hectic excitement of all of us getting ready at the same time in the morning?" I ask my uncle Nick the Tuesday after New Year's Day, stepping over his outstretched legs in the kitchen on my way to the coffeepot.

He yawns and rubs the rust-colored stubble on his chin, which he hasn't had a chance to shave yet, since Ellie is still in the bathroom. We've been back in Sturgis for more than three weeks, but with school starting today, it's the first time everyone in the house has been on the same schedule. "No. Did you guys multiply overnight? I swear there were two girls when I went to sleep, and at least four fighting over my bathroom this morning."

"*Our* bathroom," I remind him, draining the last of the coffee. Then I turn for the refrigerator, until I'm stopped short by Uncle Nick's outstretched hand.

"You weren't about to take the last of the coffee without

replacing it, were you?" he asks in a tone that aims for forbidding but doesn't quite pull it off. He pushes his Buddy Holly glasses up on his nose and adds, "There are rules in this house."

I duck past him, open the refrigerator, and grab the half-and-half. "Your rules are not my rules, beloved uncle."

"Then my coffee is not your coffee, cherished niece. Give it back."

"Too late." I pour a healthy dollop of cream into my coffee and hold it up. "This coffee is no longer lactose free."

"You're the worst," he says with a long-suffering sigh, and I stick my tongue out at him as I dash upstairs to finish getting ready.

Uncle Nick is only seven years older than me, and he's always been more like an older brother than an uncle. My grandfather and his second wife, Uncle Nick's mom, retired to Costa Rica when Nick was in college, so he moved in with us. A year later we left for Chicago, and my parents, who decided to hang on to the Sturgis house in case they needed to come back, asked Uncle Nick if he wanted to keep living there.

He did, and for the most part it worked out, except that Dad spent a lot of time on the phone with Uncle Nick nagging him equally about home maintenance and college, since Uncle Nick couldn't settle on a major. He tried coding, film studies, and political science before finally graduating with an accounting degree, which he's never used, because it turns out he hates accounting. Now he's enrolled in a master's program for teaching, which I think he'll be great at—he used to help out at Saint Ambrose when he was in college—but Dad can't give him a break.

"When are you going to start collecting a paycheck?" he

asked Uncle Nick last week. I love my father, but he can be a stereotypical scientist sometimes; blunt to the point of being cruel. He doesn't realize how demoralizing it is to watch him dismiss someone who doesn't have their entire life mapped out by the age of twenty-four.

Uncle Nick is doing his best to put up with us, but he'll probably move out soon, which is yet another strike against the Sturgis house. I forgot how drafty and cold it is in the winter, how small the closets are, and the fact that the electrical system wasn't built for the twenty-first century. Every time I enter my bedroom, I worry that the chain of power strips I've plugged into my single outlet will have blown a fuse.

Not today, though; the laptop on my desk still displays the Saint Ambrose website. I logged on last night to double-check my class schedule, and then went down a rabbit hole of scrolling through old photos from 2017 to 2018, when Mr. Larkin taught there. After his death, the police interviewed all our administrators and teachers, which made sense—Mr. Larkin had last been seen in his classroom, and he'd died in the woods behind Saint Ambrose. Even Uncle Nick, a lowly classroom assistant, had to give a statement. But nobody ever truly questioned whether one of Mr. Larkin's colleagues had had a problem with him, any more than they ever suspected Shane, Charlotte, or Tripp.

"Stronger together," I murmur, my gaze lingering on a picture of our head of school, Mr. Griswell, pointing to a banner with the school motto. "Were we?"

"Were we what?"

I glance up to see Ellie entering my room, a towel wrapped around her head. She doesn't actually care about the answer, though, because she immediately follows that question up with "Hey, do you have a white T-shirt? I forgot how see-through the uniform shirts are. My only clean bra is black, and this school does not deserve to see it."

I get up and rummage through my dresser. "Sounds like you're as excited as I am," I say, extracting a shirt and tossing it into her waiting hands.

"At least you only have to go to Saint A's for five months. I have *years*."

"Maybe Dad will transfer back before then," I say.

She sighs. "Here's hoping."

My phone buzzes, and I pick it up from my rumpled bedspread to see a new text. Mason: *Ready for today? Excited to have you back!*

I smile and send back a heart, feeling a quick burst of relief. Most of my former friends from Saint Ambrose aren't there anymore, but Mason Rafferty and Nadia Amin still are, and when I met up with them for coffee last weekend, it was easy and comfortable and fun. Which is exactly what I need if I'm going to make it through this semester.

Ellie is right, I only have five months, but five months is an eternity if you don't have anyone except your fourteen-year-old sister to hang out with. Especially when all my friends back home in Chicago are blanketing social media with nostalgia already: *Last winter break! Last softball season starting up soon! Who's ready for the last MLK weekend at Four Lakes? Sign-ups coming for the senior trip!* Izzy, Jackson, Olivia, Sanjay, and

Quentin are all going along with life like nothing has changed and I wasn't ripped from our supposedly unbreakable group of six.

I know I can't blame them. It's not their fault I had to move, and it's not like I expected them to start wearing all black and boycotting social events. It wouldn't kill them, though, to tag me with an occasional *We miss you!* Especially Quentin, who asked me out right before the Sturgis news broke, and then immediately backtracked once he learned I was leaving. "Long distance, right? Who needs it?" he said.

Fair point, but not exactly an ego boost.

I change into my Saint Ambrose uniform, frowning when my favorite gold charm bracelet catches on the polyester plaid of the skirt. The bracelet used to be Mom's when she was in high school, and I like the randomness of the charms—a hummingbird, a skull, a shamrock, a star, and a snowman. "These remain the cheapest uniforms ever," I mutter, smoothing down the thread that sprang loose from my skirt.

"And the ugliest." Ellie whips off her towel turban and grabs my hair dryer. "It's a good thing you didn't have to go to your *Motive* interview straight from school. They'd have taken one look at this prep school nightmare and sent you home."

"Accurate," I say, plucking my Saint Ambrose blazer off the bedpost.

Ellie plugs in the dryer and turns it on. "Are you going to tell our classmates that you're spying on them for your internship?" she yells over the roar of hot air.

"I'm not spying," I say, giving myself a critical once-over in the mirror. Ellie and I are both slight and shorter than we'd like to be, with a sprinkling of freckles and thick auburn hair we have to straight-iron into submission. We're near-twins except for our eyes; hers are brown like Mom's, and mine are green. They're also makeup smudged, and I lean forward to carefully wipe away excess mascara. "I'm observing."

That's the same line I used on my parents, who were thrilled about the *Motive* internship until I told them I'd pitched Carly on a story about Mr. Larkin. "We want you to have every opportunity, Brynn," Mom said. "Especially after what happened with—well, you know." The dick pics remain a sore subject at the Gallagher dinner table. "But you need to understand the potential impact of what you're doing. If a show about Mr. Larkin actually airs, it could be very disruptive for the Saint Ambrose community. And for you."

"I'm already disrupted," I reminded her. The move was easy for our parents; Dad's been at the same biotech company for our entire lives, so he's still working with his usual colleagues. Mom has always had a home office for her illustration work. Most of our family is here, and a lot of their old friends. They didn't get fired, wait-listed, or splashed across BuzzFeed. "Anyway, it's not like Carly agreed to do it. She barely even agreed to consider it."

Eventually they gave their blessing and let me go in to *Motive* for orientation—but not before making me promise that, as Dad put it, I'd be "ethical about what you share." I'm pretty sure he meant *about* Saint Ambrose students, though, not *with* them. As far as I'm concerned, I don't need to share anything with the near-strangers I won't see again after five months.

"So that's a no, then?" Ellie asks, shutting off the hair dryer.

She grabs an elastic from my dresser and pulls it through her still-damp hair to create a messy bun. There's no time left for straightening. "Just gonna keep everybody in the dark?"

"It's a no," I admit, and Ellie grins.

"Undercover," she says. "I like it."

CHAPTER SIX

BRYNN

Saint Ambrose hasn't changed. It's still a cluster of redbrick white-pillared buildings, surrounded by carefully manicured grounds and a wrought-iron fence that separates the campus from the small, run-down houses that dot the rest of the neighborhood. The Volkswagen that I pull into one of the last parking spots behind the main building would fall exactly in the middle of a student car ranking; we're surrounded by everything from brand-new BMWs to rusty death traps that are so old, whatever emblem they might've once had has long worn off.

There's a small group of boys huddled next to one of the back stairwells, smoking. "Maybe you can find a hot new Saint Ambrose boyfriend while you're here," Ellie murmurs as we approach. "Plaster him all over social media and show Quentin what he's missing."

"Awesome. Can't wait to plunge into the Saint Ambrose

dating pool," I say dryly. "Are you going to find a new girl-friend too?"

"I was the dumper, not the dumpee," Ellie reminds me. "I have nothing to prove."

Most of the boys ignore us as we get closer, but one of them lifts his head to watch us. He's tall and solidly built, with a crew cut and the smudge of a beard along his chin, and he elbows one of his friends. "We got some new girls," he says, then lifts his chin toward me. "What's up, beautiful? Are you an elite, or are you a dreg?"

That startles me enough that I pause with one foot on the bottom step. "Sorry?"

"Are you an elite, or are you a dreg?" he repeats, scanning me up and down so thoroughly that I'm very glad to be wearing a coat.

"I have no idea what you're talking about," I say, continuing up the stairs.

"Elite," one of the other boys says, and they all laugh.

"What the hell," I mutter to Ellie as I pull open the door.

"He seems nice," she says, slipping through. "I see potential there."

Inside there's a flurry of activity as Ellie and I check in at the main office, receive our locker assignments and our schedules, and get directions to the auditorium even though we've been there hundreds of times before. "Enjoy your first day at Saint Ambrose," says a woman I've never seen before, who clearly missed the "returning" part of our transcripts.

"Should we part ways and head for our respective lockers, or just bring our coats to morning assembly?" I ask Ellie as we enter the stream of students in the hallway. Everyone's navy, gold-buttoned blazer has the Saint Ambrose crest on the left breast pocket, like a brand. *Stronger together.*

"Bring our coats," Ellie says, clutching my arm with an uncharacteristic flash of vulnerability.

I spot familiar faces as we walk, but it's like gazing at people through a distorted mirror; everyone's just different enough from what I remember that by the time I recall their names, I've already passed them. It leaves me with a disoriented feeling, until we turn a corner and nearly bump into someone who's instantly recognizable.

"Oh," Charlotte Holbrook says, stopping short. "There you are."

"Here I am?" I reply, confused. Charlotte is as stunning as ever, with her pale blue eyes, luminous skin, and perfect bone structure. Instead of the Saint Ambrose regulation white oxford uniform shirt, she's wearing one with subtle lace on the collar that complements the pearl-and-crystal headband holding back her shiny chestnut hair. Everything about Charlotte Holbrook is designed to make mere mortals feel plain, awkward, and underdressed.

"Brynn Gallagher," Charlotte says, like I need to be introduced to myself. "I saw your name on the class roster and was wondering if it was actually you, or just somebody with the same name. But here you are." Before I can repeat her words again, she gives us a small smile and says, "Welcome back."

Then she's gone—heading in the wrong direction, I think, until I watch her fling her arms around a dark-haired boy. I can't see enough of him to be sure it's Shane Delgado, but if so, Charlotte finally got her man.

"Imagine just walking around all day with that face," Ellie

whispers as we continue forward, funneling into the auditorium amid a sea of navy and plaid. "How would you get anything done?"

"Brynn!" someone calls, and I turn to see Mason Rafferty standing in the second row of the auditorium seating with his hand in the air. Mason is a head taller than most of our classmates—unreasonably tall, he used to say—with longish dark curls and a gap-toothed smile. He cups his hands around his mouth to amplify his voice above the buzzing crowd and adds, "We saved you a spot."

I catch sight of Nadia beside him and push my way toward them, happy to feel included. "Is there space for Ellie too?" I ask when we reach the row.

"Of course," Mason says, plucking a coat off a couple of empty chairs. "Hello, Eleanor. Nice to see you again. Still tearing up the flute?"

"Hello, Mason. I don't know if *tearing up* is the correct technical term, but sure," Ellie says, and they grin at each other. Mason and Ellie have always gotten along well—queer bonding, Ellie used to say whenever I'd reminisce about him in Chicago. She was ten when we moved, and not fully aware of who she liked, but she'd always been more comfortable around Mason than any of my other friends.

While Mason and Ellie catch up, I settle in beside Nadia. "How does it feel to be back?" she asks in her faint British accent. She was born in England and didn't come here until she was ten, after both of her parents died in a car accident and she had to move across the Atlantic to live with her aunt and uncle. They have a beautifully restored antique colonial house in Stafford, but I'm not sure it's ever truly felt like home to Nadia. "Is everything as you remember?"

"Not exactly," I say. "What's a dreg?"

"A drag?" she asks quizzically. Mason takes the seat next to me, his coat on his lap and his long legs stretching beneath the chair in front of him.

"No, a *dreg*. When Ellie and I were coming inside, some boy asked us if we were"—my brow wrinkles at the memory—"an elite, or a dreg."

"Ah," Nadia says, rolling her eyes. "I see you've already been introduced to our growing class divide."

Ellie leans over from her seat beside Mason. "Do people seriously call each other that?"

"Not most people, no," Nadia says, pushing back a strand of dark, blunt-cut hair. "But Saint Ambrose has gotten a lot more . . . extreme in some ways since you left. They relaxed the scholarship standards, so we have a lot more local kids in the Upper School who aren't quite as academically inclined. There's some resentment between them and the wealthier students."

"The elites?" I ask, eyebrows raised as I look between Mason and Nadia. "So which are you guys?" Nadia's family is comfortable but definitely not wealthy, and Mason lives a few streets away from me in Sturgis. Scholarship all the way, for him.

"We're Switzerland," Nadia says. "And we think it's silly. But you can't tell that to the Colin Jeffries of the world." Her eyes stray to look over my shoulder, and I turn to watch the same boy who accosted us on the stairs shove his way toward the back of the auditorium. "It would spoil his image of himself as unfairly maligned by the powers that be."

"Who are the powers?" I ask.

Nadia inclines her head toward the entrance. "There go the top three."

Somehow I know who I'm going to see before I actually do. It's Charlotte, of course, as regal as a queen with her arm tucked firmly in the arm of the handsome boy beside her, who is definitely Shane Delgado. On her left is another tall, broad-shouldered boy with burnished blond hair, who I would have taken for an equally pampered private school prince if I hadn't spent hours hanging out in his seventies-décor house. "So Tripp Talbot is elite now? Did his father win the lottery or something?" I ask, before realizing that admitting I recognize him gives away my social media stalking.

Mason smirks knowingly. "Tripp is elite by association," he says. "The rules make no sense, obviously, but that's dreg logic for you."

"So great to be back," I say, slumping down in my chair just as Saint Ambrose's head of school, Mr. Griswell, takes his place behind a podium onstage. There's a cloth-covered easel to his left, and a glass of water in front of him that he takes a long sip from.

"Do people still call him 'Grizz'?" Ellie asks.

"Always," Mason replies.

Grizz's hair has gone full-on gray, but other than that he's exactly as I remember him: impeccably dressed with a sweater vest beneath his suit jacket, short in stature but imposing in presence, and sporting a year-round tan. "Welcome back, Saint Ambrose," he says, leaning forward so the microphone can fully project his words in the now-hushed auditorium. "I hope your winter break was restful, and that the holidays energized you for the semester ahead. We're thrilled to have you back, because we are, as always, stronger together."

I tune him out as I gaze around me, taking in the familiar details along with what's new; the soaring ceiling rafters are decorated with a few more blue-and-yellow championship banners, the plain gray curtains that used to frame the stage have been replaced with lush navy velvet, and all of our seats look freshly upholstered. Faces I once knew are starting to come into sharper focus—Katie Christo, who was a sort-of friend until she started calling me "Trippstalker" after Tripp's gym outburst; Martina Zielinski, a straight-A student who's probably on track for valedictorian; and Pavan Deshpande, who was my first kiss behind the science building in seventh grade.

"And there's one last thing." I force my attention back to Grizz as he raises his voice; the volume of chatter in the room has steadily increased as students have grown restless. "This year we mark a sad anniversary in our school's history. It's been nearly four years since eighth-grade teacher William Larkin died, leaving behind a rich legacy of achievement and dedication to his students. Our assistant head of school, Ms. Kelso, is heading up a committee to plan a memorial garden that will be unveiled later this spring, and I urge those of you with room in your schedules to volunteer."

I straighten in my seat. *Memorial garden committee?* Oh, hell yes. That's the perfect opportunity to get information about Mr. Larkin without being obvious about it.

Ellie leans over Mason again. "Do you have room?" she whispers. "I think you do."

"Shut it," I hiss as Mason tilts his head, curious.

"In the meantime," Grizz continues, gesturing toward the

easel beside him, "in our tradition of honoring distinguished faculty, we've commissioned a portrait of Mr. Larkin that will hang in the administrative hallway. It is my great pleasure to reveal that portrait today." He removes the cloth from the easel with a flourish, then recoils as the auditorium fills with a loud mixture of gasps, hoots, and confused buzzing.

"What on earth?" Nadia leans forward, squinting. "What does that say?"

I've always had better eyesight than her. "Asshole," I reply, staring at the bright red letters scrawled across Mr. Larkin's face and partially obscuring his signature lemon tie.

"Oh no," Nadia says as Grizz tries to quiet the room with booming assurances that the person responsible for such a disgraceful act will be found and punished. Mason has gone pale, as though the entire situation is making him physically sick, and I remember how much he always looked up to Mr. Larkin. "Who would do something like that?"

Ellie tugs at one of the strands of hair slipping from her bun, eyes on the stage as Grizz, still shouting, replaces the cloth. "What a warm welcome back to Saint Ambrose, huh?" she says. "Population: messed up."

CHAPTER SEVEN

TRIPP

My head is pounding when I wake up at six a.m. on Wednesday morning. All I want to do is go back to sleep, but I force myself to toss the covers aside and climb out of bed. The only thing I hate more than running is how I feel when I *don't* run.

I dress quickly, unplug my phone from its charger, and root around in the top of my bureau for my earphones. No luck. They're not on my desk or the floor either, so I grab my sneakers and head for the living room, the shaggy green carpet muffling my footsteps. Our house is a split-level that my dad inherited from his parents, and it's barely been updated since the seventies. One of the last things my mother did before she left was strip away the loud floral wallpaper and paint every room a different, jewel-toned color. I can still remember her standing in the middle of the dining room when she'd finally finished, paintbrush in hand, gazing accusingly at the walls like they'd broken a promise. "This is no better," she said.

Even then, I knew she wasn't talking about wallpaper.

She never got around to yanking up the rug. Just as well. It's ugly but insulating, which matters when you're not allowed to set the thermostat any higher than sixty-five degrees. My steps slow as I near the kitchen, and I yawn so hard that my jaw cracks. The bitter smell of burnt coffee wafts toward me, which it shouldn't, since I'm the only one up in the—

"Morning," a voice calls, startling me so much that I drop my phone onto my foot. It hits on exactly the wrong spot, and pain radiates through my toe as I retrieve it.

"Jesus, Dad!" I hobble toward the kitchen and glare at him. "You scared the crap out of me. What are you doing here?"

He's wearing a T-shirt one of his buddies gave him as a joke that reads *Peaked in High School,* and I guess you have to give him credit for running with it. My father was a sort-of star football player when he was my age; good enough that his name is on a couple of plaques at Sturgis High, but not so good that anyone recruited him to play past that.

Dad rubs one hand over his thick, graying hair before taking a sip of black coffee. "I live here, remember?"

I spot the cord of my earphones beneath a jumble of silver on the table—Dad's key ring, which takes up way too much space because it's full of random discs that he calls his "lucky medallions." I used to like them when I was a kid, partly because there was something comforting about the jingling noise they made, and partly because I still believed in luck back then. Now I avoid looking at them as I tug my earphones free.

"Yeah, but why are you up?" I ask. Dad works the night shift as a security guard at Sturgis Hospital and comes home about an hour before I get up for school. He sleeps most of the day, and I don't usually see him until nearly dinnertime.

"Working at Home Depot later this morning," Dad says through a yawn. "No point in going to sleep for two hours."

"Back-to-back? Why?" Dad's occasional Home Depot shifts are usually on the weekend, to avoid exactly this scenario.

"Car needs a new transmission," he sighs.

That's life in the Talbot household. My father works hard, but at jobs that don't pay much and offer zero stability. He's been laid off more times than I can count. On the one hand, you have to give the guy credit for plugging along, always landing something right before things fall apart. On the other hand, it'd be nice not to have to choose which bills to pay every month.

We don't talk about that, though. There are a lot of things we don't talk about.

"I'm gonna run," I say, stuffing the buds into my ears. "See you." Whatever Dad says in return is drowned out by my playlist, and I pull the hood of my sweatshirt over my head as Rage Against the Machine propels me out the door.

My feet automatically carry me on my usual path: down my street, a half mile until I pass Sturgis High School, and then a left onto Main Street. The upper section of Main is the best part of Sturgis, full of old Victorians that look good no matter how badly their paint is peeling. I steadily increase my pace for the next mile until I reach the end of Main Street. I'm at top speed now, the fastest I can comfortably run for any length of time. My limbs pump, smooth and purposeful, as endorphins course through me and fill my veins with a buzzy sense of well-being.

This is why I run. Because it's the only time I ever feel that way.

At this hour almost everything on Main Street is closed, even Brightside Bakery. The streets are quiet and nearly deserted; I can only see one car in my peripheral vision as I near the crosswalk. I don't slow down, since pedestrians have the right of way, but whoever's driving decides to be a dick and speeds up to blow past me before I can cross. "Asshole," I mutter, pulling up short on the sidewalk.

Then I do a double take as I catch sight of the driver. They pass in a flash, and I blink at the bumper, confused and disoriented. *No. It can't be.* The car is a nondescript gray sedan I've never seen before, with a New Jersey license plate.

It can't be.

I keep going and turn onto Prospect Hill. My heart thumps harder as I struggle to maintain my pace against the incline, and my lungs start to burn. Music pounds in my ears, urging me forward even though everything in me wants to slow down, until all of a sudden it's interrupted by a text tone.

I shouldn't look in the middle of the hardest part of my run. But that flash of familiarity in the gray car makes me pull out my phone, because there's no one else who ever texts me this early. I stop abruptly, panting, and steel myself for what I might see. It's not what I was afraid of, though. It's actually worse.

The text is from an unknown number, and the message is a single word.

Murderer.

CHAPTER EIGHT

TRIPP

"Who would do this?" Charlotte demands at lunch, brandishing her phone like an accusation. "How dare they? It's obscene!"

"It's a stupid joke," Shane says. He leans back in his chair and puts an arm around Charlotte's shoulders, but for once she's too distracted to melt into him. "That whole portrait thing has everyone riled up."

"Well, they should make up their minds," Charlotte says tightly. "Do they hate Mr. Larkin, or do they hate us? If we're *murderers,* then you can't have it both ways, right?"

"Stop acting like this is supposed to make sense," I say, hoping I sound as nonchalant as Shane. If Charlotte knew how much that text freaked me out, she'd only spiral more. Besides, I started feeling better—less targeted, anyway—when I realized Shane and Charlotte got one too.

"I hate being falsely accused." Charlotte flings her phone onto the table and folds her arms tightly across her chest. "It brings back *memories.*" Shane and I both blink at her, confused, until she says, "Hello? The class-trip money? People said I was a thief."

"No one ever actually believed that," Shane reassures her.

Charlotte looks more than ready to argue the point, so I quickly change the subject. "I wonder how whoever sent this got our numbers?" I say.

Shane shrugs. "School directory? The office has them. Wouldn't be hard."

"So it's somebody here," Charlotte says, her eyes narrowing as they flick across the cafeteria. "One of the dregs, probably."

"Come on, Charlotte. Don't jump onto that train," I say. The term *dregs* makes me uncomfortable, and not only because the guy who started it, Colin Jeffries, lives two blocks away from me in Sturgis. If there's such a thing as a *dreg* at Saint Ambrose, I'm it. Shane and Charlotte keep forgetting that, maybe because they've never been to my house. Even when they pick me up to go someplace, I meet them at school. That started in eighth grade, when I was an asshole who was embarrassed about where I lived, and somehow it never stopped.

Yes, it's weird. But it's probably weirder that they've never questioned it.

"Drop it, okay?" Shane murmurs as the table starts to fill up. Abby Liu puts her tray next to mine, lowering halfway into a chair, before springing back up with a frustrated sigh. "Ugh, I forgot to get a drink," she says. "Anyone else need anything?"

"Could you find me another apple?" Charlotte asks, frowning at the one on her tray. "This one has a bruise." It looks fine to me, but Charlotte is like that fairy tale about the princess and the pea—always pointing out flaws that nobody else notices.

"Sure," Abby says, twisting her shiny dark ponytail over one shoulder. "Tripp?"

"I'm good, thanks," I say.

Charlotte watches Abby walk away before turning to me with a knowing smile. "She's into you," she says.

I snort. "You say that about everyone."

"Can I help it if everyone is into you?" Charlotte asks, flipping her hair over her shoulders. The *except me* is implied. For the moment, at least, the *Murderer* text seems forgotten. "And you need a girlfriend. You've been single for way too long."

"Nobody *needs* a girlfriend," Shane says, earning a hard look from Charlotte. "I just mean, leave the guy alone, babe. Tripp can get plenty of action if he wants it."

"Don't be a Neanderthal," Charlotte huffs, scanning the tables around us. "Hmm," she adds, her expression turning thoughtful. "Brynn Gallagher got pretty, didn't she?"

I don't follow her gaze. It's funny how Charlotte is the hottest girl in school, but if you had to say why, you'd be stuck, because even though she's the total package, there's nothing about her that stands out. Not to me, anyway. With Brynn, on the other hand, everything stands out: the green eyes, the light dusting of freckles, the coppery hair. But noticing that feels like a bad idea, so I act like I didn't hear Charlotte and say, "Here comes Abby with your apple."

Charlotte puts on a bright smile as she plucks the shiny red apple from Abby's outstretched hand. Then her expression dims into disappointment as she sets it carefully next to the other one. "This is bruised too, but thank you anyway."

I can't hear, exactly, what Shane mutters under his breath, but it sounds a lot like *fucking impossible to please.*

*   *   *

Hours later I'm in the Saint Ambrose greenhouse, at the edge of a group of kids I barely know, while waiting for Ms. Kelso, because I'm afraid Regina really will fire me if I don't sign up for this goddamn memorial garden committee.

There's no one here to talk to, so I distract myself by scrolling through my phone. For some reason I still haven't deleted the *Murderer* message; maybe because I keep wondering if there might be some kind of clue as to who sent it, but that's pointless with a blocked number. Before I can get rid of it, though, a text comes through from a familiar, unwelcome number.

Lisa Marie: *Still an early-morning runner, huh, Trey?*

I shut my eyes briefly. It's always "Trey," like my mother needs her own special version of a nickname, and it's a bonus that I happen to hate it. The driver of the gray sedan that sped past me this morning wasn't a mirage after all. This day just keeps getting better.

A second text forces my attention back to my phone. *Want to get coffee after school? I saw a cute bakery on Main.*

You mean the bakery I work at? I almost type, but think better of it. It's not as if my mother would bother to remember that I have a job now. Besides, I don't owe her an instant response just because she decided to show up out of the blue and cruise the streets of Sturgis, instead of giving me a heads-up like a normal person. Lisa Marie thinks this kind of thing is fun, that she's bringing an exciting spot of color into the drab life she left behind.

But I think it's bullshit, and I'm tired of playing her games.

"Hello, hello! So sorry I'm running behind!" Ms. Kelso

64

bustles in with a few people behind her, her arms filled with folders. "What a pleasure to see so many of you here. I'm grateful, and thrilled to be working with all of you on this important project."

She opens one of her folders, pulls out a bunch of stapled papers, and hands them to the kid closest to her. "Take one and pass it along, please. This is an outline of how I'm thinking the process will go, but I welcome any and all feedback." Then her eyes settle on me, and her entire face lights up. I'm a favorite of hers, even though I've done nothing to deserve it. "Tripp, you made it after all! I'm so happy you decided to join us."

"Sure," I mumble, ducking my head as I take a handout and pass the rest to whoever's next to me, without looking at them. I don't need any more curious glances; I've been getting them since I showed up in the greenhouse. I'm the guy who found Mr. Larkin, after all.

"I'm thinking about this in phases," Ms. Kelso continues. "First there's planning. We need to decide what the garden should contain, both in terms of plantings and some kind of object like a bench or a plaque. We're going to have to price out those options. And then . . ."

It's hot in the greenhouse, so I unzip my coat and look around me as Ms. Kelso continues to talk. There are too many plants here, I decide. I don't like it. I haven't liked being surrounded by this much green since that day in the woods.

No. Not thinking about that.

Usually it works; the memory threatens to surface, and I push it down. But this time, maybe because I'm in the middle of an overheated faux woods, I can't. For a few seconds, everything around me fades. All I can see is trees, their trunks gnarled and their branches twisting every which way, blocking the sunlight and hemming me in. Someone is screaming, making it impossible to think, and I *have* to think.

"Tripp?"

I blink until my vision clears. Ms. Kelso is staring at me, which probably means everyone else is too.

"Did you hear me?" she asks. "Are you okay with heading up that subcommittee?"

Fuck. What subcommittee? What have I gotten myself into? I should just accept that Martina Zielinski is getting the Kendrick Scholarship, not me, and then I can leave this leafy hellscape and never come back. Except for the part where Regina would either fire me or kill me. Possibly both. "Yeah, I guess," I mumble, dropping my eyes back to my handout. The words swim in front of me, impossible to read.

"Wonderful," Ms. Kelso says. "You and your co-chair will make a great team."

Co-chair? Ms. Kelso is smiling at someone to my left, the person I shoved the handouts toward without a glance a few minutes ago. I look now, and find myself staring into Brynn Gallagher's bright green eyes.

"Hi, partner," she says.

CHAPTER NINE

BRYNN

"Brynn. Question for you. How many murders did Patty LaRusso commit?"

"Um." I look up from my Excel spreadsheet to see Lindzi Bell, one of the associate producers for *Motive*, leaning expectantly into the doorway. "Well, she was involved in three deaths, but one of them was ruled an accident. So, technically two."

It's my third week at *Motive*, and so far my schedule seems to be "whenever you can show up," as Lindzi puts it. Lindzi is my supervisor, and I spend most of my time here in what she calls the Pit—a windowless room with a long table where a dozen research assistants sit behind laptops—working on projects like cataloguing female serial killers.

Lindzi shakes her head, sandy curls bouncing as she rolls up the sleeves of her perfectly fitted wrap top. She's thirty-ish with a face full of freckles, and dresses like she just came from a very expensive yoga class. The kind where you wear all your best jewelry. "Let's delete her. Two's not enough to make the cut."

The guy next to me, a gangly hipster named Gideon, mutters, "Way to slack, Patty" as I dutifully remove Patty LaRusso from the spreadsheet.

Lindzi ignores him, eyes still on me. "Also, I wanted to talk to you about the roundtable we're having in Scarlet later," she says.

When I first started working here, I only understood about half of what Lindzi said, because a lot of her conversation takes place in shorthand. But now I speak the language of *Motive* a little better. I know that roundtables are meetings where producers give updates on stories in progress, and Scarlet is the big conference room next to reception. All the conference rooms are named after characters in Clue. "Try to avoid holding meetings in Mustard, if you can," Gideon told me on my first day. "The table is always sticky. No one knows why."

"What about it?" I say eagerly, spinning in my chair.

Today's roundtable is a big deal for me. I gave Lindzi my Mr. Larkin summary as soon as I arrived, and she got back to me a few days later with notes. "I like it. There's something there," she said, and I felt a quick, happy burst of pride. Then last week she suggested I introduce the story at the next roundtable.

"Are you serious?" I gulped. "*Motive* is going to cover Mr. Larkin?"

"That's not what *introduce* means," she said kindly. "It's just a chance to get more input on an early concept, so don't get too excited."

"You sure you want me to do it?" I asked, then immediately regretted the question. I needed to be confident, not tentative.

"Why not? It's your idea," she said. Then she winked. "Also, to be honest, it's going to be a pretty sparse roundtable with a light agenda. A lot of people are traveling, or still on vacation. So consider it a practice run among friends."

Now Lindzi crosses her arms and leans against the doorway. "So, it turns out that today's roundtable is going to be a lot less casual than I thought. Ramon d'Arturo is here for it."

All the research associates murmur "Ooooh" in unison as I blink at Lindzi.

"Who's Ramon d'Arturo?" I ask.

"New senior exec, joined a few months ago from ABC. His job is to get us picked up by a bigger platform." Lindzi lowers her voice and adds, "Ramon and Carly clash a lot. He's all about *growing the brand,* and his ideas can be pretty old-school. He also loves to poke holes in stories, so I'm thinking today might not be such a great day to present William Larkin."

"What? No, it's fine," I insist, my stomach plummeting at the thought of all my careful preparation going to waste. "I don't mind. Critique is part of the job, right?"

Lindzi looks doubtful. "It's not part of an internship, typically. You were only on the roundtable schedule in the first place because . . ." She trails off at my expression, which is probably in the range of *crestfallen.*

"Because you didn't think anyone would be there to hear me?" I finish.

"It's for your own good, honestly," Lindzi says. "I hate presenting in front of Ramon, and I've been a producer for five years."

"I want to do it," I say stubbornly, even though I'm not sure that's actually true.

"Let me see what Carly thinks," Lindzi says. Then she's gone, bracelets jangling as she waves to someone in the hallway.

Gideon heaves a mournful sigh. "It was nice knowing you, Brynn."

"What? How bad can it be?" I ask. "I'm just introducing an idea."

"Oh, you sweet summer child." Gideon shakes his head. "There's no *introducing* when it comes to Ramon. I can guarantee you, if William Larkin is on the roundtable agenda, Ramon already knows more about his case than you ever will."

"That's impossible," I protest. "I was Mr. Larkin's student."

"As I said," Gideon says, "it was nice knowing you."

"I'm ignoring you now." I turn back to my female serial killer spreadsheet, trying to pretend his words haven't caused an anxiety spike.

I keep working until a few minutes before four-thirty, when I make my way to Scarlet. There are ten leather chairs around the table, mostly filled by producer types like Lindzi. Already it's a much bigger meeting than the "practice run among friends" Lindzi originally described. She waves to me while patting the empty chair beside her, and the butterflies in my stomach take full flight.

"Carly said go ahead," she murmurs as I approach.

"Great," I gulp. No backing out now.

I take a seat just as Carly strides into the room, deep in conversation with a tall man with salt-and-pepper hair and wire-rimmed glasses. My first impression of the two of them is that they match; even from a distance, I can tell he's the kind of person who commands a room without even trying. Carly catches my eye and flashes a smile before settling into a chair at the head of the table. The tall man takes a seat beside her, smoothing his tie down his chest.

"Okay, everyone," Carly calls out, and the chatter instantly dies down. "Ramon is joining us all the way from New York for today's roundtable, so let's give him a warm welcome." The tall man inclines his head, as a chorus of hellos and a smattering of applause fill the room. "Excited to have your input, as always, on what I think are some very interesting concepts." Carly gazes around the table until her eyes settle on me. "Most of you know our intern, Brynn, who's sharing a story idea for our consideration today. It's one where she has a personal connection, since the victim in question was once her teacher. Brynn, do you want to start us off with the William Larkin case?"

Oh God. Nothing like getting right to it. "Of course," I say, opening my laptop.

Ramon peers at me over his glasses. "We're letting interns pitch stories now?" he asks in a deep, rich voice.

I swallow nervously as Carly says, "We're a flat organization, Ramon. Ideas can come from anywhere, and personally, I love the initiative. Go ahead, Brynn."

"Okay," I say, but my voice is a lot shakier than it was ten seconds ago. *Relax,* I tell myself. *Just do everything you practiced last night.* "I thought we could start out by meeting Mr.—by meeting William Larkin in his own words."

I stab at a key on my computer. A video springs to life on the whiteboard in front of the room, and there he is—my former teacher, wearing a white shirt and his lemon tie. Mr. Larkin is seated in my old classroom, smiling at whoever's pointing a camera at him. "I enjoyed working at the Eliot School," he says, brushing a lock of wavy dark hair out of his eyes. "But

Saint Ambrose is something special. I love this school's commitment to educating students from every walk of life to such exceptionally high standards."

I pause the video and say, "William Larkin recorded that for Sturgis Cable Access in March 2018. A month later, on April 12, he was dead, found bludgeoned to death in the woods behind Saint Ambrose." I hit another button, and a collage of photos fills the screen. Mr. Larkin's staff directory photo, our eighth-grade class picture, and several candid shots—him helping Mr. Solomon haul a bag of fertilizer during recess, serving chili at the All-School Potluck, and manning a booth at the annual book fair. "He was a popular teacher, beloved by all his students, and he was also—"

"A void," Ramon d'Arturo breaks in.

A few people inhale sharply, and my cheeks instantly flame. "I'm sorry?" I say. My hand goes instinctively to my charm bracelet, and tugs at the familiar links.

"Ramon," Carly says tersely. "Brynn was speaking."

"I apologize for interrupting," Ramon says. "But there's a core issue we need to address." He gets to his feet, grabs a marker from the ledge below the whiteboard, and writes *WHO CARES?* in giant capital letters over Mr. Larkin's head.

My jaw drops as Carly says, "She was just telling you that."

"She's telling me he was a good teacher," Ramon says. "Which is wonderful. But normally when we pursue a story of this nature, there's a grieving family looking for answers. Parents who share childhood memories. A fiancée or partner who lost the love of their life. Siblings pointing the finger at people they never liked. But William Larkin?" He shrugs. "His body was identified by his roommate. The local papers interviewed his colleagues, not his family. Because apparently they don't exist."

"Wait, what?" I blurt out.

Ramon's brow furrows. "You didn't know that?"

"I . . ." Am at a loss for words.

"Did your teacher ever mention his family in class?" Ramon presses. "Or a close friend? A girlfriend, maybe?"

"Um." All eyes are on me again as I search my memory. Surely he must have, and yet . . . absolutely nothing comes to mind. When Mr. Larkin talked to us, it was always *about* us, and it never occurred to me to question that. I just assumed it was his job to care more about his students than himself. I didn't even think about his family and friends while I was pulling my roundtable presentation together, which now seems like the most amateur of oversights.

Lindzi was right; I should have backed out when I had the chance.

"No," I admit. "Never."

Ramon nods. "I'm not surprised. The Sturgis Police couldn't find any relatives, and none came forward. Details of the burial were handled by the Saint Ambrose staff. Like I said, the man was a void."

I'm not sure which is worse—that it took Ramon less than five minutes to expose me as a true-crime novice who neglects basic research, or that he keeps calling Mr. Larkin a *void*. I want to defend Mr. Larkin, or maybe myself, but Carly speaks up before I can do either.

"And that's a story, isn't it?" she asks. "Why was this handsome, intelligent young man, who was well-liked by his students and his colleagues, so isolated?"

"It's not our story," Ramon says. "*Motive* needs the personal element for our viewers to care, and it's going to take far too many resources for us to even scratch the surface here. My recommendation is that we kill the idea." I wince, because there's something awful about hearing that word while looking at Mr. Larkin's smiling face. Almost like he's dying all over again.

"You're not giving it a chance, Ramon," Carly says. "What about the kids involved? They were barely questioned, and I don't think it's a coincidence that some of them have very wealthy and prominent parents—"

"There's one more thing," Ramon interrupts. He smooths his tie down his chest, gold cuff links flashing, and even though I've never played poker, I'm suddenly reminded of someone who's about to reveal a winning hand. "One of my Vegas sources tells me that Gunnar Fox is chasing the same story."

Everybody reacts as though Ramon just tossed a heap of garbage onto the table. Faces twist, nostrils flare, and more than one person says "Ew." A half dozen side conversations break out as I unlock my phone and hastily Google the name. Results come up quickly: a former Las Vegas sportscaster who was fired for sexual harassment and who recently launched a true-crime show called *Don't Do the Crime* that he broadcasts on YouTube and his Facebook page. Basically a *Motive* copycat with a skeevy host and no credibility.

"Why on earth would Gunnar Fox be chasing this story?" Carly demands.

"According to my source, he claims to have some kind of inside scoop," Ramon says. "But it doesn't really matter why, right? The point is, if you move forward, you'll be wrestling with that pig for interviews. You'll get dirty, and he'll like it. There are too many other stories worth your talent to waste time on this one." His eyes flick toward me, and if he wanted to make me feel an inch tall, mission accomplished.

Carly levels a penetrating gaze at Ramon, but all she says is, "Noted. Let's move on for now. Tucker, do you want to tell us about the Echo Ridge case?"

I slump in my seat as Lindzi frantically scratches a note on her pad and shoves it in front of me. *DON'T FEEL BAD,* she wrote in all caps. *HE'S LIKE THAT WITH EVERYONE.* I give her a wan smile and push the pad back toward her, trying to refocus my attention on the rest of the meeting. She's right; all the other pitches get picked apart, though none as badly as mine. When the roundtable is finally over, I hurriedly grab my stuff, eager to go back to the relative safety of the Pit even though Gideon's "Told you so" is waiting for me.

"Brynn!" Carly's voice stops me in my tracks. When I look up, her eyes are on her phone as she adds, "I need to take this call, and then I'd like a quick sidebar with you and Lindzi in Mustard. Wait for me there, please."

"Ugh, Mustard," Lindzi mutters, and my heart plummets as I follow her out the door and down the hall. Carly didn't sound happy, at all. Instead of impressing her, I embarrassed her, and probably ruined my shot at journalistic redemption.

"I'm out of here, aren't I?" I blurt out when Lindzi shuts the door behind us.

"What?" She blinks in confusion while setting her laptop on the chair beside her, then holds out her hand when I move to put mine on the table. "Don't. It'll stick."

"Can't someone just, you know, clean that?" I ask, momentarily distracted as I balance my computer and notebook on my knees.

Lindzi heaves a deep sigh. "Believe me when I say we have tried."

The door flies open then, and my pulse picks up when I see Carly's face. She looks angry, and when her mouth opens, I brace myself for the words *You're fired.* Instead she closes the door, leans against it with her arms crossed, and spits out, "That asshole needs to learn who's in charge around here."

CHAPTER TEN

BRYNN

"What?" I ask as Lindzi tries and fails to suppress a grin.

"Who is he to interrupt my staff in the middle of a presentation?" Carly asks, starting to pace the room in her mile-high heels. "To interrupt *me*? And question my judgment, like I'm some kind of novice who needs guidance and not the person who single-handedly built this show from the ground up?"

"Preach it," Lindzi says under her breath.

Relief floods my veins as Carly's words sink in and I realize her anger isn't directed toward me. "You don't agree with what Ramon said about Mr. Larkin?" I ask.

"I didn't get where I am by letting some corporate hack tell me what to do," Carly says. She flings herself into a chair and exhales loudly, visibly composing herself before adding, "Let's take some preliminary steps on this story. Lindzi, I want you to get in touch with the Sturgis Police and see what evidence they're willing to share."

I manage not to bounce out of my chair, but just barely, as Lindzi picks up her laptop and starts typing. "Aye, captain," she says.

"And put a call for information on the website," Carly continues. "William Larkin's name, picture, age at his death, the date he died, and the hotline email."

Lindzi pauses in her notetaking, brows raised. "If William Larkin goes up on the website, Ramon is going to know . . ." She trails off as Carly's expression gets steely again.

"That we're pursuing a story?" Carly asks coolly. "Which is the lifeblood of this organization and the reason everyone involved with it, including him, has a job? Good."

"Good indeed," Lindzi says, returning her eyes to her screen.

I gaze between her and Carly, hardly able to believe what I'm seeing. Two brilliant, sought-after professional journalists are giving their full attention to Mr. Larkin's story—all because of a suggestion I made. Well, and the fact that a guy Carly doesn't like just shot me down in flames, but I'm going to focus on the positive for now.

"What can I do?" I ask.

Carly wrinkles her brow. "Maybe poke around a little on those kids from the woods," she says. "What are they up to now? What are their families up to? That kind of thing."

I nod, thinking back to the Saint Ambrose memorial garden committee meeting from earlier today. I didn't show up there expecting to see Tripp Talbot, and spent the first ten minutes of the meeting annoyed that he was ignoring me before I had the chance to ignore him. Then Ms. Kelso put us together, which was worthwhile for the expression on his face alone. It looks like that's not the only benefit of being stuck with my old nemesis, though.

"Already on it," I say.

Later that night, I'm still filled with nervous adrenaline and unable to sleep. I tried briefly around eleven o'clock, then gave up and picked up my phone, which is a treasure trove of Google results on the Delgado and Holbrook families. What Shane's and Charlotte's parents are *up to,* apparently, is making even more money.

Mr. Holbrook's company is a venture capital firm best known for funding a popular dating app. The Delgados co-own a real estate development company, and churn out press releases on what seems like a weekly basis. I've already scrolled through the past two years' worth of news, and now I'm checking out what they had going on the year Mr. Larkin died. DELGADO PROPERTIES COMPLETES SALE OF EIGHT-ASSET NEW HAMPSHIRE PORTFOLIO, DELGADO PROPERTIES LAUNCHES GROUNDBREAKING MIXED-USE PROJECT, DELGADO PROPERTIES ANNOUNCES RECORD YEAR FOR CHARITABLE CONTRIBUTIONS. . . .

I copy some of the links to a spreadsheet that I've labeled *Larkin Research,* which is my process for every story I've ever worked on: dump all the details I can find into one document and look for patterns. What's repeated? What stands out? But already my Larkin spreadsheet looks different, almost chaotic, and I'm reminded of what Carly said when we first met: *You do realize we're not the* New York Times, *though, right? True-crime reporting is a very specific niche, and if you aren't passionate about it—*

I didn't let her finish, but I think I understand what she meant. You need passion, because crime—especially murder—comes from the deepest, darkest part of the human heart. It's almost impossible to think about for too long, unless you're desperate for answers.

My head is starting to ache. *Time to sleep,* I think, but instead I switch to social media to see what my Chicago friends are up to. Izzy's posted a new TikTok of her dog, and I reply with the heart-eyes emoji. Olivia's latest Instagram post is a pretty solo shot that's getting a ton of comments. When I go to add mine, I see a string of fire emojis from none other than the mouth-breather himself, basketball captain Jason Pruitt. I click on the single reply to his comment, which is from Olivia: *Go away.*

"Solidarity, sister," I say, feeling a burst of gratitude for my friend. I click on Jason's page, and my temper rises at a photo of him spinning a basketball on one finger. When *Motive* breaks Mr. Larkin's case wide open, Izzy and Olivia will make sure everyone at my old school knows I was behind it, and then they'll realize exactly how wrong they were about me.

A light knock sounds on my door, and I glance at the clock beside my bed. It's almost two in the morning, and there's only one other person in the house who's ever up this late. "Come in," I say, and the door cracks to reveal Uncle Nick.

"Thought I heard you," he says. He's not wearing his glasses, and his face looks unfinished without them. "Can't sleep?"

"I'm doing research," I say, closing out Instagram before Uncle Nick can notice me creeping on Jason's page. "Hey, when you were at Saint Ambrose, did Mr. Larkin ever mention his family? Or a girlfriend, or anything like that?"

"Did he . . ." Uncle Nick cocks his head, puzzled. "Not that I can think of. What's the urgency? I thought *Motive* had Will's story on the back burner?"

"There's been, um, renewed interest," I say. And I hope that's all he'll ask, because I don't want to have to explain the whole Ramon d'Arturo fiasco.

"Oh really?" Uncle Nick raises his brows. "Have you told your parents that?"

"Not yet. It could still turn out to be nothing. But, you know." Jason Pruitt's smug face looms in my brain, uninvited. "I'm trying to do a good job. Impress people, hopefully."

"You should pitch your boss on what happened in Carlton. That was right next door. Well, a couple towns over." I blink at Uncle Nick, and he adds, "Oh right. You guys were still in Chicago then. It was a big local scandal—three kids skipped school and wound up finding their classmate's dead body. Like *Ferris Bueller's Day Off* but with murder." He sighs at my still-blank look. "You really need to watch that movie sometime. Anyway, look it up."

"I will," I say. "So, nothing about Mr. Larkin that you can tell me? What about Tripp? Did you ever talk to him about what it was like to find Mr. Larkin in the woods like that?" I didn't, since Tripp and I weren't on speaking terms anymore.

"No, but I'm sure he was horrified. Traumatized. They all must have been." Uncle Nick folds his arms and leans against my doorframe. "Listen, I know this is exciting for you, but . . . don't lose sight of what your father said earlier, okay?"

"Meaning what?"

"Be ethical about what you share," he says.

"Since when do you listen to Dad?" I counter.

The corners of my uncle's mouth quirk. "Basically never, and look where it's gotten me. Still living with him at the age of twenty-four. So—learn from my mistakes, okay?" He yawns and scratches his chin. "And get some sleep. I need to do the same."

"Okay. Good night," I say, and wave as he shuts the door. Then I unlock my phone and go back to the Delgado Properties website. I'm still on the charitable donation press release, and I skim until I find a quote from Shane's dad. *"Delgado Properties is proud to support local businesses and services with more than ten million dollars in charitable contributions," says founder and co-president Marco Delgado. A full list of donations is provided in the company's annual 10-K report.*

The last few words are linked, and when I click, it launches a PDF file. I nearly shut it down, because those are incomprehensible on a phone, but then I see a name I recognize: *Saint Ambrose School.* Shane's dad's company gave $100,000 to the school the year Mr. Larkin died. I make a mental note to check whether they make that kind of donation every year. Then my eyes stray to the listing below Saint Ambrose, and I inhale a sharp, surprised breath.

Sturgis Police Foundation: $250,000.

TRIPP

FOUR YEARS AGO

Shane is a crappy partner. Even though he forgot his binder, along with most of Ms. Singh's instructions, he seems to think he should lead this leaf-gathering expedition. "Not that way," he announces when I start to follow a forked path to the right. "This way."

"Why?" I ask.

"We should go near the fire pit." There's a hollowed-out area farther into the woods, close to Shelton Park, where the Upper School kids have bonfires sometimes.

"Why?" I repeat. "That's nothing but pine trees."

Shane's eyes get shifty. "I told somebody I'd meet them there."

"Who?"

"Charlotte," Shane says, and I groan. Leave it to Shane Delgado to turn a science project into a date.

"Yeah, well, have fun with that. I'm going this way."

"No, don't!" Shane says. Too quickly. When I turn, I'm surprised to see that he almost looks nervous. "I don't want to go by myself."

"Why not?" I ask. I'm pretty sure every other guy in our class would jump at the chance to be alone in the woods with Charlotte Holbrook.

"Because Charlotte is—a lot." A muscle in Shane's jaw twitches. "You know how some girls want to, like, own you, practically? She's like that."

I can't relate. Girls don't want to own me; they look right through me. Except Brynn, but she looks at me like I'm her brother, and that's worse. Or she used to, anyway, before I embarrassed her in gym class yesterday. Today she hasn't looked at me at all, which is exactly what I wanted, so there's no point in whining about it.

"I didn't come here to be your third wheel," I tell Shane. I put my earbuds in, turn the music on my phone up to drown out any protest he's about to make, and keep following the forked path to the right. As far away from the fire pit as I can get.

CHAPTER ELEVEN

TRIPP

You can't ignore me forever, Trey.

Try me, I think. Then I drop my phone beside the cash register at Brightside Bakery and go back to sweeping the floor.

It's been more than twenty-four hours since I saw Lisa Marie cruising the streets of Sturgis, and I still don't know why she's here. I assume she's staying with her high school friend Valerie, since that's where she always lands when she breezes through town, but I haven't asked. I haven't answered a single message. I don't see why I should.

Except, maybe, to avoid the kind of barrage I'm getting right now. My phone keeps buzzing until Regina, who's seated behind the counter writing signs for tomorrow's specials, clears her throat. "Thought your friends knew better than to bother you when you're supposed to be working," she says with mock severity.

"It's not my friends," I say, leaning the broom against the

wall beside a sleeping Al before grabbing my phone. I silence it and scroll through my mother's follow-up messages.

How about dinner Friday night at Shooters?

I love that place.

My treat.

I'll be there at six.

"Of course you will," I say out loud. Shooters is more a dive bar than a restaurant, and Lisa Marie is all about the happy hour life.

Regina puts her marker down. "I know that tone," she says. "What's going on with Mom?"

"You mean Lisa Marie?" I scowl. "She's here and she wants to get dinner."

"Well, that sounds nice," Regina says.

"There's nothing *nice* about it."

"What does Junior say?"

"Not much." When I told Dad that Lisa Marie was back in town, he just pressed his lips together, like she's not worth a bigger reaction.

"I know you've been burned, Tripp," Regina says in a too-kind tone that I hate, because it means she feels sorry for me. "But maybe this time will be different."

When my mother left home, she did it in stages. First she spent the weekend with Valerie, and then she moved into a motel on Route 6. She'd been gone a week when I decided to ride my bike there and convince her to come home. It was an October afternoon, crisp and sunny, and I remember feeling relieved as I pedaled along the narrow strip of road that passed for a bike lane. I just had to promise to be a better kid, and everything would go back to normal.

As soon as she answered my knock, though, all the hope drained out of me. My mother looked different, silhouetted by the dim lighting of her room. Her hair was up, and she was wearing more makeup than I was used to, but it wasn't just that. The lines around her mouth had vanished, her eyes were brighter, and her shoulders were straighter.

She looked *happy.* Like leaving us was the best thing she'd ever done.

Still, I'd gone there with a mission, and I was going to see it through. Lisa Marie listened while I told her all the things I'd do differently once she came back. Then she took me to the vending machine outside and let me pick my snacks—a Coke and a packet of Lay's potato chips—before we settled back into her room, one of us on each of the twin beds. "Here's the problem, Trey," she said, "I'm kind of done with this whole mothering thing."

I didn't even know what to say to that. How can someone just be *done?* I was afraid to ask, so all I said was "But you're a good mother." I was about to open my potato chips, but I was nervous and accidentally squeezed them hard, crushing them.

"We both know I'm not," she said as I hurriedly shoved the chips behind my back. It felt ominous to have ruined something she'd given me before I'd had the chance to enjoy it.

"I want you to come home, Mom." I still called her that then; we didn't enter the "Lisa Marie" stage of our relationship until she'd been gone a few years.

"I'm not going to do that," she replied, and the certainty in her words chilled me. "Listen, Trey, you need to understand something." She blew out a sigh then, long and deep. "I never planned on being a parent. I always had the feeling I wasn't cut out for it, but Junior wanted a baby so much that I agreed to give it a shot." *Give it a shot.* Like I was an unusual flavor of ice cream. "I've been trying my best, but this day-in, day-out stuff?" She shrugged. "It's not for me. I've had enough."

Eight years later, I still can't believe she said that to a nine-year-old. Of all the things my mother has done to me over the years, being honest might be the worst.

The bell on the door jingles, and Al raises his head as a girl in a gray coat and slouchy black hat enters. She pulls off the hat, sending her auburn hair flying in all directions with static, and I realize with a sinking heart that it's Brynn. When she suggested after Ms. Kelso's meeting in the greenhouse that we should get together to start planning the layout for Mr. Larkin's garden, I didn't think she meant *today.*

"Who is this majestic bundle of fluff?" she asks, holding out a hand to Al. He glances at Regina—Al is too well-trained to approach even friendly customers without permission—and springs up when she nods. He trots toward Brynn and leans against her with his full weight, tail wagging. I'm surprised he doesn't knock her over; Brynn is as tiny now as she was in eighth grade. "A wisp of a girl," Dad used to call her. "With a big mouth." Which might sound as though he didn't like her, but he did.

"Hello, you're beautiful," Brynn croons to Al, vigorously rubbing his neck like she knows it's his favorite spot. "Yes, you are."

"That's Al. The owner's dog," I say warily. "Look, I know you wanted to talk committee stuff, but I'm working, so . . ."

Brynn looks up and catches sight of Regina, who's leaning over the counter watching us. "Hi," she calls. "Are you the owner? I love your dog."

"I am. And he loves you," Regina says. "Don't be flattered, though. He's not picky." Brynn laughs, and Regina glances between us like she's waiting for an introduction. When none comes, she says, "You go to school with Tripp?"

"Yeah," Brynn says. "In middle school, and again as of last week. My family moved away from Sturgis for a while, but we're back now." She gazes around, taking in the white subway tile, pale wooden tables, tasteful light fixtures, and framed sketches of baked goods. "This is new, right? Well, in the past four years at least. It's gorgeous."

"We opened two years ago," Regina says with a pointed look toward me. "Looks like Charm School over there forgot his manners, so I'll have to ask. What's your name, hon?"

Brynn approaches the register, Al at her heels, and takes Regina's outstretched hand. "I'm Brynn Gallagher."

"Regina. Nice to meet you, Brynn. What brings you here? Coffee?"

"No. Well, I'd love some, but I was actually hoping to catch Tripp for this garden project we're doing at Saint Ambrose—"

"Except I'm working," I repeat, picking up the broom again and brushing it over the gleaming floor. "We'll have to talk later."

Too late. Regina's already perked up. "Did you say *garden project*?" she asks, looking at me with dawning approval. "As in Mr. Larkin's memorial garden?"

"Yes," Brynn says. "You know about it?"

"Oh, I know about it." Regina steps out from behind the

cash register and plucks the broom from my hand. "The floors are clean. Take a break, Tripp, and work on your project with the young lady. What kind of coffee do you want, Brynn? On the house."

"Really? Thank you, a latte would be great," Brynn says.

Regina goes back behind the counter and fires up the espresso machine as Brynn heads for a high table by the window and hops onto a stool. She shrugs off her coat, pulls a notebook and pen out of her bag, and turns to see me still standing where Regina left me. "Oh, for God's sake," Brynn says, rolling her eyes. "Would you get over yourself and sit down for ten minutes? It's not like I'm asking you to be my *boyfriend.*"

Fantastic. I was really hoping that would come up, and by *really* I mean not at all. But Brynn is back to rummaging in her bag as I take the stool across from her. "I was thinking we should have a mix of annual and perennial plants," she says, pulling out her phone. "And things that bloom at different times of year, and some evergreens. So that it always looks nice, even in winter. Thank you," she adds as Regina brings over her latte.

"Whatever," I say, earning a hard look from Regina. "I mean, yeah. Sounds good."

"We could choose plants that have meaning," Brynn says, head bent over her notebook. "Like forget-me-nots. Yellow tulips for friendship. Or rosemary, for remembrance. What else?" She looks up expectantly.

"I don't know anything about plants," I say.

"Well, it's not like I garden in my spare time either," Brynn says. "That's why Google exists." She takes a sip of her latte.

"And experts. Is Mr. Solomon still the Saint Ambrose ground-skeeper?"

"No, he retired. The new guy is only part-time, and he's kind of an asshole. You could ask Mr. Solomon, though," I say, thinking back to my run-in with him a couple of days ago. "He loves talking about that shit."

"*I* could?" Brynn asks, eyebrows raised. "Because I'm a one-woman subcommittee?"

I suppress a sigh. "*We* could. He actually just asked me to stop by, so . . ."

"Perfect. Do you have his number?"

"No. It's not like we hang out. I just see him downtown sometimes."

"I'll ask Ms. Kelso," Brynn says, jotting a note. She taps her pen on the table, pinning me with those unnerving eyes of hers. "So how've you been, Tripp? What's new?"

"Not much," I say.

She waits a beat, pen still tapping, before saying, "This is the point in our polite conversational break where you ask me how *I've* been."

The corners of my mouth almost turn up, but I stop them. I'm not trying to encourage friendliness, here. "How've you been, Brynn?"

"Really good." If she doesn't stop tapping that pen, I'm going to grab it and throw it behind the counter. "Right up till the moment I had to move away from the high school I've attended for three and a half years and finish my senior year with a bunch of strangers."

"We're not strangers," I say. "You know most of us."

"Not anymore." She finally puts the pen down, thank God. "I wouldn't have recognized you if someone hadn't pointed you out. You've changed a lot."

"People tend to do that between the ages of thirteen and seventeen."

"Almost eighteen," she says. "Next month for you, right?"

I nod. My birthday's not hard to remember; it's February twenty-ninth, which means I only celebrate the actual day every four years. The last leap year that Brynn was around, she gave me a travel mug that said *Being My Friend Is the Only Gift You Need.* I lost the top years ago but still use it to hold pens.

She sips her coffee, then puts it down before asking, "Is it weird, being part of the memorial garden project?"

"No." I say it brusquely, since I don't plan on talking about anything related to this project other than plants, but Brynn keeps going.

"It must have been awful, finding Mr. Larkin. We've never talked about it."

Of course we haven't. I made sure, four years ago, that Brynn and I would never talk again. But she doesn't seem to care anymore that I embarrassed her in gym class. If anything, she strikes me as kind of amused about it now.

"I don't talk about it with anyone," I say.

"Not even Shane and Charlotte?"

Especially not Shane and Charlotte.

But I just shrug, and Brynn adds, "I have to admit, I was surprised to see you guys had become such good friends. Does Shane still take naps in the class coatroom?"

"No. Come on. We're practically adults," I point out, before honesty compels me to add, "He stopped fitting on those benches in ninth grade."

Brynn laughs, almost spitting out her coffee, and I grin as I hand her a napkin. For a second it's almost like we're friends again, cracking up at her kitchen table over homework. Then she wipes her mouth and says, "So you're an elite now, huh?"

My smile fades. "Jesus. Not you too."

"I'm only repeating what I hear." She tucks a strand of hair behind her ear. "Saint Ambrose has changed a lot since middle school."

"They'll let anyone in now," I say, and wow, that made me sound like a dick.

Brynn's lips quirk. "How elitist of you."

"Being an elite isn't a *thing*," I growl. Obviously. If it were, I wouldn't be taking a long shot at a scholarship by making nice with Brynn Gallagher and talking about tulips.

Both of our phones buzz then, and I look down at mine. *I'm having a party Saturday,* Charlotte texted. *Your presence is both requested and expected.* I send a thumbs-up, and she adds, *I'm inviting Brynn.*

God damn it. *Don't,* I text back. Charlotte replies with a bunch of question marks, and I add, *She's a pain in the ass.*

Charlotte sends a shrug emoji. *Too late.*

I look at Brynn, who's holding up her phone. "Charlotte's having a party, huh?" she says.

"Yeah, but I can't make it," I say, rubbing the callus on my thumb.

"Me either," Brynn says. "It's nice to be asked, though." She finishes her coffee and looks toward the counter, but Regina has disappeared into the back with Al. "Would you tell Regina

93

I said goodbye, and thanks again for the coffee? I have to get a move on or I'll be late picking Ellie up from her flute lesson."

"Sure," I say, relieved.

"I'll let you know about Mr. Solomon," Brynn says, dropping her phone and notebook into her bag before looping it over her shoulder. She puts on her hat, covering up her distracting hair, and adds, "Just one more thing." Before I can respond, she leans forward until her lips are just inches away from my ear, and her breath tickles my neck as she whispers, "You're a bad liar, Tripp Talbot. Always have been."

CHAPTER TWELVE

BRYNN

"This is the one class where you're not only allowed but encouraged to use your phone," Mr. Forrest told us at the start of my media technology elective on Friday afternoon. So naturally, everyone's heads are bent over theirs as he talks about emerging platforms. If the other students are anything like me, though, they keep getting distracted by existing platforms.

I'm on Charlotte's Instagram page, which is unlocked now that she's accepted my follow request. I'm scrolling through it to see what a Charlotte Holbrook party is like. Because of course I'm going tomorrow night, even though I told Tripp I wasn't. *Poke around,* Carly said.

I checked Delgado Properties' annual giving over the last ten years, and the one and only time they ever gave money to the Sturgis Police Foundation was the year Mr. Larkin died. I texted the information to Lindzi, who replied *Interesting! Let me see if I can find the actual date of the donation.* But I haven't heard back from her yet.

Media technology is the only class I have with Shane and Charlotte, and I glance at the corner of the room where they're clustered with Tripp, Abby Liu, and another boy and girl I don't know. I'm as far away from them as I can get, trapped in a corner next to Colin Jeffries. He's wearing an overpowering amount of cologne that doesn't cover the stench of cigarette smoke wafting from his clothes, and he keeps restlessly tapping his foot on the floor, too close to mine. This is my punishment for showing up at the last second before the bell rang, when every other seat in the classroom was taken.

"So, here's what we're going to do," Mr. Forrest says, and I force my attention back to him. He turns to the whiteboard and writes *Nike, Apple,* and *Purina* on one side, and *TikTok, YouTube,* and *Instagram* on the other. "You're going to partner up, and then you're going to pick a company and a platform. Find a promotional video for your chosen company on your chosen platform, and be prepared to share with the class what you like and dislike about it."

My eyes stray to the elite corner—I can't help using the name; it's weirdly catchy—where Charlotte drapes herself over Shane, and Abby turns a hopeful smile toward Tripp.

Tripp, who lied like a rug yesterday about not being able to go to Charlotte's party. I know this because he always rubs his thumb and forefinger together when he lies. He's done it ever since he was a kid, although I'm not sure anyone else has ever noticed. If only he hadn't been clutching a volleyball with both hands in gym class four years ago while he reamed me out, I could've known for sure whether he actually believed what he was saying.

It's useful knowledge to have up my sleeve. When I was in eighth grade, I accepted everything Tripp, Shane, and Charlotte said about Mr. Larkin's death. I was mad at Tripp, sure, but I couldn't imagine that he'd lie about something so important. But Carly and Lindzi are starting to rub off on me, and suddenly I'm questioning everything.

What do you know, Tripp? I think as he gives Abby a thumbs-up and her smile widens. *And what did you do?*

"Everybody, pair up," Mr. Forrest says.

Mason is in this class too, but he's several rows away. By the time I catch his eye, he offers an apologetic shrug, already moving his chair closer to Pavan Deshpande. Who *also* would've been a good partner, because Pavan remains cute and, from what I can recall, was a solid kisser for a seventh grader. Quick and light, with zero attempt at tongue.

"Wanna be partners?" a voice rumbles from my right.

Oh God. It's Colin Jeffries, the original dreg. I'd feel bad about calling someone that, if it weren't what they called themselves. My eyes dart away, searching for an escape hatch, but everyone else in the class has already paired up. "Sure," I say, suppressing a sigh. "Do you have a preference for which company, or—"

"I don't give a shit," Colin says.

Off to a great start. "Well, I pick Purina, because dogs. As for platform—"

"YouTube," Colin says, and if he interrupts me again, I'm going to walk away and insert myself between Mason and Pavan. Rules be damned.

"Fine," I say through gritted teeth.

There's a moment of blessed silence while we both stare

97

at our phones, and I let my blood pressure settle down with a puppy video. Then Colin has to ruin it by saying, "You should wear your skirt shorter."

I know, even before the words escape my mouth, that I'm going to deeply regret engaging with him, but . . . "Excuse me?" I ask.

"You know." His eyes linger on my knees, making my skin crawl. "Some of the girls here hike their skirts up, shorter than they're supposed to be. You should do that."

"If I'd wanted your fashion advice, I'd have asked for it," I say icily. "But I didn't, since it's none of your fucking business."

Colin snorts. "Typical elite bitch."

"You throw around a lot of labels for someone who's so rude," I snap. "Maybe the people you call *elite* just don't want to talk to you."

"Whatever," Colin grunts, turning back to his phone.

To hell with him. I'm reaching for my bag so I can join Mason and Pavan, when Mr. Forrest calls, "Anyone have anything to share yet?" He started walking around once we broke into pairs, but now he returns to the front of the room and gestures to a laptop perched at the edge of his desk. "Feel free to connect your phone to the whiteboard and show us what caught your eye, even if you haven't done a full analysis of the content yet," he says.

There's a chorus of "no" throughout the room, because we've barely gotten started, until Colin calls out, "Yeah, sure. There's something that *caught my eye.*"

"What are you doing?" I protest as Colin gets to his feet. "We haven't talked about anything yet."

"Don't worry," he smirks, with a leering wink that makes

me want to bleach my eyeballs. "I got this." I look away, repulsed, and catch Tripp watching us from across the room with a furrowed brow. As soon as our eyes meet, his flick away. He bends his head toward Abby and says something that makes her glance my way.

I glare daggers at Tripp, even though he's no longer looking at me. Jerk. It's not like I *chose* Colin.

Colin plugs his phone into the cable dangling from Mr. Forrest's laptop, and a paused YouTube video fills the whiteboard.

"Okay, Colin, great," Mr. Forrest says. "But that doesn't look like—"

Colin taps his phone, and too-loud music makes everyone jump. Then a man's face comes into focus: cleft chin, broad nose, steely gray eyes that are too close together, a head full of thick hair that's suspiciously brown for somebody with that many wrinkles. A sense of déjà vu hits me—*I've seen him before, and recently*—right as the man announces, "I'm Gunnar Fox, and you're watching *Don't Do the Crime,* the only true-crime show that takes a no-holds-barred look at what it means to literally get away with murder."

Mr. Forrest cocks his head, frowning. "This is off topic."

"Wait for it," Colin says.

The camera pans back to show Gunnar Fox striding purposefully at a weird angle, like the ground beneath him is tilted. "This spring I'm launching a new series called *Killer Kids*—about boys and girls on the periphery of murder cases who might not be as innocent as they seem. We're starting next week with a dead prep school teacher in Massachusetts whose wealthy thirteen-year-old student left fingerprints on the murder weapon, yet walked away"—Gunnar pauses and stares directly into the camera—"scot-free."

And then, to my shock, Shane's face pops up on-screen. It looks like a Saint Ambrose yearbook photo; he's in his navy blazer and striped tie, smiling confidently, just like the real-life version would.

Real life. Which, I have to remind myself, is happening now. Shane's barely ten feet away from me, staring blankly at the whiteboard screen as Colin sneers, "Anyone want to explain why we're letting murderers walk around this school?"

Images flash on the screen: police tape, the chalk outline of a body, and a leafy redbrick campus that's not actually Saint Ambrose. Whoever pulled these shots together did it sloppily, with crappy production values to boot. For a second there's total silence in the room, and then everyone starts talking at once.

"What is *wrong* with you?" Charlotte shrieks, her voice rising above the noise. "Turn it off!"

"Colin, for God's sake—" Mr. Forrest makes a move for his laptop, but Tripp is faster. I didn't even see him get up, but he's suddenly at Colin's side, pulling the phone from Colin's hand and disconnecting it with a vicious yank.

"You're an asshole," Tripp hisses as the whiteboard screen goes blank.

"Give me my phone!" Colin orders, reaching for it. Tripp leaps nimbly backward, and Colin stumbles from his own momentum, banging his knee hard against the leg of a desk. His face twists as he rears one arm back and takes a wild swing at Tripp that misses by a mile.

"Boys, stop!" Mr. Forrest tries to come out from behind his

desk, but he's not looking where he's going and gets tangled in a bunch of cable wires. He twists left, then right, but only makes it worse and nearly falls over. "Do not touch one another!" he orders, hopping on one foot as he tries to extricate himself.

"Nice punch," Tripp says tauntingly, holding Colin's phone over his head. Nearly everyone is on their feet now, forming a semicircle around Tripp and Colin—except Shane, who's still frozen in his chair. "Want to try again?"

"If I do, I'll end you." Colin makes another futile grab for his phone that Tripp easily dodges. "You were in those woods too. You and—"

He turns toward Charlotte, and Tripp moves with him. "Eyes on me, Colin," Tripp says, pulling the case from Colin's phone and tossing it to the ground. Then he throws the phone itself into the air, and catches it one-handed. "Or I might accidentally drop this while you're not looking."

"You better not, you murderer," Colin snarls. "Bunch of psychopath elite freaks, all three of you. Think you can kill a teacher and get away with it."

"Fuck you," Tripp says, eyes glinting as he transfers Colin's phone to his left hand and curls the right one into a fist. His face is suddenly a hard mask, his temper taking over to the point where he almost looks like a different person. And for a second—just a split second—I can imagine him losing control and doing something terrible.

The thought should make me recoil, but instead it propels me out of my seat. I push through my classmates with one thought: *Stop him before he does something he can't undo.*

"Tripp, don't!" Abby calls. Her arms are fastened tight around Charlotte, who's glaring furiously at Colin, like she's hoping to incinerate him with her eyes. "You'll get expelled. He's not worth it!"

"Fight!" a boy yells, and a bunch of other people pick up the chant: "Fight, fight, fight, fight!"

Mason slips into the hallway, probably to get help, because Mr. Forrest is useless. He hollers, "Everyone, settle down! This instant!" at the top of his lungs, while yanking a cable from the wall in yet another frustrated attempt to break free. A loud whine of feedback fills the room, a girl screams, and Colin and Tripp keep circling one another as I reach Tripp's side.

Tripp pulls back his arm, and I lunge for his sleeve. After that, everything happens at once: I grab air, because Shane has materialized behind Tripp to drag him away; Colin lets out a wild-banshee cry as he stumbles forward with another flailing punch; and when I turn to face him, he's both off balance and much too close.

Then the side of my head explodes with pain, and I go down.

"Explain this to me again. Like I'm five," Uncle Nick says after picking me up from the nurse's office an hour later. He had to take a Lyft here, so he could sign me out and drive my Volkswagen home. The nurse wouldn't let me leave without an adult family member, and Uncle Nick was far and away the best choice. The administration knows him from when he used to work as a teaching assistant, plus he's a grad student with a flexible schedule. "I'm not supposed to tell your parents you got punched in the head because . . ."

"Because they'll freak out," Ellie finishes from the back seat.

"Not a good reason," Uncle Nick says. "You could have a concussion, Brynn."

"The nurse says I don't," I say, although her exact words were *You're not currently showing symptoms, but they don't always present right away, so make sure you're evaluated by your family doctor.* Close enough. "It's not like I blacked out or anything."

As soon as I hit the ground, I tried to get up, but Mr. Forrest, who'd finally freed himself from the cables, wouldn't let me. He got another teacher to take over our class and brought me to the nurse's office with Mason's help, even though I insisted I could get there on my own. Now I have a headache, and a bruise on my temple that my hair helpfully covers, but that's it.

"Jesus," Uncle Nick mutters, braking extra hard at a red light. "What the hell is happening at that school? It never used to be like this."

"Gunnar Fox happened," I say. "He's a parasitic hack with no journalistic credibility whatsoever." That's a direct quote from Lindzi.

"Okay, but doesn't that tell you something? Reopening old wounds about Will is setting people on edge," Uncle Nick says. "Maybe you should tell *Motive* to take a step back."

"*Motive* is nothing like *Don't Do the Crime!*" I protest.

"Your parents should be the judges of that," he says.

Ellie lets out a disappointed *tsk*. "Way to sound like Dad, Uncle Nick," she says.

"My niece. Got punched. In the *head*," he replies.

My sister leans forward between the front seats. "Do I need to remind you about the vase incident, Uncle Nick?" she asks.

He groans. "Ellie. Come on. I was sixteen."

"And I was *six*," Ellie reminds him. "But I still took the

blame after you knocked over Mom's favorite vase when you got drunk at Dad's birthday barbecue."

"I shouldn't have let you do that," Uncle Nick says. "That was a terrible, irresponsible move on my part. And look where it's gotten me. Covering for a couple of teenagers."

"Leave me out of this," Ellie says loftily, settling herself back against her seat. "I'm an observer and occasional consultant in this drama. Not a participant."

"So you're covering for me, Uncle Nick?" I press.

There's a long beat of silence, during which, I suspect, Uncle Nick pits the angel on his shoulder who's insisting that his brother needs to know, against the devil who's reminding him that Dad can be a judgmental jerk. "Only if you let me take you to Urgent Care to get your head checked out," he finally says. "No driving until we do."

"Thank you!" I say. I'd hug him—if I didn't want to prove my maturity by not making him accidentally swerve into the other lane. "You're the best. I love you."

"I'm a pushover, is what I am," Uncle Nick grumbles. "Just promise me you'll keep your distance from the kids involved in this mess."

"I promise," I say, mentally crossing fingers while I reply to Charlotte's worried text.

I'm fine. Can't wait for tomorrow night!

Don't tell Tripp I'm coming, though. I want it to be a surprise.

CHAPTER THIRTEEN

TRIPP

"Your father said we should start without him. He'll be a little late for dinner," Ms. Delgado says to Shane, settling herself at the end of their massive dining room table. Shane and I are on either side of her; I'm eating here instead of at Shooters with my mother, and I've already silenced my phone so I don't have to hear her indignant texts coming through. "He's on the phone with Edward. That video won't be up for long."

I don't know who Edward is, but I'm guessing a lawyer. The Delgados have at least a dozen of those. I guess it comes with the territory when you own one of Boston's biggest real estate development firms.

"Great," Shane mutters, dropping his napkin onto his lap. Our plates are full of roast chicken, green beans, and some kind of fluffy grain, prepared by the Delgados' personal chef. Of all the things money can buy you, having every single meal look and taste this good without lifting a finger has to be one of the best. "It's not like the internet is forever or anything."

Ms. Delgado puts her hand on his. She's dark-haired and elegant, and looks so much like Shane that it's hard to believe he was adopted. "At least he didn't use your name," she says. Shane just snorts, and Ms. Delgado turns to me. "Thank you for what you did, Tripp. You've always been such a good friend to Shane."

I duck my head and dig my fork into—whatever this grain is. Couscous, maybe? "It was nothing. I should be thanking him. I'd probably be expelled if he hadn't pulled me back."

That didn't hit me, fully, until about an hour after the whole thing went down—that I could've thrown my entire future down the drain for Colin Fucking Jeffries. Not just the Kendrick Scholarship but the scholarship that's keeping me at Saint Ambrose. After putting in twelve years at that damn school, I would've ended up with a diploma from Sturgis High School. If they'd even take me. At least I know, now that Colin put Shane, Charlotte, and me on blast in front of our entire media technology class, who sent the *Murderer* texts.

Ms. Delgado's mouth tightens, which is another way that she and Shane look alike. It's usually the only way you can tell they're mad. "Marco and I would never allow that to happen," she says, with the full confidence of someone who's used to getting what she wants. "But we'll certainly be pushing for it with regard to Colin Jeffries. He should never have been let into Saint Ambrose in the first place." She takes a sip of wine and adds, "How is that poor girl doing? Brianne, was it?" Ms. Delgado rarely pays attention to Saint Ambrose kids who aren't friends of Shane. She and Charlotte have a lot in common that way.

Shane doesn't bother to correct her. "Charlotte says she's fine."

"You should check on her yourself," Ms. Delgado prods gently. She's talking to Shane, but a hot spike of shame runs through me. *I* should check on Brynn, considering that punch was meant for me. I've been avoiding it, though, because texting Brynn feels like opening a door that needs to stay shut. She puts me off balance in a way that I hate.

"I will," Shane says.

"I meant now." Ms. Delgado cuts a green bean in half. "I think we can relax the no-phone rule at the table so you can do the gentlemanly thing."

"Fine," Shane sighs, pulling his phone from his pocket. "But I need to get her number from Charlotte. I don't have it."

That does it; I can't be the only jerk who doesn't check on Brynn. I take my phone out, ignoring the pileup of texts from Lisa Marie, and open my contacts. *Brynn Gallagher* is still there, but it's entirely possible she deleted me years ago or has a different number now. In case of either, I write, *Hey, it's Tripp. Sorry about what happened today, hope you're okay.*

There. Done. Politeness achieved.

Mr. Delgado comes in then, silver hair glinting beneath the light of the chandelier. He's at least twenty years older than his wife, but unbelievably fit for a guy in his sixties. I play squash against him sometimes at the country club the Delgados belong to, and he never gets winded. "Sorry, Laura," he says, planting a kiss on his wife's cheek. "That took longer than I thought it would."

"Everything all right?" she asks.

"Edward will be lodging a defamation suit against that Las

Vegas hack," Mr. Delgado says, taking a seat beside Shane. I've always appreciated the fact that, even though the Delgados have a ridiculously oversized table for a family of three, they don't actually sit twelve feet apart from one another. "That should keep him off our backs."

Ms. Delgado looks like she has a few follow-up questions about that, but all she says is "And the video is down?"

"Soon," Mr. Delgado says, nostrils flaring. I can tell it's massively frustrating to him that he can't just write a check and make it disappear.

My phone buzzes in my pocket, and for some reason I'm sure it's Brynn. It would be rude to ignore her after an injury, so I violate the Delgado no-phone policy once again to check my texts. Sure enough, she sent a picture of her making a face and holding her hair away from the impressive bruise on her temple. *Should've been you,* she wrote.

I don't know whether to wince or laugh. The bruise isn't funny, obviously, but her expression is, and she clearly feels well enough to mess with me. *Sorry about that,* I text back.

Want to make it up to me?

That's a loaded question if I ever heard one. *How?*

I talked to Mr. Solomon and he invited me to stop by tomorrow at two. Can you come?

My shoulders relax. It's not how I'd choose to spend my Saturday afternoon, but it could be a lot worse. *Sure,* I reply.

CHAPTER FOURTEEN

TRIPP

"I might have exaggerated a little," Brynn says when I get into her Volkswagen the next day. It's so clean that I'd think it was brand-new, except for the fact that it doesn't have that new-car smell. Whoever normally sits in the passenger seat—Ellie, probably—is a lot shorter than me, so I have to adjust the seat all the way back. Once I do that, I turn to look for my seat belt.

"About what?" I ask.

"Well, technically I didn't talk to Mr. Solomon. I left him a message."

I freeze halfway to buckling myself in. "You left him a— hold on. Are you telling me he's not expecting us? We're just showing up?"

A red alert starts chiming on Brynn's dashboard as she backs out of my driveway. "You need to fasten your seat belt," she says calmly. "And yes, that's what I'm telling you."

"We can't do that," I protest.

"Why not? You said he invited you. Plus, he might never check his messages. A lot of people don't, and then where would we be?"

"Not barging in on the guy, for one thing." The beeping sound is driving me crazy, so I finish fastening my seat belt even though I'd rather get out of the car entirely. "You know, for somebody who called me a liar, you sure like to play fast and loose with the truth."

"I didn't call you a liar," Brynn says. "I called you a *bad* liar."

Yeah, she did, and it's been bugging me ever since. Why would she say something like that? Maybe she was just looking for an excuse to rattle me, which she seems to enjoy. I guess I can't blame her, and it's not like I'm going to ask. Instead I settle for a grumpy, "I wouldn't have come if I'd known."

"You owe me. I took a punch for you." She adjusts her knit hat, which is pulled down so low, there's no possibility of seeing whether the bruise has gotten worse. She looks perfectly healthy, though, her cheeks pink from the cold and her eyes bright and clear.

Which I'm noticing as a clinical observation, to make sure a concussed person isn't driving me around town, and not for any other reason.

"You shouldn't have been next to me," I say, before realizing it's the ultimate dick move to blame someone for getting punched. Plus, I remember Brynn's hand brushing my sleeve just before Shane pulled me away. She was there because she was trying to stop me from making a giant mistake. "Sorry. That was out of line. I'm just . . ."

Rattled. You rattle me, Brynn. Always have.

"It's fine," Brynn says, waving a hand. "Bygones. And I

know I'm being a little pushy with Mr. Solomon, but it would be nice to give Ms. Kelso something positive on Monday. She's had a rough week."

"What do you mean?" I ask.

"Well, first there was Mr. Larkin's portrait. That really upset her. She was in charge of having it done, and she feels responsible for what happened because she didn't keep it somewhere secure. It was just backstage in the auditorium, where pretty much anyone could have gotten to it," Brynn says. "But also, when I asked her yesterday for Mr. Solomon's number, she mentioned that somebody had trashed all the flyers she'd made for the memorial garden committee."

"Threw them out?" I ask.

"No. Scribbled over Mr. Larkin's face in every single one. Well, *scribbled* sounds kind of harmless, doesn't it? It was more like . . . angry red slashes."

"Well, shit." I'm quiet for a beat, absorbing that. "Somebody really didn't like Mr. Larkin, huh?"

"Ms. Kelso thinks it's directed at her."

"Seriously?" I ask. I can't picture it; Ms. Kelso is like everyone's favorite grandmother. Even the self-proclaimed dregs don't give her a hard time. "Why would she think that?"

"I guess she can't imagine anyone hating Mr. Larkin that much." Brynn makes a turn onto Spruce Road, the long, winding street that leads to Mr. Solomon's house. Most Sturgis kids know where he lives because his house backs up against the soccer fields, and we'd always pass it on our way to buy ice cream after practice. He usually worked in his garden on weekends, and would wave as we passed. "Especially since he's been gone for almost four years. I mean, can *you* think of a reason?"

111

I don't like the way she asks the question; like there must be a sinister answer that only I know. "Nope," I say shortly, and shift in my seat to look out the window.

We drive in silence until Brynn passes a mailbox with the number thirty-nine on it and says, "Here we are." She slows to a crawl and turns into the unpaved driveway. I flip the sun visor up, expecting to see the same pristine little bungalow I remember, but that's not what's in front of us. The yard is littered with tools, debris, and an oversized blue tarp half-covered with ice. The flower boxes beneath the windows, and two large planters flanking the stairs leading to the front door, are full of dead plants. "Um. Are we sure he still lives here?" Brynn asks, pulling to a stop beside a rusty black pickup.

"*We* aren't sure of anything," I say. "This is your field trip." She bites her lip, looking worried enough that I relent and say, "Yeah, he lives here. That's his truck."

"Okay, well, here goes nothing," she says.

We climb out of the car and approach the front stoop, stepping over a scattering of loose bricks that look as though they've been there for a while. Brynn presses the yellowing doorbell, and a loud chime sounds. We wait in silence for a minute, and she presses again. This time I hear a clattering noise from somewhere inside, but nobody comes to the door. "Mr. Solomon?" Brynn calls, cupping her hand beside her eye to peer through the dusty windowpanes next to the door. "It's Brynn Gallagher from Saint Ambrose. Are you home?"

"If he is, he doesn't want to talk to you," I finally say. "Let's go."

"Not yet," Brynn says. "I could swear I heard someone. Maybe we should try the back door." She doesn't wait for an answer, just troops down the stairs and rounds the corner of the house. After a moment's hesitation, I follow.

Mr. Solomon's backyard is worse than the front, filled with half a dozen rusted wheelbarrows, and empty planters stacked so high that they're tilting dangerously. The space used to be open when we were kids, but now it's surrounded by a short wooden fence. Brynn is standing at the gate, brow furrowed as she fumbles with the latch.

"What are you doing?" I call, lengthening my strides. "You can't just open that."

"It's the only way to get to the back door," Brynn says, head down. "I don't understand how this works, though."

I forgot how hopeless Brynn is at anything that requires spatial awareness. "You pull and lift," I say, popping the latch. "But I don't think—"

There's a loud click from the direction of the house. Brynn's hand seizes mine, and clutches so tight that it hurts. She's gone completely rigid, eyes fixed in front of us. When I follow her gaze, I find myself staring into the barrel of a shotgun.

"Oh shit," I breathe. My heart gives a panicky leap, and my mouth goes dry. I've never seen a gun before, except behind glass at a museum. This one, even from twenty feet away, looks cannon-sized and deadly. A half dozen thoughts crowd my brain all at once. *I'll miss Regina and Al. I haven't seen my mother in two years. I never got to leave Sturgis. I never made up for any of the things I did wrong, and I never apologized to . . .*

"Brynn," I say, my voice hoarse. "I'm really sorry."

"For what?" Brynn hisses, squeezing my hand even tighter. "Did you know this was going to happen?"

"No, I just . . ." I don't know how to finish that sentence.

Seconds tick by with no sound except for our breathing, and my tunnel vision expands to take in the man in front of us. He's short and white-haired, dressed in a checked flannel shirt that's too big for his frame, and even though his face is half-hidden by the barrel of the gun, my heart rate slows as I process who it is.

I never would've expected Mr. Solomon to pull a gun on anyone, so all of this is new territory, but I'm reasonably confident he won't pull the trigger.

"Mr. S!" I call. "It's Tri—it's Noah Talbot. You asked me to come by, remember?"

"Thieves!" he barks out. "Think you can sneak around and take what's mine?"

"No. Definitely not." Somehow, without my even realizing it, I've put up the hand that Brynn isn't holding, like an old-time bank teller getting robbed. "We just wanted to talk to you."

"Goddamn thieves and trespassers," he snarls. Then he lowers the gun a fraction, like my words finally sank in. "Wait. Noah?" he asks doubtfully. "Is that you?"

"It's me," I confirm. "Could you maybe put the gun all the way down?"

He ignores the request and jerks his head toward Brynn. "Who's this?"

Brynn calls, "Brynn Gallagher, Mr. Solomon. I went to Saint Ambrose, remember?"

"No," he says shortly. But he finally lowers the gun, and both Brynn and I exhale noisily. "Why are you trying to break into my garden?"

"Yeah, Brynn, why are you?" I mutter, which earns me a glare.

"Well, actually, Mr. Solomon, we wanted to talk to you about gardens." She glances around us at the ruins of what used to be Mr. Solomon's pride and joy. "The school is putting one together for Mr. Larkin, like a memorial garden? Tripp and I—I mean, Noah and I—are in charge of plantings, but we don't know what to choose. We don't know what's good for something like that." Mr. Solomon just stares at her without moving a muscle, and Brynn shoots me a helpless look. I don't know how she thought this was going to go, but I'm sure she didn't picture shouting questions over a gate at an armed man. "So, we thought we'd ask you." It's not a question, exactly, but her voice lilts hopefully at the end.

"I'm busy," Mr. Solomon says.

"Oh, sure," Brynn says. "We should've—I should've called. Well, I did call, but . . . anyway. We could come back? Another time, maybe?"

"You can come back," Mr. Solomon says, his voice finally softening. "Always nice to see Saint Ambrose kids. But I'm not talking to you about any goddamn garden."

"You're not?" Brynn asks doubtfully, gazing around at Mr. Solomon's wasteland of a backyard. "Do you not, um, like gardens anymore?"

"I like them fine," Mr. Solomon says. Brynn's eyes cut toward me, confused.

I shrug, mouthing, *He's not all there.*

She finally notices that she's still holding my hand, and drops it like I'm burning her, which makes me annoyed that I didn't pull away first. "I might not have explained things right," she says. "The garden we're doing is a memorial garden for Mr. Larkin, to celebrate his—"

"I know what a memorial garden is," Mr. Solomon interrupts. "And I'm not interested in helping you with this one." Mr. Solomon tucks his gun under his arm and turns for the door, calling, "Take care, Noah," over his shoulder. "See you at Brightside."

"What the hell?" Brynn murmurs. She raises her voice and calls, "Why not?"

Mr. Solomon is at the door now, and at first I think he's going to ignore her. But instead of reaching for the knob, he pauses with one hand on the railing, and half turns to face us.

"Because that son of a bitch got what he deserved," he says. Then he walks inside and slams the door behind him.

CHAPTER FIFTEEN

BRYNN

"He said *what*?" Nadia asks.

We're playing Ping-Pong in my basement on Saturday evening, me and Nadia versus Mason and Ellie. Ellie's taking a break from flute practice, and the rest of us are killing time, because while I don't know for sure what time a party at Charlotte Holbrook's house should start—since she didn't bother to tell me—I'm pretty sure it's not eight o'clock.

"That son of a bitch got what he deserved," I repeat.

Ellie sends the ball back to Nadia's side, and I lunge for it because Nadia is staring at me, openmouthed. I miss, and the ball goes flying off the table. Uncle Nick is sitting a few feet away, sifting through my parents' old record collection because he too is going to a party, and it has an eighties vinyl theme. He leans to one side, scoops the ball out of a corner, and tosses it to me.

"Are you sure he was talking about Will?" Uncle Nick asks.

"I don't know who else he could have been talking about," I say, handing the ball to Mason so he can serve.

Mason takes it but makes no move to start playing again. "Maybe he was confused. You said he didn't recognize you, right?"

"Right," I say. "He didn't seem to know Tripp at first either. But then he did, and he seemed fine after that. Until he . . . said what he said."

"That's horrible," Nadia says. "Poor Mr. Larkin. First the portrait, and now this. This whole week has been such an affront to his memory."

Ellie taps her Ping-Pong paddle against her palm, thoughtful. "Do you think it's possible that you guys didn't know Mr. Larkin as well as you think you did? Maybe he wasn't totally nice all the time."

I give her a hard look. Ellie's the only person in the room besides Uncle Nick who knows about my internship, and she's the only one who knows about Ramon d'Arturo's *The man was a void* comment. She's hitting a little too close to stuff I'm not ready to share. "I knew him plenty well," I say. "And everybody at Saint Ambrose loved him. Including Mr. Solomon."

Uncle Nick leans back on his heels, a Blondie album in one hand. "Don't put Will too far up on a pedestal, Brynn," he says. "The guy was only human, like the rest of us. He could get into it with people."

"Get into it?" I repeat. "What does that mean?"

"You know." Uncle Nick keeps digging through the pile until he extracts a Simple Minds album. "Yessss. Score," he says happily. "Don't, don't, don't, don't, don't you forget about me."

"Nerd," Ellie says.

I clear my throat. "Actually, I *don't* know," I say. Uncle Nick just blinks at me, clearly having lost the thread of our previous conversation, so I add, "What you meant when you said that Mr. Larkin could get into it with people."

"Argue. Lose his temper," Uncle Nick says. "Not with you guys," he adds when my eyebrows rise. "But with parents. I'd hear him every once in a while, when I was doing after-school homework help. Sometimes it turned into an actual shouting match."

"Shouting match?" Nadia asks. "With who?"

"Most of the time I couldn't tell," Uncle Nick says. "I was trying to mind my own business. But I saw Laura Delgado storm out of there more than once."

"Shane's mom?" I ask. I don't know Ms. Delgado well, but every time I've seen her, she's been smooth and unruffled. "I never took her for a shouter."

"She wasn't one of the shouters," Uncle Nick says. "But she was upset, which is my point. Will had a way of pressing buttons. Maybe all this media attention is opening old wounds." Then he seems to realize what he just said—*all this media attention,* including the potential *Motive* story that nobody else except Ellie knows about—and hastily adds, "Or maybe you just caught Mr. Solomon on a bad day. Getting old sucks, or so I've heard." He gets to his feet, wincing a little as something cracks, and Ellie smirks.

"Hurt your back, Grandpa Nick?" she asks.

"Go play some Mozart," he retorts. "All right, I'm heading out. How about you?"

I glance at the clock on the wall; it's barely eight-thirty. "I think it's still too early."

"You've got a designated driver, right?" he asks, in that semi-stern tone he thinks makes him sound like Dad.

Nadia plucks the ball from Mason's hand and bounces it neatly on her paddle. "That's me," she says. "Always."

Mason looks like he can't wait to leave my basement. "You say that like we go to parties every weekend," he says. "This is the first party we've been to *all year.*"

"It's January eighth," she reminds him.

"I was including New Year's Eve in that equation."

"Well, don't," Nadia says. "New year, new social slate."

It's possible that, in our efforts to look too busy and important to show up early, we ended up being a couple of hours late.

"Well, this is quite the rager," Mason says as Charlotte's enormous, contemporary-style house comes into view at the end of her mile-long driveway. The front of the house is almost entirely windows, and every room is packed full of people talking, drinking, and dancing.

"You're not going to be allowed inside if you use that term," Nadia says.

"I'm guessing her parents aren't home," I say, which is another detail Charlotte failed to mention.

"I don't think I should go any farther," Nadia says, slowing the car to a stop. "It looks like people are blocking one another in, and I don't want to get stuck. I'm going to pull onto the grass." Cars are parallel parked on either side of Charlotte's driveway, and Nadia adds her Subaru station wagon to the end of the line.

I lean forward from the back seat to thump both of them

on the shoulders. "All right. Let's see what an elite party is all about."

"Only if you stop calling it that," Nadia says.

Mason pouts as he gets out of the car. "Stop policing our vocabulary."

We make our way down the rest of the driveway, weaving through cars that are parked much too closely together. When we reach the house, we all pause, eyes roving across its front. Nadia is the first to say it: "Where's the door?"

It's a fair question, because everything looks like a giant window. Then a boy rushes from inside toward one of the panes and pushes it outward. He barely makes it past us before he falls to his knees and vomits into a shrub. Music pulses from the open door as Mason catches hold of the slim silver rod that passes for a doorknob and says, "Thanks for the assist."

"Should we help him?" Nadia asks, looking over her shoulder.

I wrinkle my nose. "With what?"

The boy gets up then, still clutching a Solo cup in one hand, which he waves at us as he staggers back through the door. "This," he slurs, "was one too many."

"Auspicious start," Mason says. "Let's go."

The first thing I notice as we're absorbed into a crush of people is that we're underdressed. Well, Nadia and I are. The boys are in casual clothes, but most of the girls are wearing cute cocktail-style dresses. Some of them are in heels, but more are barefoot, like they kicked off their shoes a while ago.

"Abby," Nadia calls, and I turn to see Abby Liu leaning against the wall in a short red dress, fanning herself. "You look so pretty. Is this supposed to be semiformal?"

A different type of person than Abby might smirk about

how we're obviously second-tier guests, but she smiles kindly. "Oh, no, it's just something a few of us did for fun. How often do we get to dress up, right?" She fans herself again. "I was about to grab a drink. You guys want something?"

"Yes," Mason says, nodding eagerly. "I would like that very much."

"They're in the kitchen," Abby says. "Follow me."

I tap Nadia's arm. "You guys go ahead," I tell her. "I'm going to find a bathroom." My friends leave with Abby, and I wander through the crush of people until I see a long line of girls in the hallway that can only mean one thing. I join them with a sigh, thinking how much easier life must be when you can just saunter outside and find a tree. By the time I finish my turn and make my way into the kitchen, my friends are nowhere in sight.

Charlotte is, though. She's wearing a shimmering bronze dress, her hair pulled back on one side with a jeweled barrette. She's using a ladle to scoop red liquid from a crystal bowl into cups, and when she catches sight of me, she waves and holds one up. "Punch?" she asks.

"Thanks," I say, taking it. "Your house is amazing."

"Oh." Charlotte blinks around her kitchen—which is twice the size of mine and has top-of-the-line everything—like she's never really thought about it before. "It's okay, I guess." I can't help but let out a snort, and her lips curve into a small smile. "That came out wrong. I just wish it were closer to school, sometimes. I'm jealous of the kids who can pop home for lunch."

I've never *popped home for lunch* in my life. But she's been nice to me all week, so I tell her, "Well, if you get desperate, you can always come to my house."

"Your house?" Charlotte looks baffled at the concept, like it hadn't occurred to her until just now that I continue to exist when I'm out of her sight. Then her hostess mask slips back into place and she says, "You're the sweetest."

Aaand, we're done. "Is Tripp around?" I ask.

"He is," Charlotte says, scooping more punch. "But I wouldn't go looking for him if I were you. He's having a bad night."

"A bad night? What do you mean?"

Charlotte squints critically at the neat line of cups in front of her. They all appear to be holding the exact same amount of liquid, but she tops two of them off. Then she frowns and dumps the contents of one of them back into the crystal bowl. "It's not easy, you know," she says.

"What isn't?" I ask, my patience thinning at her vague-talk.

Charlotte seems to realize it, and finally meets my eyes full-on. "Seeing what we saw," she says. "Back then. It doesn't leave you."

"Oh," I say, surprised at her honesty and a little ashamed that I forced it. Sometimes I get so deep into reporter mode that I forget I'm dealing with actual people. I take a long sip of punch, which isn't quite sweet enough to mask how strong it is. "Yeah, of course."

"Everybody has their own way of dealing," Charlotte says. "Tripp's is that sometimes he drinks a little too much when something sets him off." Her face hardens. "Like a demented old groundskeeper turning positively feral."

123

"He told you about Mr. Solomon, huh?" I ask.

"He did," Charlotte said. "And I told *him,* I think being on that committee is a terrible idea." She gives me a pointed look, as though I'm the one who recruited him. "Scholarship or no scholarship."

"What scholarship?" I ask.

"I don't know what it's called," Charlotte says. Of course; she doesn't need to know anything about scholarships when she lives in a house like this. "But there's a big community service requirement, so—" She breaks off as a group of girls descends upon the orderly line of punch cups. "One at a time, please," she chides, and I take the opportunity to slip away.

I check my phone and see a text from Mason that reads *GORFF IS HERE I LURV HEM,* so I can only assume that (1) Mason, a notorious lightweight, has been hitting the punch hard, and (2) he's found his crush, Geoff. I catch sight of Nadia's pink sweater in a knot of girls and decide that my friends are doing fine on their own for now.

I make my way through the house. A room with a huge arched ceiling and a massive television on the wall seems to be where people are drinking the hardest, but if Tripp's having a bad night, he's not going to be in a crowd. I don't know the current version of Tripp all that well, but I know where my old friend would be. So I go outside, shivering without the coat I dropped in a pile somewhere, and gaze around at the much smaller groups of people standing in Charlotte's spacious backyard.

There's a covered pool, a fountain, and an immaculate-looking shed that's practically a small house. The property is ringed by a wrought-iron fence broken up with evenly spaced stone pillars, all the same size and shape except for the one farthest away. When I get closer, the irregularity morphs into the outline of a person. Tripp is sitting on top of the narrow platform, his legs dangling and his left hand clutching a nearly empty bottle of whiskey.

I stop at the base of the pillar and call up to him, "How'd you get up there?"

Tripp blinks slowly at me, and I'm pretty sure he didn't see me coming. "Climbed," he says. He's coatless and his blue button-down shirt is half-untucked, the sleeves rolled up. His tousled blond hair looks silver in the moonlight; his shadowed features are as fine and chiseled as a statue's. *He's beautiful*, I think, before shoving the thought away and replacing it with a more appropriate descriptor. *And very, very drunk.*

"Charlotte says you're having a bad night," I say.

"Charlotte is mistaken," Tripp says, taking a long swig from the bottle. When he finishes, there's barely an inch of liquid left. "I'm having a *great* night."

"Have you thought about how you're going to get down?"

He shrugs, unconcerned. "Jump."

"You're at least eight feet off the ground."

"And I'm six feet tall, so . . ." Tripp shrugs again. "I only have to jump two feet."

"That's not how it works," I say.

Tripp finishes his bottle and points it at me. "You're fun at parties, Gallagher. Always knew you would be."

"I'm just trying to—" Then I gasp, my heart jumping into my throat as Tripp suddenly launches himself off the pillar.

125

For a second I can't breathe, waiting for the horrific splat that's sure to come, but he lands on his feet with barely a quiver, the bottle still in one hand. He sets it on the ground before bowing deeply, and the fact that he still doesn't lose his balance makes my temper spike. "Asshole!" I say, socking his shoulder. Which probably hurts me more than it hurt him, because he is *solid*. I shake my hand and back away, glaring. "You scared me."

Tripp brushes his hair out of his eyes. "Why?"

"You could've broken a leg! Or worse. And then—"

"No," Tripp says, advancing toward me until he's close enough to touch. He's almost a foot taller than I am, and I have to crane my neck to see his face. "I mean, why do you care?" I don't answer right away—words have deserted me, for some reason—and he adds, "You can't stand me."

"That's not true," I say automatically, because that's what you say to a drunk person exhibiting self-destructive tendencies. It takes a few beats for me to realize I mean it.

"It should be," Tripp says.

I study his face. He looks tired and sad; there's none of the raw anger I saw when he nearly punched Colin Jeffries. *That's not who he is,* I think, and then I push the thought away, because how do I know, really? Were we ever truly friends, if he could've dropped me so easily? But Charlotte's offhand remark about the scholarship keeps circling through my brain, reminding me how precarious Tripp's home life always was, and probably still is, no matter how together he seems on the surface.

I don't understand, suddenly, why I'm here. Well, I *understand* it—reconnaissance for Carly—but it doesn't feel right anymore. There's no way I can tell her about this conversation;

I can't offer up Tripp's pain like it's just another sound bite. But there's still something I'd like to know, for my own sake.

"Why did you apologize to me?" I ask.

His forehead knits. "Huh?"

"Today, at Mr. Solomon's. You said you were sorry."

"Right. Yes. I am."

"For what?"

Tripp's voice is steady, and if I hadn't seen copious evidence to the contrary, I'd almost believe he was sober. "For what I said in eighth grade. In gym class. It was a lie. Which you already know, obviously." He huffs out a humorless laugh. "I'm a *bad liar.*"

"Then why did you say it?"

"Because." His Adam's apple bobs once, then twice, as he looks at the ground. "I needed you to hate me."

"Why?" I ask. "Because you'd suddenly decided to hate *me* back then?"

Tripp looks up then, his eyes capturing mine. "No, Brynn. I didn't hate you back then. And I don't hate you now." He enunciates each word slowly and carefully, like he needs to make sure I don't misunderstand him. "Not even a little bit."

"T!" The booming voice behind us makes me jump. I turn to see Shane heading our way, wearing a big grin and a determined expression. "Time to come inside, don't you think, bud?" I step back, self-conscious about how close together Tripp and I were standing, and Shane gives me a curt nod. "Hey, Brynn, how's it going? I'll take it from here."

"Take what?" I ask.

"Tripp's having a bad night," Shane says, sounding like

Charlotte's echo as he lifts Tripp's empty bottle from the ground with two fingers. His free hand curls around Tripp's bicep. "You can't take anything he says right now too seriously."

"We were just talking," I say, feeling weirdly defensive. I try to catch Tripp's eye, but he's looking at the ground again.

"No, totally, I get it," Shane says. "But talking's over, okay?"

He doesn't wait for me to answer before steering Tripp away.

CHAPTER SIXTEEN

TRIPP

My mother finally wore me down, but not so much that I'll show up on time.

I'm exactly fifteen minutes late to meet Lisa Marie at Shooters on Sunday evening, because I've made a deal with myself. If she's not there yet—which she won't be, because she's never on time—then I'll leave. I have my text all planned: *Sorry, couldn't wait. See you next time you're in town.* Then I'll go home and collapse into bed, because my head is still pounding from last night at Charlotte's house.

Which I can barely remember, except for the part where I almost told Brynn—what? Too much? Everything? Thank God Shane came along when he did.

I knew I shouldn't have texted Brynn. That moment of weakness after Colin punched her in the head has caused nothing but trouble.

Anyway, it's good to have a solid plan when dealing with

my mother. So I'm annoyed when the hostess leads me to a booth where Lisa Marie looks like she's been sitting for some time, judging by the almost empty bottle of beer in front of her. Not only was she not late, but she might've been early? This doesn't bode well. At all.

"Get stuck at work?" Lisa Marie asks as I slide onto a cracked red vinyl cushion. Shooters is one of those places that keeps changing ownership—first it was Steady Eddie's, then Midtown Tavern, then the optimistically named Paradise Lounge—but nobody ever bothers to update the interior. It's always been my mother's go-to spot in Sturgis, and I still think of it as Steady Eddie's because we used to go there every Saturday when I was a kid.

"Yeah," I say, accepting a menu from the hostess. If finishing my Kendrick Scholarship application with Regina's prodding could be called *stuck at work.* She gave me a stamp, then left a line of customers waiting so she could march me to the mailbox down the corner from Brightside Bakery to make sure I actually mailed it.

"Think positive thoughts," she told me as I slid the envelope through the slot.

"I'm positive I won't get this," I said.

Regina patted my arm with a sigh. "Attaboy."

Now, a server appears beside the booth. "Something to drink?" she asks me.

"Just water."

Lisa Marie rolls her eyes. "Have a soda. Live a little."

"I like water," I say evenly.

"You folks ready to order, or do you need a minute?" the server asks.

"Several minutes," I say, since I'm not even sure I'm staying for dinner.

"Ugh, really? I'm starving," Lisa Marie whines. When I don't reply, she turns to the server and asks, "Could we get a basket of bread or something?"

"Coming right up," the woman says.

Lisa Marie nudges my foot with hers. "I'm getting the burger," she says.

Instead of opening my menu, I lay it on the table and lean against the back of the booth, letting my eyes settle on hers. I know that makes her nervous; my mother has always hated prolonged eye contact. She looks about the same as she did the last time I saw her two years ago—too much like me for comfort—although her hair has gotten blonder and her teeth are blindingly white. Also, are her lips bigger? I think they might be.

"How's Junior?" she asks.

"*Dad* is fine," I say. It annoys me that she never calls him *your father*, like the title is as pointless for him as *mother* is for her.

"And how's school?" she asks.

No. We're not doing this. "Why are you here?"

Lisa Marie finishes the last of her beer and glances out the window. "Still not a fan of small talk, huh?"

"Nope," I say. I might be acting calm, but I don't feel it. I'm always jumpy around my mother, wondering what form her particular brand of dysfunction is going to take this time.

The server reappears with my water and a basket full of rolls, with foil-wrapped butter. "I'll take another one of these too, please," Lisa Marie says, holding up her beer bottle. Then she grabs a roll, tears it in two, and smears an entire butter packet over one half. "So you're applying to colleges now, huh?" she asks.

"Applied," I say. "It's done."

"When do you find out if you get in?" she asks, before taking a big bite of roll.

I slowly unwrap my straw. "A few months."

She's silent for a beat, chewing, then swallows and says, "What about the money part? How are you paying for it?" Another bite of roll leaves a line of butter along her lip, and she lifts her napkin to wipe it off.

"To be determined," I say.

She raises her brows. "You need help?"

"Of course," I say, wondering why she's wasting my time with this when I already spent months bugging her to fill out the goddamn FAFSA forms already. She finally did, which is all the help I've ever expected from Lisa Marie.

"Well, that's why I'm here," she says.

Something tugs at my chest then, and it takes a few seconds to realize that I just felt a small rush of hope in my mother's presence. I push it down, immediately. I don't trust it. "To help me?" I ask. "With what?"

She rolls her eyes, like it should be obvious. "Paying for school."

The server returns then with Lisa Marie's beer and asks, "You ready to order?"

"God, yes. I can't wait another second," my mother says, and rattles off her burger order.

"I'll have the same," I say. My voice is a low rumble, because my throat has gotten kind of thick all of a sudden. Stupid hope.

We hand over our menus, and when the server leaves, Lisa Marie folds her hands on the table and gives me a big, overly white smile. I almost return it, until she says, "There's an exciting opportunity I want to tell you about."

The lump in my throat dissolves instantly. That sounds like an infomercial, not an offer to cover part of my tuition. "Really," I say.

"So, you know, I meet some pretty interesting people in the casino," she says. "And sometimes we end up talking for a while, about more than whatever game they're playing."

Oh Christ. Does she have a new boyfriend? Does she want me to meet him? Even if he's rich and generous, I'm not sure I can stomach that. "Okay," I say.

"So last month I met this guy"—I close my eyes briefly, but they pop right back open when she continues—"and as it turns out, he knows Sturgis."

"Knows it?" The skin at the back of my neck starts to prickle. "Why?"

"Well, he's a true-crime reporter, and—"

I don't need to hear the rest of her lead-up. "Gunnar Fox," I say flatly. I should've made the connection as soon as Mr. Delgado called him a *Las Vegas hack*. It's a big city, but my mother has the kind of negative energy that would pull someone like him right in.

Her eyebrows rise. "You know him?"

"I saw the hit piece he did on Shane, yeah," I say. "*Killer Kids?* Classy."

"Gunnar is looking to revolutionize the true-crime genre away from the stale, overproduced shows that dominate the airwaves," my mother says, like she's some kind of Gunnar Fox puppet getting its strings yanked. "Everything the networks churn out now is just same old, same old. There's no pizazz, you know?"

"Because they're crime shows," I say. "About dead people."

Lisa Marie waves a dismissive hand, as though she's sweeping away the negativity that's keeping me from seeing the big picture. "He has a vision."

I grab a roll, just to have something to rip apart. "Am I the next Killer Kid, then? Is that what this is about?" I ask. "You're giving me the heads-up that Shane didn't get? Thanks a lot. I'll be sure to plan my day around getting slandered on YouTube."

"Don't be ridiculous," Lisa Marie snaps. "That Delgado boy's story has never added up, and it's about time somebody called him on it. But you're different. I told Gunnar, there's no way my son would protect a thug like that unless he was afraid for his life."

"You told him *what?*" I stare at her, disbelieving. "I never said anything like that, to you or to anyone else. It's not true. So you're just making shit up now?"

"You didn't say it because you felt like you *couldn't,*" Lisa Marie says earnestly. "I've finally realized that. But you're safe now, Trey. You have people looking out for you, and you can tell your side of the story."

"Jesus Christ." I stuff a too-big hunk of roll into my mouth, briefly fantasizing that I'll choke and she'll have to stop talking. Who am I kidding, though? She wouldn't.

"That's where the opportunity comes in. Gunnar knows what your story is worth, and he wants to pay you. Ten grand to be a guest on *Don't Do the Crime. Ten thousand dollars.* And that was just the starting offer. I bet we could get it higher. Can you imagine?"

Yes, I can. That's almost enough to cover a year's worth of room and board at UMass, and after that, who knows? I could worry about that once I'm not in Sturgis anymore. But as soon as I've finished swallowing, I say, "No."

Lisa Marie's brow furrows. "What do you mean, *no*?"

I keep shredding my roll into smaller and smaller pieces. "I mean I'm not going to lie on television, and if I were? I wouldn't do it with your pal Gunnar."

"Oh, come on, Trey. You haven't even thought about it—"

"I don't have to think about it. The answer is no."

"If you don't tell your side of the story, he'll tell it for you."

I pause, mid-tear. "Is that a threat?"

"Of course not. But don't you want to control your own narrative? Gunnar thinks it would make for amazing television. And he's not the only one doing something on Mr. Larkin, by the way." Lisa Marie takes a sip of beer. "He heard a rumor that that *Motive* show is going to cover it too. You know the one? With the host who just moved to Boston. That type of show always picks an angle, and if they haven't gotten in touch with you, guess what?" She tips the bottle toward me. "You're the angle." Then she puts on her most persuasive voice. "Honey, I haven't even told you the best part," she says. I almost laugh, because since when does she call me *honey*, but then she adds, "We'd be doing this together."

The server arrives with our burgers and slides plates in front of us while asking questions about ketchup and drinks that I can't answer because my mind has gone blank. Then it slowly fills back up, like data populating a spreadsheet, and I understand everything. Why my mother is here, why she suddenly cares about my college career, and why she looks like a camera-ready version of her usual self.

Once our server leaves, I say, "Gunnar Fox offered you money too, didn't he? Was it the same amount? No, probably half. But we're a set, so without me, you get nothing. Am I right?"

Her shifty expression is all the confirmation I need, even before she says, "Gunnar is very interested in my contributions too."

"Your *contributions*?" I almost laugh. "What would those be? You weren't even around when Mr. Larkin died. You'd been gone for years."

"I was in town," Lisa Marie says. "I remember the atmosphere. Very tense."

I stare at her. "You were not in town. You were in Vegas, like always."

"I came back for the Saint Ambrose spring concert, remember?"

Right. The spring concert, where participation is mandatory for all students even if you've never sung a note in your life. It's always held in late March, which never actually feels like spring in New England. "You came back for Valerie's birthday," I say. "The concert just happened to be the next night, and Mr. Larkin died two weeks later."

"I was still there, at Valerie's." She has the grace to flush a little then, because she'd made a big deal about having to leave as soon as the concert was over. "I ended up not feeling well when it was time to go to the airport, so I stuck around."

"For two weeks? And you didn't tell anyone?"

"I had the flu," Lisa Marie says with a delicate sniff. "I didn't want you to catch it."

God, she's such a liar. I don't know which is worse—that my mother came all the way from Las Vegas to try to pimp me out on television, or that I believed, even for a minute, that she came for me.

When I dropped the Kendrick Scholarship application into the mail today, I thought, *I'd do anything to win this.* But what I really meant was, *I'd do anything to get out of Sturgis next year.* It turns out that's not actually true, though. I'd rather live in Regina's spare room for the rest of my life than hand thousands of dollars to the woman who abandoned me eight years ago and never looked back.

I push the remains of my roll aside and grab my hamburger. "Give Gunnar my regards, and tell him he can fuck himself," I say, taking a huge bite of burger as I exit the booth.

"Noah Daniel Talbot! You don't understand what you're giving up. Get back here and have a mature conversation," Lisa Marie calls after me. She's finally using my actual name—my full name, no less—but it's too little and much too late. I wave goodbye over my shoulder with my burger, and keep walking.

CHAPTER SEVENTEEN

BRYNN

"That's certainly an interesting development," Carly says.

It's Wednesday afternoon, and I've just finished briefing her and Lindzi about everything that's happened in Sturgis since the infamous roundtable meeting. Well, almost everything. "Which part?" I ask, because even leaving out my conversation with a drunken Tripp, we've covered a lot of ground, between Colin Jeffries, the Gunnar Fox video, the vandalism of Mr. Larkin's portrait and Ms. Kelso's flyers, and my visit to Mr. Solomon's.

"'That son of a bitch got what he deserved,'" Carly says thoughtfully, tapping her pen on her notepad. We're in one of the smaller *Motive* conference rooms, Peacock, which is my favorite because it has cushiony armchairs for seating. She gives me a wry smile. "Not to say that the rest of your update hasn't been full of surprises. Are you sure you're all right?"

"I'm fine," I say. I was a little wary of telling Carly that I'd been hit by Colin, or had had a shotgun aimed at me, because in my experience, that's the kind of thing that makes authority figures want to lock you away for all eternity. But Carly and Lindzi took everything in stride, like it's all just another day at work. And I suppose for them it probably is.

"Good." Carly leans back in her chair and steeples her fingers beneath her chin. "And you say Mr. Solomon had never made that kind of statement before?"

"Not that I've heard," I say. "But Tripp says he's kind of senile, so maybe he was confused."

"Entirely possible," Carly agrees. Her eyes gleam. "You don't suppose Mr. Solomon could have *done* it, do you?"

"Done what?" It takes a few seconds for what she means to sink in. "Killed Mr. Larkin? Oh my God, no. No way."

"That was a very quick denial," Carly says. "Why?"

"Because he's a sweet old man!" I say.

"Who pulled a gun on you," she points out.

"He thought we were trespassing."

"Still. It's quite the overreaction."

"How could he kill someone like Mr. Larkin, though?" I ask. "Mr. Solomon was old and frail even back then."

Lindzi speaks up. "It wouldn't have taken all that much strength, actually. The murder weapon is less heavy than you might expect."

I blink at her. "It is? How do you know?"

"Because we got evidence photos from the Sturgis Police yesterday." My jaw drops as Lindzi adds, "Sorry. I would've told you straightaway, but your update was way too interesting. Have a look." She taps a few keys on her laptop and spins it toward me. Before I have time to prepare myself, there it is—

the jagged, blood-soaked rock that ended Mr. Larkin's life. The first thing that strikes me is that Lindzi is right; it's not nearly as big as I imagined. I pictured a boulder, almost, something of such significant mass that nobody could survive being hit by it. But in reality, it's only about twice the size of my hand.

"There were no fingerprints except for Shane's, so the killer was probably wearing gloves," Lindzi says. "Not surprising, since the temperature was barely forty that day."

She enlarges the photo, one finger tracing the edge of the rock on-screen. "William Larkin was struck in the back of the head," she says. "Right at the base of his skull. Kind of like a rabbit punch in boxing, which is banned because it's so deadly." Bile threatens to rise in my throat then, and I have to swallow a few times to force it down as Lindzi keeps talking. "The person who did this might have been skilled, or they might have made a lucky shot. Well, an unlucky shot, obviously, for William, who either was unaware that anyone was behind him or was in the process of walking away from them. Whatever happened, the blow that killed William wasn't self-defense."

"Lindzi," Carly says in a forbidding tone. "You can't deliver a monologue like that without warning. Brynn is positively green."

Lindzi looks up with a chagrined grimace as she catches sight of my face. "Sorry. I get carried away sometimes."

"It's okay," I say, tugging at my bracelet. But I want to stop looking at the rock, so I add, "What else do you have?" Then I wish I'd kept quiet, because I'm suddenly terrified that she'll show me pictures of Mr. Larkin's body.

Instead she pulls up a photo of a thin silver chain. "The police wouldn't share everything. But there's this. William Larkin was wearing it when he died—well, not *wearing* it, exactly, because it seems to have broken when he was struck. But it was inside his shirt."

"Really?" I ask, squinting at the screen. "I've never seen that before. I wouldn't have taken him for a jewelry kind of guy." There's a thumbnail photo on Lindzi's desktop of a man who's too small to see clearly, and I ask, "Who's that?"

"Your principal," Lindzi says, enlarging what turns out to be a *Sturgis Times* article. "Or your head of school, I guess. That's what they call them in private schools, right?"

"Sometimes, yeah," I say.

The picture is of Grizz in the Saint Ambrose school office, beaming as he holds up a large turquoise envelope covered with stickers. The headline reads, *Weekend Car Wash Pushes Saint Ambrose Fundraising Efforts Over the Top.* "And the mysterious money envelope," Lindzi says. "The class-trip money that was stolen was in a smaller Saint Ambrose envelope, and then that plus the donor list was put inside the turquoise envelope and kept in the school office." She smiles wryly. "Not very secure, especially after that photo op. Anyway, police found the Saint Ambrose envelope in Charlotte Holbrook's locker, but not the turquoise envelope."

"I've seen that before," I say, frowning at Lindzi's screen.

"The article?" she asks.

"No, the envelope."

"At school, probably, right?" Lindzi says.

"I don't think so," I say slowly. "Well, maybe, but . . . it feels out of context."

"Out of context how?" Carly pounces, like my answer is of profound importance. And then I feel foolish, because I honestly have no idea.

"I don't know," I admit. "Maybe I just didn't realize what it was for."

"Well, it was never found after it went missing," Carly says. "Although all the money was accounted for in the smaller envelope found in Charlotte's locker." She taps her pen again, thoughtful. "You said Charlotte claimed she didn't know how it got there, right?"

"Yeah," I say.

"Did you believe her?"

"I mean . . . yeah," I say slowly, casting back to my eighth-grade mindset. "Everybody did. For one thing, she didn't need it. But even if Charlotte had been some kind of kleptomaniac back then, I don't know why she would have kept the money sitting around in her locker. It had been missing for more than two weeks before Mr. Larkin died, so she would have had plenty of time to put it someplace else."

"Any repercussions for her at all?" Carly asks.

"No," I say. "Grizz—Mr. Griswell, I mean—wouldn't even let me report on it for the school paper. He said we all needed to heal."

Carly snorts as Lindzi asks, "What was the timing? Mr. Larkin was killed, and they found the money the next day?"

"Two days later," I say.

"How would someone have gotten Charlotte's locker combination?" Lindzi asks.

"They wouldn't need it," I say. "They could've just slipped the envelope inside—our lockers have big vents in front. We used to use them to leave notes for one another." That became a sore point for me after the gym class incident, when Katie Christo started dropping off mocking notes about my alleged crush on Tripp. *Trippstalker,* she wrote on one, drawing a heart-eyes cartoon version of me staring at Tripp.

Tripp, who's been avoiding me all week at school, and hasn't answered any of my *How are you feeling?* texts. Tripp, who never unconsciously touched his finger and thumb together at Charlotte's party Saturday night, which means he was telling the truth.

I needed you to hate me.

Why? Because you'd suddenly decided to hate me *back then?*

No, Brynn. I didn't hate you back then. And I don't hate you now. Not even a little bit.

"So if it wasn't Charlotte, who do you think took the money?" Carly asks. "And why would they frame her?"

"What?" I blink, and give myself a little shake to bring my mind back. *Focus, Brynn.* "I'm not sure."

Carly turns to Lindzi. "It'll be interesting, when we get to the interview stage, to hear what the police theories were about that theft. And whether they think there's any connection to William Larkin's murder."

Lindzi nods, eyes on her phone. "Here's something else that's interesting." She holds it up. "I just heard from the public relations department at the Sturgis Police Foundation. The Delgado Properties donation was made on April 30, 2018. So about a month after the money went missing, and eighteen days after William Larkin died."

"Convenient timing," Carly says. "And that's the only year they ever donated?"

"Yup," Lindzi says.

Carly's gaze sharpens. "Those kids know more than they're saying."

My stomach gives an uncomfortable twist. I'm sure she's right, and for a second I'm equally sure I don't want to know the truth. Part of me is stubbornly clinging to the eighth-grade image of my heroic classmates, leading police to Mr. Larkin so the wheels of justice could start to turn. Except, of course, they never really did.

"Have you gotten any tips yet about Mr. Larkin?" I ask. "From the website?"

"We had a few technical difficulties, so his section just went up yesterday," Lindzi says. "So far it's nothing but junk, which isn't unusual. Once it's been live for a week or so, we should start getting higher-quality information."

"All right." Carly checks the slim Rolex on her wrist. "This has been a good discussion, but I need to break. It's almost time for me to get on the phone and do battle with Ramon."

"About Mr. Larkin?" I ask.

She gives a rueful chuckle. "About everything. Listen, Brynn. I appreciate all you've shared to date, but please be sure to keep your distance from Richard Solomon. I don't like what I heard today."

I nod, and after she leaves, Lindzi says, "Brynn, you can finish up working in here if you want. Nobody has it booked for the rest of the day, and I noticed the Pit was kind of crowded."

"Thanks," I say.

"I'll share the photo file with you too," she says, gathering her laptop to her chest. "I promise there's nothing more gory than the rock in there."

I spend my final hour at *Motive* putting the finishing touches on Lindzi's female serial killer spreadsheet. The round-table for that story is coming up next week, and Lindzi's been cramming like it's a final exam so she doesn't get caught off guard by another unexpected Ramon d'Arturo appearance. It's past five o'clock when I finish, and I take my phone out to check for texts.

My group chat with Izzy and Olivia has gotten a little quiet recently, but it's not dead yet. I answer that first, giving my input on Izzy's latest boyfriend drama (*His mom does like you, that's just her face*) and Olivia's semiannual question about getting bangs (*DO NOT*). I have a bunch of notifications from Mason, who spent most of Charlotte's party hanging out with Geoff and is now overanalyzing every syllable of their conversation. Nadia wants to make plans to study for an upcoming math test, and Ellie sent a clip of her playing "Despacito" on the flute that's so good, all I can do is send back a string of applause GIFs.

Nothing from Tripp.

It's not as bad as I thought, being back in Sturgis, except for the part where Tripp Talbot is as big a thorn in my side now as he was at the end of eighth grade. When we're talking, he annoys me. But when we're not talking, that's somehow worse.

My laptop is still open, and before I finish packing up, I navigate to the main *Motive* drive and open the William Larkin folder. Lindzi was true to her word; she gave me permissions to access a subfolder labeled Photos/Images. I take pictures of everything in the file with my phone, then click on the Sturgis Cable Access video I played during my short-lived roundtable presentation. "I enjoyed working at the Eliot School. But Saint Ambrose is something special," Mr. Larkin says on-screen.

I pause the video, open Google, and type in *Eliot School.* The web address pops up, leading me to an aerial shot of a redbrick campus in Providence, Rhode Island, surrounded by vibrant fall foliage. I click on *About Us* and read the mission statement and the at-a-glance section before pulling up a biography for the head of school. The first sentence reads, *Jonathan Bartley-Reed has served as head of the Eliot School since July 1, 2013.*

There's a phone number at the bottom, and I lift my phone to dial it. I'm not expecting an answer, since it's past five o'clock, but someone picks up on the second ring. "Jonathan Bartley-Reed's office," a woman says.

"Oh, hi." I'm stumped for a beat, but recover. "Is Mr. Bartley-Reed available?"

"I'm sorry, he's left for the day. Can I take a message?"

"Yes. Could you tell him that Brynn Gallagher from"— *where should I say that I'm from? Motive? No, probably not*— "Saint Ambrose School in Sturgis, Massachusetts, wanted to speak with him?"

"Of course, Ms. Gallagher. And what is this in regard to?"

"A former employee."

"Very well. Could I get your number?" I recite it, and she says, "I'll ask him to return your call at his earliest convenience. Have a lovely evening."

"Thanks, you too," I say, and hang up.

I stare at the paused video on my laptop screen. Mr. Larkin is perched at the edge of his classroom desk, just like he used to do every time he'd give me a pep talk in eighth grade. *When life hands you lemons, make lemon cake.*

"I'm trying," I say to the empty room.

CHAPTER EIGHTEEN

TRIPP

"These were supposed to be *over,*" Charlotte says tightly, glaring at her phone. "Colin had his little show. Why is he still bothering us?"

"You sure this is Colin?" I ask, deleting my own brand-new *Murderer* text. "It would be a bold move under the circumstances." Colin is currently at home, suspended, waiting for what everyone is pretty sure will be a cut-and-dried expulsion hearing.

I could have been waiting right along with him, instead of spending my Thursday study period in the library, and I send a silent thank-you Shane's way. Maybe we're not such surface friends after all, because that's twice he's saved my ass in under a week.

I only have a hazy memory of him dragging me back inside Charlotte's house Saturday night, but I do remember Charlotte herself bringing me up to her bedroom and insisting that I lie down on her couch, even though I tried to tell her my pants were muddy. I was very, very worried about that. "It's all right," she said, in a highly un-Charlotte way. "I'll take care of it in the morning. What's a little mud between friends?"

Shane shrugs, oblivious to where my mind has wandered. "It's not like Colin has a functioning brain or anything," he says.

Charlotte frowns, fidgeting with the edge of an open textbook that she hasn't looked at once since we got here. "I don't like this," she says. "Any of it. I keep checking that horrible channel to see if there's anything new there."

"Which channel?" I ask.

"You know." She wrinkles her nose. "That Fox creature."

Shane flings an arm across the back of her chair. "I told you, babe, my dad took care of him," he says. "Gunnar Fox is buried under an avalanche of lawsuits." His tone is typical breezy Shane Delgado, but there's a tightness to his expression that makes me think Gunnar Fox rattled him more than he's willing to let on. It's not the first crack I've seen in his golden-boy aura lately, and it makes me nervous. If Shane can't handle the pressure from all this renewed interest in Mr. Larkin, what the hell hope do Charlotte or I have?

Charlotte shifts restlessly in her seat, and I wonder if she's thinking the same thing. "But what did your mother say, Tripp?" she asks. "That *Motive* is doing a story too? That show is actually legit."

"Yeah," I say. "But you can only believe about half of whatever Lisa Marie says, so there's a good chance she made it up."

"Why would she do that?" Charlotte asks.

"To convince me to do what she wants."

"That's very toxic behavior," Charlotte says, and I snort out a laugh.

"If you ever meet my mother, Charlotte, you'll realize what an understatement that is."

"You're not doing it, though, right?" she presses.

"Doing what?"

"The interview," she says, frowning. "Gunnar Fox is trying to use you. He'd probably say all kinds of awful things once he got you in front of a camera."

She doesn't know the half of it. I haven't told her and Shane the rest of what Lisa Marie said: "That Delgado boy's story has never added up, and it's about time somebody called him on it. But you're different. I told Gunnar, there's no way my son would protect a thug like that unless he was afraid for his life." Neither of them need to hear that.

Before I can reply, Shane says, "Of course he's not doing it."

Charlotte instantly relaxes. "Good," she says with a relieved sigh, like she doesn't even need confirmation from me now that Shane has weighed in. I feel a flash of irritation that everything's decided, apparently, just because they say so. It's not like you could pay me any amount of money to talk to Gunnar Fox, but sometimes I wonder what life would be like if I didn't spend almost every waking moment at school flanked by the king and queen of Saint Ambrose. That makes me—what? Their court jester? Or some kind of knight, maybe whose sole value lies in keeping the two of them safe.

Probably neither, but I've run out of royalty metaphors.

"I've changed my mind about Brynn Gallagher, by the way," Charlotte says, flipping a page in her textbook. "I don't like her for you anymore, Tripp."

I'm relieved at the change of topic, although I'm not sure this one is much better. "Sorry, what? You don't *like* her for me?"

"I don't want you to date her," Charlotte explains patiently, like I'm a child with minimal comprehension skills.

"I wasn't planning on it." Was I?

"Good," Charlotte says in the same satisfied tone, which annoys me all over again.

"What's your problem with her?" I ask.

"I told her to leave you alone Saturday night, and she did the opposite," Charlotte says.

Sounds exactly like Brynn. "You're not her boss, Charlotte," I point out. "She doesn't have to do what you say."

"It's not only that," Charlotte says. "I Googled her. Do you know she wrote about *erections* for the newspaper at her last school?"

"Wait. What?" I start laughing, positive that she's joking. Except Charlotte never jokes.

"I'm serious. Well, actually, it was mostly a photo collage. Look." She holds out her phone, and I recoil.

"Charlotte, I'm not gonna look at a bunch of—"

"It's just the BuzzFeed coverage," she says. "Everything else is blurred out."

I take her phone, and start snickering hard enough that Shane leans over my shoulder to take a look. "Come on. Brynn obviously didn't do this," I say. "It's some kind of prank."

"Her name is there," says Charlotte. Mistress of the obvious.

"Yeah, which is what would make it funny to whatever asshole did this," I say. But it's impossible to explain humor to Charlotte, even bad humor. She never gets it.

"Charlotte's right, though," Shane says, handing her back her phone. "Brynn's more trouble than she's worth."

I'm about to protest—*How the hell do you know what she's worth?*—but I'm tired, suddenly, of arguing with the two of them. Tired of them, period. So when I catch sight of a flash of auburn hair between the stacks to our left, I don't hesitate. "Be right back," I say. I get to my feet, and take a little too much pleasure in sauntering away from Shane and Charlotte. Right toward the person they just told me to avoid.

Brynn is on her tiptoes, trying and failing to reach something on the top shelf. She huffs in frustration and puts her hands on her hips, looking around for a footstool, before she catches sight of me leaning against the end of the stack.

"What do you need?" I ask.

"Middlemarch," she says. I pluck it off the shelf and hand it to her. "Thank you. I'm glad your hands are working again." I raise my eyebrows, and she adds, "I assumed they were broken since you didn't answer any of my texts."

"Sorry," I say. "I've been busy."

"Oh, me too," she says. "I can't text anyone either because I haven't had ten seconds to spare in the last five days."

I lean against the stacks again, arms crossed. "So what you're saying is, you've been counting the days since you heard from me."

She gets a little pink. "No. I'm saying common courtesy takes very little time, so you should give it a try."

"I'll do that," I say. "Right after I finish going through your body of work at your former school paper. And when I say *body*, I mean that literally."

"Oh good. Great," Brynn says, rolling her eyes. "So glad you came across the dick pics. The pinnacle of my journalistic career. I hope you found my in-depth analysis insightful."

"I learned a lot," I say, and she huffs out a reluctant laugh.

"I'm sure it goes without saying that I didn't actually post those."

"Don't burst my bubble."

She smiles and tucks a strand of hair behind her ear. "So, listen, if you had returned any of my texts, I'd have told you that I'm meeting with Wade Drury after school tomorrow. The new groundskeeper?" she adds at my confused look.

"I know who it is, but why? I told you he's an ass."

"Well, Mr. Solomon wasn't very helpful, was he? Maybe Wade will have some suggestions for the memorial garden. If nothing else, he's unlikely to be armed." She hikes her back-pack strap higher onto her shoulder and adds, "You're welcome to join me. If he *does* pull a gun, it won't feel the same if you're not there."

"Wouldn't miss it," I say, a little surprised to realize that's true.

"Greenhouse, three o'clock," Brynn says. "See you then."

She turns to leave, and I call after her, "Does this mean I'm forgiven? You don't hate me for being a lazy texter?"

Brynn pauses and looks over her shoulder. "I don't hate you, Tripp," she says, a small smile playing at her lips. "Not even a little bit."

CHAPTER NINETEEN

BRYNN

"Have fun," I tell Ellie, yawning as we pull open the doors to Saint Ambrose on Friday morning. She has an early orchestra rehearsal, so I had to wake up at six-thirty instead of seven to drive her to school, and I'm already missing that half hour of sleep.

"I won't," Ellie sighs, swinging her flute case. "Most of the violinists are new, and they sound like dying cats." We reach the auditorium and she asks, "Want to listen?"

"After that lead-in? No thanks. I'm going to the library." I could use the extra time before class starts to go over my notes about Mr. Larkin.

"Suit yourself," Ellie says, and I wave before heading for the stairs, relishing the fact that I don't have to push through throngs of students to get there.

The library has always been my favorite place at Saint Ambrose. It's on the top floor of the main building, painted a bright white that never seems to fade. One of the walls is nothing but windows, streaming sunlight into the reading area and turning the scarred wooden furniture the color of honey. It's right next to the *Saint Ambrose Sentinel* office, and when I was in eighth grade I used to alternate between the two as writing spaces.

I'm expecting the library to be empty, but the first thing I see when I step inside is that my favorite table already has an occupant: Charlotte Holbrook, frowning in concentration as she writes something down in her notebook.

I pause in the doorway, debating a change in plan. I didn't miss the dirty look Charlotte shot me yesterday while I was talking to Tripp in the stacks, and I'm pretty sure she's mad that I found him at her party after she'd told me not to. But then she glances up at me, and I don't want to look like I'm leaving because of her, so . . .

"Hey," I say, and flash my best attempt at a carefree smile as I take a seat at the opposite end of the table. "How's it going?"

Her lips thin, and all I get in return is a curt nod. Looks like our brief bout of camaraderie is over. Note to self: Charlotte doesn't like being disobeyed.

I take out my Mr. Larkin folders, and we sit in silence until my phone rings, earning me a cold look from Charlotte even though it's not quiet hours. I meet her gaze evenly, thinking, *I can talk if I want,* and swipe to answer without fully registering that it's a Providence phone number. "Hi, this is Brynn."

A rich baritone fills my ear. "Brynn, this is Jonathan Bartley-Reed from the Eliot School returning your call."

"Oh, hi," I say, flustered. I shouldn't have picked up. I want to ask Jonathan Bartley-Reed about Mr. Larkin's time at the Eliot

School, but I can't do that with Charlotte watching me like a resentful hawk. "Thanks so much for getting back to me," I say.

"Please forgive the delay. I've been inundated since the start of the new year," he says with a deep chuckle. "How can I help you?"

"Um." *I'll just take the call in the hallway,* I think, standing so quickly that I bang my knee hard against the table. I let out an involuntary grunt of pain and drop back into my chair, holding my knee, as Charlotte smirks.

"Is everything all right?" Jonathan Bartley-Reed asks solicitously.

"Yeah, I was just . . . Sorry. I hit something. Anyway, I was hoping to talk to you about a former employee of yours. About his . . ." Charlotte is still staring at me, making it impossible to think. "Flower preferences."

"I'm sorry?"

"We're doing a memorial garden for William Larkin at Saint Ambrose, and—"

"Excuse me," Mr. Bartley-Reed interrupts. "Are you a student?"

"Yes, but—"

"All right," he says, his tone turning patronizing. "While it's always a pleasure to hear from students, I'm afraid I'm not the correct person to speak with for a school project. I'll pass your name along to one of William's former colleagues, and they'll follow up about your memorial garden. Have a good day." Then he hangs up on me.

"Thank you so much," I say to the empty line, because no way am I letting Charlotte know I've just been dismissed. "Yes. Yes, that's right." I pause for a few beats. "That's so incredibly helpful. . . . What's that? . . . Oh, of course, I'd be happy to call back then. . . . It's been a pleasure speaking with you too," I finish, finally lowering my phone.

Charlotte looks like she's not buying it for a second. "Well, that went much better in the second half, didn't it?" she says.

My temper rises, but I manage to keep my voice calm when I ask, "Do you have a problem with me, Charlotte?"

"Yes," she says, which is more bluntness than I expected from her. "I think you should stay away from Tripp."

"I'm not sure why that's your business."

"Because he's my friend."

"Mine too," I say, even though I'm not 100 percent sure that's true.

"He doesn't need the complication of a relationship right now," Charlotte says.

"A relationship? I'm not interested in a *relationship* with Tripp."

I'm not 100 percent sure that's true either. Even though it should be, considering everything I don't know about what Tripp did four years ago. Still, an image flashes through my mind of him leaning against the bookshelf yesterday, blue eyes crinkled at the corners while he teased me. His blazer neatly pressed but his tie a little askew, in a way that made me want to reach up and fix it. Or maybe use it to tug him closer. I'm undecided on what the best course of action would have been.

Charlotte rolls her eyes, like she knows exactly what I'm thinking. "If you can't be honest, then there's no point in talking about any of this, is there?" she asks. Which sounds like her cue to start ignoring me again, but her gaze remains locked on mine, challenging.

"You don't even know me," I say.

"I know Tripp," she says, tossing her hair. "And I know guys."

Now it's my turn to roll my eyes. "I hate to break it to you, Charlotte, but having a single relationship with your middle-school sweetheart doesn't make you an expert." I feel angry and off balance suddenly, wishing I could have this conversation with someone who's not simultaneously judging me and belittling me, and frustration turns my words sharp. "It actually makes you kind of sheltered. So maybe don't try to give advice when you're incapable of making a move without Shane."

As soon as the words spring from my mouth, I regret them. I can't tell Charlotte to mind her own business when it comes to Tripp, and then bring up Shane like that. But before I can apologize, she surprises me by standing up, walking the length of the table, and perching on top of it beside my stack of books. Her beautiful face is utterly expressionless as she asks, "Do you know what it's like to have boys treat you like you're some kind of prize?"

"Um." I hesitate, not sure if she actually wants a response, until silence stretches between us long enough that I'm forced to admit, "No. I do not."

"The first boy I ever had a crush on told me I looked like a fairy princess," she says. "He never wanted to talk to me, though. Just stared at me like I was some kind of *object*. It's been like that my entire life—or worse, because sometimes the attention gets really creepy. I think I was eleven when the Upper School boys started catcalling me."

"Really?" I ask, horrified. "That's gross."

"I know," Charlotte says. "It's dehumanizing. Shane's always been different, though. He barely noticed me at first. I was the one who had to chase *him*." She almost giggles, her eyes bright and shining with devotion. "It was a nice change of pace, and so was the fact that he treated me—*treats* me—like an actual person. So if being with him makes me kind of sheltered, you know what? Good. Bring it on."

"Charlotte," I say cautiously. I'm not sure what prompted this burst of confidence, or what she expects me to say in return. "I'm sorry that guys are . . . awful, sometimes. And I shouldn't have brought Shane up like that. It's not my business. Look, I'd really like for you and me to . . ." What's the phrase I'm searching for here? "Get along."

Charlotte gives me a serene smile. "We'll get along fine as long as you don't mess with my boys."

Her *boys*? "Plural?" I sputter. "I thought we were talking about Shane."

"Tripp's important to me too," Charlotte says, and even though this is one of the strangest conversations I've ever had, it's still nice to know that Tripp has clearly never tried to hit on her. "And he's not as strong as he seems. He needs someone to look out for him."

Who appointed you? I think, but I know there's no point in saying it. Or continuing this conversation. "Understood," I say, shuffling the papers in front of me. "I've got a ton of work to do, though, so . . ."

Charlotte takes the hint and hops off the table. "And I'm going to make a Starbucks run before class starts," she says. Then she frowns at my scattered notes. "Why do you have that?"

I follow her gaze to a defaced poster of Mr. Larkin that I've been keeping in my files. "Oh, um . . . I passed it in the hallway on my way here, and felt bad about leaving it up," I lie, hastily closing my notebook before she catches sight of anything related to *Motive*. "I can't understand why anyone would do something like that."

"Can't you?" Charlotte says.

I blink at her. "What, you can?" Then my stomach drops, thinking about the conversation we just had. "Charlotte, was Mr. Larkin somebody who treated you . . . Did he . . ."

"Oh no," Charlotte says decisively. "Nothing like that." She returns to her chair and gathers her books, and I breathe a sigh of relief until she adds, "There's more than one way to be awful, you know."

"Huh?" I ask, but she's already turned for the door.

My eyes drop to Mr. Larkin's lemon tie, still visible beneath the red slashes on the garden committee poster, as I think about everything I've heard or seen over the past week. *The man was a void. That son of a bitch got what he deserved. There's more than one way to be awful.* And I wonder, with another uncomfortable twist of my stomach, whether I ever really knew my favorite teacher at all.

TRIPP

FOUR YEARS AGO

Music blares through my earphones, drowning out my restless thoughts as I gaze around me, disoriented. I thought I knew these woods, but when I left Shane, I went farther down the path than I usually do, and it stopped being a path a while ago. Now would be a great time to ask someone with a better sense of direction than me which way to turn, but I can't.

I'm completely alone in the woods.

I can't text Shane; even if we'd exchanged numbers, which we haven't, there's no reception here. "It's fine," I mutter to myself, but my words are swallowed by the music, and suddenly it feels ominous that I can't hear anything around me.

I pause my playlist and pull out my earphones, listening to the chirping, rustling, crackling noises of the woods. I look upward, searching for the sun, because it should be dropping to the horizon soon, setting over our school. The canopy of trees above me is dense, but I think—no, I know—it's brighter to my left.

I turn that way, and within a few minutes, I hit an incline, much steeper than the path I've been following so far. I know where I am now; it's the ridge near Shelton Park, the most elevated part of the forest. I've gotten even farther off track than I realized, and I'm a lot closer to the fire pit, where Shane and Charlotte are meeting up, than I wanted to be. Still, I'm relieved that I'm no longer completely lost. I was right all along; school is to my left.

I'm about to follow the sun when I hear a rustling sound, lower to the ground this time, and the loud snap of a twig.

Then the screaming starts.

CHAPTER TWENTY

TRIPP

From a distance, I think the girl at the bulletin board Friday afternoon is Brynn: same height, same hair, same way of standing with her hands on her hips and her head cocked. But then she turns at my approach, and the illusion is gone; Ellie Gallagher doesn't look a thing like Brynn. It's interesting how eyes can transform an entire face. "What's up, Ellie?" I ask.

"Hi, Tripp," Ellie says before returning her gaze to the bulletin board. She taps two pieces of paper in succession and says, "Seeing these next to one another gives me an idea." *These* refers to a messed-up poster of Mr. Larkin and a flyer for the Winter Dance. The theme is Glow Up, and there's a picture of a neon cityscape with matching stars.

"Really?" I ask, bemused.

"Really," she confirms. "Do you think anyone would mind if I took them?" She doesn't wait for an answer before carefully removing both from the bulletin board and tucking them into her backpack. "Okay, well, see you," she says, giving me a cheery wave before taking off down the hallway.

I watch her go with a mix of confusion and approval. Ellie was always a weird little kid, and it's good to see she hasn't changed.

"You're supposed to be meeting me at the greenhouse now," says a voice over my shoulder.

There's the real Brynn. Green eyes and all. "I could say the same thing," I reply. "You're late. I'm beginning to think you don't care about this subcommittee as much as I do."

"*Nobody* cares about this subcommittee as much as you do," Brynn says, falling into step with me as we walk toward the exit. "I've been meaning to talk to you about it, actually. You're getting a little obsessed."

I laugh, surprised at how *light* I feel around Brynn. I haven't felt that way since . . . eighth grade, probably. We pass Abby Liu in the hall, whose eyes flick over us as she gives a small, regretful smile, and I feel a quick tug of remorse. Did I lead her on, somehow? I don't think I did, but it's hard to know how other people interpret things. I shake it off and answer Brynn, "It's not *obsessive* to text your co-chair seven hundred fern pictures. Speaking of which, did you have a favorite?" Brynn snorts as I lift my phone, ready to continue the joke, but there's an actual text waiting for me.

Lisa Marie: *That little shit Shane Delgado is causing problems for Gunnar.*

The smile falls from my face, and Brynn notices. "Everything okay?" she asks.

I text *Good* to Lisa Marie and say, "It'll be better when my mother goes back to Vegas."

We stop at the exit, and Brynn tightens her scarf before pushing through the door. It's been an unusually mild January, but it's windy today, and she clutches her hat with one hand and glances up at me. "She's here?" she asks.

"Yeah," I say shortly, heaviness settling around my shoulders like it never left. Lisa Marie is the ultimate mood killer.

"How is, um . . ." Brynn shoves her hands into her coat pockets, suddenly tentative. "How's that going? With her?"

"Better than ever," I say sarcastically. "You remember that bullshit video Colin played in class?"

Brynn scowls. "I remember."

"Well, in a fun twist, turns out Lisa Marie knows the asshole who made it, and tried to bribe me into doing a show with him," I say. "Which I turned down, obviously. But it would mean a payday for her too, so she won't leave it alone."

"Oh my God, really?" Brynn looks stricken. "That's horrible. I'm sorry."

Instantly I wish I hadn't said anything. I hate pity, and I especially hate it coming from her. "It is what it is," I say, silencing my phone before shoving it into my pocket. "Mr. Larkin is a popular guy all of a sudden. Lisa Marie says another show might be working on something too. *Motive*, I think. Do you know it?"

"Um." Brynn shoves her hands deeper into her pockets as the greenhouse comes into view. "Yeah, I know it."

"Guess this memorial garden better be ready for prime time," I say, unable to keep the bitterness out of my voice. Four years. Four years of keeping my head down, working hard, and trying to do the right thing, whatever that is, to make up for one very wrong thing. I thought I was *this close* to leaving Sturgis behind, but it's starting to feel as though having that hope was the universe's way of fucking with me, extracting payback by letting me roll a boulder almost to the top of a hill before I lose my grip and it crushes me.

I'm not getting out. I'll be standing in those woods behind Saint Ambrose forever, making a decision that I was way too young to make, and maybe the worst part of all is that I don't know if I'd choose differently today.

"Tripp?" Brynn's hand touches my arm. "We don't have to do this now."

"Oh, no, let's do it," I say in a strident, mocking tone that I can't seem to control. "It's happening. Let's make a mother-fucking *garden*." I clap my hands together like an asshole, because why not alienate everybody?

"That's what I'm talking about, brother," says a lazy voice in front of us, and I realize we've reached the greenhouse. Wade Drury stands before us in snow overalls, even though it's not snowing, and a battered baseball cap that reads *Live Free or Die*. He spits onto the ground, and all the spite drains out of me. This guy's a dick, so if I continue being a dick as well, the laws of math state that Brynn's going to be outnumbered. "This little lady must be Beth," he adds with a sardonic tip of his cap.

Brynn presses her lips together before responding. "It's 'Brynn,' actually."

"Jesus. You kids and your names," Wade says, and snorts. "Your parents should've just named you 'Bentley' and called it a day. Or 'Beemer.'"

"I'm sorry, what?" Brynn asks, turning bewildered eyes to me.

"I tried to tell you," I say.

Wade claps his hands together, kind of like I just did. "So what's the deal? You're making a little garden for a dead guy and Google's not your friend? It's too much work for a couple of rich kids, so why not waste Wade's time?"

"Wow." Brynn blinks a couple of times before turning back to me. "I didn't think I'd have to admit this within the first thirty seconds of this meeting, but—you were right, Tripp."

"Good talk, Wade," I say before taking Brynn's arm and steering her away.

"Well," she says. "I guess expert consultation isn't going to be a thing."

"No, you know what?" I say, suddenly eager to make up for how I acted on the walk over. There's nothing like being confronted with the Wade Drurys of the world to make you realize you haven't hit rock bottom, and don't want to. Plus, I can't drive away the only person besides my fifty-year-old boss who makes me feel even a little bit happy. "We should go back to Mr. Solomon's. He'll be more prepared to see us this time, and I think we can soften him up. We don't need to talk about Mr. Larkin. Just let Mr. S get going on plants, and we'll have everything we need."

"What, *now*?" Brynn asks.

"No, I have to be at Brightside in half an hour. Tomorrow?"

She bites her lip. "I'm not supposed to go back there."

"Says who? Your parents?"

"Um, yeah," Brynn says, looking a little . . . shifty? But before I can ask her what's up, she squares her shoulders and says, "You know what, though? Never mind. It's not a big deal. Let's do it."

CHAPTER TWENTY-ONE

BRYNN

It's interesting, the things you learn about yourself in a new environment. For instance, I never thought watching someone haul boxes would make them more attractive until I saw Tripp doing it at Brightside Bakery on Saturday afternoon.

"Close your mouth," Mason says, gently tapping my jaw as Tripp disappears into Regina's storage room with the last of the supplies that UPS dropped off beside the front door. "All that drooling is putting me off my croissant."

My cheeks warm as Nadia says, "Okay, but in her defense, have you seen his arms?"

"I have been enjoying the show, yes," Mason says, taking a sip of coffee. "But quietly, subtly, and with dignity. Brynn could learn a few lessons from me."

"Shut up," I mutter before stuffing a piece of Pop-Tart cake into my mouth. I swallow and add, "Speaking of dignity, Mason, how's Gorff?"

The tips of his ears turn red as Nadia laughs. Mason's giddy, incomprehensible drunken texts about Geoff the night of Charlotte's party have become our favorite thing to tease him about. Sometimes I like to text him screenshots in class just to watch his ears get scarlet.

"SKSKSKKS GORFF IZ STAKIIING MEEEEE," Nadia says, reciting the most classic of the Gorff texts. "What did you mean by that, Mason? Was he staking you? Is Gorff under the impression that you're a vampire?"

I tap my chin, thoughtful. "Or was he stalking you? Was that a cry for help?"

"Maybe he offered you a steak?" Nadia asks.

"All right, yes, you're both hilarious," Mason says sourly. "And you're officially disinvited from my dance circle when *Geoff* and I go to the Winter Dance together."

"Your dance circle?" I ask.

"There's going to be black lights," Mason says. "It's my true medium." Then he does a strange little chair shimmy before finishing the last of his coffee. "Too bad you'll miss it."

"I don't think it's possible to miss that," I say.

"Speaking of." Nadia gets a little red herself, which almost never happens. "I was thinking of asking Pavan, but I wanted to check with you first, Brynn. Would you mind?"

"Pavan Deshpande?" I blink at her, confused. "Why would I mind?"

"Well, you kissed him once. Does taking him to a dance violate the girl code?"

"I kissed him in seventh grade," I remind her. "So no. But it's sweet of you to ask."

"Will you be taking Box Stud?" Mason asks as Tripp returns to the counter.

"Shhh," I mutter, and my stomach twists. I missed an opportunity yesterday; when Tripp brought up *Motive,* I should have told him that I worked there. But I couldn't bring myself to do it when he was so upset about his mother, and the moment passed.

Now it hits me with a prickle of guilt that I haven't told Mason and Nadia either. For no good reason, other than the fact that I didn't tell them from the beginning. I'm not sure why; maybe because I never expected them to become more than lunchtime friends. But they are, and I need to come clean, especially now that Carly is full steam ahead on gathering information about Mr. Larkin. It's only a matter of time before someone from Saint Ambrose catches wind of the fact that he's on the *Motive* website, and once they do, the news will spread like wildfire.

I'm taking a deep breath, preparing myself to start, when Tripp suddenly materializes by our table. He smells like sugar, and he's still in short sleeves, with the flannel shirt he took off while moving boxes draped over one shoulder, so my concentration vanishes.

"Ready?" he asks. We're heading to Mr. Solomon's after his shift.

"Is she ever," Mason says, and another moment passes. It's all right, though, because I should probably explain *Motive* to Tripp before I explain it to anyone else.

"Let's go," I say, reaching for my coat. I'll tell him in the car.

* * *

I did not tell him in the car.

I was going to, really. But then Uncle Nick called from Vermont, where he's using the family ski pass on a weekend trip with his college buddies, because he can never keep track of the activation code. "I texted it to you before you left," I complain.

"I know, but I must've deleted it by mistake. It's not there."

"Well, I'm driving and I can't look for it. Check your email, because I definitely sent it to you at some point in the past three months."

"What would the subject be, do you think?"

"Oh my God, Uncle Nick. Try *activation code.*"

By the time he finally tracks it down, I'm pulling up beside Mr. Solomon's truck. "You're a lifesaver, cherished niece," Uncle Nick says before disconnecting.

"Sorry," I say to Tripp as I shift into park. "My uncle's kind of disorganized."

"No problem. Hey, listen. Before we leave the car, there's something I've been meaning to talk to you about." Tripp turns to face me, a smile tugging at the corners of his mouth, and I'm suddenly very aware of how close we're sitting. Close enough that I could brush away the lock of hair that's threatening to dip into his eye, if I wanted to.

Don't blush. "What's that?" I ask. Cool and casual, that's me.

"Let's concentrate our efforts on the front door, this time."

Oh. Right. What did I think he was going to say? "Good call," I say as we climb out of the car and close our doors. I consider, briefly, raising the subject of *Motive* before we reach the door, but it's nowhere near a long enough walk. Plus, I'm starting to get anxious about seeing Mr. Solomon again, wondering if he'll be the kindly man I remember from Saint Ambrose, or the one who went off about Mr. Larkin after aiming a shotgun at us. "Let's just keep ringing the bell until—" Then I stop short at the top of the stairs, causing Tripp to bump into me. He puts a hand on my waist to steady us both before moving to my side, and I ask, "Is the door open?"

"Huh. Yeah," Tripp says, gazing at the sliver of space between the door and its frame. He pushes lightly on it, and the door swings wider with a loud creak. "Mr. Solomon?" he calls. "It's Tr—Noah Talbot. You there?" There's no answer, and no sound at all from inside. "Maybe he's out back?"

"I'll check," I say. I quickly jog around the corner of the house, taking care to keep a safe distance from the gate. But Mr. Solomon is nowhere in sight. I return to Tripp, who's pushed open the door another few inches. "He's not there," I report.

"Okay, well . . ." Tripp stands with his hands on his hips, jaw twitching. "Maybe we should go in and make sure he's okay. And let him know his door is open. Can't imagine he did that on purpose."

"Probably not, but do you think that's a good idea? I mean, he was mad enough when we were just trying to open his gate."

"We'll announce ourselves," Tripp says, grasping the knob to open the door fully. "Mr. Solomon," he yells. "It's Noah and Brynn. Your door was open. We're coming in, okay?"

The returning silence makes the hairs on the back of my neck stand up. Everything about this feels wrong. I glance back to the driveway at Mr. Solomon's truck, hoping that maybe he's in the driver's seat getting ready to go somewhere and we just failed to notice him. But the truck is empty, and so is the dark hallway we step into. A threadbare striped rug covers the floor, and a pair of boots sits askew on a shoe tray pushed against the wall. The space is dusty, and I sneeze before calling out, "Mr. Solomon, are you there?" I don't like how high and thin my voice sounds.

"Have you ever been here before?" Tripp asks, pausing at the edge of a staircase. The short hallway in front of us branches in three directions; the kitchen is straight ahead, a dining room to the right, and a living room to the left.

"No," I say as we move toward the kitchen. It's empty but the overhead light is turned on, and so is the half-full coffeepot I spy on the counter. "He's not in here. And he should have heard us by now if he were on the first floor." I retrace my steps to the stairway, and pause with one hand on the banister. "Mr. Solomon?" I call. "Are you home?"

"Maybe we should go upstairs," Tripp says.

"Yeah, maybe," I say, turning to look over my shoulder into the living room. "We could—"

And then everything stills—my words, my steps, my heart—when I see it. The edge of a stockinged foot jutting out from behind a chair, just in my line of vision. "Oh no," I breathe, and Tripp freezes at my tone.

"What," he says, every line of his body tensing.

Go over there, I command myself, staring at the still foot, but my legs refuse to obey. *Just walk.* In my head, my voice sounds like the soothing, singsong one I used on toddler Ellie when she was having a bad dream. *Open your eyes. I'm with you. You're okay.*

"You're okay," I murmur, and finally start moving. "You're okay." I don't know who I'm talking to, but the closer I get, the more positive I am that I'm wrong on all counts. I'm focused with laser precision on the sock, and when I'm fully inside the living room, I notice a hole in the heel. Somehow, that's what forces a choked sob from my throat, even before my eyes finally take in the rest: Mr. Solomon lying still, his neck bent at a horribly unnatural angle, and his head resting in a puddle of dark red blood.

"Mr. Solomon," I gasp, falling to my knees beside him. "Are you . . . can you hear me?" Of course he can't; his open eyes are so lifeless that I know he's past hearing anyone, but I can't stop babbling. "I'll get help. I'll call for help. Did you fall? Mr. Solomon, did you fall?" He's lying in front of his fireplace, and the sharp edge of the mantel above it is also stained with blood. I scramble for my phone in my pocket, but it's not there. It's in my bag. Where is my bag? I must have dropped it at some point. I look behind me and spot it on the ground a few feet away, and as I lunge for it, I see Tripp.

He's rigid and ghostly pale, his eyes almost as blank as Mr. Solomon's. "What did you do?" he asks in a ragged voice.

"I—what?" I ask, bewildered. "What do you mean?" I don't understand the question, since we've been together this whole time and I very obviously didn't do anything to cause the horrific scene in front of us. Is he talking to Mr. Solomon? Tripp doesn't reply, and I can't wait for an answer. I grab hold of my bag's strap and drag it toward me. "We have to call for help. Maybe someone can help. . . ."

Tripp sinks to his knees, staring directly at Mr. Solomon, but somehow it feels like he's not really seeing him. "I have to think," he says, putting his head in his hands.

"Tripp, I—" I'm lost. He's not okay, obviously, but Mr. Solomon is a lot less okay, so that needs to be my priority now. I finally locate my phone in the depths of my bag, but my hands are shaking so hard that I nearly drop it. "I'm going to call 9-1-1," I say. Whether that's to reassure Tripp or myself, I'm not sure.

"Stop screaming," Tripp says hoarsely. His head is still in his hands. "I can't think when you're screaming like that."

"I'm not screaming," I say, verging on tears. "I'm trying to use my *fucking phone*." I finally manage to dial, and within a few seconds a cool voice says, "9-1-1, what's your emergency?"

"Someone's hurt," I choke out, my eyes darting between Mr. Solomon and Tripp. One of them is perfectly still, and the other is rocking on the floor muttering to himself. I want, desperately, to help them both, but I can't. I don't know how.

I don't know how to help anyone.

CHAPTER TWENTY-TWO

TRIPP

White walls, bright lights, the strong smell of ammonia. "Vitals are fine," says a voice. There's a tug on my eye and an even brighter light. "Pupils look fine. There's nothing physically wrong with him, so I'm thinking post-traumatic stress."

"I'm not surprised," says another voice. "This is the worst kind of déjà vu."

A hand squeezes my shoulder. "Tripp, you're going to be fine, I promise, but we're having trouble reaching your father. Who else can we call?"

I don't know what they're talking about, or why they need my dad. But I do know the answer to that question, so I give it.

"No one," I say. "There's no one else."

A couple of hours later, I'm sitting in a room at the Sturgis police station with Regina. I'm back to myself enough to know that Brynn called her and she closed the bakery to be here. "You didn't need to do that," I said when Regina told me. "I could have . . . I should have just asked them to call Lisa Marie."

"No," Regina said. She's always been the biggest supporter of me giving my mother a shot, but even she couldn't put a positive spin on the suggested Gunnar Fox interview. She patted my hand, which is like a tackle hug for Regina. "Not for this."

She met me at the hospital, where I was taken along with Mr. Solomon's body, because apparently I lost my shit when I saw him. I don't remember that part, though. I don't remember anything past Brynn's hand on the banister, and the look on her face when she said, "Oh no."

Regina says that's a blessing. "Nobody needs to remember that," she said when I told her. I'm not going to be much help to my old friend Officer Patz, though, who takes a seat across from us and regards me with something that almost looks like compassion.

"How are you holding up?" he asks.

"Fine," I say automatically.

"You don't need to talk to me right now," he says. "We can wait till you feel better, or till your father is able to be present."

"He's asleep," I say. "He won't be up for hours. It's fine. I'll talk to you now. I don't want to come back."

Officer Patz looks at Regina. "You think he's up for this?"

She pats my hand again. "If he says so. But why are the police involved, Steven? I thought poor old Dick fell and hit his head."

Poor old Dick. Mr. Solomon, the guy who used to grow gigantic flowers and wave to everyone after soccer practice. I know, in theory, that he's dead, but it hasn't sunk in yet. It doesn't feel real.

"He did," Officer Patz says. "But there may be robbery involved as well. We can't find his red fishing tackle box. You know the one?" Regina nods; she's gotten paid out of that tackle box more than once. "Maybe that's related, maybe it's not, but we're going to treat the house as a crime scene until we know more. We've talked to Brynn Gallagher, who was very helpful, so I think we have most of what we need. Anything Tripp can add is gravy."

I haven't seen Brynn since Mr. Solomon's house; not consciously, anyway. I know she was at the hospital, but I don't remember any of that. I feel sick, suddenly, imagining what I must have looked like through her eyes. Way to fall apart in a crisis, Talbot.

But it's not just shame making me nauseated. It's not knowing what I might have said while I was out of it. *What did I say?*

"I don't know what I said," I say abruptly, lifting my eyes to meet Officer Patz's.

He reaches for a pen with too much eagerness. "About what?"

No. I can't ask him. What the hell was I thinking? "I don't know what I *saw*," I amend. "I can't remember."

"I know. We spoke with the doctor who evaluated you. Your memory may come back at some point, but there's no reason to push it, especially not today. Let's just go over your approach and entry to the house, okay? Maybe you noticed something that Brynn missed."

I do my best, but I can tell from Officer Patz's resigned

expression that I'm not adding anything useful. After a certain point, he stops bothering to take notes and just nods along with my ramblings. "Okay, well, the good news is, Brynn Gallagher has an eye for detail," he finally says, snapping his notebook shut. "I guess that comes in handy for a student journalist."

"Former student journalist," I say.

"Well, but she has that internship," Officer Patz says.

"What internship?" I ask. I glance at Regina, who looks equally puzzled.

"With *Motive*," Officer Patz says. "You know, the true-crime show? She told us all about it during our interview. Interesting, because we've been talking with one of their producers about—" He breaks off then, frowning as he takes me in. "You didn't know that?"

"No," I say, my hands curling in my lap so tightly that my knuckles turn white. "I didn't know that."

CHAPTER TWENTY-THREE

BRYNN

I have screwed up on all possible fronts.

With my parents, who are livid that I didn't tell them about being punched or having a gun pulled on me. All of that came out while I was talking to the police, so I needed to come clean with them too. With Uncle Nick, who's suffering their wrath for keeping my secret. With Carly, who told me very specifically not to return to Mr. Solomon's and is catching hell from Ramon d'Arturo for, as he put it, "letting a kid lead you into a potential PR nightmare." With Nadia and Mason, who are hurt that I didn't tell them about the *Motive* internship.

And with Tripp, I'm guessing. But I don't know, since he hasn't returned any of my calls or texts. I tried stopping by Brightside Bakery this morning after church, but only Regina was there, and she shook her head when I approached the cash register. "Tripp's not here, hon," she said. Al thumped his tail but didn't get up, like even he's disappointed in me.

"Is he okay?" I asked.

"Physically, he's fine."

"What about everything else?"

"I'll let him tell you that himself," Regina said. Kindly, but firmly.

The only person who doesn't hate me is Ellie, so that's who I'm hanging out with in my room while my parents are on the phone with Carly, discussing whether and how I should be allowed to keep working with *Motive*. Ellie brought in her old magic kit, like she's ten years old, and she's poking through its contents while I lie on my bed and stare at the ceiling.

"On the plus side," she says, "this makes the dick pics look like nothing."

"Too soon," I grumble, turning onto my side so I can stare out my window instead.

I expect another flip remark from Ellie, because that's her go-to when she's trying to cheer someone up, but instead she exhales a soft sigh. "I know," she says. "It's okay to just feel crappy for a while. I do. Poor Mr. Solomon."

The lump in my throat gets bigger, and tears sting my eyes. "He had a hole in his sock," I say, and that does it. The tears spill over. I don't know why that small detail in particular makes me feel so sad, but every time I think of it, my chest aches. Ellie's arms steal around me as I curl into the fetal position, sobbing so hard that the rest of me hurts too.

"At least he had a long life, you know?" Ellie sniffs, stroking my hair. "And a good one. I think he was happy. Maybe it was even a kindness, before he got more confused and couldn't live on his own. I don't think he ever would have wanted to leave that house."

"What if he was scared?" I choke out. "At the end? And he was all alone, and . . ." I trail off, crying harder. It's been twenty-four hours since we found Mr. Solomon, and I can't seem to stop crying for more than a couple of hours at a time. Finally I understand how Tripp must have felt in the woods four years ago.

"He wasn't alone," Ellie says. "You were with him." She's not right in any meaningful sense, because Mr. Solomon was long gone when we got there. But I held on to his hand while I waited for the EMTs to arrive, my other arm extended so I could grasp Tripp's knee, which was the only part of him I could reach. It felt ridiculous, but I couldn't let either of them be without human contact.

I sit up, wipe my face, and take a couple of deep, shuddering breaths. "I messed up so badly. You were right, Ellie," I say. "I should have told people what I was doing with *Motive* from the start."

My sister screws up her face. "I'd like to take credit, but I don't think I ever actually said that. I'm pretty sure I aided and abetted you on all fronts." She shrugs and brushes a stray lock of hair from my face. "It'll be okay. People just need time."

"I hope so," I sigh, and pick my phone up from my bedside table. My last text is from Nadia, in response to the string of apologies I sent: *I guess I just don't understand why you'd hide something like that.*

I don't have a good answer. What can I say? *I wasn't planning on getting invested in our friendship again—my bad!* I came back to Sturgis with a chip on my shoulder, treating the five months I had to spend at Saint Ambrose like an unwelcome bridge to someplace better. I didn't realize how much that attitude had seeped into my interactions with people until I found myself in my bedroom with only my sister for company.

"Tripp still won't talk to me," I say.

"I think you're going to have to be patient on that one," Ellie says. "After what happened with his mom, this probably feels like Gunnar Fox all over again." She must see my face crumple, because she quickly adds, "I'm not saying it *is* like that. I'm just saying it might possibly *feel* like that." She picks at a stray thread on one of my pillowcases and adds, "I don't know if it's the worst thing in the world to get some distance from him, though. If things with Mr. Larkin's death aren't what they seem, well, Tripp was front and center to all that, wasn't he? And you have to admit, he acted weird at Mr. Solomon's house. I know it was traumatizing and all, but didn't he say something like, 'What did you do?'"

"Yeah," I say. "And he told me to stop screaming, even though I wasn't. It felt like he thought he was looking at Mr. Larkin, not Mr. Solomon."

"What did Tripp say to you at Charlotte's party, again?" Ellie flops onto her stomach with my pillow under her arms. "Something like, *I needed you to hate me*?"

"Yeah," I say. "But he was talking about what he said in gym class. That happened before Mr. Larkin died."

"Hmmm." Ellie squints. "Okay. So what's your theory?"

"About what? What happened to Mr. Solomon, or what happened to Mr. Larkin?"

"Both. Either."

"I don't have one yet. I'm still gathering information."

Ellie rolls her eyes. "Weak sauce, Brynn. You need to be more like that Ellery girl."

A few days ago, Ellie walked in on me while I was watching a YouTube interview with Ellery Corcoran, the girl who helped solve the Echo Ridge murders that Tucker, one of the producers at *Motive,* wanted to cover. Carly deemed the story *old news,* but I was interested enough to look it up.

"At first I suspected the dead girl's boyfriend, because it's always the boyfriend, right?" Ellery said on video as Ellie walked in. "Then I thought it might be my mother's old boyfriend. Two of them, actually. Or my neighbor, or my friend's sister, or a couple of different classmates . . ."

"Wow," Ellie said. "She's thorough."

"She's all over the place," I said, but I couldn't help liking Ellery. She was filled with what Carly talked about in our interview: *passion.* Meanwhile here I am, carefully documenting bits and pieces of data without ever reaching a conclusion. True-crime journalism really is different from anything I've done before; the stakes feel impossibly high. And I'm a little afraid of what I might learn—about Mr. Larkin, or Tripp, or somebody who's not even on my radar yet.

All I say to Ellie, though, is "I'm working on it."

"Well, whatever's going on, you have to admit that Tripp is sketchy." She's right, obviously—I've known it all along, even while I keep getting closer to Tripp—but I can't help frowning, and Ellie smirks a little. "Sorry for thinking your boyfriend is sketchy."

I toss a pillow at her head in response, and when she ducks, it hits the cover of her magic kit. "Why do you have that, again?" I ask. "Revisiting your childhood?"

She sits up, brightening. "Oh, no. That's for a project."

"What project?" I ask.

"Not telling," she says in a singsong voice. "I need to work alone for this one."

"Work alone?" I repeat. "What are you—"

My phone rings, cutting me off, and I grab it, hoping for Tripp, Nadia, or Mason. But it's a Providence number. I briefly consider sending it to voicemail, but since that's where the Eliot School is located, curiosity gets the better of me and I answer. "This is Brynn."

"Brynn, hi. My name is Paul Goldstein. I'm an English teacher at the Eliot School in Providence. Headmaster Bartley-Reed gave me your number. I hope it's okay that I'm calling on a weekend?"

"Yeah, of course," I say, edging back on my bed until I'm propped against the headboard. Ellie mouths, *Who is it?* and I wave her away. "Thanks for getting back to me."

"No problem. I understand you're doing some kind of memorial for Will Larkin? And you're looking for input on . . ." He pauses, like he's checking notes. "Flowers?"

"Um, yes and no." After everything that happened with Mr. Solomon, I couldn't care less about plants. "I mean, if you happen to be aware of any that he liked, that would be nice to know, but mostly I was hoping you could share some memories. What it was like working with him, that kind of thing."

"Sure," Paul Goldstein says. He sounds like Mr. Larkin; the kind of teacher who gamely rolls with something anytime a student seems to be showing initiative. "Well, first off, Will was a brilliant English teacher. He knew the classics inside and out, but he was big on bringing modern authors into the classroom too." Paul goes on for a while, describing Mr. Larkin's teaching style, and all I can think about is Ramon d'Arturo's words: *The man was a void.* Paul Goldstein couldn't be nicer, taking time out of his Sunday to share recollections, but he's not telling me anything I don't already know.

"That's so helpful, thank you," I say when he pauses for a breath. "I loved having him for a teacher, so what you're saying really resonates. I was wondering, also, what kind of stuff he liked to do outside of class? As students, we never got to see that side of him."

"Well, to be honest, I couldn't really tell you," Paul says. "Will kept to himself. He rode his bicycle to school, so I know he was an avid cyclist."

I pinch the space between my eyes. *An avid cyclist.* Fascinating. I can practically see Ramon d'Arturo falling asleep in his chair as we speak. "Did he talk much about his family?"

"No, I can't say that he ever did," Paul says, and I feel a sharp stab of disappointment until he adds, "Well, just once."

"Oh?" I sit up straighter. "When was that?" Ellie, who's been watching me this whole time, perks up at my expression. She leans close to me, listening in.

Paul chuckles. "Staff party. When everyone is a little more forthcoming than usual, thanks to the liquid refreshments. Don't mention that part," he adds hastily.

"I won't," I promise.

"Will had taken the Saint Ambrose job by then, so he was leaving in a few weeks. I asked him what the attraction there was, because, you know . . ." He hesitates. "No insult meant to Saint Ambrose or Sturgis or anything, but it's not quite, well, the setting—"

"It's a dump," I say, hoping my impatience doesn't show in my voice. "It's okay, you can say it. We all know it."

"No, no," Paul says, but he chuckles again. "It's just that Eliot is considered a plum assignment in private-teaching circles, so I was curious why someone would choose to leave a job like that so early in their career. I asked Will, 'What drew you to Saint Ambrose?'"

"What did he say?" I ask.

"Well, at first he said all the typical stuff about a progressive educational environment, students from diverse walks of life, what have you. Then somebody bought another round—again, don't mention that, please. I don't want to give the impression that teachers at Eliot are a bunch of lushes. After he'd finished his drink, Will leaned over to me and said, 'You want to know the real reason I'm going to Saint Ambrose, Paul?'"

"What was the real reason?" I ask as Ellie mimes biting her knuckles.

"He said, 'I want to be at the same school as my brother.'"

CHAPTER TWENTY-FOUR

TRIPP

I get up early Tuesday morning after the long weekend to run, same as always. When I get home, I shower, eat breakfast, brush my teeth, and get dressed for school on autopilot. Oxford buttoned, tie knotted, navy blazer shrugged over my shoulders. The only difference from a typical day is this: I fill a flask with my father's Jim Beam before I head out the door, and turn in the opposite direction from the road that takes me to Saint Ambrose.

I can't face school. I call the main office as I walk, put on my father's voice, and tell them I'm home, sick. Nobody will be surprised. Everyone knows what happened at Mr. Solomon's on Saturday; my phone is full of messages from people I don't want to talk to.

Including Brynn. *Especially* Brynn.

Who I'm not thinking about, now or ever again. She had the fucking nerve to call *me* a bad liar? She's the worst liar of anyone, spying on the entire school for *Motive*. I hope she has an absolutely shit day of reckoning for that, and I'm almost sorry I won't be there to see it.

Not sorry enough to show up, though.

I don't know where I'm going, exactly, and it doesn't help that I've finished almost half the Jim Beam before I've gone a mile. "Slow down," I lecture myself after I stumble over a pothole on the side of the road. Although, that's the town's fault, really, for letting this pile of crap known as Sturgis keep falling apart. Still, it's probably not a bad idea to get off the road, and that's when it catches my eye: the arched stone entrance to Sturgis Cemetery. Maybe this is where I was headed all along. Where Mr. Solomon will be soon, and where Mr. Larkin was laid to rest four years ago even though he's not from here.

It never occurred to me, until now, to wonder why he wasn't buried someplace else.

I know where his grave is, sort of. It takes some wandering to find him, because it's not like I come here all the time. Twice a year, maybe? I don't bring flowers or anything when I do. I just stand beside the grave, like I am now, and read the inscription on his headstone. *To unpathed waters, undreamed shores.* It's Shakespeare, Ms. Kelso told us at the funeral. I think she might've picked it.

Then I say the same thing I always say: "I'm sorry."

I don't usually follow that with a whiskey chaser, but I also don't usually come here three days after finding a dead body, so—exceptions have to be made.

"I think I'm cursed," I find myself saying. That's new.

The wind picks up, tossing my hair into my eyes, and I push it back. I didn't bring a coat, for no good reason except

I didn't feel like wearing one, and I should probably be cold. I'm not, though. I'm just numb.

"I don't know when it started," I tell Mr. Larkin's tombstone. "Maybe with you, but maybe before. When Lisa Marie left. Or when two people who never should have gotten together in the first place had a kid they didn't want."

I drop heavily onto the grass. The ground is cold and hard beneath me, ridged with clumps of half-frozen dirt. When I set my flask down, it falls right over. Good thing I had the presence of mind to screw the cap back on. "That's not fair, though," I tell Mr. Larkin's grave. "My dad wanted me. He just didn't know what to do once he had me."

I'm pretty sure my father has never been more grateful for our opposite schedules than he was this weekend. He kept apologizing for sleeping through the hospital-slash-police-station portion of the day, but I could tell he was relieved too. Almost as much as I was. "You feeling better?" he asked when we were finally face to face on Saturday evening. "Need anything? To talk to someone, or . . ."

"I'm fine," I said.

Less true words have rarely been spoken, but Dad just nodded. "Regina was probably a good person to have around," he said.

He's right; she was. And that scared me, because what am I supposed to do when I lose Regina? I will eventually, because that's how it goes.

"Melodramatic," I tell Mr. Larkin's grave, and then I feel the need to clarify. "Me, not you. You're not melodramatic. You're just . . ."

Dead. Still. Always.

I shove myself to my feet unsteadily, clutching the flask in one hand, feeling sick and desperate to get away. But where am I supposed to go? I'm surrounded by nothing except gray stone and bare branches. Then my eye catches a spot of color—a familiar bright blue house, one I used to ride my bike past when my mother was in town because I thought she might see me and invite me inside. Valerie's house, where Lisa Marie is now.

Lisa Marie. At least she's up-front when she's doing a television show about my dead teacher, unlike some people.

It seems like a really good idea, suddenly, to go see my mother. Which should probably be my first clue that I'm a lot drunker than I realized. The second clue is that when I get to Valerie's front door, I can't find the doorbell, so I just twist the knob, and it turns. I push the door open and step inside.

I don't know much about Valerie, other than the fact that she went to high school with my mother, is divorced with no kids, and cuts hair at Mo's Barber Shop. She's always been friendly enough to me, calling me "sweetheart" whenever I see her. Occasionally I wonder if that's because she can't remember my name, but it's better than getting called "Trey."

Her house is a split-level like mine, but it's a lot nicer. There's art hanging on the walls, a lot of brightly colored throw pillows, and a rug from this decade. It's also quiet; the only thing I hear is the sound of a shower running. I'm sitting on Valerie's plush couch, looking around me and wondering if it's her or my mother getting ready, when I spot a distinctive floral phone case on the coffee table. I recognize it as Lisa Marie's, and there's a small flip phone beside it.

Unless Valerie prefers outdated technology, I'm pretty sure it's a burner phone. "What are you up to?" I mutter, reaching for Lisa Marie's iPhone first. When I lift it, the screen lights up with a text.

Gunnar: *Love it. Can we try it with tears?*

The last time Lisa Marie was in Sturgis, she made a big deal out of storing my face recognition in her security settings while we were out to lunch—"so I can have a little piece of you with me at all times," she said. She was on her third beer by then, and apparently she hasn't changed her settings since, because the phone unlocks when I tilt it toward me. The *Try it with tears* message is the latest in a long string between her and Gunnar Fox. It's in response to a video she sent last night, and I click to launch it, and tap play. Lisa Marie pops up on-screen, seated at this very couch, wearing a demure floral blouse and a pained expression.

"I think I knew, from an early age, that Noah wasn't like other kids," she says. "I was always so afraid of his temper. It's why I left. When I heard about his teacher, all I could think was—is this it? Did what I've been afraid of for so long finally happen?"

I pause the video. *I think I knew, from an early age, that Noah wasn't like other kids.* Is this real? Is it true? Is this who I am and I just can't see it? It fits, right? Maybe bad things keep happening not because I'm cursed but because I *am* a curse. Even my own mother thinks so.

I try to restart the video, but the phone slips in my hand and I end up back in the text string between Lisa Marie and Gunnar. There are lots of them, too many to read, so I start somewhere in the middle.

Lisa Marie: *He won't do it. I've tried everything.*

Gunnar: *I need this, Lee.*

Gunnar: *I need to nail Shane Delgado before his father's lawyer nails me.*

Gunnar: *Don't Do the Crime could shut down for good if this keeps up.*

Gunnar: *The kid's a fucking psycho, I know it. But they guard him like a prince.*

Lisa Marie: *I don't know what you expect me to do.*

Lisa Marie: *I tried my best.*

Lisa Marie: *My kid is a stubborn little shit.*

Gunnar: *What if we take another angle?*

Lisa Marie: *???*

Gunnar: *All three of them in it together.*

Gunnar: *Noah isn't the witness, you are.*

Gunnar: *He's a bad seed who found a partner in crime with Delgado, and you can't cover for him anymore.*

Gunnar: *I'll pay you what I was going to pay him.*

Bile rises in my throat, and I choke it down. The words start swimming in front of me, but not before I manage to screenshot them and text them to myself, along with the video. When I'm done, I pick up the burner phone. There's no passcode on this one, and only a handful of outgoing texts. All of them are a single word: *Murderer.*

Two of the texts went to my number. I don't know Shane's and Charlotte's numbers off the top of my head, but when I look them up in my phone, they match the other outgoing texts. Turns out Colin Jeffries didn't send the *Murderer* texts after all. My mother did.

I'm so caught up in looking between the phones that I don't hear when the shower stops running, or much of anything else until an outraged voice says, "What the hell are you doing here?" I look up to see Lisa Marie in a fuzzy blue bathrobe, a white towel wrapped around her head, and an incredulous scowl on her face. "Did you just break into Valerie's house?" she demands.

"No," I say. "It was open." My words are thick and slurring, so I try to talk slowly, although I don't think it's helping much. "But I broke into your phones."

"Give me those!" She's on me in an instant, snatching both phones, and I don't resist because I have what I need. Well, almost.

"Here's what I don't understand," I say. "And mind you— I am a little drunk, which might be exasperating the issue." That's not the right word, but whatever. "I get that you were willing to lie about me being a murderer for money, after I wouldn't lie about Shane being a murderer for money. What I don't get, though, is why you sent the three of us texts calling us murderers before I'd even told you no. And how did you get Shane's and Charlotte's cell phone numbers?"

"My goodness," Lisa Marie says, studying me. "You are *wasted.*"

"That's not an answer."

She snorts. "You won't even remember the answer, will you? Gunnar got the numbers. He has his ways. And those texts were just for color. Gunnar wanted to paint a picture of you being lumped in with the other two, to the point where you were being unfairly harassed. But you messed it all up."

"So, just so I'm clear. *You* unfairly harassed me."

"We were building a story line, Trey," she says. "You would have come out of it smelling like a rose if you'd just listened to me."

"Don't call me that," I say.

She frowns. "What?"

"Don't call me 'Trey.' It's not my name. It's not even my nickname."

"It's *my* nickname for you."

"Yeah, well." I get unsteadily to my feet, wishing I were more clearheaded, because once I say what I have to say, I'm never going to speak to her again. "You lied on camera and said I've been a killer since the day I was born for ten thousand dollars, so guess what? You don't get to call me anything. The only thing you get to do is fuck off."

I head for the door with Lisa Marie at my heels. "All you had to do was *listen* to me!" she says. "I wanted to work with you, not against you. But you have to be so stubborn, so goddamn high-and-mighty, like you actually belong at that snotty little school you go to. You never even asked why I needed the money. I have medical problems, Trey. And crappy insurance and maxed-out credit cards, and Junior is no help whatsoever. So maybe, before you run around guzzling booze and judging people, you could think about *that*."

I thought I was done talking to her, but it turns out I have one more thing to say. I open the door, turn to brace myself against the frame, and face her one last time.

"Try it with tears," I say before slamming the door.

CHAPTER TWENTY-FIVE

BRYNN

It's been almost a week since Tripp and I found Mr. Solomon's body, but I still haven't seen or heard from him. He hasn't been at school, which is one of the many things keeping my stomach knotted with worry lately, and he's not answering any of my calls or texts.

Messages from Charlotte, on the other hand, are piling up fast and furious on my phone:

Tripp is nowhere to be found.

I blame you.

Shane and I want to stop by his house, but we don't know where it is.

Where is it?

Just because I'm asking you for a favor doesn't mean I've stopped blaming you.

I put my phone down without answering her. How in the hell, after four years of friendship, does she not know where

Tripp lives? If that weren't so weird, I'd almost be tempted to give her his address, because he certainly didn't answer the door when I stopped by. But it feels like another betrayal to hand out information that Tripp could've shared a hundred times by now if he'd wanted to.

Anyway, I'm supposed to be working.

I hung on to my internship by the skin of my teeth. The rules I have to follow now are many: I can't be involved in any news stories, I've lost privileges for everything except my own hard drive, and I'm not allowed inside the Pit anymore. Even worse, the call for information on Mr. Larkin has come down from the *Motive* website.

When I tried to tell Carly about what Paul Goldstein had said—that Mr. Larkin took the Saint Ambrose job so he could be at the same school as his brother—she held up her hand before I could get out more than a couple of words. "Stop right there," she said. "That story has caused enough trouble already. We should've listened to Ramon and killed it already."

I didn't dare protest.

My only jobs now are to help update the website, proof-read documents, and compile media clips. It's tedious and I hate it, but it's better than getting fired. I have to report to a new supervisor, a public relations manager named Andy Belkin. Before I was banished from the Pit, Gideon told me that the research associates call him "Blandy."

"So, these packets you put together?" I jump when Andy appears over my cubicle wall, as though my resentful musing summoned him. Andy is a short-sleeve-button-down-shirt kind of guy, and today he's wearing a pale yellow version. His brow furrows as he holds up one of the stapled clip packets I put on his desk fifteen minutes ago. "For the next set of clips, I'd prefer a corner staple."

"A what?" I ask.

He points to the staple, which runs parallel to the top of the page. "You did a straight staple, and I prefer a corner one." He picks up my stapler and angles the paper so his staple creates a triangle in the top corner of the page. "See? Like that. Except, obviously, higher, because in this particular instance I had to work around your existing staple."

Kill me. Just kill me, Andy, and get it over with. "Okay."

"Do you want me to leave this with you as a reference?"

"No, I think I've got it, Andy. Thank you."

He disappears, and I lower my head onto my desk so I can bang it ever so slightly.

It's only Friday, but I feel like I've already lived a lifetime this week. A sad, boring, isolated lifetime. Monday was a brief respite, since it was Martin Luther King Day, but on Tuesday I felt like I was on trial—*Saint Ambrose v. Brynn Gallagher*—with the entire school giving me the evil eye as I walked through the halls. *Spy* was the nicest thing people called me. I hid out in the library every free moment I could, including lunch.

Wednesday was a little better, though. While I was loading my books into my locker before the first bell, Nadia came up beside me and tapped my arm. "Why did you eat in the library yesterday?" she asked. "Did you think we wouldn't let you sit with us?"

"Um." That was exactly what I'd thought. "I didn't want to put you in a bad position or anything, so—"

Nadia rolled her eyes. "You're today's gossip, Brynn. Pretty soon you'll be yesterday's news. That's how it goes around here, and Mason and I never pay attention to stuff like that. It would be nice, though, if you'd make an effort to show us that you're sorry for keeping us in the dark. Besides texting it."

She was right, obviously. While I'm grateful that Nadia and Mason haven't abandoned me, I miss the easy camaraderie we had, and I'm not sure how to get it back.

In summary, I probably deserve the purgatory of stapling dozens of media packets to Andy's precise specifications. But I still don't like it.

When I finish my next set of clips, I head for an empty conference room, close the door, and pull out my phone. Carly wouldn't let me talk about Mr. Larkin's maybe-brother today, so that's an itch I still feel the need to scratch. I press a name in my contacts, and wait until a wry voice says, "What now, sort-of-cherished niece?"

"Did Mr. Larkin have a brother at Saint Ambrose?" I ask Uncle Nick without preamble. "Anyone you met, or heard about, when you worked there?"

"What?" He sounds bewildered. "A brother? No. Why?"

"I talked to a teacher at Mr. Larkin's old school who said Mr. Larkin told him he was going to Saint Ambrose to be at the same school as his brother. Which is weird, right? It's the first I've ever heard of a brother."

"Are you kidding me?" My uncle's voice gets uncharacteristically cold. "After everything that's happened, you're still snooping around about Will?"

My throat goes dry. I called Uncle Nick without thinking, assuming I could talk to him like I always have. "I got in touch with Mr. Larkin's old school before Mr. Solomon died, and they only just got back to me—"

"You're unbelievable, you know that?" Shame keeps me silent, and he lets out a snort. "I stuck my neck out for you."

"I'm sorry—" I start, but I'm talking to dead air. He hung up on me. My uncle, who almost never loses his temper, finally snapped.

I should've known better; I've already caused enough trouble for Uncle Nick with my parents. Mom, especially, was furious that he hadn't told them about Colin hitting me at school. She spent half the weekend glaring at him, and muttering things like "I don't recall signing up for having a third teenager in the house, but apparently that's what I've gotten."

I take the long way back to my cubicle, past Lindzi's office, because I can't help but hope that if she sees me, she'll wave and call me in like she used to. I might be wrong, but when Lindzi passed by Scarlet while Carly was laying down the law, the look she gave me through the window seemed sympathetic. I could use a friendly face right about now. As I near her office, though, I can hear her on the phone, so I linger in the hallway to see if she sounds close to wrapping up.

"So do you not even want to talk about it?" she asks. A pause, and then, "I know, Carly. I don't disagree, but the tip seems legit. What if people have been looking at the entire Larkin story from the wrong angle? What if the *police* did?" My ears prick up as she adds, "Look, just let me email it to you, okay? And we can go from there."

Email it to me too, I think as Lindzi hangs up the phone. She would have, a week ago. There's a clatter of keyboard noise, and then she bursts out her office door, heading so quickly in the opposite direction that she doesn't notice me. I stare after her, then into her office.

Her laptop is *right there*. It hasn't even had time to auto-lock.

I glance over my shoulder at the deserted hallway, and take a couple of steps toward Lindzi's office. Then a couple more. And then—

"There you are, Brynn." Andy's nasally voice makes me jump, and when I turn, he's waving a stapled packet at me. "Really nice job with these, except I thought I told you I wanted them double-sided?" He hands it to me with an expectant look. "These are very important documents that the production staff needs to help them understand the competitive landscape. They need to be perfect."

"I . . ." I take the handout automatically, but I can't look away from Lindzi's laptop. So near, and yet so far. "I'm sorry, I don't remember that."

"It's all right, but let's go ahead and redo them, okay? Why don't you come with me, and I'll show you where you can find some more paper?"

My shoulders slump as I prepare to follow him. But then—I can't do it. I can't let the opportunity pass. "Andy," I say, a little breathless. "Can I meet you back at my cubicle? I was actually headed for the bathroom just now."

"Oh." His face puckers, but only for a second. "Of course."

"Thanks. I'll be quick." I wait for him to round the corner, then dash back to Lindzi's office. It's still empty, and her laptop is still unlocked. I put Andy's media packet on the desk and angle Lindzi's screen toward me. Microsoft Outlook is open, and I navigate to her sent folder to see the last email she sent: *Larkin (?) Background*, to Carly Diaz. I open it and forward it to the junk Gmail address I use when I don't want to give my real one online. Then I hear voices, much too close, and one of them sounds a lot like Lindzi. There's no time to delete what I sent, so I'll just have to hope that Lindzi doesn't notice.

There's also no time to leave her office.

I shove her laptop back to where I found it—I think—grab Andy's packet, and spring as far away from the desk as I can. "Hi!" I call cheerfully when Lindzi enters, waving the sheaf of paper at her. "Andy wanted me to give you this."

"Oh my God, Brynn, you scared the life out of me," Lindzi says, putting a hand over her heart. She takes the packet and frowns. "Why did he want me to have this?"

"He . . ." What had Andy said? "He said you need it to evaluate the competitive landscape."

She rolls her eyes. "That's a bit of a stretch, but thanks."

"You're welcome," I say, and hustle out of there so I can finish stapling packets until it's time to go home and check Gmail.

Lindzi's notes are rapid-fire and precise, just like her.

> Most of the tips that came in through the website were useless, but there was one that said, "Looks like a guy I used to know, but his name was Billy Robbins." I followed up, and this person claimed he grew up in New Hampshire with someone who looked a lot like William Larkin. I wondered if there was a name change at some point, and searched court databases in all six New England states.
> I found a strong possibility: a young man who

changed his name from William Dexter Robbins to William Michael Larkin eleven years ago.

Then I searched the name William Robbins. There are a lot and none seemed right, but I did find this article about a New Hampshire man named Dexter Robbins. Attached.

Please read and let me know what you think.

Lindzi

I click on the attachment and open a *New Hampshire Union Leader* article that's fourteen years old:

LINCOLN MAN REPORTS WIFE AND TODDLER SON MISSING

Grafton County Sheriff's Office detectives have put out an alert for 26-year-old Lila Robbins and 3-year-old Michael Robbins of Lincoln after Lila Robbins's husband, Dexter, 42, reported them missing upon returning from a hunting trip with his 15-year-old son from a previous marriage.

Dexter Robbins states that his wife and son were last seen in their home on Friday, March 5, when Robbins and his older son left for a cabin in the White Mountains belonging to a friend of Dexter Robbins.

Robbins was unable to provide a more current photo of his wife than her high school yearbook photo. One neighbor of the couple says they're not surprised that Lila and Michael are gone.

"Dexter rules that family with an iron fist," said the neighbor, under the condition of anonymity. "We barely saw Lila. I'm surprised he left her alone for a weekend. He didn't let her go anywhere except church."

The Robbins family are members of a fundamentalist church located in Cross Creek, New Hampshire, that, among other things, does not believe its members should be treated with modern medicine. "Michael has asthma, but Dexter wouldn't do anything about it," the neighbor said. "Poor kid was gasping every time I saw him.

"If Lila saw her chance to leave," the neighbor concluded, "I don't think anyone would blame her for taking it."

I sit back against the headboard of my bed and study the two pictures accompanying the article; a grainy photo of a young woman with bleached-blond hair and heavy makeup, and one of a small, dark-haired boy being carried in the arms of a teenage boy. The caption for the first photo reads, *Lila Robbins, age 18.* The second says, *Michael Robbins, age 3, with his half brother, William.* Neither of the boys' faces is particularly clear, but I could almost imagine, if the older boy's sullen mouth were turned up in a smile, that he might look a little like Mr. Larkin.

Dexter Robbins's older son, William, was fifteen years old when this article was written. Four years ago, he'd have been twenty-five, just like Mr. Larkin was when he died. The other boy, the toddler who disappeared with his mother, would have been thirteen when Mr. Larkin died, and seventeen now. My age, and my classmates' age.

I want to be at the same school as my brother.

CHAPTER TWENTY-SIX

TRIPP

Mr. Solomon's funeral is on Friday, but I don't go to it.

School is on Friday too, but I don't go to that either. Or to work. It's interesting, how you can just stop doing things and the world keeps right on going. That would've been useful information to have before I wasted so much energy on stuff that turned out not to matter anyway. All that time, I could have been doing nothing.

I did go to the liquor store on Saturday, because Dad's out of alcohol, but the woman behind the counter laughed me out of the place. Joke's on her, though, because a guy in the parking lot was happy to buy me whatever I wanted for a twenty-dollar tip. "Here you go," he said. "Don't drink it all at once, Prep." I've taken to wearing my Saint Ambrose blazer as a coat because I don't mind the cold, and also, I can't find my actual coat.

Joke's on him too, because I *did* drink it all at once.

Dad leaves me notes. I don't read them. I told him I have a fever.

Sometimes I take out the video Lisa Marie made, and the screenshots from her phone, and think about sending them to Shane so Mr. Delgado can destroy my mother and Gunnar Fox in one fell swoop. It feels like that might be satisfying, in a way that nothing else is, except for the part where Mr. Delgado would have to hear what she said about me.

I think I knew, from an early age, that Noah wasn't like other kids.

Lisa Marie was lying, but also she wasn't, because what regular kid would do what I did and then live for four years like nothing happened? I still don't remember seeing Mr. Solomon's body, but that must be what finally dragged me out of denial and dropped me straight into hell.

Lisa Marie just reminded me that I belong there.

Mostly, though, I curl up on our couch and I sleep, making up for all the sleep I haven't gotten for the past four years. That's the thing nobody ever tells you about being involved in a murder: it tends to keep you up at night.

"Tripp. Tripp! Wake your sorry ass up."

Somebody is shaking my shoulder, hard. I groan and crack open my eyes, then immediately close them when light sears my eyeballs. I don't need to see a face, though. I know that voice.

"You smell like a brewery and you look like shit," Regina says.

"Nice to see you too," I mumble.

"Fever, my ass. I knew you were lying. Sit *up*." She drags me into a seated position. "I closed the bakery for you. The least you can do is sit the hell up."

"I didn't ask you to do that."

"No, you just left me in the lurch for a week so you could drink yourself senseless." She slaps my cheek, but not hard enough to hurt. "Listen. I know you saw something terrible last week, and it made you think of that other terrible thing you saw. I know your mother is a toxic mess and your father checked out a long time ago. All of that is a shame. But you're not the only person who's ever gone through a hard time or been dealt a shitty hand, Tripp Talbot. You've got a roof over your head, a good education, and the sense God gave you. That's more than a lot of people have. So get up and get moving. If you're gonna lie around all day, you can do it in the storage room and feed Al while you're at it." She wrinkles her nose and puts some space between us. "But first, take a goddamn shower."

She's right about that part. The shower's overdue, so I stumble upstairs, peel off days-old clothes, and turn the water up to scalding hot. For a few minutes, as water pounds my skull and my shoulders and the clean scent of soap and shampoo surrounds me, I think that I can maybe do what she says. I dry off, brush my teeth, and put on fresh clothes. Even though my head is pounding and my hands are shaking, I feel a little bit normal. Then I look in the mirror, at my shadowed eyes and stubbled jaw, and all I see is *him*.

I think I knew, from an early age, that Noah wasn't like other kids.

Regina's a good person. The best one I know, and she

shouldn't have to deal with *him*. So when I hear her go into our downstairs bathroom, I grab my Saint Ambrose blazer, shrug it on, and take off out the front door.

As usual, I don't know where I'm going. My house is on a main road, and I start across the street without looking, only to have a car swerve around me, honking loudly. "Jerkoff," I mutter, even though it was my fault. Another car approaches from the opposite direction, but much more slowly, and its headlights flash when it gets close.

I know that Range Rover; I've ridden in it dozens of times. The driver's-side window rolls down, and Charlotte pokes her head out. She's wearing a white coat with a faux-fur hood, bright red lipstick, and an exasperated expression.

"Shane and I have been looking for you everywhere," she says. "Get in."

CHAPTER TWENTY-SEVEN

BRYNN

Ellie comes into the kitchen Saturday night when I'm elbow-deep in batter, using a spatula to beat it with all the arm strength I can muster because I can't find the electric mixer. Half our kitchen stuff is still boxed up from the Chicago move. "What are you doing?" she asks, fastening an earring.

"Making chocolate-chip cookies," I say, wiping my brow and smearing grainy batter across my forehead. Then I go back to attacking the dough. "I thought I could drop them off at Nadia's and Mason's houses tomorrow. You know, like a gesture of friendship."

Ellie sidles up to the counter and tries to stick a finger into my batter, but I swat her away. "Okay, but isn't Nadia gluten-free?" she asks.

I keep stirring until her words sink in. "God damn it," I say, letting the spatula fall into the batter. "You're right. Ugh.

Why am I such a terrible friend?" I lift the bowl like I'm about to dump it into the sink, but Ellie stops me.

"You can still make them for Mason," she says. "And you're not a terrible friend. You just don't pay attention to that kind of stuff."

"I should, though," I say, slumping against the counter. "Details are supposed to be my *thing*. How can I say I want to be a journalist when I can't even remember that one of my best friends is allergic to gluten?"

Ellie shrugs. "Book smart isn't people smart," she says.

"When did you get so wise?" I mutter.

But she's right about Mason; he could use some cookies. He sobbed on Nadia's shoulder like his heart was broken all the way through Mr. Solomon's funeral yesterday. When I shot her a quizzical look, she whispered, "They used to be close." Which feels, again, like the kind of thing I should have known.

"I have always been so," Ellie says breezily. "You just never appreciated it until your social circle shrank to"—she gazes around the kitchen with an expectant air, like she's waiting for party guests to arrive—"me." I flick a dish towel at her, and when she darts away, her skirt swishes and I notice how cute she looks.

"Why are you all dressed up?" I ask.

"I'm going to the movies with Paige Silverman," she says, glancing at the clock on our microwave. "Her mom will be here any minute."

"Is this a date?" I ask.

"Mayyyyybe," Ellie says coyly. "If she's lucky." A horn beeps outside, and she lunges for the bowl and snags a fingerful of cookie dough before I can stop her. "That must be them," she says, sticking her finger into her mouth. Then she makes a face and spits the dough into the sink. "Brynn, ew. How much salt did you put in this? It's horrible."

"I put what the package said," I say, picking up the discarded chocolate-chip bag so I can peer at the back. "A tablespoon."

"Let me see." Ellie takes it from me and shakes her head. "*T-s-p* means 'teaspoon,' not 'tablespoon,' you nitwit. You put in three times as much salt as you should have."

"God *damn* it," I say with a rush of fury that I realize is out of proportion for the situation, even as I slam the bowl into the sink. This time Ellie makes no attempt to stop me.

"Buy him some Chips Ahoy! instead. On that note, have a good night!" she calls on her way to the door.

I sink into a chair at the kitchen table when she's gone, contemplating all the poor life choices I've made recently that have left me home alone on a Saturday night with no company except oversalted cookie dough. I lift my phone and flick through my texts in case I missed a new one, but I didn't. Then I open my Gmail and read the *Union Leader* article again, even though I know it by heart.

If Mr. Larkin is really William Robbins from New Hampshire, is Michael Robbins, the little boy, the brother Mr. Larkin told Paul Goldstein about? The one he took the job at Saint Ambrose for? If yes, there's a good chance that Mr. Larkin was talking about one of my classmates. But he must not have made contact, because whoever it was didn't say anything when Mr. Larkin died.

I keep studying Lila Robbins's high school yearbook photo, torn between thinking she looks familiar and thinking I just *wish* she looked familiar. Lila was generically pretty at age eighteen, but who knows what she looks like now? If she was twenty-six when she disappeared fourteen years ago, she'd be forty now.

I Googled *Dexter Robbins* last night, and couldn't find any results except the minutes of a town hall meeting three years ago where he was vehemently opposed to a property tax increase. Lila Robbins is a ghost; the only mention I could find of her was the *Union Leader* article about her and Michael's disappearance. If Dexter is still looking for them, he hasn't gone to the press about it since that first article painted him in such a bad light. Lila and Michael are nowhere to be found. Maybe because, like their neighbor insinuated, they don't *want* to be found.

I open my camera and scroll through the evidence photos I took, back when I had access to *Motive*'s files. There's the bloody rock that still makes me shudder. The silver chain that continues to confuse me, because I never saw Mr. Larkin wear anything like that, or any jewelry at all. And the turquoise, sticker-covered envelope that—

Oh. Oh my God.

The memory crashes over me like a wave and leaves me just as breathless. I know where I saw the envelope now, and it definitely wasn't at Saint Ambrose. I leap to my feet and grab for my keys because here, *finally*, is something I can do.

When Charlotte answers her door, she is not, to put it mildly, happy to see me.

"I'm not having a party," she says, although she's certainly dressed for one. Our home-on-a-Saturday-night wardrobes are nothing alike, so I'm guessing she has Shane in there somewhere. Charlotte is wearing a glittery black top over jeans; her lips are bright red and her eyes are dusted with shimmery powder. I, on the other hand, realize I still have cookie dough on my forehead, which I hastily rub off when I see her eyes stray toward it. "And even if I were—"

I stick my foot in the door before she can close it. "I'm looking for Tripp," I say.

"Haven't seen him," Charlotte says coolly. She's a much better liar than Tripp is, so I might have believed her if Regina hadn't told me that she saw him getting into a black Range Rover this afternoon. I've seen Charlotte's car in the Saint Ambrose parking lot, and it's not the type I typically catch sight of in Tripp's neighborhood.

"Charlotte, please. It's important."

"Oh?" She lifts perfectly shaped brows. "It was important when I asked for his address too, but you wouldn't give it to me."

"Okay, but seriously, how do you not know that?"

"Bye, Brynn." Charlotte tries closing the door again, and I wedge my foot in farther.

"Can you just tell him I'm here?"

"You should try texting him."

"I *did*," I say, my frustration growing. "He's not answering."

"Then take a hint," Charlotte says, and this time she manages to shut the door in my face. After that, since the entire front of the house is windows, I get to watch her ponytail swinging as she walks away from me and disappears around a corner.

"Ughhh," I mutter, kicking her front stoop. I knew this

was a long shot, but I was still hoping Tripp might come to the door.

I make it about halfway to my car before I turn and look at the house again, hands on my hips. Tripp wasn't inside the last time I went looking for him at Charlotte's house, so maybe he isn't now either. I creep along the side of the house, hoping I can get into the backyard from there, but it's all fenced. I wander for a few yards until I catch sight of a light burning in Charlotte's fancy shed. Or maybe it's not a shed after all.

Tripp must have climbed the fence in order to get onto that stone pillar he was sitting on the last time I found him here. If he can do it, surely I can too.

I don't see how I can scale the wrought-iron part of the fence, though; the spikes on top look as though they could impale me. The stone pillar seems like a better bet, but the rim around the bottom is too low to the ground to provide much of a boost. I cling to the flat top of the pillar and try digging the toes of my boots into the rough stone as a foothold but only manage to get myself about six inches higher. As soon as I try to move, I slide right back down.

The only way to the top, apparently, is by doing a giant pull-up, and I now recognize the flaw in my plan. Tripp is a foot taller than me and has a lot more arm strength. Still, I have to try. I'm clinging to the flat top of the pillar, muscles tensed, when a voice slurs, "What—and I cannot stress this strongly enough—the *fuck* are you doing?"

CHAPTER TWENTY-EIGHT

BRYNN

"Looking for you," I pant, releasing the pillar and dropping gracelessly to the ground. Tripp is on the other side of the fence, in a T-shirt and his Saint Ambrose blazer, his jaw unshaven and his hair mussed. "I thought you might be in that—shed, or whatever it is, so I was trying to get over the fence." I dust my palms together and add, "That last part was probably obvious."

"Did you consider using the gate?" Tripp asks, in that careful voice he puts on when he's trying to sound less drunk than he is. He reaches out a hand to tug at something a few feet to my right, and a section of the wrought-iron fence swings outward. I'm very glad, suddenly, that it's too dark for him to see the heat rising in my cheeks.

How, given what I came here for, can he still make me blush?

"You know I don't like gates," I say, stepping through before he changes his mind.

Tripp looks me up and down with those long-lashed eyes of his, frowning. "I'm mad at you," he says slowly. "But I don't remember why."

"Probably wasn't that bad, then," I mutter, scuffing the toe of my boot into the ground.

"Why are you here, Brynn?" he asks.

I could ask him the same question, but I don't know how much time we have before he either decides to sic Charlotte and Shane on me or stops making sense. "I need to talk to you. Do you want to go into the shed for a minute? You look cold."

Tripp turns to look at the building behind him. "It's not a shed," he says. "It's a guesthouse. And I'm not cold." He watches me shiver for a bit and adds, "But you are, so fine."

Once we enter the guesthouse, I can't believe I ever called it a shed. It's beautiful inside, most of the space dominated by a living area that contains a sectional sofa flanked by leather armchairs, with a heavy oak coffee table in between. Bookshelves line one wall, and a tall bronze lamp casts a warm, buttery circle of light onto the richly colored carpet.

Tripp staggers a little and shrugs off his blazer before collapsing into a corner of the sofa. I take off my coat and perch a few feet away from him. I'm a little surprised by his lack of resistance, but I also don't think he was being facetious when he said he couldn't remember why he was angry with me. He's obviously not doing well, and it makes my chest constrict even though I know, finally, why I haven't been able to trust him fully.

"Okay," I say. "I need to talk to you because I remembered something. About the class-trip money that went missing in eighth grade." I pause, looking for some kind of signal that the topic means something to him, and I don't think I'm wrong that he stiffens a little.

"There were two envelopes," I continue. "A small envelope that held the money. That was found in Charlotte's locker. And a bigger, turquoise one covered with stickers, that held the smaller envelope plus the donor list. That was never found. But I saw it, after the money had gone missing." I wait a beat for his reaction, but there's nothing this time. "I saw it in your room while we were doing homework."

"No, you didn't," Tripp says instantly. Then he rubs his thumb with his finger, and I feel a spark of triumph. *Liar. Caught you.* But the spark dies as quickly as it came, because— all of a sudden Tripp has a motive for keeping Mr. Larkin quiet, doesn't he? If he stole that money years ago, and Mr. Larkin found out about it . . .

No. I'm getting ahead of myself. I haven't asked nearly enough questions, and besides, I keep circling back to what Tripp said in Mr. Solomon's house, when he seemed to be flashing back to Mr. Larkin's death. *What did you do?* Not *What have I done?* I think his raw, horrified voice in my head is why I came looking for him without hesitation, never imagining that pushing for the truth might be dangerous. That *he* could be dangerous. I'm pretty sure that the only person Tripp is dangerous to, especially right now, is himself.

"Yes, I did," I say. "I know what I saw." I swallow hard and add, "Did you take the money, Tripp?"

He runs a hand across his temple, then over his scruffy jaw and the back of his neck. "I'm so tired," he says heavily.

"Of what?" I ask.

"Everything."

"Did you take the money?" I repeat.

He drops his hand to his lap and says, "Yeah, I took it. What can I say? I'm sorry. It was dumb." Then he rubs his thumb again, and relief floods through me. *Goodbye, motive.*

"No, you didn't," I say.

His eyes flash with surprise. "I just told you I did."

"And I'm telling you that I know you didn't. Was it Charlotte?" We can do this by process of elimination, I guess.

"Okay, yeah, it was. I'm just trying to look out for her. She didn't mean any harm." His fingers move again, and it's honestly shocking to me that he doesn't realize he does this. Every single time.

"Nope," I say. "Not her either."

He frowns. "What are you playing at, Brynn? You ask, I answer, and you tell me I'm lying. Why are you even here if you don't believe a word I say?"

"Because I'll know when you're telling the truth," I say.

Tripp huffs out a humorless laugh. "You will, huh? Because you're magical like that."

Who is he protecting? The envelope was in his house, so the list of people who might have put it there is short. I could run through all his friends, I guess, but it probably makes sense to start closer to home. "Was it Lisa Marie?" I ask. I don't really think that Tripp would lie for his mother, and she was in Las Vegas anyway, but I want to test his reaction.

He answers immediately, his hand still. "No."

"Was it your dad?" I ask.

"No," he repeats, and rubs his thumb.

"Bingo," I say softly.

Unlike me, Tripp has never been a blusher, but now his

cheeks stain a deep red as his mouth drops open. "How the hell are you doing that?" he breathes, too startled to fake anything. Then he tries to recover, stammering that he was just messing with me, but he's nowhere near sober enough to pull it off.

"I'm not going to tell on your dad, Tripp." I say it with a pang, because solving the theft might be a key puzzle piece in the overall mystery, but I've never been more sure of anything than this: Tripp needs to talk about what happened back then. "I just want to know. How did the money end up in Charlotte's locker?"

He drops his head into both hands and falls silent for a long minute. I'm about to ask again, when he looks up and says, "Swear you won't tell?"

I cross my heart. "I promise."

"I found it the weekend before Mr. Larkin died, when I was looking for a hammer in the basement," Tripp says. "It was under my dad's workbench. I knew what it was, right away. He must've taken it during that whole shelf fiasco, you know, when he was building them for Grizz and then he unbuilt them? I brought it up to my room and tried to figure out what to do. I decided I'd bring the money back to school and slip it into the office when no one was looking, but I lost my nerve and left it at home on Monday. Which is when you saw it."

He knots his hands together so tightly that the veins in his forearms bulge. "I lost my nerve on Tuesday and Wednesday too. Then Mr. Larkin died, and I didn't go to school on Thursday. It felt like that fucking envelope was staring at me all day. So on Friday I was finally like, 'I have to get rid of this goddamn thing, no more stalling,' and I brought it to school. I thought I could be sly and drop it in Grizz's office when nobody was looking. I was almost there when I saw the cop he'd brought in to search our lockers. I didn't know what he was there for, but I panicked anyway. I took the little envelope out of the big one so I could dump it into the nearest locker, which turned out to be Charlotte's. Then I put the big envelope through the shredder in the art room."

"And you never told Charlotte?" I ask.

"I never told anybody," he says.

My mind is spinning. It's awful that his dad took the money, but—this can't be why Tripp has been spiraling, right? It's not enough. There's something else going on. I'm trying to figure out the best way to worm more details out of him, when Tripp shifts in his seat to face me. "That's why I said all that stuff to you," he says.

"That stuff . . . ," I start, and then I get it. "In gym class."

"Yeah." He swallows hard. "I knew you saw the envelope the night before. I was afraid you'd write about it for the *Saint Ambrose Sentinel* and my dad would wind up in jail. I tried to make it so nobody would believe you if you covered it. So they'd think you were just making stuff up to get back at me. Or maybe you'd be too embarrassed to try."

"I didn't even realize what the envelope was," I say. "Not till recently."

"Cool." Tripp hangs his head. "Glad I alienated you for no reason whatsoever."

"You could've talked to me about it," I say. "We were friends, remember?"

"Sure," he says, shrugging. "But you cared more about the school paper than about me."

"That's not true!" I protest, stung. Tripp just snorts. I want to keep arguing, but . . . the thing is, I was pretty black-and-white in my thinking back then. Maybe I wouldn't have cared *more* about the paper, but I definitely would have felt a strong urge to finish the story. I probably would have thought that since telling the truth is objectively the right thing to do, everything would turn out fine. So all I finish with is "You could've been less brutal in gym class."

Tripp's gaze is focused on the circle of lamplight on the rug. "I don't even remember what I said," he mutters. Then he rubs his fingers together.

"Yeah, you do," I say, and he collapses against the sofa.

"How?" he asks plaintively, his voice ragged.

"Why'd you pick that particular lie?" I ask.

It doesn't matter, I guess, but I'm curious.

Tripp lets out a bitter laugh. "I might as well tell you, right? You'll know if I don't, because you're some kind of goddamn truth wizard." He rakes a hand through his hair. "I was freaking in love with you back then, Brynn, and I was afraid that if I didn't make you hate me so much that you'd never talk to me again, I'd end up spilling everything. There was a small, stupid part of me that almost *wanted* to give you that big scoop, because it would make you happy. Messed up, right? I had to get rid of that part."

His hands don't move.

I fall silent, and Tripp snort-laughs again. "I finally shut you up, huh?"

"You were— You never said anything," I stammer.

"Why would I? You didn't like me that way. And let's not

forget that I was thirteen and basically a disaster. But there you go, Brynn. There's your truth. Are you satisfied?"

"No," I say, and he blows out a sigh. "I'm sorry, but none of that is bad enough for—all this." I wave a hand around him. "You haven't been to school or work in a week, and I'm pretty sure you haven't been sober for that entire time either. You look terrible." That last part's not true, actually, but he *should* look terrible, which is the important point. "You're hiding out in Charlotte's guesthouse. It can't just be because your dad took some money or because you . . . liked me and then cut ties with me." I can't bring myself to say *love;* that was the alcohol talking, and anyway, it was four years ago and we were kids. "What aren't you telling me?"

What did you do? Who was that question for? That's the key to everything, and right now there are only three people I can think of: Shane, Charlotte, or his dad.

"No," Tripp says, softly but firmly.

"No what?"

"No more," he says.

"Tripp, I really think you have to—"

"I don't." His gaze suddenly sharpens into a glare. "I remember why I'm mad at you. You work for that TV show. You've been using me this whole time, haven't you?"

"No," I say. "I haven't, I swear. I'm really sorry that I didn't tell you about *Motive.* I should have. But I never shared anything you told me with them." He just shakes his head, and I add, "I'll quit, Tripp. I will send an email and quit right now if you'll tell me what happened to make you this upset."

"No, you won't."

"I'm doing it." I pull up Carly's email and type, *I'm so sorry, but I have a conflict of interest and can no longer work as an intern at* Motive. *Thank you so much for the experience. I appreciate the opportunity and will always be grateful.*

I show Tripp my screen, and his lips twist. "You won't send it."

I take a deep breath—*here goes nothing, goodbye, internship, you were great while you lasted, until the Blandy Era anyway*—and press send. Then I open my sent folder and show it to him. "See?"

"That was stupid," he mutters. "I never said I'd tell you anything."

"I know," I say. "But I want you to know you can trust me."

He looks away. "There's nothing more to tell."

I don't need to see his hands to know that's a lie. "Just give me a chance, Tripp. Please. Don't you think it would help you feel better?"

"I don't know," Tripp says, his voice hollow. "I don't think I'll ever feel better, to be honest. I don't think I should."

There doesn't seem to be anything I can say to convince him, but I can't just give up either. I move closer until I'm right next to him, and take his face in both of my hands, feeling the sharp planes of his cheekbones and the soft scruff at his jawline as I pin him with my gaze. "Tripp, if you don't let whatever is inside of you out, I'm honestly afraid that it's going to kill you. And soon."

He jerks his head away, eyes burning into mine. "Don't do that," he says hoarsely. "Don't—you can't touch me like that when you know how I . . . Fuck." He slumps against the sofa, eyes closed, and I shove down the part of me that wants to ask, *When I know how you what?* This is not the time for that conversation. "I'm so tired," he says. "Of all of it."

I don't say anything, because I can't think what else to say. I've used every tool in my limited arsenal of persuasion. So I just sit there, quietly, for so long that I think Tripp must have fallen asleep. And then, when I'm about to touch his sleeve to see if he has, he says, eyes still closed, "It started right before the leaf project."

TRIPP
FOUR YEARS AGO

I'm almost out the door at Saint Ambrose, getting ready to meet up with Shane by the woods for our leaf project, when I hear them.

"There's no mistake. Someone saw. A kid finally came forward to tell their parents, and the parents told me."

It's Mr. Larkin, talking to someone in his classroom. I'm about to keep walking when a familiar voice stops me in my tracks.

"You sure the kid was telling the truth?" my father asks.

I stop and press against the wall, even though there's no one around to see me. I stayed after for extra help in math, and everyone else is long gone. Dad never mentioned coming here, and I don't know why he *would* come, unless . . .

"It's a reliable source," Mr. Larkin says. There's a long pause, and then he says, "Are you trying to deny it? If you are, I can get the police involved—"

"No," Dad says heavily. Another pause, until he adds, "I'm not denying it. I'll get it back to you, okay? Every last cent."

Shit. Shit. Shit. My heart starts pounding as I clutch the strap of my backpack tighter—my stupid backpack that, once again, doesn't have the turquoise envelope inside. I waited too long to return it, and now Mr. Larkin knows. *He knows.*

"It's not that simple," Mr. Larkin says.

"Why not?" my father asks.

"Because it's theft. The administration needs to know, and so do the authorities."

No, no, no, no, no, no, no.

A hard edge creeps into my father's voice. "You just said you wouldn't get the police involved if I—"

"I never said that," Mr. Larkin interrupts.

"Come on, Will," my father says, and I can almost hear him swallowing his anger before adding in a calmer tone, "Can't we keep things between us?"

"No," Mr. Larkin says. Curt and dismissive, like he won't even consider it.

"You don't understand what this will do to Tripp. It's not just about the money. It's—"

"Tripp isn't my concern," Mr. Larkin says in the coldest tone I've ever heard him use. He barely even sounds like the same person.

They keep arguing, and my stomach keeps churning until Mr. Larkin finally says, "All of this sounds like a *you* problem, Junior. Not a *me* problem. Now, if you'll excuse me, I have someplace to be."

I flatten myself behind the trophy case as he storms out. "You don't get it, Will," Dad calls after him, his voice hoarse and almost desperate. "You can't do this!" He steps into the hallway, hands on his hips as he watches Mr. Larkin walk away. "You can't do this," he repeats in a quieter tone.

My heart pounds as I slowly back around the corner without my father seeing me, and slip out a side door. I make my way outside, and when I reach the parking lot, my eyes hit on an unwelcome sight: Mr. Larkin, walking toward the exact same woods where I'm supposed to be. I freeze in place, indecisive. I don't want to run into him, not after everything I just heard. Should I go back inside and talk to my father? But the thought makes me too nauseated to consider for long, so I keep walking.

Mr. Larkin does the typical adult thing—instead of hopping the fence, he walks all the way to the edge of Saint Ambrose, where there's a break between our fence and one of a neighboring yard. I head for the kids' shortcut, which is a low, sagging bit of fence that's easy to jump. I toss my backpack over, then wait a few minutes to make sure that Mr. Larkin is well on his way to wherever he's going.

Tripp isn't my concern, Mr. Larkin said. The words shouldn't hurt as much as they do, because I have a much bigger problem. Tomorrow, the entire school will know that my father is a thief.

The bell rings, signaling the end of after-school help at Saint Ambrose, and I take that as my cue to haul myself over the fence. Then I make my way to the birch grove, where I'll be able to see Shane when he arrives.

Shane, of course, is late, and we argue until we finally split up. It's a relief to be alone, listening to music while adding leaves to my collection, until I realize I've lost track of where

I am. I pull out my earbuds, get my bearings at the ridge near Shelton Park, and start to make my way back to Saint Ambrose.

Then the screaming starts.

I crash through trees to follow it, and stop short when I see something blue among all the brown and green. Charlotte's coat. Her hands are covering her mouth, but they're not doing much to muffle her screams. Shane is standing next to her, a big rock in his hands and a dazed expression on his face. He's looking down, staring at the ground, at . . .

Oh God.

Mr. Larkin is lying on his back, unnaturally still, his eyes wide open and staring at nothing. The leaves beside his head are stained red. "Is he . . ." I trail off and step closer, even though every cell in my body wants to run away.

"I don't know what he is," Shane rasps out. He's still clutching the rock, and it's . . . Holy hell, it's literally dripping with blood. Shane's hands are smeared, and I watch in horror as a spatter of red lands on his Saint Ambrose chinos.

Maybe Mr. Larkin tripped, I think. He tripped, and hit his head on that rock. But somehow it doesn't look like that. It doesn't look like that at all.

"Shane," I say in the calm tone I use when I'm trying not to scare my neighbor's neurotic Chihuahua. "What did you do?"

"Nothing," Shane says in the same hoarse voice.

"Why do you have that rock?" I ask.

"I . . . It was next to him."

Something glints on the ground beside Mr. Larkin. I kneel for a closer look, and my heart jumps into my throat. For a second I can't breathe, can't do anything except stare at the bright silver disc nestled among the leaves. "My lucky medallions," Dad always calls them when he twirls his key chain on one finger.

Why is one of my father's medallions next to Mr. Larkin's dead body? Because Mr. Larkin has to be dead, right? I haven't dared to feel for a pulse, but nobody could be this still for this long unless . . .

Charlotte hasn't let up. "Stop screaming," I say tightly. "I can't think when you're screaming like that."

She starts gasping then, struggling mightily to get herself under control, as I quickly palm the silver disc and stuff it into my pocket. I glance at Shane to see if he noticed, but he's staring at the bloody rock in his hands. "I heard yelling," he says suddenly. "Like, people arguing. Then it got quiet, and . . . I saw Mr. Larkin. Just lying there."

My blood, already running cold thanks to the silver medallion, turns to ice. "I heard yelling," Shane said.

I heard yelling earlier too.

A series of images flashes through my brain. The things I heard and saw: Dad and Mr. Larkin arguing, Mr. Larkin cutting him off and heading for the woods. And the things I imagine: Dad following, finding Mr. Larkin, losing his temper, and doing something horrible.

Something you can't take back.

Now what? I have to think. My dad—he didn't mean to do this, I know it. He was just trying to . . . God, he was trying to protect me, wasn't he? He'd told Mr. Larkin, "You don't understand what this will do to Tripp." He must have come here to plead his case again, and lost his temper at exactly the wrong moment.

It was an accident, I'm sure of it. But that doesn't matter

when someone's dead, right? They'll take Dad away, and then they'll take me away too.

I push the medallion farther into my pocket as I carefully scan the ground for anything else my father might have left behind. When I'm satisfied that there's nothing, I return my attention to Shane. We lock eyes, and his are suddenly a lot clearer.

"I heard yelling," he repeats, and my gut twists. Does he realize what he heard—or *who*? I can't let him speak the words and make them real.

"No, you didn't." I didn't plan on saying that, but as soon as I do, I know it's the right move. Well, not *right*—nothing about this is right—but it's my only choice. Shane's not an independent thinker. He's a go-with-the-flow kind of kid who's always happy to follow someone else's lead, and right now I need him to follow mine.

Shane blinks, and I add, "Do you know how this looks, Shane? You're holding the rock that must've been used to kill Mr. Larkin. Your fingerprints are all over a murder weapon." I can only hope my father's aren't too. But—no. He was wearing gloves when I saw him in the hallway, and he would've kept them on outside. There shouldn't be anything that ties him to the scene, as long as I can keep Shane contained.

"I didn't . . . It was . . ." Shane drops the rock with a thud, startling Charlotte so much that her sobs catch in her throat. She sniffs and shakily wipes her eyes as Shane adds, "Mr. Larkin was already like this. All I did was pick it up."

"I believe you," I say. "But if you go around telling people you heard an argument in the woods that nobody else heard"— I glance at Charlotte to see if she's going to contradict me, but she's still wiping her eyes—"and meanwhile your hands are covered in blood? You'll look guilty. Like you're making stuff up." Shane swallows visibly, staring at his hands, and I press my advantage. "You could go to jail for killing Mr. Larkin."

Charlotte blanches as Shane gulps, "Really?"

"Really. It happens all the time," I say, like I'm some kind of crime expert instead of a terrified kid.

Charlotte clutches Shane's arm, pulling him close. "We can't let Shane get arrested," she says urgently, and I say a quick prayer of thanks for Charlotte's Shane obsession. If we were with any other kid, she's bossy enough to argue with me—and ask questions, maybe, about why I'm laying it on so thick. But Shane? Shane, she just wants to protect.

"We won't," I say. "We just need a single, simple story. We'll tell everybody that we went into the woods together, that we never heard or saw anybody else, and that we found Mr. Larkin just like this. Shane picked up the rock without thinking, and then we realized that we needed to get help. Right?" They both nod. "Good. Now pay attention, because details matter and our stories have to be identical. Here's what we're going to say."

CHAPTER TWENTY-NINE

TRIPP

I can't believe I told her.

I've managed to keep that story inside for almost four years, and now Brynn Gallagher, of all the damn people, knows that my father killed Mr. Larkin and I covered it up. With a naïve, childish, boneheaded plan that *actually worked.* For weeks afterward, I was afraid the pressure would get too intense for Shane and he'd cave. Or that Charlotte, once I accidentally framed her with the class-trip money, would change her story to deflect attention.

But nothing like that happened. Shane, Charlotte, and I became sympathetic, almost heroic witnesses, and nobody—with the possible exception of Officer Patz—ever suspected that we were really just a bunch of well-rehearsed liars. "We tell the police our story," I'd told Shane and Charlotte, "and then never, ever talk about it again. Not to each other, and not to anybody else. That way we won't accidentally say the wrong thing."

Sometimes I still can't believe we got away with it. That none of us ever slipped up, or got tired of the pretense, or reached the point where the truth clawed its way out no matter how hard we tried to shove it down.

Until now.

I can't look at Brynn, can't stand the thought of what her expression must be. And then dread starts seeping through my entire body, curling around my heart and lungs until it's almost impossible to breathe. She's going to tell someone; of course she is. How could she not? What have I done, what have I done, what have I done . . .

"Tripp, no!" Brynn is shaking my arm. I pull away, still unable to look at her. "That's not what happened. It couldn't have happened."

"Your magic truth compass is broken, Brynn," I say bitterly. "It happened."

"No," she says, tugging harder at my arm. "You need to listen to me. My dad and I—we were at school then too. I was working late at the school paper and he picked me up. Only, when he tried to restart the car, the engine wouldn't turn over." Her voice is rushed and urgent, her words tumbling over one another. "So he got out of the car and looked around for somebody who might have jumper cables. There was no one in the parking lot, so I went back into Saint Ambrose to see if I could find a teacher, and I saw your dad."

"Saw my dad *what*?" I ask, stomach churning.

"Standing near the trophy case. I asked him for help, and

he came outside with me. He got jumper cables out of his trunk and connected them to our car."

"What . . . what time was that?" I say thickly.

"I told you. After school."

"But when after school?" I press. Dad's always been in semi-decent shape, and he can move fast when he wants to. When he *needs* to. If Brynn's dad's car broke down even half an hour after my father and Mr. Larkin argued, none of this matters. "What exact time?"

"I don't know, but . . ." Brynn scrunches her face for a few agonizing moments, and then her expression clears. "Oh! The after-school bell rang right after I asked your dad for help, so it would have been . . . whenever that is. Three-thirty, maybe?"

"The after-school bell rang," I repeat. I stare at my sneakers, remembering how I hopped the fence right after that bell—just a few minutes behind a very much alive Mr. Larkin. "You're sure?"

"I'm positive," Brynn says. "Because your dad said, 'Looks like you've been saved by the bell' like a giant dork." She attempts a smile I can't yet return, and adds, "Turns out it wasn't the battery, so my dad called a tow truck, and yours took me home. He hung out with me and my mom and Ellie for a while, till my dad got back from the garage. He was there when the police called. Tripp, my God." When I finally look at Brynn, her eyes are equal parts sympathetic and horrified. "How could you not know that? Didn't he tell you where he was?"

"He said . . . he said he was at Saint Ambrose to drop off an invoice, and then he started to say something else, but . . . I interrupted," I say. Every time my father said a word in the police station, unless it was about me, I tried to stop him.

234

I couldn't keep the police from talking to him on their own, of course, so he probably explained the car breakdown then. I never asked, though. For months, every time he tried to bring up that day, I put him off. I was looking at my father through such a distorted lens that everything about him seemed shifty and wrong. All my attention was focused on making sure that Shane, Charlotte, and I had our stories straight, that I never let it slip that my father had argued with Mr. Larkin right before he died, and that nobody knew about—

"The medallion," I say abruptly. "The silver disc I found next to Mr. Larkin's body. I thought . . . I could've sworn that belonged to my dad."

"Well, maybe it did," Brynn says. "He could have lost it another day, although it's strange that you'd find it right there, right then." Her eyes take on a sudden gleam. "Hold on. Mr. Larkin was wearing a silver chain when he died. It was broken, so . . . the medallion could've come off when he was attacked." She twists in her seat, newly animated. "Do you still have it?"

"I don't know." As soon as I got home and had a minute alone, I shoved the medallion into the back of a drawer without looking at it. I haven't looked at it since, so it's entirely possible that it's still there, but I can't pivot that fast. Not when there's this much at stake. "Brynn, look, I need you to . . . You gotta be totally honest, okay? Are you *sure* my dad never left you guys? Not at any point?"

"I'm positive. I was with him, and so were my parents. My dad came forward to let the police know he'd been in the parking lot that day, and he told them what happened with our car. He was basically a witness to your dad's alibi. Not that anybody thought he needed one, because he *didn't*. Oh my God."

Her hands are in mine now, squeezing hard. "I can't believe that you've been thinking all this time that your dad killed Mr. Larkin. All you had to do was *ask*. If you and I had still been speaking, I'd have mentioned that he helped us out. Your dad might be a thief, but he's not a murderer."

He's not a murderer.

The story I put together four years ago was just that— a story. Not real life. I should be flooded with joy and relief now, but everything inside me is numb. I don't feel any better. I still feel cursed.

"But I covered it up," I say. "Or I thought I did. I was willing to—I let Mr. Larkin go to his grave, and I never said—"

I'm starting to slump down into the cushions again, but Brynn pulls me upright. "No," she says firmly. "Don't torture yourself with a new crime before you've even let yourself accept that the old one wasn't true. You were thirteen, you loved your dad, and you were scared. You didn't have anyone except him, which is a terrifying position for a kid. So don't keep drinking yourself into oblivion because you decided to protect him. It doesn't make you a bad person. Besides," she adds, releasing my hands as though she suddenly decided she shouldn't be holding them. "We have a different problem than that to consider."

"Oh really?" I huff out a non-laugh. "A bigger problem than me fake perjuring myself over my teacher's murder?"

"Yes," Brynn says. "Because here's the thing. A big part of the reason Shane didn't get into trouble back then—even though his fingerprints were all over the murder weapon—is that you said he and Charlotte had been with you the whole time. That the three of you arrived at the woods together, that you never lost sight of one another, and that you found Mr.

Larkin together. You weren't friends with Shane back then, so nobody believed that you would lie about what happened. Meanwhile, you thought you were protecting your dad, but he didn't actually need it." Understanding seeps into my fuzzy brain, and I gape at Brynn as she finishes, "The person you ended up protecting, after all that, was Shane."

There are a lot of things I should say to that, probably, but the only one I can think of in the moment is, "Well, fuck."

The guesthouse door rattles then, and we both jump. It swings open with a loud creak, sending a blast of frigid January air our way, and for the first time all week, I feel the cold. A silhouette appears, and morphs into a familiar figure once he steps inside and leans against the doorframe. His gaze flicks between Brynn and me before finally settling on me.

"What's going on, T?" Shane asks.

CHAPTER THIRTY

TRIPP

"Hey," I croak out as Brynn springs back to her own cushion. My mouth is desert-dry all of a sudden, my head is pounding, and my muscles ache. It's like all the abuse I've been putting my body through for the past week has finally caught up with me. "What are you doing?"

"What is *she* doing, is the question," Shane says, lifting his chin toward Brynn.

"I came to apologize," Brynn says, tucking a leg beneath her. I didn't even have a chance to notice that she was practically in my lap until she was already gone. "About the show. And to let Tripp know that I quit. I'm not working for *Motive* anymore."

"Good for you. If that's even true," Shane says, crossing his arms. His face is like a mask, his expression cold and forbidding. How much did he hear? "Still doesn't explain why you're here when my girlfriend told you to leave."

"It's my fault," I say. My mind might be sluggish, but I feel pretty confident in that statement. Most things are my fault.

"I was just going," Brynn says, getting to her feet. She turns to me. "I think you should come with me, Tripp. Your dad will be worried."

"His dad's at work," Shane replies before I can. "Tripp is fine where he is. Charlotte and I are looking out for him, so how about you mind your own fucking business?"

"Hey," I start, but Brynn is already speaking.

"Is it *looking out for him* to leave him by himself with a fully stocked bar?" she asks, sweeping her arm toward a side table covered with liquor bottles.

"He wanted to be alone," Shane says, jaw twitching.

I blink, and for a second I see the Shane of four years ago, smaller but still one of the biggest kids in our class, his eyes empty and his hands covered in blood. *All I did was pick it up.* All this time, I thought I was using Shane as a shield for my father. It never occurred to me that it might be the other way around, and I still can't wrap my brain around that. He's being a dick right now, sure, but he's still my friend.

Isn't he?

"That's not the most important part of what I said," Brynn snaps.

"You have a lot of opinions for someone who shouldn't be here," Shane says, advancing toward her with a menacing look in his eye. Brynn takes an involuntary step back, and I finally manage to heave myself to my feet beside her.

"Leave her alone, Shane. She's just trying to help."

"You're whipped, T," Shane says scornfully. "She's using you."

"I'm not—you have no idea what you're talking about." If

239

only. That would've been a much better way to drown my sorrows. "Look, thanks for coming to find me today. And giving me some space to crash. But . . ." I was about to say *Brynn's right,* but that'll just set him off again. "I need to get home. I have to talk to my dad."

Good thing Shane doesn't have Brynn's magical truth-serum abilities, because that was a lie. I mean, I have to talk to my father eventually, but . . . I don't even know where to start. Our relationship underwent a massive shift four years ago, then shifted back within the past five minutes, and he doesn't know about any of it.

"And say what?" Shane asks.

His voice is challenging. How much did he hear? I still can't tell.

"Just check in," I say. "He's been worried."

Shane lifts his eyebrows. "And you suddenly care because . . . ?"

Because he's not a murderer. Surprise! Maybe you are, though?

No. That's nuts. Just because Dad didn't kill Mr. Larkin doesn't mean Shane did. I'm overtired, and if I stay here any longer, I'm going to start saying some of this stuff out loud.

"I'm heading out," I say. "Tell Charlotte I said thanks—"

And then, with a few quick steps, Shane is right in my face, fists curled at his sides. We're almost exactly the same size, except I'm a little taller and he's a little bulkier. I don't know who would win in a fight, because we've never fought.

"Seriously?" I ask.

"You're forgetting who your friends are," Shane says in a low voice.

"No, I'm not. I just have more than two friends."

"We took you in when nobody gave a crap about you," Shane hisses.

"You *took me in?*" I'd laugh if he didn't look so pissed. "I'm not an orphan."

His lip curls. "Could've fooled me."

"Stop!" a commanding voice calls from the doorway. Shane steps away before my brain can process his last comment and tell the rest of me, *Yeah, let's hit him for that.* Charlotte strides forward, and I should thank her, because if I'd taken a swing at Shane, he'd probably have kicked my ass. But she glares at me before I can say a word. "I see you've picked your side," she says icily.

I rub my aching temple. "There's not a side, Charlotte."

She lets out a sound that's too polite to be called a snort. More like a *hmmph.* "There's always a side. And she needs to get off my property," she adds without looking at Brynn.

"I'm going." Brynn heads to the door, clearly happy for the cue.

I don't want to leave like this, but I'm starting to think there's not going to be a better way, especially after this night of revelations. For a second, when Shane and I were staring one another down, I was seized with a sudden, paranoid certainty that he wouldn't *let* me leave.

"Thanks for everything," I mumble as I pass them.

Charlotte gives another elegant huff. "See you next time you fall apart."

Brynn doesn't say anything until we're at the gate. "Wow," she whispers when I unlatch it and we step through. "That was a lot." I don't reply, and she adds with a backward look over her shoulder, "Do you think Shane heard us?"

"I don't know," I say.

"My car's in the—"

Before she can finish, I trip over a root and go flying. Brynn tries to grab my arm and keep me from falling, but all she manages to do is go down with me. "Ow." She winces, rolls to one side, and springs into a crouch. I just lie there, though, too disoriented to move.

"Remind me not to take you along the next time I want to make a quick getaway," she says, and holds out her hand before adding, "Come on. I know you need rest, but not here."

I grasp her palm and sit up, but tug her closer before she can pull me the rest of the way to my feet. "Hey," I say. "Thank you. Seriously. I'm not—I don't know if I'll ever be able to averagely thank you for what you did for me tonight."

She raises her brows. "Averagely?"

"Yes."

"Do you mean *adequately?*"

"I'm trying to have a moment, Brynn," I grumble.

Her eyes twinkle. "Maybe you shouldn't have it in Charlotte's yard, though."

"Okay. Fine." I get to my feet, still holding on to her hand. "Just know that I am very grateful. I'm bursting with so much gratitude, I could kiss you."

Brynn freezes, eyes wide. Oh. Right. I might've—no, I *definitely* told her I used to be in love with her, so it's possible she thinks I mean that I literally want to kiss her. It's also possible I do mean that.

She recovers with a wry smile. "Sober up first, okay?" she says. "Then we'll talk."

CHAPTER THIRTY-ONE

BRYNN

"More coffee, hon?" Regina approaches with a pot held aloft, Al trotting at her feet.

"Yes, please," I say, and she tops me off while ignoring Tripp's empty cup.

"Once again," he says humbly, "I am very sorry."

"Al and I forgive you, but that doesn't mean we're ready to talk to you," Regina says coolly, just as Al pokes his nose into Tripp's leg to demand a scratch. "Traitor," Regina tells the dog, then goes ahead and gives Tripp more coffee before returning to behind the counter.

"Thank you for not firing me," he calls after her.

We're at Brightside Bakery on Sunday morning, but Tripp is just a customer today since Regina doesn't want him working until, as she puts it, "You've gone at least twenty-four hours without making a damn fool of yourself."

He's clean-shaven, clear-eyed, and neatly dressed, and he

smells like some kind of citrusy soap. His entire demeanor is so much lighter than it's been since my first day back at Saint Ambrose that any lingering doubts about what I came to tell him disappear. I clear my throat and say, "Tripp, listen. After everything that happened last night, I've been thinking, and . . . I have some ideas about Mr. Larkin that I want to run by you, but only if you're okay with that. Would you rather I drop it?"

"Drop what?" he asks.

"Mr. Larkin. The case. Everything."

Tripp's brow furrows. "Like—we never talk about him again?"

It sounds a lot like a certain pact in the woods, but I'm not about to point that out. "I won't talk about him with anyone, if that's what you want," I say.

When I lay in bed last night, unable to sleep, Tripp's words in Charlotte's guesthouse kept running through my brain: *You cared more about the school paper than about me.* He truly believed that, and it hit me with an aching sense of regret that I don't want to be the same single-minded girl Tripp knew in eighth grade—or the girl who bulldozed through Sturgis last month in a desperate attempt to prove herself. I've never felt more alone than I did when people were mad at me for being sneaky about working at *Motive,* which was bad enough. But it's been worse to realize how much my tunnel vision hurt my friends, my family, and especially Tripp.

That's the part I still need to make clear. "You're much more important to me than a story, Tripp. I'm sorry I never showed you that before now."

Tripp is quiet for a while, eyes on the floor. "I'm sorry too," he finally says. "About what I said to you in gym class, obviously, but also about . . . everything else. I used to go to Mr. Larkin's grave a few times a year, to apologize for how he'd never get any justice because of me. But even while I was standing there, talking to his headstone, I knew it was just a bunch of empty words. It wouldn't change anything."

"You visited Mr. Larkin's grave?" I ask, my heart breaking a little at the mental image. "That must have been hard."

"It was the absolute least I could do." Tripp grimaces before meeting my gaze. "You don't have to drop it, Brynn. Go ahead. Tell me your ideas."

"Okay, well, here's the thing." I take a deep breath before pulling the *Union Leader* article up on my phone. "Do you remember when I said last night that your lie protected Shane, not your father?" Tripp nods, and I explain everything I've learned so far: that Mr. Larkin had a brother at Saint Ambrose, that he may have changed his name from "William Robbins," and that if he did, he could have been the son of a controlling New Hampshire man whose second wife took off with their toddler son and hasn't been heard from since. "I'm thinking that the little boy who disappeared, Michael, might be one of our classmates. The age is right, so I was trying to think of kids who might fit, and then I thought of . . ." I blow on my coffee as Tripp takes my phone. "Shane."

"Shane?" Tripp repeats, eyes glued to my screen.

"Yeah. We've only known him since kindergarten, and he doesn't live in Sturgis, so we have no idea what his life was like when he was a toddler."

"He was adopted," Tripp says. "From the foster system."

"Maybe," I say. "Or maybe that's just a cover story." Tripp blinks, startled, and I add, "Maybe Laura Delgado is really Lila Robbins, and she wanted to hide their identities. She's the right age, approximately. Early forties."

"So are half the parents at school," Tripp points out. "And there are lots of kids at Saint Ambrose from other towns. Kids with families we don't know anything about."

"Right. But here's the thing . . ." I hate to state the obvious to the new and improved Tripp, but: "Only one of them was found standing over Mr. Larkin's body with the murder weapon."

Tripp studies the photo of Lila Robbins for a beat, his brow furrowed. "This isn't Ms. Delgado," he says, but his voice isn't entirely certain. "I don't think so, anyway. Even if she dyed her hair, this girl's nose is too big."

"Noses can be changed," I say. "And the name 'Laura' isn't all that different from 'Lila,' if you were going to change your name and wanted to keep it close."

"But that kid—Michael Robbins, he had asthma, right? Shane doesn't."

"Are you sure? Do you know everything about him?"

Tripp's jaw muscles tighten before he admits, "No. We don't—we're not the kind of friends who'd tell one another stuff like that. I've never seen him with an inhaler, though. And he plays lacrosse. You can't do that with asthma, can you?"

"You can if it's well managed. Plenty of elite athletes have asthma." I tap my chin thoughtfully. "It can be invisible, so it's probably not a great clue to follow. Plus, it's not just that. My uncle Nick told me that he heard Mr. Larkin and Ms. Delgado arguing, back when Uncle Nick was our classroom assistant in eighth grade."

"Arguing? About what?"

"He wasn't sure. But the timing is interesting, isn't it? That's right around the time when Mr. Larkin could've told her he knew who she really is."

Tripp releases a long exhale. "So you think Shane is some missing kid from New Hampshire who killed his own brother?"

"It's one theory."

"And Charlotte is just—what? Fine with it? Never said a word?"

"Charlotte might not have been there," I point out. "You have no idea how long they'd been together before you got there. But even if Charlotte saw everything, it's possible she'd cover for him. That she's still covering for him."

Charlotte has always been devoted to Shane; that's nothing new. What *is* new, though—at least to me—is how almost fanatical the two of them are about keeping Tripp close. But after they tracked him down when he was at his most vulnerable, they left him alone. On the one hand, you could argue that they were giving him space. On the other, you could argue that they didn't so much want to *help* him as keep him quiet. It seems like every time Tripp has "a bad night," as Charlotte told me at her party, they try to keep him quiet.

"But remember what I told you Shane said that day?" Tripp asks. "He heard yelling. I thought he was talking about my dad and Mr. Larkin, but—maybe there really was a drifter. Maybe everything happened exactly like the police said back then." He

247

swallows hard. "Except, you know, the part where I covered up evidence."

"You accused Shane of making the yelling up," I counter. Tripp opens his mouth to protest, but before he can, I add, "I know you only did that to protect your father, but you might have been right. That's genuinely the kind of thing somebody would say if they were trying to deflect attention. Did *you* hear yelling?"

"I had my earphones in, listening to music for most of the time. I didn't hear anything until I took them out and heard Charlotte scream."

"Did she hear yelling?"

"I don't know," Tripp admits. "I never gave her the chance to say. I shut the entire conversation down because I wanted them to follow my lead."

"There's a good chance Shane was covering for himself," I say. "I mean, he was at the scene when Mr. Larkin died. That's something Carly always says—*proximity matters.*"

"Okay, but if you put it that way, the whole school had proximity." When I tilt my head, puzzled, Tripp adds, "Kind of. I mean, the woods are right behind Saint Ambrose. People from school hike there all the time. Teachers, even. But nobody ever suspected . . . Grizz, for example. Or Ms. Kelso."

"Ms. Kelso? Really?" I ask, even though my mind ran along a similar track when I first started rethinking everything I thought I knew about the case. I wondered if, maybe, there was bad blood between Mr. Larkin and a coworker that I never noticed.

"Or your uncle," Tripp says.

"Uncle Nick?" I frown. "Why would anybody suspect *him?*"

"Proximity," Tripp repeats. "Was he working that day?"

I don't want Tripp getting sidetracked with something that doesn't matter, just because he doesn't want to have *this* conversation. Instead of answering, I take my phone back and enlarge the *Union Leader* article. "Look, my point is that Shane could've been terrified," I say. "Dexter sounds like a control freak who dominated his wife and let his kid suffer. If Shane was in this great new life, with him and his mom feeling safe with Mr. Delgado, maybe he was afraid Mr. Larkin would lead Dexter Robbins to them, and everything would explode."

Tripp looks a little green. "Jesus. Killer kids, getting away with murder. You're telling me Gunnar Fox was actually right?"

"Well, there's a lot more nuance involved, but . . . maybe?" Last night, as I drove Tripp home from Charlotte's, he told me about Lisa Marie's video—the one where she pretended to believe that Tripp could've killed Mr. Larkin. When we got to his house, I had him text her to warn that if the video ever goes public, Tripp will contact *Motive* and show them Gunnar's messages offering to pay Lisa Marie for lying. "Have you heard back from Lisa Marie?"

"Not yet." Tripp grimaces. "This is so messed up. Do you really think it's possible? I mean, Mr. Delgado is like a guard dog with his family. Couldn't he just have sent a bunch of lawyers after Dexter Robbins? That guy would never get custody, or visitation, or whatever Shane might've been worried about."

"I don't think we can be sure about that," I say. "Parental rights are a big deal, and Lila Robbins taking a kid from his father could be seen as kidnapping, even if there's a good reason. Plus, if Ms. Delgado really is Lila Robbins, we have no idea how much she told her new husband. Maybe he *actually* thinks Shane was a foster child. I wonder if . . ." I think back to all those defaced posters of Mr. Larkin. "Maybe Shane is the one who's been writing all over Mr. Larkin's face on the garden committee posters. Like, seeing his presence at school again, after the trauma of everything that happened in the woods that day, is too much for him."

"Shane's not a graffiti kind of guy," Tripp says. "If he didn't want to look at something, he'd rip it down."

"Maybe," I say. "But that's all sidebar, anyway. The main thing is . . ." I hesitate, not wanting to push him so far that he thinks I wasn't sincere about dropping the case. He was so regretful about Mr. Larkin earlier that I want to make sure he's considering all the angles. "At some point you should tell someone that you weren't with Shane and Charlotte the whole time." I almost say *tell the police,* but we haven't even gotten into the whole Delgado Properties $250,000 donation to the Sturgis Police Foundation yet. I'm not sure who we can trust to be objective when it comes to this case, but I'd put my money on Carly first.

A flush darkens Tripp's cheeks. "I know," he mutters, hanging his head. "I'm just not ready yet. Because then I'd also have to tell them my dad took the money, right? And he and I haven't even talked about that, and—"

"It's okay," I say quickly, relieved that he's at least considering it. "You don't have to do anything right now." I take his hand in mine, and it twitches beneath my fingers. I let go instantly, chagrined that I keep forgetting what he told me in Charlotte's guesthouse: *Don't—you can't touch me like that when you know how I—*

It's still not the right time to complete that thought. I wonder, fleetingly, if it ever will be, because I'd really like to know. "It's just good to keep sharing information," I say, letting my palms rest on my knees. "We've already learned so much more about Mr. Larkin than I ever thought we could. And if we can get answers about something that happened such a long time ago . . ." I sit straighter in my seat as a new thought occurs to me. "If we can do *that,* maybe we can even get answers about—"

And then I stop, realizing that I almost raised yet another painful subject. "Other stuff," I finish limply, before taking a sip of lukewarm coffee.

"Other stuff?" Tripp eyes me steadily. "That's not what you were about to say."

I take another sip. More of a guzzle, really. "Yeah, it was."

"Come on, Brynn. We're being honest from now on, right? What other stuff?" When I don't reply right away, he adds, "Are you under the impression that I can't handle whatever it is, because I've been in freak-out mode ever since you got back to Sturgis?"

"Possibly," I admit.

"I got that out of my system. I can take it."

I shoot him a worried look. *He's not as strong as he seems,* Charlotte said during our library showdown, but then again . . . I don't believe that. Charlotte has no idea what Tripp has been carrying for the past four years. "Well, it just hit me that the one thing we haven't talked about yet when it comes to Mr. Larkin is, um . . . Mr. Solomon," I say.

"Mr. Solomon?" Tripp recoils, but more like he's confused, rather than flashing back to finding our former groundskeeper's body. "Why would we?"

"Because the police aren't sure whether he fell and hit his

head or was pushed. And if he ran his mouth about Mr. Larkin to us, he might've done it with other people too. Maybe the wrong people."

Tripp blinks. "But it was a robbery."

"That could've been a distraction."

"Are you saying . . ." He shakes his head decisively. "Look, there's no way Shane did anything to a harmless old man, okay? There just isn't."

"That's not what I'm saying." And I'm *definitely* not saying that Tripp told his friends what Mr. Solomon said to us, even though I know he at least told Charlotte. I'm not trying to cause a relapse, here. "It's just that Mr. Solomon died under mysterious circumstances after talking about Mr. Larkin, so . . . like I said, it's good to keep sharing information."

Tripp is silent for a moment, then reaches abruptly into his pocket. "Okay, well, on that note . . . I found it." I can't help it; I let out a small gasp when he lays a silver disc on the table. "The medallion. The one next to . . . you know."

"Mr. Larkin's body," I whisper, and he nods. I pick up the disc; it's about the size of a quarter and has a small hole on top, like it's meant to be worn on a chain. There's an emblem of a snarling dog with the words *Mad Dog Tavern* on the front, along with the words *Bite First.* The back is engraved with the name "Billy," in large block letters.

"You were right," Tripp says. "That's Mr. Larkin's name, so it must've been his." He hunches his shoulders. "I wish I'd looked at it more closely back then. That would've saved me, and everybody else, a hell of a lot of trouble."

"Did Shane or Charlotte see you take this?"

"I don't think so."

I study the medallion, frowning. "I never heard anyone call Mr. Larkin 'Billy,' but it could've been a childhood nickname. Even if he did change from 'William Robbins' to 'William Larkin,' it would still fit." The emblem of the dog is raised, and I run my thumb across it. "Have you Googled *Mad Dog Tavern*?"

"No," Tripp says. His lips quirk. "Figured I'd leave that to you."

I put down the medallion, open Google, and type the tavern name. "There are a few Mad Dog Taverns," I report, scrolling through the results. "Including one in North Woodstock, New Hampshire." I pause and tap my chin, thoughtful. "That's pretty close to Lincoln, where Dexter Robbins is from. What if—God. Do you think *Dexter* could've been in the woods that day? And that's who Shane heard arguing with Mr. Larkin?"

"The woods are getting crowded if he was." Tripp picks the medallion up and turns it over in his hand. "I could ask Shane, I guess. Do you think I should?"

"Break the pact? I'm not sure we want to open that Pandora's box with Shane, especially after the way he acted last night. It might be better to do more digging first." I hit the directions button and pull up Google Maps. "Mad Dog Tavern is only two hours from here, so . . ."

Tripp looks up with a half smile. "So, what?"

My stomach flutters. I've searched my middle-school memories and can't conjure up any feelings beyond friendship for Tripp from back then; as much as I liked him, I didn't think about him that way. But now is different, and not only because I lose my train of thought every time he smiles. Despite everything that's been piled onto his shoulders for the past four years—and even before that—he's not bitter. He's still hopeful, and hardworking, and loyal, and funny, even if that last one is mostly at my expense.

I pluck the medallion from Tripp's hand and attach it to my key chain, then dangle the set of keys in front of him. "So how would you feel about a road trip?" I ask.

CHAPTER THIRTY-TWO

TRIPP

The stark January landscape flashes by my window as Brynn and I drive to New Hampshire. I'm lost in thought, trying to absorb everything she just told me about Shane, but it's impossible when I still haven't fully absorbed the truth about my father.

It's not as though I've been afraid of him for the past four years, or worried that he'd hurt someone else. Even when I believed he'd killed Mr. Larkin, I *also* believed it was a single, horrific mistake that he'd never repeat. Still, the thought that he'd done it—and that I'd made myself complicit by covering for him—poisoned everything between us to the point where I've spent most of high school avoiding him.

This morning, before I left to meet Brynn at Brightside Bakery, I was louder than usual getting ready, half hoping that I'd wake Dad up. For the first time in years, I wanted to talk to him. I don't know what I'd even say—how do you tell someone you thought they were capable of *that*? I'm not sure I can go there, but it would've been nice to . . . I don't know. Look at him with different eyes, I guess.

He can sleep through anything, though, and he did. Before I left the house, I typed out a text that said *Can we talk sometime this week?* then instantly deleted it. He wouldn't know what to do with that. It would only freak him out.

So I don't get any texts from my father while we cruise along 93 North, but Charlotte keeps lighting up my phone.

You were very rude last night, she writes.

You can still come to the Winter Dance with me and Shane, though.

Unless you're planning on bringing Brynn.

I don't know what to think about Charlotte, or what she really knows about what happened that day in the woods. I have no idea if Shane and Charlotte were together when they found Mr. Larkin. I always assumed that they were, but I was wrong about a lot of things. In her messages, though, she sounds the same as ever: a little imperious, a little bossy, and a lot over-invested in the Saint Ambrose social scene. I'm comfortable with that person, so for now, at least, I'm going to consider her texts at face value.

I wasn't planning on going to the Winter Dance, or, if I did, on bringing anyone, but . . .

I steal a glance at Brynn, who's driving like she's lost in thought. We've been quiet for almost half an hour, listening to music, but it's a good kind of quiet. The kind you don't have to fill with bullshit because you're afraid of it stretching so long that the other person starts asking questions you don't want to answer.

Brynn knows all my worst truths now. She's the one who pulled them out of me and held them up to a light I didn't even think existed. And she's not just tolerating me this morning; she's giving me those cute sideways looks that make all my nerve endings buzz. I've been telling myself for weeks that those looks don't mean anything, since I'm not supposed to have good things. But maybe they do, and maybe I am.

You're much more important to me than a story, Tripp. If you didn't know Brynn, that wouldn't sound like much of an opening, but since I do . . .

"Charlotte's speaking to me again," I report.

Not what I meant to lead with, but oh well.

"That's good," Brynn says. She sounds like she means it, even though there's been tension between her and Charlotte for a while. "I hope she doesn't hold last night against you."

"She texted about the Winter Dance," I say. *Nice pivot.* "Are you going?"

"Ah," Brynn says. Her face falls. "Well, I was planning to tag along with Nadia and Mason and their dates, but I don't know if that would be much fun. For them. They're kind of mad at me for not telling them about *Motive.*"

"Maybe you could quit again," I say. "That was a hell of a gesture." She huffs out a laugh, and I add, "Or you could go with me."

I feel a brief stab of guilt, because Charlotte's had my back for years, and I'm not trying to piss her off. But she doesn't get to choose my friends—or my girlfriend.

Brynn briefly takes her eyes off the road to meet mine. "Are you asking?"

"Are you making me ask twice?"

"No," she says, tucking her hair behind her ear. "To the second question, I mean. Yes to the first. If you want."

"I want," I say. It comes out a little more fervent than I meant it to.

"Okay, good." She flashes a quick smile and pulls off the road, announcing, "We're here."

Mad Dog Tavern is a squat, gray building with a dark red door and a sign featuring the same snarling dog from the medallion. There are a lot of Harleys parked in the lot beside the building; they outnumber the cars almost two to one. It's a pretty full parking lot for a Sunday afternoon. "I guess it's a biker bar?" Brynn says doubtfully.

"Looks that way," I say glad I managed to find my winter coat instead of pulling on my Saint Ambrose blazer yet again. We're going to stick out badly enough as it is, if we're even allowed inside. "You sure you want to go in?" I ask.

"I just drove for two hours, so yes," Brynn says, turning off the ignition. As we get out of the car, she adds, "If nothing else, I need to use the bathroom."

"Enter at your own risk," I say as a couple of guys emerge and linger in front, talking. They look exactly how you'd expect a biker to look: burly and leather-clad, with thick beards and impressive mullets. I feel a spike of nerves, suddenly wishing I had Shane with me, but as soon as we get close, one of them pulls the door open and steps back.

"Young lady," he says, with exaggerated politeness that could come off as mocking without the friendly grin. "And good sir."

"Keep an eye on your girl in there," the other one says to

me with a wink. They both look like they think we're hilarious, and possibly twelve.

"That could have gone much worse," Brynn murmurs as the door falls closed behind us.

I blink, letting my eyes adjust to the sudden darkness. The only light is coming from the windows, streaming pale sunlight onto the scarred wooden floors. One side of the room is all pool tables, and most of them are in use. The other side is a mix of booths and cocktail tables in front of a long bar with the words *Bite First* carved into the middle.

"Oh, hell no," the woman behind the bar says as we approach. She's plump with gray-streaked dark hair, wearing a tight black T-shirt that shows off serious tattoos. The one on her right forearm spells out *Fiona* within a vine-and-floral design. "I don't care how good your IDs are. You two are underage."

"We're not here to drink," Brynn says, giving her a sweet smile. "Your tattoos are beautiful. Is your name Fiona?"

"My daughter's," the woman says. "I'm Rose, the owner. And who are you?"

"I'm Brynn, and this is Tripp."

"And what can I do for you, Brynn and Tripp, if you're not looking for a drink?"

Brynn leans against the bar. "I was hoping to talk to someone about Dexter Robbins."

Rose's eyebrows rise. "Dexter doesn't own the place anymore, hon."

Brynn and I exchange glances, and I try not to look as shocked as I feel. Even though Brynn's instincts have been dead-on about a lot of things, I still figured this was a wild-goose chase.

I definitely wasn't expecting a hit right out of the gate. "Oh, that's okay," Brynn says, sounding flustered. "I wasn't actually looking for him, per se. . . ."

Rose rests her forearms on the bar. "Then why'd you ask about him?"

"Well . . ." Brynn takes a breath, and I can almost see her steeling herself to go all in. "I'm an intern with a true-crime show called *Motive,* and we're looking into the death of a man named William Larkin." She delivers the half-truth smoothly—to me, at least. I still can't figure out how she caught out my lies so easily last night.

"William Larkin?" Rose shrugs. "Never heard of him."

"He might have changed his name," Brynn says, pulling out her phone. I catch a glimpse of the photo she pulled up—Mr. Larkin's official Saint Ambrose picture—before she holds it out to Rose. "But this was him. Four years ago."

Rose, who's been a combination of amused and bored since we got here, suddenly goes rigid. Her eyes widen as she takes Brynn's phone, and her expression gets tense. "Is this some kind of joke?" she asks.

"No, of course not," Brynn says quickly. "I would never joke about something like that. The picture is of William Larkin. He was our eighth-grade teacher at Saint Ambrose School in Sturgis, Massachusetts. We learned recently that he might previously have been named William Robbins?" She's doing a pretty good job of sounding like she knows what she's talking about, until her voice lilts nervously at the end.

"Billy." Rose draws the name out slowly, still frowning. "Billy is dead?"

"You recognize him?" Brynn asks.

Rose swallows hard and hands back Brynn's phone. "I gave him that tie when he was a kid, as a joke. Life hands you lemons, you know? I guess he finally grew into it."

"He called it his lucky tie," Brynn says, and Rose closes her eyes. "Could we . . . Do you think we could talk to you about him?"

"Hold on," Rose says, turning to the row of bottles behind her. "You two might not be able to have a drink for this conversation, but I sure as hell can."

"I bought this bar from Dexter," Rose tells us a few minutes later, when we're settled in a booth with a basket of greasy tortilla chips and some drinks. Beer for her, and soda for us. "After he got religion and decided drinking was a sin. Which is bullshit, if you ask me." She raises her bottle. "The Jesus I believe in would have a beer with you."

"Amen to that," I say, and Brynn kicks me under the table.

Rose points the bottle at me. "Not you specifically. Jesus respects the drinking age."

Brynn clears her throat. "Were you friends with Dexter?"

"We ran in the same circles," Rose says, and shrugs. "The biking community around here is close, and Dexter rode back then. I always liked his kid better than him. Billy was a sweet little guy. Lonely, though. No momma. She died when he was a baby. He hero-worshipped his dad, but I don't think Dexter paid him much attention. He thought raising kids was women's work, the sexist creep, so he left Billy pretty much on his own."

She crunches a chip. "Then Dexter got married again, got religion, and decided to get rid of the Mad Dog. I didn't see much of him after that, but Billy would come by sometimes. I think he was lonely, still. Dexter had another kid by then and had gotten all zealous about being the spiritual leader of his new family. Rumor had it he might've taken that too far. A lot too far."

"Like this?" Brynn asks, showing Rose the *Union Leader* article.

She nods. "Lila and Mikey going missing was a big deal around here, until stories started coming out about how Dexter practically kept that poor woman a prisoner and wouldn't treat Mikey's asthma. People didn't look too hard for them, after that." She takes a swig of beer. "It's a shame Lila didn't take Billy with her, but I suppose she couldn't. He wasn't her biological son."

Brynn's the journalist here, but I'm curious too. "So when did Mr. Larkin change his name?" I ask. It feels weird to call him by a name Rose doesn't know, but calling him "Billy" would be even weirder.

"Well, I never knew that he did," Rose says. "We fell out of touch, like you do when kids get older and have their own lives. The last time I saw him, he was a junior in college. He stopped by for a quick hello on his way someplace else. Told me he'd cut ties with his father, which felt like good news, although I wondered how long it would last. It was nice to see him, but . . ." She trails off and picks at a hangnail. "He was different. Harsher than he used to be."

"What do you mean?" Brynn asks.

Rose's lips twist. "Billy was charming as all get-out, like always, but the sweetness was gone. Maybe life had beat it out of him. Or Dexter did." When Brynn and I exchange horrified glances, she adds hastily, "Not physically, I don't think. In all the other ways that count, though. Billy spent his life trying to impress his dad and getting nothing in return, especially after Mikey was born. Mikey would be . . . maybe your age now." She squints at us, thoughtful. "Very young to be working for a TV show, in other words."

"I know," Brynn says. "To be honest, I was hired partly because I pitched a story about Mr. Larkin during my interview." She darts me a guilty look, and I shrug. *Water under the bridge.* "But it's been hard to find an angle on his personal life. Nobody could find any family or friends when he died. I don't know how hard they looked, though." Brynn frowns and breaks a chip in half. "I mean, we got a tip about the name change pretty fast."

Rose sighs heavily. Having to tell her about Mr. Larkin's murder was the worst part of the conversation, by far. "What a damn shame. I had no idea. I never heard about that, not from the news or from Dexter, neither. I wonder if he even knows." She takes a swig of beer. "How on earth did you know to come here, if no one could find his family?"

"Because of this," Brynn says, taking her keys out of her bag and holding up the silver medallion. "It was Mr. Larkin's, but it was only, um . . ." She darts a glance at me. "Recently found."

Rose reaches out a hand to touch the medallion, turning it so the *Billy* engraving is facing her. "Lila had this made," she says. "When Billy turned thirteen. She knew he loved this place. She had one made for Mikey too, but said Billy had to hold on to it until Mikey was older. Did you find that too?"

"No," I say. And I looked carefully. Did I miss something?

I guess it's possible, but if I did, the police should have found it afterward. "Just the one."

"I have to ask," Brynn says, leaning forward. "Is there any chance—could Dexter Robbins, possibly, have been the one to kill Mr. Larkin? Would he do that to his son?"

"Oh Lord," Rose says. "I'd like to say no. But Dexter was capable of some dark stuff. I wouldn't have thought he'd treat Lila the way he did either."

"Where is Dexter now?" Brynn asks.

"I don't know." Rose shrugs. "Haven't seen him for years. Last I heard, he was still big into church but working at a pawnshop. Not sure how that's more godly than a bar, but okay. I doubt he's changed much, so Lila was right to stay gone." She picks up a chip and points it at us. "Men like Dexter are a hornet's nest. Why poke it if you don't have to, right?"

CHAPTER THIRTY-THREE

BRYNN

"You missed the turn for one-twelve," Tripp points out.

"I know," I say.

"Let me guess." He drums his fingers on the center console. "On purpose?"

"I just thought, since we're here . . ." I make a sharp left into a strip mall parking lot, heading for a storefront I noticed on our way to Mad Dog Tavern.

Superior Pawnshop.

"Brynn, come on," Tripp says when I park in front of it. "What are you up to?"

"Maybe this is where Dexter Robbins works," I say. "It's right down the street from the bar he used to own."

"Are you out of your mind?" Tripp twists in his seat to glare at me. "You heard Rose. Don't poke the hornet's nest."

"I'm not trying to talk to him or anything," I say. "If he's still as religious as he used to be, he's probably not even working on a Sunday. Which makes today the perfect time to check up on him. Then I can find him later, if I need to."

"Why would you need to?" Tripp asks, frowning. "I don't care what you think Shane, or whoever, might've done. You can't send this guy after him. Besides, you said it yourself at Brightside—maybe Dexter Robbins was in the woods that day. Maybe he killed Mr. Larkin, and we should stay the hell away from him."

"I will," I say. "I just want to know more about him."

Tripp doesn't look convinced, but all he says is, "Well, you're on your own. Leave me out of this." I hesitate, wondering if he's regretting giving me the go-ahead to keep digging into Mr. Larkin, until he smiles and lightly pushes my shoulder. "Go, already."

"I'll be quick," I say, and dart out the door.

I've never been inside a pawnshop before, and this one is nicer than I expected. It's long and narrow, with glass cases lining either side and a booth in the back with a neon sign above it that reads LOANS. One wall is hung with guitars, the other lined with shelves filled with different types of electronics. There are almost a dozen people inside already, browsing the cases, and two workers behind the counters wearing navy *Superior Pawn* T-shirts. One of the employees is a woman and the other is much too young to be Dexter, so my shoulders—which I didn't even realize were rigid—relax as I approach the woman.

"Can I help you?" she asks.

"Hi. I was wondering if Dexter Robbins works here?"

"Nope," she says without a flicker of recognition.

"Are there other pawnshops nearby?" I ask.

"Near-ish, if you're driving." The bell over the door jangles as someone else walks in, and her eyes drift over my shoulder. "It's not my job to help you find them, though."

"Fair enough," I say, wondering how many more pawnshops I can visit before Tripp's patience wears out.

Turns out the answer is three.

"All right," Tripp finally says when I climb back into the car after having a friendly, but ultimately fruitless, conversation with the owner of Empire Pawn & Music. I never realized, until the past hour, how much business pawnshops do in used guitar sales. "Enough. I have stuff to do, and this isn't getting you anywhere. Things would go a lot faster if you went home and just called every pawnshop in New Hampshire."

"That is . . . a good point, actually," I admit. "Can I make just one more stop, though? The guy at Empire said there's another place right down the street."

Tripp slumps against his seat. "If this counts as our first date, I'd like to go on record as saying it sucks."

I grin at him, because he's very cute when he's annoyed. And also when he's not. "It doesn't count," I say.

"Good," Tripp says, closing his eyes. "Then I have no qualms about asking you to wake me up when it's over."

It takes less than five minutes to arrive at the appropriately named Last Chance Pawnshop, and its parking lot is much less crowded than any of the others. The only other vehicle in sight is a faded red pickup truck that's parked directly in front of the window. I park a few spots away from it, and Tripp opens his eyes as a tall, bearded guy wearing a bright red baseball cap and a gray sweatshirt comes out the front door carrying a bulging trash bag. The man tosses it into a nearby dumpster, brushes his hands together, and goes back inside.

"Place is hopping," Tripp observes. "This is definitely the least popular pawnshop in central New Hampshire."

"Yeah," I say, feeling strangely reluctant to leave the car. There was something comforting about how busy the other pawnshops were; here I feel too conspicuous. But it's my last stop, so . . . "I'll be right back."

There's no bell on the door, but it opens with a loud, prolonged squeak of the hinges. The man who took the trash out is the only person in the shop, positioned behind a streaky glass case that holds an assortment of watches. "Help you?" he says, adjusting his baseball cap enough for me to notice that his hair is dark and peppered with gray like his beard.

I wasn't able to find any photos of Dexter Robbins online, but this guy looks around the same age, which makes me wary of mentioning the name. "I was, um . . ." My mind goes blank as I approach the counter, so I grasp at the nearest straw. "Wondering if you buy jewelry?"

Red Hat smirks. "Did the gigantic neon sign in the window not give you a hint?" he asks, pointing behind me.

I don't need to turn. WE BUY GOLD flashed in my face while I was opening the door. "Right. Sorry," I say, forcing a smile that he doesn't return. I push up my left coat sleeve, exposing my charm bracelet. "What do you think I could get for this?"

"Lemme see," he says.

I meet his eyes for the first time. They're flat and cold, flicking across my face without much interest. He can probably tell at a glance that I won't actually sell anything, just like I can tell

I'm not going to learn anything helpful here. We have no use for one another, and I don't like his vibe, but I still find myself holding out my wrist.

He snorts and makes a beckoning motion with his palm. "I'm gonna need to take a closer look than that."

Reluctantly I unclasp my bracelet and drop it into his hand. He lays it across the counter and pulls a jeweler's loupe off the shelf behind him. While he bends over the bracelet, I scan the scattered paperwork that's piled beside him. It looks like a bunch of receipts, for items that people have either dropped off or bought, but I'm having a hard time reading them upside down. I inch a little closer, just as he looks up.

"Fourteen karat," he says, eyes glinting. They're not brown like I first thought; they're hazel. Like Mr. Larkin's were. My heart stutters in my chest as he adds, "Feels light. I can weigh it, but there's probably less than ten grams of gold here. Ballpark one twenty-five, maybe."

"Oh, okay. That's not as much as I was hoping." Suddenly the only thing I want in the world is to have the bracelet back on my wrist. I pluck it from beneath the loupe, not caring if I'm being rude, and drop my keys onto the counter so I can fasten it. "Thank you for checking, but I'll hang on to it after all."

He shrugs. "Up to you."

The clasp is delicate and hard to close, and Red Hat yawns while I wrestle with it. Just as it finally catches, I glance down at my keys and realize, stomach churning, that I forgot I'd attached the Mad Dog Tavern medallion to them. It's lying flat on the glass, snarling dog emblem down, the *Billy* engraving clearly visible. I freeze, hand still at my wrist, and steal a glance at Red Hat, hoping his eyes have gone back to his paperwork.

They haven't. They're fastened on the medallion, which shines brightly beneath the harsh fluorescent lighting. "What the—" he starts, face creasing into a frown.

I lunge for my keys and manage to scoop them up right before he does. He stares at the empty space where they were, then at me, and gooseflesh erupts across my arms. His eyes are narrowed into slits, and every line of his face looks like it's been etched from stone. "Where the hell did you get that?" he rasps. "Who are you?"

I don't hesitate. There's a counter between us, and I'm going to make full use of that barrier because I'm absolutely positive I don't want to have this conversation. I turn on my heel and run for the door, fling it open, and dash for my car. By the time I hear a shout behind me, I've already unlocked the doors and slid behind the wheel.

Tripp is reclined in his seat, eyes closed, and he startles at how loudly I slam the door. "What's up?" he asks, bringing his seat back into the upright position as I shove my keys into the ignition. As soon as the engine catches, I throw the car into reverse and back up much too quickly. Red Hat is out of the pawnshop now, and starts running straight toward us as I shift into drive. That's enough to make me turn the wheel sharply, slam on the gas, and tear out of the parking lot.

"Brynn, what the hell?" Tripp asks, staring behind us as I drive over a sidewalk in my haste to get onto the road. "What's that guy's problem?"

My throat has closed to a pinprick, and I can't speak until a glance in my rearview mirror reassures me that no one is following us. Still, I accelerate well past the speed limit, wanting to put as much space as possible between my car and the Last

Chance Pawnshop. "I think that might have been Dexter Robbins," I say.

"What?" Tripp asks. "Why?"

Oh God. It kills me to admit how careless I was, but . . . "I put my keys on the counter, and he saw the Mad Dog Tavern medallion. He, um, seemed to recognize it."

"Recognize it how?"

"He asked where I got it."

"Maybe he just liked it. They're kind of cool."

"Yeah, except . . ." My head pounds, and I wish I could go back and relive the last fifteen minutes of my life—never go into Last Chance Pawnshop in the first place or, at the very least, put my damn keys into my pocket. "The logo side was facedown, and the *Billy* side faceup. That's what caught his attention. And he was . . . angry."

"Well, shit," Tripp says. "That's not good." I turn onto Route 112, and he adds, "I don't think he's following us, though. There's nobody around except a Lexus, and . . ." He waits for it to pass and reports, "The driver's a woman, by herself. You didn't give your name, did you? Or leave anything behind?"

"No," I say, my pulse starting to slow. "I handed over my bracelet at one point, because I was acting like I might sell it, but I got it back."

"That's all right, then," Tripp says. We're both silent for a few beats until he adds, "You got what you wanted, right? If that was him, you can find him again."

"I guess," I say, but I know I won't. Even though there are now miles between me and Red Hat, and my heart rate has almost returned to normal, I don't feel silly for running away.

I feel like I escaped a predator, because that's exactly what he looked like when he saw the medallion. His entire demeanor changed in a flash, from bored to flat-out menacing. As much as I want to know what happened to Mr. Larkin, it turns out there's a limit to how far I'll go.

CHAPTER THIRTY-FOUR

BRYNN

"What is that?" Mason asks when I plop the cardboard box between him and Nadia during lunch period on Monday.

"A diorama," I say, spinning it so he can see. "From fifth grade. Remember? Mr. Hassan had us recreate a scene from a book with the people we'd most like to go on an adventure with. I picked *The Lion, the Witch and the Wardrobe,* and you guys."

"Oh my gosh," Nadia says, laughing as she peers into the display. "You kept this?"

"I did. You wouldn't believe how much Saint Ambrose stuff is in my attic." I dug the diorama out of a box yesterday after I got back from New Hampshire, determined to use some of my still-buzzing energy for good instead of chaos.

"Look at how cute I am," Mason says, examining the mini-Mason. "My hair is so *bouncy.*" Then his brow furrows. "Wait. Weren't Katie Christo and Spencer Okada in here too?"

"Yeah, but Spencer went missing at some point, and I ripped Katie out in eighth grade after she started calling me 'Trippstalker,' " I say. Then I reach into my backpack and pull out two Tupperware containers. I put the one with a red cover in front of Nadia, and the blue cover in front of Mason. "And these are chocolate-chip cookies. Gluten-free for you, Nadia. They have a normal amount of salt."

"Okay," Mason says, looking puzzled. "Good to know."

Nadia picks up her Tupperware container. "What's all this for, Brynn?"

"An apology," I say. "I know I'm not the most thoughtful person, but I really do value your friendship. I always have. I'm sorry I wasn't honest about my internship—which I quit, by the way—and I hope you can forgive me."

"Aw, look at you. So much personal growth." Mason gives me a one-armed hug and accidentally detaches mini-Mason from the bottom of the diorama. "Oops. Can I hang on to this, though? I like my sweater vest."

"You're all yours," I say with a hopeful look toward Nadia.

A smile tugs at her lips. "If I tell you we stopped being mad a week ago, can we still keep the cookies?"

"Yes," I say, as one of the biggest knots in my stomach untangles. "Does this mean we can all still go to the Winter Dance together?"

Nadia rolls her eyes. "We were always going. You're so dramatic. Why'd you quit the internship, though?"

Ugh. As much as I'd love to be totally straightforward, I can't tell her that without getting into a whole lot of stuff that I promised Tripp I wouldn't. "Long story," I say. "By the way, I have a date for the dance now. Sort of."

Mason's brows shoot up. "Does that have anything to do with the fact that Tripp Talbot has finally resurfaced in the hallowed halls of Saint Ambrose?"

"It may," I say. "I tracked him down." A couple of trays rattle beside us as more people join the table, and I shift my diorama to the side to make room.

"Tracked him down?" Nadia repeats. I put a finger to my lips as one of our new seatmates shoots us a quizzical look.

"It's too bad you got rid of Katie, really," Mason says, tucking his diorama self into the front pocket of his backpack. "She was an oracle."

Two days later I'm sitting cross-legged on my bed after school, organizing my notes on the Mr. Larkin case. I'm feeling much calmer than I was after meeting maybe-Dexter, to the point where I almost think I overreacted. *Almost.* Not enough to call the Last Chance Pawnshop and confirm that he works there, though.

Ellie comes in and flops down dramatically beside me, flinging an arm across her face. "Mom's going to be a chaperone for the dance on Saturday," she moans.

"What?" I ask, eyes on my laptop.

"They were short, so the PTA put out a call, and she answered," Ellie says, and sighs. "So awkward."

"Really?" I ask, giving her my full attention. My parents and Uncle Nick have been slower than Tripp and my friends to accept my apologies, but maybe this is a sign that Mom, at least, is thawing. "That's great. What did she say?"

Ellie makes a face. "Um, that she's going? It wasn't exactly a long conversation. I cut it short so I could come here to commiserate, but you've let me down with your weirdly chipper attitude." She raises herself on one elbow to peer at my laptop. "What's so interesting?"

I pull up the picture of eighteen-year-old Lila Robbins again. "Does this look like Ms. Delgado to you? Even a little bit?"

Ellie rolls over to look at my screen. "She looks like somebody," she says finally. "But like a lot of somebodies. She has one of those faces. Could be Ms. Delgado, I guess, but I haven't seen her in a while. Have you told Carly about all this?"

"No," I say. "She wants to get together next week, but it's complicated. I was never supposed to see the *Union Leader* article, remember? Plus, Tripp's not ready to talk about his dad taking the money, but if he *doesn't* talk about that, then he *also* can't talk about the fact that he doesn't actually know what Shane and Charlotte might have done to Mr. Larkin before he got there." I explained the whole story to Ellie—after getting Tripp's permission—because she already knew so much that I was afraid I'd let something slip. Besides, I told him, he could think of it as practice: another person knows the truth, and the world doesn't end. Ellie took everything in stride, like she always does, and she's been helping me brainstorm ever since.

"A tangled web," Ellie says.

"Indeed," I sigh, closing the cover of my laptop.

"Would it be helpful to know who's been vandalizing Mr. Larkin's picture?" Ellie asks, tugging at the end of her braid.

"Yeah, sure," I say. "But Ms. Kelso's pretty much given up on that. She's not even putting up committee posters anymore."

"Hmm," Ellie says. Her eyes glint in a way I don't like, but before I can ask her what she's talking about, she springs to her feet and heads for my dresser. "Do you have any crosses or, like, rosaries?" she asks. "I'm going for an eighties Madonna theme at the dance."

"I do not," I say, reaching once again for my laptop.

"Just chunky jewelry, then?"

"Take whatever you can find," I say, navigating to Lila Robbins's senior class picture again. Closing it and reopening it has become something of a habit, because every time I do, I hope that *this* will be the moment—the moment when I can say with 100 percent certainty that she's Shane's mother. But certainty keeps eluding me, even though, as I study her face once again, I'm more positive than ever that I know her.

I just don't know *how*.

CHAPTER THIRTY-FIVE

TRIPP

"Tripp!" The voice coming from our kitchen startles me when I get home from school Wednesday afternoon, because I'm used to silence when I open the front door. "You want to get your ass in here and explain this?"

Probably not. I don't know why my father is awake or what he's yelling about, but that's never a good lead-in.

"What's up?" I ask, dropping my backpack onto the floor and leaning against the kitchen doorframe. Then I freeze, because I can barely see my father behind all the empty liquor bottles he has lined up in front of him at the kitchen table—the ones I drained last week and shoved back into the cabinet under the sink, with the hazy thought that I'd replace them one of these days. I left the beer he keeps in the fridge alone, so I didn't think he'd notice anything else.

"What's *up* is that I went looking for drain cleaner when

I got home this morning and found these," he says. "None of which were drunk by me."

"Ahh. Yeah," I say, rubbing the back of my neck awkwardly. Beyond that, words fail me, because my father looks ready to explode, and that's never good.

"*Yeah?*" he echoes. "You're raiding my liquor cabinet now?" When I don't reply, his scowl deepens. "What the hell is going on with you, Tripp? These were full last week. Did you have a party or something, or did you . . ." He trails off, understanding dawning in his eyes. "Or did you drink all these on your own? You were on the couch every damn day last week. Were you even sick?"

I've put it off as long as I could, but I guess we're doing this.

"I wasn't sick," I admit, dropping into a chair across from him. "And yeah, I drank them all on my own."

"Jesus, Tripp." He still looks angry, but now it's mingled with concern. "Why on earth would you do that?"

"Things haven't been going great," I say.

He snorts out a harsh laugh, scraping one hand over his jaw. "Sounds like that's an understatement. I didn't know . . ." He picks up one of the bottles and turns it around in his hand, gazing at the label like it holds some kind of answer. "What didn't I know?"

I swallow hard. "You remember when Mr. Larkin died?"

Dad blinks. Whatever he might've been expecting me to say, it wasn't that. "Of course I remember."

"Well, there's been a lot of stuff happening around that lately. Memorial projects at school, and a couple of TV programs looking into it—"

"Wait, what? Really?"

That's a whole other conversation, but we need to have this one first. "Yeah, really. So I've been thinking a lot about what happened back then, and the thing is, Dad . . ." I look into his weary, puzzled eyes. *We're doing this.* "I know about the class-trip money."

He tilts his head, bemused. "The class-trip . . ." A flash of understanding crosses his face, along with an emotion I can't decipher. "Right. The stolen money," he finishes.

"Yeah. I, um, I found it here. Under your workbench." I can't look at him for this part, so I stare at the cracked linoleum. "And I tried to bring it back to school, but I got nervous and dumped it into Charlotte's locker, so that's where Grizz found it."

"Ahh," Dad says, his voice heavy with regret. "I wondered if you were the one who brought it back to Saint Ambrose, but you never said anything, so I hoped it was . . . Well. That would've been too much to expect, I guess." I finally raise my eyes, because I don't understand his reaction, and he adds, "But why did that upset you so much, after all this time?"

"Everything with Mr. Solomon happened, and—"

"Oh God, of course." My dad flushes, and for the first time since we started talking, he looks ashamed. "*Of course.* Jesus, you saw the poor guy lying dead in his living room, and I just let you fend for yourself afterward, didn't I?" His voice gets rough. "I'm sorry, Tripp. I've gotten way too used to how good you are at looking out for yourself. I would've drunk a whole cabinet worth of liquor too."

There's a brief moment when I think, *Actually*—when I'm on the brink of telling him what the real problem was, and what I believed about him for almost four years. Then I let the moment pass, because I can't imagine any scenario where he's not gutted by that information. Instead I say, "I just want to understand why, Dad. Why'd you take the money? I mean, I know we could always use it, but we're not—"

"Tripp," Dad interrupts. "I didn't take it."

I blink at him, confused. "But you just said . . ."

Except he didn't say he'd taken it. He said, *I wondered if you were the one who brought it back to Saint Ambrose, but you never said anything, so I hoped it was . . . Well. That would've been too much to expect, I guess.*

Of course. *Of course.*

"Lisa Marie?" I ask.

He nods. "She grabbed it at your spring concert. I didn't know that at the time, of course. She was supposed to leave the next day, but she didn't. Kept hanging on at Valerie's." His jaw twitches. "I ran into her in the supermarket a week later, which pissed me off, because she'd barely spent any time with you while she was here. I went by Valerie's to give her a piece of my mind, and she had the damn envelope sticking out of her bag. Didn't try to hide it, even though every parent at school knew it was missing by then."

I stare at him, wordless, as he continues, "So I brought it home. I was trying to figure out the best way to give the money back, when it disappeared and turned up at school. I told myself your mom must've had a change of heart, that she stopped by to apologize when I wasn't home, and she took the money and returned it."

Dad huffs out a mirthless laugh at whatever expression is on my face. "Yeah, I know. That's about as likely as pigs

281

learning to fly, but I wanted to believe it. Mostly because the only other option was that you'd found it, and I didn't want to have that conversation with you. I'm sorry, Tripp." He exhales in a gust. "I've avoided a lot of hard conversations with you over the years."

"But . . ." I'm sifting through my memories, trying to make sense of them. "Mr. Larkin . . . he was looking into the theft, and he . . ." No. I can't tell Dad I overheard that argument; it'll bring us way too close to the truth of what I was willing to believe.

Dad picks up without me having to finish, though. "He knew it was your mom. A kid saw her and came forward. I tried to convince Will to keep quiet. Not just because it'd be rough for you at school if people found out your mom took the money, but also . . . all I could think was how hurt you'd be if you knew she was around that whole time and never stopped by to see you. Will wouldn't budge, though. I was furious with him at the time, but in retrospect, of course he was right." Dad heaves a sigh. "Then he died before he could say anything, and I took the coward's way out and kept quiet."

He *kept quiet.* That's my father's gravest sin. Not murder, and not even theft. Keeping quiet because he didn't want me to know how little my mother cared. Which doesn't even register on my mental checklist of Reasons Why My Life Sucks, because last week she conveniently showed me herself. The only surprise is that she wasn't lying at Shooters when she told me she'd been in town when Mr. Larkin died.

"I'm sorry," I say. "I shouldn't have thought it was you."

"Why not?" Dad asks. "It's not like I ever told you what was going on. What were you supposed to think, when you found that money in our house? The thing is, Tripp—I haven't known what to say about your mom for a long time. I don't understand her. I could never explain why she acts the way she does, so I stopped trying. And that not-trying spilled over to almost everything else between you and me, and . . . here we are." He raps one of the empty bottles with his knuckles. "You skip a week of school, drain an entire cabinet full of hard liquor, and I don't notice. You don't have to be sorry for anything, but I do. I am."

"I kind of do, actually."

Actually. Here's that moment again. *Actually, Dad, I thought you did a lot worse than theft, and that's why I've basically ignored you for four years, and spent every waking moment trying to leave Sturgis and get as far away from you as possible.*

"No, you don't," he says emphatically, with more of a spark in his eyes than I've seen in a long time. "I'm not letting you feel bad about any of this, Tripp. I'm the adult in this situation, and you get to be the kid. At least one of your parents should let you be the kid. Better late than never, right?"

I haven't felt like a kid since that day in the woods, and it doesn't seem like the kind of thing you can get back. Still, I meet his gaze, swallow hard, and say, "Right."

"Okay," Dad says. He gets to his feet and gathers all the empty bottles in his arms. "How about I recycle these and we order some Golden Palace for dinner?"

He gives me a tired, tentative smile that I mirror back. "Sounds great," I say.

The moment passes again. Maybe this time for good.

CHAPTER THIRTY-SIX

BRYNN

"How do I look?" Ellie asks, posing in my doorway.

"Cute. And surprisingly like Madonna," I say, slipping on my shoes. My sister is wearing a flouncy black dress and boots, her hair is teased, and there's a pile of silver necklaces around her throat. "*Why* Madonna, again?"

"I was going through all the old albums Uncle Nick brought to eighties night and got inspired. Plus, when you're Madonna, people expect you to dance with them." Before I can ask why that matters—my sister has never been shy about dancing with whoever she likes—she steps into my room and adds, "You look pretty. We're, like, opposite. Good and evil."

My dress is short, sparkly, and pale silver, and my hair is flat-ironed straight. So yes, we contrast with one another, but I'm pretty sure no one's going to mistake Ellie for the evil Gallagher sister. I've been trying to keep a low profile all week, but memories at Saint Ambrose are longer than Nadia said. At least I'm not braving the Winter Dance on my own. "You sure you don't want to squeeze in with us?" I ask. Tripp should be here soon, and then Mason will pick us up in his mother's minivan—along with Nadia, Pavan, and the legendary Geoff.

"Nah, I'll just let Uncle Nick take me," Ellie says. Our mother came down with a bad cold and is currently doped up on NyQuil, so Uncle Nick heroically gave up his Saturday night to be a chaperone in her place. He twirled me in a nerdy dance when he told us, so I think I might finally be forgiven. "He has to be there early, and Paige is on the committee, so I can help her finish setting up." She blows me a kiss and grabs the bag at her feet before turning for the staircase. "See you there."

"Bye," I say, and plug my straightener in again for a final pass through my hair.

When I'm done getting ready and head downstairs, my father is hovering in the hallway. "I haven't seen Tripp in a while," he says, adjusting his glasses. Dad and Uncle Nick are like Ellie and me; they look enough alike that if they were closer in age, they'd get mistaken for one another. Uncle Nick is essentially a younger version of Dad with more hair and trendier eyewear. "It'll be nice to catch up."

Oh God. My father's idea of *catching up* with my friends is making science jokes that aren't funny to anyone except him. "I think I'm supposed to meet him outside," I say, checking my phone. Tripp just pulled into our driveway—he has his dad's car tonight—and Mason is only a few minutes behind.

"I'll say a quick hello," Dad says, matching me stride for stride toward the door.

"Dad—" My protest is cut short when the bell rings.

"Always knew that kid had manners," Dad says, grinning as he pulls the door open to reveal Tripp in a navy suit, his blond hair more neatly combed than I've ever seen it. "Hello, Tripp, come on in. Good to see you."

It is *very* good to see him, because wow, he looks great. Shane Delgado might be the king of Saint Ambrose, but Tripp is definitely strong competition in the suit he has on. His blue eyes sparkle as he takes me in before shifting his gaze to my dad. "Hi, Mr. Gallagher. How've you been?" Then his eyes go straight back to me. "You look amazing, Brynn."

"You too," I say, blushing as I grab my coat.

Dad asks Tripp about his father, and school, and it's so remarkably cringe-free that I don't even lunge through the still-open door when I see headlights flash behind Tripp's car. "Mason's here," I say. "We should go."

"Have fun. Be safe. Let your uncle know if you need anything," Dad says. We're halfway down the steps before he adds, "And whatever you do, don't trust atoms."

"Dad, no," I moan, at the same time Tripp asks, "Why?"

"Because they make up everything!" Dad says, before closing the door with a satisfied smirk.

"So close," I sigh.

"You know, I kind of missed the science jokes," Tripp says. He grabs my hand, which is a nice surprise, as the van door slides open and Pavan sticks his head out.

"You guys get the way back," he says. "Sorry."

"Weren't you two a thing once?" Tripp murmurs in my ear. "Should I be jealous?"

"You should," I whisper back. "Pavan was smooth for a twelve-year-old."

"Smoother than me, anyway," Tripp says, keeping hold of my hand as I step unsteadily into the slightly-too-high-for-me van.

Mason and Geoff, who's in the front passenger seat, both turn as Tripp and I squeeze into the back row. "Don't you two look nice," Mason says. "You know Geoff, right?"

"Of course." I wave to Geoff, who reminds me of a teenage Chidi from *The Good Place,* before locking eyes with a grinning Nadia. Then I mime zipping my lips, because there's no reason to embarrass Mason on his first date.

"I also answer to 'Gorff,'" Geoff says, and I almost choke on my surprised laugh.

"This is going to be a good night," Mason says as he backs out of my driveway.

I hope so. I feel loose and happy for the first time in a while, not to mention fluttery every time my eyes meet Tripp's. He's taken my hand back, and is letting his thumb run lightly across my palm while he jokes with Pavan and Nadia, and I have goose bumps even though it's warm in the van.

It's not as though everything is suddenly perfect. I'm worried that by being with me tonight, Tripp is risking friendships that mean a lot to him, and I'm nervous about seeing Shane and Charlotte. But I'm going to try to forget all that, and all of my theories, and just have fun. It would be a crime to waste how good Tripp looks in that suit.

The Saint Ambrose parking lot is nearly full when we arrive, and Mason has to slam on his brakes as a red pickup truck swerves in front of us to snag an empty spot. "Okay, fine," he mutters, easing the van into a crawl behind a half dozen of our classmates walking toward the entrance. "Didn't realize parking was going to be a competitive sport."

"There," Nadia calls as a Volvo backs out of a nearby spot.

Mason inches carefully in between the lines and exhales a loud sigh of relief when he shifts into park, then turns around and says, "Let's go make some memories, kids."

Pavan opens the door, and everyone climbs out. As Mason locks up, I take Tripp's hand to follow the group in, but he resists the pull of my hand. "Hold on a sec," he says, leaning against the side of the van. His hands steal around my waist. "Can I get five minutes alone with you?"

"What for?" I ask as my stomach executes a slow flip. Tripp licks his bottom lip, and my eyes follow the movement with a little thrill. It seems ridiculous, suddenly, that we've spent all this time together and haven't kissed once.

"Pavan might be smooth," he says, pulling me closer, "but I liked you first."

A tingle runs up my spine, and I think, suddenly, of the way Nadia and I used to text a GIF of Michael Scott from *The Office* yelling "It's happening!" anytime something we'd been waiting for finally came to pass.

It's happening. Maybe I haven't been waiting as long as Tripp has, but all of a sudden it feels like it.

"Seventh grade is earlier than eighth grade," I remind Tripp, tilting my head up. He's so tall, it's a good thing I'm wearing heels.

"I liked you since sixth," he says.

"Oh really?" My hands move up to his chest and lightly grasp the lapels of his suit. It's chilly out and he's not wearing a coat, but he doesn't seem to notice the cold. "Three years of homework sessions, and you never said a word."

My tone is teasing, but his gaze is intense when he replies, "Those were torture."

I want to keep talking about this forever, and I also want—more. It's the most agonizingly wonderful tension I've ever felt. "That's a long time to like somebody and not do anything about it," I say.

The corners of Tripp's eyes crinkle. "Well, there was a break in my pining once you moved away."

I try to fake pout, but I can't pull it off. My mouth refuses to turn down. "A break, huh?" I ask. "Till when?"

"Probably that day at the greenhouse."

I raise my eyebrows. "When Wade Drury made fun of my name?"

"No. Before that. When Ms. Kelso put us together on that committee. Which I guess was"—he pretends to check a watch—"the first time we talked since you left."

It's getting a little hard to breathe. "That was fast," I say.

"What can I say? I'm nothing if not consistent." His eyes go soft as he pulls me closer, which I didn't think was possible. I thought I'd eliminated all the space between us already. "Brynn. Can I—"

"Yes." Before he can say anything further, I press my lips to his. My arms wind around his neck, and his hands grip me more tightly, lifting me off my feet as the kiss deepens. Instantly I'm breathless; Tripp isn't just kissing me like someone who's wanted to do that for years. He's kissing me like it's the *only* thing he's ever wanted. I meet him with the same intensity, feeling feverish as my fingers twine in his hair, every new kiss so charged and fiery that it's almost too much. If he lets go of me, I'll fall straight to the ground.

Fortunately, he doesn't let go. At least, not until a loud beep cuts through the blood pounding in my ears and somebody hollers, "Get a room!"

I pull back as Tripp gently lowers me to the ground, just in time to see the taillights of Charlotte's Range Rover pass us. Of course. Nobody knows how to ruin a moment better than Charlotte Holbrook. Although, to be fair, she's not the one who yelled.

"Sorry," Tripp says, as breathless as I am. He rakes a hand through his hair, looking dazed. "I didn't mean . . . God, that was . . ."

"I'm not sorry," I say.

A slow smile spreads across his face. "Me either."

I force myself to take a step back, because now that I'm more aware of my surroundings, I realize we have a much bigger audience than Charlotte and whoever was in her car. It feels like half the school arrived at once, and most of my classmates are smirking as they pass me and Tripp. "We should probably go inside, though, huh?" I ask.

"If we have to," Tripp says, smoothing a lock of my hair away from my face before taking hold of my hand again. I float along beside him until we get inside the main building and my practical side takes over. Nerves, plus mussed hair and what is probably now a complete lack of lip gloss, require a bathroom pit stop.

"I'll meet you in there, okay?" I say, reaching up a thumb to wipe the pink sheen from Tripp's mouth. "I need the restroom."

"Okay," he says, giving me a quick, sweet peck on the lips

that shouldn't make me swoon as much as it does. Turns out I have it *bad*.

The restroom is full of excitedly chattering girls, but they're mostly there to gossip and fix makeup, so there's no line. Once I've gone to the bathroom, I wash my hands, run a brush through my hair, and reapply my lip gloss.

Back in the hallway, music pounds from the gymnasium, but before I can head that way, something catches my eye at the end of the corridor. It's a poster of Mr. Larkin with, once again, angry red slashes across the face.

I walk toward it, skirting around a desk that's been shoved against the wall beside the poster. Which is odd, come to think of it; there's never been a desk in this hallway before. Even weirder, a single red marker lies on top of it, its cap off to one side, like somebody quickly defaced the poster and then took off. But why would a marker be here in the first place? Did Mr. Larkin's vandal bring their own and leave it behind, or . . . ?

"There you are!" I look up to see Ellie half walking, half dancing her way toward me, jewelry jangling with every step. She stops when she reaches the desk, hands on her hips as she examines the defaced poster. "Oh good," she says. "Look at that."

"I'm looking," I say. "Why is it good?"

"Because." She picks up the marker and winks. "My trap worked."

CHAPTER THIRTY-SEVEN

TRIPP

I lean against the wall in the gymnasium, letting my eyes adjust to the scene in front of me. Black lights are in every corner of the room, illuminating a huge cityscape made from neon paper that covers one side of the gymnasium. The dance committee was handing out fluorescent bands at the entrance, and most of my classmates are wearing the bands looped around their wrists or necks. Anyone wearing white or bright colors is glowing. Neon balloons bob around the room, adding to the surreal effect, but I'm only half paying attention. I keep scanning the room for Brynn, because I'm not sure I can go much longer without kissing her again.

Those five minutes outside Mason's van might have been the best of my life.

I spot Brynn's light dress weaving through the crowd toward me, and start grinning like an idiot, until I notice that she isn't alone. It's not that I don't like Ellie, but I'd like her better if she were someplace else right now.

As Brynn approaches, though, I can see that her smile looks a little strained. "Ellie is doing something," she says when she stops at my side.

Before I can ask what she's talking about, Ellie grabs my right hand. I'm too startled to protest as she turns my palm like she's reading it, then drops it and does the same thing to my left hand.

"He's good," she reports.

I blink at her, confused. "What was that for?"

She holds up her own right palm, which glows with some kind of bright green residue. "I'm looking for my match."

"I can't believe you checked Tripp," Brynn says, folding her arms tightly across her chest. "I told you he was fine."

"Sorry, but I couldn't take your word for it," Ellie says. "You're not exactly your most objective self when it comes to him."

"Is someone going to tell me what's going on?" I ask.

"Go ahead," Brynn says, lifting her chin at Ellie. "This is your brilliant plan."

"You say that like it's *not* brilliant," Ellie pouts. Then she turns to me. "I used my old magic kit to coat a red marker with ultraviolet powder and left it next to a poster of Mr. Larkin. So that anybody who used the marker to write on his face would have a hand like this." She holds up her palm again. "The powder makes your skin green under UV light. Or black light."

"That's . . . Okay, that actually *is* kind of brilliant," I admit.

Ellie beams, and I frown as I realize what that means. "Hold on a sec. Are you saying you thought *I* might've done it?"

"No exceptions," Ellie says. "Speaking of." She reaches for Brynn, who scowls at her.

"Oh, *come on!*" Brynn protests.

"I can't play favorites," Ellie says sternly, twisting Brynn's hands in hers before releasing them. "Okay, you're good."

"Any suspects?" I'm amused, even though this isn't how I wanted to spend my first few minutes on a dance floor with Brynn—who, by the way, looks stupid-cute when she's annoyed with someone other than me. I wrap my arms around her and kiss the top of her head, and she relaxes against my chest.

Ellie makes a face. "Ew, heteros," she says.

"You can leave anytime," Brynn reminds her.

"I can't, though," Ellie says, looking to our left. "I need Tripp to get me into the royal court." I follow her gaze and see Shane and Charlotte surrounded three-deep by their friends. *Our* friends. "It's elite central over there, and they're our primary persons of interest."

Here we go again. "I'm telling you, scribbling on posters isn't Shane's style," I say.

"You're thinking of him as Shane Delgado, though," Ellie points out. "Not Michael Robbins."

"Shhh," I hiss, even though there's nobody close enough to hear her over the music. It's still impossible for me to believe that Brynn's wild theory is right. The whole idea is surreal— that Shane, Saint Ambrose's resident golden boy, could also be Dexter Robbins's son. And Mr. Larkin's half brother. "It's not like they're talking to me now, anyway."

"Oh, please." Ellie rolls her eyes. "You're telling me those people wouldn't part like the Red Sea if you walked through them?"

Brynn threads her fingers through mine. "That makes you sound so powerful," she teases, looking up at me and fluttering her lashes. And I guess that's that, because I'm suddenly incapable of saying no to her even when she doesn't directly ask for something.

"Fine, but prepare to be rejected," I say.

Ellie grins, undaunted. "That's the spirit."

Turns out Ellie was right; force of habit means that everyone gets out of my way as we near the group surrounding Shane and Charlotte, until Charlotte herself turns with an imperious lift of her chin. "Well, look who it is," she says, tightening her grip on Shane's arm. She's wearing a white dress that's glowing under the black light, and her hair is pulled back into a complicated twist that's half braid, half bun, with lots of sparkly pins holding it all together. Her eyes sweep over Brynn and me, ignoring Ellie completely. "Saint Ambrose's newest It Couple."

"Hey, Charlotte. Can we call a truce?" I ask. Not just to buy Ellie time either. Regardless of what's happened lately, or what Charlotte might know, she's been my friend for years. "I was in bad shape at your place, and I'm sorry if I was ungrateful. I'm doing better now."

"I'm sorry too," Brynn offers. "I shouldn't have come to your house like that."

Charlotte, who thawed the tiniest bit when I spoke, gets full-on icy again. "You're not sorry, Brynn," she says, flicking her gaze toward the arm I still have slung around Brynn's shoulders. "You got exactly what you wanted."

"Oh my God, I love this song!" Ellie cries suddenly, and before anyone can react, she's latched on to Shane. He's too startled to protest as she lifts one of his hands in the air, then reaches for the other. "Come on, let's dance!" she says, flipping his palm in her hand.

Charlotte is still clinging to Shane's arm, and pulls him backward out of Ellie's reach. "What's wrong with you?" she hisses. "Don't touch him."

"You should dance too," Ellie says, lunging for Charlotte's hand. She'd have better luck prying open a steel vise than removing Charlotte from Shane, though.

"Stop it. Go *away*!" Charlotte's shriek is out of proportion for the situation, even though Ellie has gone from quirky to flat-out weird pretty fast.

"Babe, chill," Shane says.

Ellie seems to understand that it's time to cut her losses, and releases Charlotte's wrist. "Sorry!" she says, stepping back and fanning herself. "Sometimes my love of dance gets the best of me." Then she darts past me and Brynn, murmuring "Not him" before disappearing into the crowd.

"She was dropped on her head as a child," Brynn says, watching Ellie make her way to their uncle and grab his hands. Ellie wasn't kidding about the *no exceptions* part. "A lot."

"So." I clear my throat, wondering how to fill the awkward silence that's suddenly descended between the four of us. Well, not silence, exactly, since the music is still blaring, but it's awkward as hell. "You guys having a good time?"

Charlotte glares daggers in Ellie's direction. "I was until that little freak came over."

"Hey," Brynn protests at the same time Shane wrenches his arm away from Charlotte and says, "Jesus, *enough*. She's just a kid."

His voice is loud and his words are a little slurred; his face is flushed and sweaty. He's been drinking, which isn't unusual for Shane at a Saint Ambrose social event, but refusing to put up with Charlotte's bullshit is. She blinks at him, too startled to speak, and he growls, "I'm done with this," and stalks away.

"Done with what?" Charlotte asks. Shane keeps going, heading for a corner where the lacrosse guys are clustered, and Charlotte follows. "Done with *what*?" she calls again.

"Well, there goes their night," I say.

"I'm sorry," Brynn says. "Ellie gets these ideas—"

"It's all right," I say. "It wasn't a bad idea. And I'm glad to know Shane didn't vandalize the poster. I know it doesn't prove he didn't do something else," I add before Brynn can interrupt with another one of her theories. "Or that he isn't *someone* else. I'm still glad, though."

"I get it," Brynn says. Her eyes are on the lacrosse corner, where Charlotte and Shane are arguing.

"Come on, Brynn." I spin her so she's fully facing me, and pull her closer into a slow dance, even though there's a rap song playing. "Stop looking at Shane like you want to interrogate him. Whatever truth-telling superpower you have won't work on him."

"I know," Brynn says. "It only works on you."

"What's your secret?" I ask, and I really hope she tells me, because otherwise I'm not sure I'll be able to get rid of the nagging suspicion that she's still waiting to catch me in a lie.

She holds up a hand and rubs her thumb with her forefinger. "You do this whenever you're not being honest."

I blink. "I do?"

"Every time. You have since we were kids."

"Well, damn," I say, and she grins. "How convenient for you."

We sway for a minute until Brynn rises on her tiptoes to plant a soft kiss on my lips, her hands sliding over my shoulders and around my neck. I kiss her back, harder, relishing the fact that I know how we fit together now. My hands run up and down her back, always stopping at the curve of her waist even though I'd rather not stop at all, but her uncle's around here somewhere and we're surrounded by people, and—

"Get a room," someone says, but more politely than whoever yelled it in the parking lot. Brynn pulls away, and we turn to see Mason dancing beside us with Geoff. The music has changed to something with more of a Latin beat, and they're both keeping up with it. Although the more they come into focus, the more it seems like Mason is barely keeping up with Geoff. "You can dance, Gorff," Brynn says with a smile.

"I can," he says. "My grandparents made the whole family learn. Shall we?" He holds out a hand. She takes it and lets him twirl her around before dipping her low.

"Oh," Brynn says, breathless. "You're *really* good."

"Don't be jealous," Mason says. "He only has eyes for me."

"I'm not," I say unconvincingly as Geoff spins Brynn away. "Your timing sucks, though."

"They'll be back," Mason says. "In the meantime, let's dance." He holds out his hand, eyebrows raised like he's daring me to take it. I grin, ready to grasp his palm, and then—*fuck.*

What the actual fuck.

I freeze in place, unable to move, until Mason's jaw tightens and he drops his hand. "Whatever," he mutters. He thinks I'm being an asshole, but I'm not. I don't understand what I just saw. Or maybe it would be more accurate to say that I understand it too well.

Mason's palm is bright green. Just like Ellie's.

CHAPTER THIRTY-EIGHT

BRYNN

"Your new boyfriend is kind of a dick," Mason tells me as I lead him out of the gymnasium.

"He's not really," I say, but I can't blame Mason for thinking so. I couldn't figure out what was going on, when Geoff danced me back to Tripp and he and Mason were just standing there awkwardly, not speaking or even looking at one another. Then Geoff spun Mason away, and Tripp told me what had happened. I ran after Mason, made some kind of excuse I don't even remember to pull him away, and here we are.

My eyes scan the hallway. Where can I take Mason so that we won't be interrupted for—whatever conversation it is that we're about to have? We pass Mr. Larkin's defaced poster, and I can't bring myself to look at Mason to see whether or not he reacts. What is *happening*? What did happen? My brain is spinning between thinking there's a simple, innocent, totally unrelated explanation, and trying to slot Mason into everything I've learned over the past couple of weeks.

"Here," I say, pulling open the auditorium door. It's cavernous, but empty, and at least it's a closed space. I head for the front near the stairs that lead onto the stage, where we'll be sure to see any of the doors if they open.

"Are you going to tell me what this is about anytime soon?" Mason asks.

"Yes." I sit on the steps, and Mason folds himself beside me. "Here's the thing. You know how someone's been vandalizing posters of Mr. Larkin?"

Mason doesn't have a poker face. His eyes instantly go wide before he catches himself, and even then he blinks too fast. "Um, yeah. Of course."

Oh God. Heat rushes to my cheeks as I take a deep breath, trying to slow the sudden hammering of my heart. "Well, Ellie wanted to find out who," I say. "She hung a poster of Mr. Larkin in the hallway, and left a marker coated with ultraviolet powder on the desk beside it. So that if someone picked up the marker to write on the poster, the powder would leave residue on their hands that would show up under black light." I take Mason's hand and turn it so his palm, unmarked beneath the standard auditorium lighting, is facing upward. "Like yours did. That's why Tripp freaked when you held out your hand."

Mason snatches his hand away. "Tripp was seeing things," he says.

"I saw it too," I say. "Before we left the gym."

His jaw clenches. "I don't know what you want me to say. I picked up a marker. So what?"

So what? I really, really wish that was a valid question, but I know it's not. The whole time we've been talking, the enormity of what I missed has been making me almost dizzy. I pull my phone from the pocket of my dress and unlock it with shaking hands. "The thing is, I've been looking into what happened to Mr. Larkin. On my own, kind of, now that I'm not working for *Motive* anymore. And I found out that Mr. Larkin changed his name, and that he had a stepmother, and a half brother our age, and . . ." What did Ellie say? *Book smart isn't people smart.* I'm the most people-stupid girl in the universe. "Mason, this is your mom, isn't it?"

I hand him the *Union Leader* article about Lila and Michael Robbins, and watch his face collapse.

I should have seen it straightaway. I went to Mason's house plenty of times between fourth and eighth grade. But by then his mother was much older than Lila Robbins is in the *Union Leader* photograph, and dark-haired instead of bleached blond. Ms. Rafferty has glasses and never wears makeup, and it's possible she had a nose job. But still. The similarities should have caught my eye, and maybe they would have, if I hadn't been so focused on Shane Delgado. Plus, I didn't know that Mason's father isn't his biological father until *right this second.*

"Yeah, it is." Mason hands my phone back, eyes glassy. "I . . . I never told you about any of that because it was a long time ago, and because . . ."

"Because you didn't want me to know that Mr. Larkin was your brother?" I ask.

"Half brother," he says bitterly.

"Can you tell me what happened?" My phone is clenched

tightly in my hands, and my mind is still churning. I'm remembering more now—and one of the things I remember is that Mason and his family were in Florida visiting his grandparents when Mr. Larkin died. They didn't come back until after the funeral. Whatever desperation Mason or his mother might have felt four years ago, it couldn't have led them in the darkest possible direction. And even though there's not a single part of me that believes Mason is capable of hurting anyone, I'm shaken enough in my own perceptions to feel deeply relieved that he was nowhere near the crime scene.

"Where would I even start?" Mason says woodenly.

"Do you remember your—father?" I stumble over the word.

"Of course I do." A spark of anger animates Mason's voice. "I've lived with him for almost fourteen years. My *father* is my father."

"I know. I mean, do you remember . . . Dexter?"

"No," Mason says. His hands are knotted between his knees. "I don't remember anything. All I know is what my mother told me. She was really young, and naïve, and he didn't seem so bad at first. But he got worse, fast. I was sick all the time, I guess, and he wouldn't do anything about it. He wouldn't even let her leave the house without him."

"You have asthma," I say. It's the least important detail, I realize, and yet—it's another thing that I missed.

"I've been asymptomatic for a while," Mason says. "The chronic stuff in my lungs is still there, probably, but it doesn't bother me like it used to." He shoots me a wry look. "But yeah, I have an inhaler. I just don't use it much."

I nod, absorbing that. "So your mom left when you were three?"

"Yeah. Mom told me that we were literally locked in the house while he was gone," Mason says. "He was making the whole place a fortress. Bars on the windows and padlocks on the doors. There was only one window he didn't bother with, because he thought it was too small. But it wasn't. That's the one she used. She didn't take anything except me."

He exhales a deep, shaky breath. "Mom didn't have any family. Her parents died when she was in high school. But Mr. Solomon used to be a good friend of her dad's, so that's who she called when she got us out. He—"

"Wait," I interrupt. "Mr. Solomon, from Saint Ambrose?"

Mason nods. "He came and got us, brought us to Sturgis and helped Mom find a job and an apartment. Introduced her to my dad, even. She took Dad's name when they got married, and changed mine. And everything was fine, for a while."

"Until Mr. Larkin came here?"

"I thought he was so great." Mason's voice cracks. "The cool teacher who was actually interested in *me*. Always asking so many questions. But then one day, maybe a week before he died, he asked me to stop by his classroom after school to talk about my Shakespeare essay. I was excited, because I thought I'd done really well, and that maybe I'd get a prize or something." He shakes his head. "Instead he told me who he was."

"What did you say?" I ask.

"Nothing. I couldn't speak the whole time I was there. I just sat at my desk, totally silent, while he talked. At first I thought it might be okay, because he apologized for how things were back when I was little—apologized that he didn't do more to stop Dexter from being horrible. But he also kept calling me 'Mikey,' and trying to give me this medallion with that name written on the back. I wouldn't take it—I *couldn't* take it, because I was frozen in place—and I think that made him mad. He shoved it into my backpack and said I was a Robbins, and my mom had no right to hide me away from his father." I don't miss the way Mason's hands clench as he says *his* father. "He said . . . he said Dexter's birthday was the next week, and he was going to tell him where to find me. Can you imagine? That was the last thing he said to me before he left—'You'll be the best birthday present Dad has ever had.'"

"Oh, Mason." I slip my hand into one of his. "I'm so sorry. That must have been terrifying."

"It was." Mason lowers his voice to a near-whisper. "I must've sat there for an hour afterward, totally in shock. I didn't know what to do. I told my parents, and they talked to Mr. Solomon, and he said we should just take off again. But it would be a lot harder to do a second time, you know?"

"So Mr. Solomon knew that Mr. Larkin threatened you?" I ask. Suddenly our old groundskeeper snarling *That son of a bitch got what he deserved* makes sense. I'm not sure it's something Mr. Solomon would have said if he'd been 100 percent in his right mind, but it's not out of left field anymore.

Mason nods. "He came with us to Florida when we visited my dad's parents. I know I told you guys it was a spur-of-the-moment vacation, but it was actually this intense strategy session with a family lawyer, and then—while we were gone, Mr. Larkin died."

"And he'd never said anything to his father about you?"

"I guess he didn't get the chance," Mason says. "We kept

waiting for the other shoe to drop, but it didn't." I squeeze his hand, and he adds, "I thought I was over it, and I think I am, mostly, but . . ." He gazes around the auditorium. "I was here over winter break with student council, making posters for the class play, and the red marker ran out, so I went backstage to look for another one. I found it, and then I saw the easel with Mr. Larkin's portrait. It was covered, and I was curious, so I lifted the cloth and—I don't know. Everything went hazy for a few seconds, and . . . I did what I did."

"And kept doing it?" I ask, trying to keep my voice as judgment-free as possible. "To all of Ms. Kelso's posters?"

Mason cringes, then extends the hand I'm not holding and flexes his palm, like he's checking for the green residue we saw in the gymnasium. "I'm not proud of myself, believe me. It was a shitty thing to do to Ms. Kelso, and to . . ." He swallows hard. "To Mr. Larkin. It's not like I wanted him to die, or that I don't wish things could have been different with us. But when you've spent most of your life hiding, sometimes the pressure gets to be too much." He drops his hand back into his lap and meets my eyes. "You really had no idea before tonight?"

"None," I say. "In fact, I created an entire theory in my head where Shane Delgado was Michael Robbins."

"Shane?" Even as he winces at his old name, Mason manages a laugh. "That has to be the first and last time I've ever been mistaken for Shane Delgado." Then his expression turns thoughtful. "Funny you should say that, though, because it turns out Shane was there."

"What?" I ask, confused. "Shane was where?"

"In the classroom, when Mr. Larkin told me who he was." I gape at him, and he adds, "Well, in the coatroom. Asleep, like always. After Mr. Larkin left, I was just sitting at my desk, shell-shocked, and all of a sudden Shane stumbled out of the coatroom, yawning, and staggered past me out the door. I don't think he even noticed me."

"Wait, so . . ." I rub my suddenly aching temples. "Did he hear you? Does Shane know Mr. Larkin was your brother?"

"Well, I've always wondered," Mason says. "And I was worried for a while. I mean, he was *right there.* He's never said anything, though, or acted any different toward me." He snorts out a light laugh. "In other words, he's continued to ignore me as much as ever."

I can't even process this right now. Just when I was ready to cross Shane off my suspect list, it turns out he might've known all along who Mr. Larkin was. But . . . why would he care? What possible difference could that make to Shane? Before I can follow that train of thought, though, Mason asks, "What are you going to do?"

"About what?"

"About . . ." He makes a sweeping gesture with his hand. "All this. Are you going to—tell anyone?" His voice catches. "I'm almost eighteen. I don't think I'd have to see Dexter if I don't want to, but my mom . . . I don't know what kind of trouble she might get into, leaving the way she did, and . . ."

"Mason, no," I say quickly. "I won't say a word. It's your family's business." But even as I say it, I can't stop thinking about how I accidentally showed the *Billy* medallion to maybe-Dexter in the pawnshop. I should tell Mason about that, probably, but the relief on his face is so stark that I can't make myself bring it up.

Men like Dexter are a hornet's nest, Rose said. *Why poke it if you don't have to, right?* But I didn't listen.

"Will Ellie or Tripp say anything?" Mason asks.

"No. Ellie's a vault, and Tripp . . . he has his own demons when it comes to that day." Mason raises his brows, looking interested despite still being in a state of semi-shock, and I shove gently at his shoulder. "Don't ask. It's not my story to tell."

"You're holding a lot of secrets, Brynn," Mason says. "Be careful. That can wear a person down after a while. I should know." I just smile tightly, and he adds, "Now what?"

I unclench my lips. "Now go back to the gym and dance with your date."

Mason lets out a strangled half laugh. "Oh, sure. Why not? Dance the night away."

"Do you have a better idea?"

He sighs and gets to his feet. "Not really."

I stand too, and ask, "Can I give you a hug?"

He chokes out, "Please." We grab on to one another and hold tight, and I let him be the first to pull away. "All right," he says, wiping his eyes. "I'm gonna find Geoff. You coming?"

"In a minute," I say.

Mason gives me one more smile and says, "See you in there."

I watch him leave, then turn my attention to my phone, which is filled with check-in texts from Tripp and Ellie. My overstuffed brain is too exhausted to tell them anything except *Everything's ok. I'll explain soon.* And then—I hear something. A light rustling sound, coming from behind the auditorium curtain. I freeze, my heart pounding loudly in my ears. Before I can lose my nerve, I lunge for the curtains and sweep them aside.

A flash of white rounds a corner, and I follow. "Charlotte!"

I call out, nearly tripping over an empty cardboard box. "Stop, okay? I know it's you."

From where I stand I can see Charlotte paused, one foot on the bottom of the stairs leading backstage. The jeweled pins in her hair sparkle beneath the dim lights. "How much did you hear?" I ask, which is a ridiculous question. Of course she heard everything.

Oh God. *Now* what have I done to Mason?

Charlotte turns to face me, her flawless features so empty of expression that she looks like a statue. "*Mason* is Mr. Larkin's brother?" she asks.

"You can't say anything. Please, Charlotte. It's not safe for him." I'm babbling, my words tripping over one another as I walk toward her, slowly, my hands clasped together as though I'm praying. "You understand that, right? His father is a monster, and . . ." I pause when I get closer and spot the tear tracks on her face. "Wait," I say. "Why are you here? What's wrong?"

"Nothing. I just needed some time alone." Charlotte folds her arms stiffly but can't prevent another tear from slipping down her cheek. Then her face crumples and she says, "Shane broke up with me."

"Oh, Charlotte. I'm sorry." And I truly am. I wish we were on better terms so that I could hug her, but I'm pretty sure she'd hate that. "Maybe it's just temporary?" I offer. "He seemed pretty drunk."

"I don't think so," she says, with genuine sadness in her voice. "I'd do anything for him—absolutely anything—but he's tired, he says. Tired of being in a relationship. What he really means, though, is he's tired of *me*."

"Can I help?" I ask. "We could leave, maybe get a coffee, or—"

She vehemently shakes her head, as if the very thought horrifies her, and I'm glad I held off on the hug. "No," she says. "I'm going home. And I won't say anything about Mason, I promise." My knees go weak with relief, and I'm about to thank her profusely when she adds, "But you should knock it off, Brynn."

"Knock what off?" I ask.

"This whole—Veronica Mars thing you're doing," she says, waving her hand in a circle. "It's dangerous, and if you keep going, you might learn something you'd rather not know."

"Like what?" I ask as she turns away. "Charlotte? Like what?"

There's no answer except the tap of her heels, and then the squeal of hinges as she opens the exit door and steps outside.

CHAPTER THIRTY-NINE

TRIPP

"That's a lot to process," Ellie says when Brynn finishes telling us about Mason.

"Understatement of the century," I add. My eyes stray toward the middle of the gymnasium, where Mason is slow dancing with his head on Geoff's shoulder. All his exuberance from earlier is gone, which makes me feel like shit for being the one to set everything in motion by noticing the green residue on his palm.

Even then, though, I didn't necessarily think he'd turn out to be Mr. Larkin's secret brother. The whole time Brynn was talking to him in the auditorium, I wondered if maybe he just didn't like the guy. Or he messed up the poster on a dare.

"You guys can't say anything," Brynn warns. "I promised we wouldn't." She bites her lip, darting a glance at me. "And Charlotte promised *she* wouldn't. I hope she meant it."

"If she said it, she meant it," I say. Brynn arches a skeptical brow, and I add, "Look, I know Charlotte isn't the friendliest, but her word is good. She's never let me down. She didn't break our pact in the woods, even when I accidentally framed her for theft."

"Did you ever tell her that was you?" Ellie asks.

"Oh, hell no," I say, so quickly that she snorts out a laugh.

"I wouldn't either," she says. "She's kind of terrifying."

Brynn crosses her arms. "So we're back to square one, with no idea who killed Mr. Larkin. It wasn't Mason, it wasn't Mr. Solomon, and it probably wasn't Shane, because he doesn't have a motive anymore." She offers me a half smile. "It wasn't you—"

"Thanks for the vote of confidence," I say.

"And it wasn't your dad. So who's left? Dexter, I suppose, or—"

"Maybe this is your cue to take a break, Brynn," Ellie interrupts. "Spend a small portion of the Winter Dance actually dancing. Revolutionary concept, I know, but you could try it."

"I danced with Geoff, and look where that got us," Brynn mutters.

"You should probably stick to me," I say, and hold out my hand, but before Brynn can take it, somebody half tackles me from behind. "What the—" I get out before I realize it's Shane's arm locked around my shoulders.

"T," he slurs, dragging me toward the lacrosse corner. "Barely seen you all night. You mad at me? I didn't mean to get in your face at Charlotte's. I'm just stressed, you know?"

"I know," I say. "We're good." I let him lead me away, because maybe this is Shane's way of saying he needs to talk. "Everything okay?" I ask.

"Me and Charlotte broke up." Shane pauses midstep, one arm still slung around my neck. "She went home, and I feel bad but . . . also kinda relieved, you know?"

"I know," I say. I can't blame the guy for wanting to be single for once in his teenage life. Or maybe date somebody he didn't discover a body with. "She'll be okay."

"S'better this way. Fresh start."

"Yeah. You guys could use that."

"It's just . . . everything got so messed up that day in the woods. And you said we can't talk about it, because that's the rule, right? It's like Fight Club, except we're not Fight Club. We're the Dead Body Club." Shane exhales a long, whiskey-soaked breath. "Thassa a bad name."

"I'm sorry, Shane. I didn't mean . . ." *I didn't mean to muzzle you. I just didn't want my dad exposed as a murderer.* "Is there something you want to talk about?"

"Maybe I should've said something about the fight," he says. "Cuz, like, what if that was important? I didn't say anything, and now fucking Gunnar Fox is all—" He waves an arm, almost toppling us over.

"What fight?" I ask, righting him.

"The one I heard in the woods. I never told the police."

Here it is: the perfect opportunity to ask Shane what he heard. I know Brynn said not to open Pandora's box, but Shane is already crawling halfway out, and I have to admit—I want to know. "What about it?" I ask. "Was it . . . Did you actually hear Mr. Larkin?"

"Yeah," Shane says. "He was yelling at somebody about the class-trip money."

I gape at him, dumbfounded. *The class-trip money.* That's

exactly what I was afraid Shane was going to say four years ago, because I thought Mr. Larkin had been arguing with my father. But now I know he wasn't, so who the hell else would fight with Mr. Larkin about that? Probably not Dexter Robbins, for one thing. "What did he say?" I ask.

"I couldn't hear everything," Shane says. "I didn't wanna get too close. But then the yelling stopped and I saw somebody walking away, and . . . it wasn't Mr. Larkin."

"Did you see who it was?" I ask.

"I think so. I mean, I was kind of far off, but I'm pretty sure I recognized him."

"Who?" I ask.

Then I realize I should stop him and go get Brynn, because she's definitely going to want to hear this. Before I can, though, Shane says, "Nick Gallagher."

My heart stutters, then seems to almost stop. *"What?"* I ask, just as I hear a loud gasp behind me. I turn and—

I don't have to get Brynn. She's right there.

Her eyes are enormous in her pale face. Before I can say a word, she spins on her heel and takes off, pushing her way through the crowd. "Brynn, wait!" I call, starting after her. But Shane is still draped all over me, holding me back. I catch sight of Ellie a few feet away, looking quizzical enough that I'm pretty sure she didn't overhear anything.

"Whoops," Shane says. "I can't do anything right tonight, can I? I need a drink. C'mon, you do too." He tries to steer me toward the lacrosse corner.

"Dude, not *now,*" I say, pulling away. But by the time I manage to break free, Brynn is nowhere in sight. Ellie is weaving through the crowded dance floor, craning her neck as she looks for her sister.

I can't wrap my head around what Shane just told me. When Brynn asked, "Who's left?" on the list of suspects in Mr. Larkin's murder, I sure as hell wouldn't have said *your uncle.* I gave her a hard time at Brightside Bakery about his alibi, sure, but that was only to prove the point that anybody from Saint Ambrose could've been in the woods that day. I never actually thought Nick Gallagher was, or that he had any reason to hurt Mr. Larkin. And why would they have fought about the class-trip money? Nick didn't take that; my mother did.

None of this makes sense. I need to find Brynn and sober Shane up, somehow, and then . . . I don't know. I'll figure out the rest later.

I push my way toward the center of the gymnasium and see that Ellie is already almost at the exit. When she reaches the doorway, she pauses, looking both ways. Then a figure crowds in behind her, blocking her from my view. Whoever it is glances over their shoulder, and—

"No," I say out loud, stopping short. Even from a distance I recognize the face, and it's completely out of context.

You shouldn't be here. What are you doing?

But there's no time to ask questions. Ellie is in the hallway now. She turns right, probably headed outside to look for Brynn. I pick up my pace to try to get to her through this crowd, because the person who shouldn't be here is right on her heels.

CHAPTER FORTY

BRYNN

I spot Uncle Nick just as he opens his car door, and race across the parking lot to catch him before he can slide into the driver's seat. "Where do you think you're going?" I yell, narrowly avoiding a patch of ice that would have sent me sprawling.

His brows raise at the brittleness of my tone. "Heading home," he says. "Where's your coat? It's freezing."

I don't feel the cold. I don't feel anything. "Why are you going home?" I ask. "The dance isn't over."

Uncle Nick lifts his hand from the door to adjust his glasses. "I'm a little tired. Not as young as I used to be, you know."

He gives me a smile that I can't return. "Uncle Nick, I need—"

Somebody laughs. It's a distance behind us, and when I turn, I see that it's just a couple running hand in hand toward the greenhouse. Still, it jars me enough that I open Uncle Nick's passenger door and climb inside.

"I need to talk to you," I say.

"Okay," Uncle Nick says cautiously. He gets behind the wheel and shuts the door, slipping the key into the ignition. "Let me turn on the heat so you can warm up."

"So . . ." There's no easy way to say this; I just have to blurt it out. "Uncle Nick, were you arguing with Mr. Larkin in the woods on the day he died?"

My uncle goes still. "What?"

I pause, wanting to live for a few more heartbeats in the space where I don't know anything bad. When I stalked through the gymnasium looking for Uncle Nick, memories flashed across my brain: My uncle telling me to take a step back from Mr. Larkin's murder case. Encouraging me to look into other true-crime cases instead of this one. Saying that Mr. Larkin had a way of *pressing buttons.* It all seemed so innocent, so typical Uncle Nick trying to sound like Dad, that I never imagined he might have something to hide.

If he truly *was* arguing with Mr. Larkin in the woods that day . . . If Shane wasn't mistaken, or lying . . . then what *else* did he do? My voice shakes as I say, "Shane said that he heard you, and saw you. He just told Tripp about it."

"Ahh." Uncle Nick heaves a deep sigh. Then he turns toward me, and as soon as I catch sight of his expression, I plunge my face into my hands. "Brynn?" he says, his voice hitching. "What are you . . . Can you please . . . Look, just let me explain, okay?"

"I c-c-can't—" I gasp, unable to finish the sentence. Because after one look at my uncle, I *know.*

I know he didn't hurt Mr. Larkin, and I'm hyperventilating with relief.

"Shit, I'm sorry," Uncle Nick says. "I never meant . . . I should've said something back then, but it was all so strange. I asked Will to meet me, because, well, I'd gotten this anonymous letter the day before he died . . ." Something soft brushes against my hands, and I lower them to take the wad of tissue Uncle Nick is shoving at me.

I'm not crying, but I swipe at my eyes anyway. "A letter? From who?"

"Anonymous," he reminds me gently. "And not actually for me. It was in my mail slot at school, but somebody had sorted it into the wrong compartment—Gallagher instead of Griswell. It was meant for the head of school, but I opened it before I noticed the name on the envelope. Whoever wrote it said that Mr. Larkin had stolen the class-trip money."

"What?" I twist the tissues in my hands.

"Yeah. This person said that they'd seen him take it, and wanted him fired. I wasn't sure what to do—Will was leading the investigation, for crying out loud. I was pretty sure he hadn't actually taken the money—"

"He didn't," I interrupt. "Tripp's mom did." Uncle Nick blinks, startled, and I add, "Whole other story. Keep going."

"Well, I worried about it all night. The next day, I decided to talk to Will, away from school. So I asked him if he wanted to meet me near Shelton Park for a hike. Once we'd been walking for a little while, I told him about the letter. And he—God, it was like he turned into a different person all of a sudden. He started yelling that I was after his job, and I'd probably written the letter myself. That *I* was the one who should be fired. I couldn't calm him down or get a word in, so I just . . . left."

"You left?" I echo.

"Yeah. You know how I am with confrontation," Uncle Nick says, and do I ever. He can barely handle my dad; I can't even imagine how he'd fare against the dark side of Mr. Larkin. "I figured I'd let him cool off, try again later, and then all of a sudden—I heard he was dead." Uncle Nick swallows hard. "I didn't know what to do. It took a few days before the police got around to interviewing me, and by the time they did, the money had been found. The note seemed like a bad joke. I wished I'd never brought it up with Will, and I was afraid that if I told the police he'd yelled at me about getting me fired right before he died—"

"You'd be blamed," I say.

"Yeah. Not very brave of me, I know. But that's what happened." Uncle Nick exhales noisily, like he's relieved to finally get it out. "I didn't realize anyone had heard us. Why didn't Shane say something before now?"

I'm too emotionally drained to explain Tripp's pact in the woods with Shane and Charlotte. "Did you keep the anonymous letter?" I ask instead.

Before Uncle Nick can reply, the rear passenger door flies open, startling us both. "What the hell?" Uncle Nick yelps as I twist in my seat, speechless at the sight of Tripp flinging himself into the car. Tripp is breathing heavily, eyes wild, and at first all I can think is that he followed me and heard everything. But if that's the case—why does he look terrified? This is good news, unless he doesn't believe Uncle Nick.

"Thank God," Tripp says hoarsely, and I blink with even more confusion. Then he slams a palm against the back of Uncle Nick's seat and adds in a rush, "We need to go. We can still find her. They just left."

"Find who?" I ask, bewildered.

Tripp ignores me, staring straight ahead, hitting Uncle Nick's seat harder as he yells, "*Drive!* Now! Just go!"

"Go where?" Uncle Nick asks, his face creased with concern. "Tripp, you need to calm down for a second. Please. Tell us what's happening."

Tripp takes a deep breath, steadying himself, before he grits out, "It's Ellie, okay? We need to find Ellie. Go left out of the parking lot. I saw them turn left."

A chasm opens up inside my chest. "Ellie?" I ask shakily.

Tripp finally meets my eyes, and the fear in his makes my stomach turn. "Brynn, he's here," he says. "I don't know how, or why, but he's here, and he just fucking *took* her. Shoved her into his truck and drove away."

Uncle Nick unfreezes, shifting the car into drive and slamming his foot on the accelerator in one fluid move. He speeds for the parking lot exit as I rasp out, "Who took her?" Even though I have the sinking feeling that I already know.

Like a hornet's nest.

Tripp's jaw tightens. "The guy from the pawnshop," he says.

CHAPTER FORTY-ONE

TRIPP

"What pawnshop?" Nick Gallagher asks as he tears out of the Saint Ambrose parking lot. "And where am I going?"

"I knew it. I *knew* he was Dexter Robbins," Brynn half moans, pulling out her phone. "This is all my fault."

"What's your fault?" Nick asks. "And who's Dexter?"

"Oh God," Brynn moans, clutching his arm. "Just drive, okay?" Despite everything, the energy between them seems okay, so I'm guessing Nick had a good explanation for why he was in the woods with Mr. Larkin. But that's hardly our biggest problem right now, so I don't ask. The last thing we need is a distracted Nick. We have to find Ellie, and fast, before she gets hurt and I spend the rest of my life hating myself for not getting to her in time.

I shouldn't have stopped in my tracks, not even for a minute, when I realized the guy from Last Chance Pawnshop was standing in our gymnasium. And once he started following

Ellie, I should've shoved every dancing classmate between me and her with enough force to knock them out of my way. Because by the time I made it outside, Pawnshop Guy was already shoving her into his truck. All I could do was run after them, way too late, and then run back toward school for help. Before I got there, I spotted Brynn in Nick's car.

"She has her Snapchat location on," Brynn says breathlessly. "It looks like they're on Binney Street."

"What the hell is happening?" Nick demands. "Is Ellie okay?"

Brynn ignores him and twists in her seat to look at me, her face a picture of misery. "It's my fault," she says again. "I never should have gone there. He must—he must have seen my license plate and tracked us down. Oh my God." She puts a hand over her mouth. "Wait a minute. We saw him in the Saint Ambrose parking lot tonight, didn't we? The truck that cut Mason off. And I didn't even realize . . . But why would he take *Ellie*?"

"What. Is. *Happening?*" Nick bites out. He's driving way too fast for the back roads of Sturgis, but there are barely any other cars on the street.

Brynn turns to face front again. "Dexter Robbins is Mr. Larkin's father," she says. "He's also an abusive asshole, and I don't think . . ." Her voice breaks a little. "I don't think he knew his son was dead until . . . recently."

"Will's father?" Nick asks blankly. "I don't understand."

"Just keep—" Brynn starts, but then we're on Binney Street and I catch sight of taillights in front of us, framing a license plate that starts with a six. That's all I remember from the truck that sped past me, and I lean forward between the seats.

"That's them," I say as the lines of the truck come into focus.

"Oh, thank God," Brynn cries out. Ellie's head is visible in the passenger seat, as close to the window—and as far from Dexter—as she can possibly get.

"Now what?" Nick asks, slowing to keep a couple of car lengths' distance between him and the red pickup. "Is Ellie in danger? What does this guy want?"

"I don't know," Brynn says, sounding near tears. "Make them stop."

"How am I supposed to do that?" Nick asks. "I can't— I don't want to turn this guy reckless. Not with Ellie in the car."

"I'm calling the police," I say, pulling out my phone. Which I probably should have done in the first place, except I wasn't thinking anywhere close to clearly.

"Good idea," Nick says.

"Don't lose them," Brynn urges her uncle as I dial 911.

"He's speeding up," Nick says, following the pickup into a sharp turn. "I think he caught sight of me."

"9-1-1, what's your emergency?" a voice says in my ear.

"Yeah, there's a—someone took my friend," I say. "In their car. Truck. We're following them, and—" Nick goes careening around a corner after Dexter, and I almost drop my phone.

"Are you in a moving vehicle right now?" the voice asks.

"Yeah," I say, watching the taillights weave in front of us. I'm not sure where we are. We can't be all that far from Saint Ambrose, but the road is dark and the streetlights few and far between. I can't see anything except masses of trees on either side of us. "We're in Sturgis, I think, or maybe Stafford, but—"

"Sir, I need to ask you to pull to the side of the road to continue this conversation," the operator says.

"I'm not driving," I say. "We're following a red Ford pickup truck. The license plate is six three seven oh—"

We hit a massive pothole, and this time my phone does go flying. "Damn it," I hiss, leaning forward to scramble for it.

"This isn't safe," Nick says. "He's going too fast, and these roads are dark. We need to stop and talk to the operator."

"No!" Brynn says urgently as I claw at the floor, searching for my phone. I can't reach far enough; I'm going to have to take off my seat belt. "We can't lose sight of her. *Please,* Uncle Nick. Please don't let him get away. You can't—"

Then she screams.

There's a screech of brakes, and Nick violently yanks the wheel to one side. I'm flung hard against my seat belt as the car spins, then slams so hard into something that every part of me rattles. Brynn is still screaming, and I think I must be too, or else Nick is, but—no.

He's not making a sound.

The car has stopped, its engine running. Headlights illuminate the gnarled bark of the tree we rammed into, visible through a still-intact windshield. No airbags inflated, so either Nick's car is so ancient that it doesn't have them, or we didn't crash hard enough to trigger them. Which seems impossible, but then again . . . I'm all in one piece. When I lean forward to check on Brynn, it looks like she is too. But Nick . . .

Nick Gallagher is slumped over the steering wheel, motionless.

"Brynn," I say, undoing my seat belt with shaking hands. "You guys okay?"

"I am," she says in a small voice. "But I don't know about . . ." She twists to look at me, eyes roving worriedly across my face before she turns to her uncle and puts a tentative hand on his arm. "Uncle Nick? Are you all right?"

He makes a slight groaning noise but doesn't move. Still, relief washes through me and I start searching for my phone again. "I had 9-1-1 on the line. Let me just—"

"Tripp," Brynn says in the same small voice. "Look."

CHAPTER FORTY-TWO

TRIPP

I raise my head. At first all I see is tree trunk, but then I notice movement to the right of the headlights. The figure of a man emerges, silhouetted against a red pickup truck parked along the side of the road. The man we think is Dexter Robbins is standing in front of us, staring into the windshield. As we stare back, he lifts one hand and beckons us with the gun he's holding.

A *gun*. Shit.

Out of the car, the gesture says.

"You stay," I tell Brynn. "I'll go."

"No," she says, opening her door before I have a chance to protest, and we both scramble out of the car much too fast for people about to face an armed man. I reach Brynn's side as the guy holds up his phone and points the flashlight app at us.

"There are two of you," he says. At first I think he means me and Brynn, but then he adds, "You twins?"

"Sisters," Brynn says, shivering in her sleeveless dress. I want to put an arm around her or give her my suit coat, but I'm afraid of making any sudden movements. Unlike with Mr. Solomon, I'm pretty sure this guy's gun isn't a scare tactic. "Is she okay?"

He ignores the question and keeps the bright light shining in our direction, making it impossible for me to see anything else. "It was you at the pawnshop," he says. "Not her. No wonder she couldn't tell me a goddamn thing."

Despite everything, I feel a stab of admiration for Ellie. She could have told him a lot of things, but she didn't. "We want to talk to her," I say. Dexter lowers the phone flashlight enough that I can see Ellie moving around in the passenger seat of the red pickup truck, but there's something stilted about the motion. Like she's being restrained.

"I don't give a fuck what you want," he says.

"Are you Dexter Robbins?" Brynn asks.

"I'm asking the questions here," he says. "You had Billy's medallion. Why?"

Which is answer enough.

"I—oh God." Brynn twists her hands, then casts a despairing glance behind her at a still-unmoving Nick. "He was my teacher. I knew him as William Larkin. I don't know if you even know this, but he . . . he died, four years ago." She pauses, waiting for a reaction.

Dexter snorts. "Yeah, I know. When you came along, flashing that medallion, I caught your license plate number and had a buddy of mine at the DMV look it up. Then I looked *you* up, trying to figure out what the hell your deal was. I ended up on the website for that fancy little school of yours, and there he was—goddamn *William Larkin.* Getting memorialized with a fucking garden." I'm shocked at the disgust in his voice—there's not a hint of grief or regret, anywhere. "Good riddance to him," Dexter adds. "No traitor who cuts me off and changes his name is a son of mine. Here's the thing, though—"

His voice turns musing as he continues. "Four years ago I hadn't talked to Billy in forever. Then all of a sudden he emails me out of the blue, bragging that he found his little brother at the school where he was teaching. Said he was gonna bring him by for my birthday, but after that? I never heard from him again. Figured he was full of shit like always, especially since he'd never even bothered to tell me he was a teacher. But he wasn't lying about that after all—so I figured, maybe he wasn't lying about Mikey either."

I can't think of anything to say in reply, but Dexter isn't looking at me anyway. He's laser focused on Brynn. "My youngest son. He'd be about your age, and if I know anything about his mother, I know this: she likes to put down roots. If Mikey grew up here, he probably lives here still. I saw online that you were having a dance tonight, so I showed up. I thought I'd recognize Mikey right away, but it was too crowded."

Bitterness tinges his voice. "Or maybe he's just been gone too long. Then I saw *you*—or I thought I did—and I figured, *that girl owes me some answers.*" He snorts again. "Your sister wasn't inclined to help, so I took her for a ride to let her know I mean business. And here we are. Now I'm gonna ask you the same thing I asked her: where's my boy?"

"I—I don't know," Brynn says, and gulps. "I only had that medallion because I was working on a story about Mr. Larkin for a true-crime show. I didn't know he even *had* a brother."

"I think you're lying," Dexter says.

"I'm not," Brynn says. They stare at one another for a few seconds in unnerving silence, until she adds, "Can you please let me see my sister? And call for help? I think . . ." She casts an anxious glance over her shoulder at Nick's car. "I think my uncle is hurt."

"Hope so," Dexter says shortly. Then he cocks his head. "You got a lot to say, don't you? But it's nothing I want to hear."

"Look, can we just—" I start, but Dexter silences me with a flick of the gun.

"How about we try a different tack?" he says, his eyes returning to Brynn. "I'll ask a question, and if I don't like your answer, I'll put a bullet through your sister. We'll start small, maybe with a hand, and work our way up."

"No!" Brynn screams as Dexter starts backing up toward the pickup truck. "Stop! I'll tell you whatever you want!" I feel sick then, because of course she will, she has to—but that means exposing Mason. Whatever happens after that is going to eat her alive.

"I'm out of patience, little girl," Dexter snarls, still moving. "You and your sister are about to learn what happens to people who play games with me."

There's a second when he lowers the gun as he approaches the passenger side of the pickup, when I think—*Can I reach him in time?* And I know I can't, but I'm still poised to try when a sudden roar fills my ears. I see movement out of the corner of my eye that makes me half turn, and Brynn lets out a surprised yelp as Nick Gallagher reverses his car away from the tree and then lurches forward. We're nowhere near its path, but I grab Brynn on instinct and yank her away. Both of us tumble to the ground as the car races past us. There's a sickening thudding sound, and then total silence except for the low rumble of the engine.

"Oh my God," Brynn whispers, her face buried in my shoulder. "What did he . . . What happened?"

I sit up slowly, cradling her in one arm, and try to make sense of the scene in front of me. Nick's car is stopped a few feet ahead of us, exhaust swirling around the tires. The pickup truck is still parked beside the road, with Ellie's shadowy figure moving inside.

And Dexter Robbins is nowhere in sight.

CHAPTER FORTY-THREE

TRIPP

"Come on in, Tripp." Ms. Gallagher opens the front door with a tentative smile. "Aren't those beautiful," she adds, nodding at the flowers in my hand. "Let me get a vase for them, and I'll bring them upstairs in a few minutes. Brynn's in her room." She lowers her voice and adds, "I'm glad she agreed to see you. She's been shut up by herself for too long."

I wanted to give the flowers to Brynn myself, but Ms. Gallagher looks like she's full of nervous energy that needs an outlet, so I hand them over. "How's Nick?" I ask, kicking off my sneakers and sliding them against the wall.

Her eyes get shiny. "The signs are positive. We're very hopeful."

It's been a week since we tailed Dexter Robbins from the Winter Dance to the Sturgis-Stafford town line—where he died when Nick Gallagher slammed into him with his half-wrecked car. Nick lost consciousness almost immediately after, and he's been in the hospital ever since. He's in much worse shape than either me or Brynn, because it turns out he never bothered to fasten his seat belt before taking off after Ellie. He revived enough in the car to take out Dexter, but the combined impact of hitting both the tree and Dexter was so traumatic that doctors put him into a medically induced coma until the swelling in his brain goes down.

Which I guess it hasn't, yet.

I pulled Ellie out of Dexter's pickup truck after Nick rammed into Dexter, and used one of my keys to cut the duct tape off her wrists. "I'm all right," she said, her voice surprisingly steady. "Is Brynn?" I looked over my shoulder then, to see Brynn standing with her arms dangling limply at her sides, an empty expression on her face.

"I don't know," I said. I still don't.

That night, the police brought us to the hospital to get checked out, and Brynn was like me after we found Mr. Solomon's body: practically catatonic. It scared me, because I thought maybe she'd been hurt in the accident and no one would tell me. But then one of the nurses pulled me aside. "There's nothing wrong with her, except that she's profoundly sad," the nurse told me. "She says everything is her fault."

I understood then, because if anyone knows that feeling, it's me.

In Brynn's case, she's dealing with the domino effect of accidentally leading Dexter to Saint Ambrose. Every single bad thing that happened after that—including Dexter's death and the fact that Nick ran him over—she blames herself for.

That's what Ellie says, anyway. I haven't heard it directly from Brynn, because she's not talking to me. Or anyone else.

She's been holed up in her room since last Saturday. In some ways, it's good that she's tucked away, because Sturgis has turned into a circus since the Winter Dance. Media vans are everywhere, with reporters crowding Saint Ambrose and downtown Sturgis, breathlessly analyzing every twist and turn of the story. *Motive* had a head start, of course, and Carly Diaz has been on the air constantly. I only watched one episode, the one where Rose from Mad Dog Tavern explained what kind of husband and father Dexter Robbins had been. Mason and his mother came forward with their real identities as soon as they learned about Dexter's death, and Rose seems determined to make sure there's no blowback for Ms. Rafferty's decision to take off with Mason years ago.

I don't think there will be. With Dexter gone, there's nobody alive, anymore, who wants to see either of them punished.

Brynn told Ellie about Nick and Mr. Larkin arguing the day he died, and Ellie told the police. Which turned out to be a good thing, probably, because Shane decided he's sick of keeping quiet and did the same thing. When Officer Patz interviewed me again, I told him as much truth as I could without edging into what I'd believed about my dad. I said I'd found the *Billy* medallion in the woods but hadn't known it belonged to Mr. Larkin, and I'd lied about being with Shane and Charlotte the whole time because we'd been scared.

Both of those things are technically true, so my lies were mostly of omission. Luckily, Officer Patz doesn't have Brynn's ability to know when I'm not being honest, or maybe he doesn't care. "You were just kids," he said when I'd finished. For the first time, it occurred to me that he might always have believed that. The waves of suspicion I used to feel coming off him were probably my own misplaced guilt.

I meant to tell him that Lisa Marie took the class-trip money. I really did, but when the time came, I couldn't get the words out. Dad offered to bring me back and do the talking, but I keep putting him off. It's hard to focus on anything until I know that Nick—and Brynn—are going to be okay.

Everybody in the media wants to talk to me, Shane, and Charlotte, but we're keeping a low profile. Meanwhile, reporters are having a great time diving into the Delgados' charitable contributions—even though they, and the Sturgis Police Foundation, insist there was no quid pro quo for that big donation the year Mr. Larkin died. I don't buy it for a second; there's no question that Mr. and Ms. Delgado wanted to smooth things over for Shane back then. They've been doing it his entire life, so why would they stop when his fingerprints were on a murder weapon?

It would be a silver lining to all this, for Shane's sake, if his parents started letting him figure out life on his own. I think he can handle a lot more than people give him credit for.

I'm lost in thought all the way up Brynn's stairs until a voice calls, "Tripp." Ellie's bedroom door is open, and she's sitting cross-legged on her bed in front of her laptop. "Hi," she says, giving me a wan smile. "Brynn just woke up."

I glance toward Brynn's bedroom door, which is still closed. "Should I wait, or—"

"No, go in. She's excited to see you." Ellie looks more like she wishes that were true than that she actually believes it, which makes my heart sink a little.

"Good," I say, but don't move right away. "How are you?"

"I am . . ." She trails off before lifting her shoulders in a shrug. "About the same."

"So, a low-key badass," I say, and she snorts.

"Yeah. Such a badass, getting kidnapped from the Saint Ambrose parking lot." Ellie closes her laptop and pushes it to the side. "My parents are going to make me see a therapist, so I can relive it on a weekly basis. Can't wait."

"Maybe it'll be good, to talk to somebody."

"Maybe." She traces the pattern on her bedspread with one finger. "It's not so much what Dexter did that gets to me. I barely remember that part; it's like I disassociated the whole time I was in his truck. But everything after . . . Uncle Nick being hurt . . ." She swallows hard, then makes a face. "Ugh. Sorry. It's not like *you're* getting paid to listen to this crap."

"I don't mind," I say.

Ellie waves me away. "Go see Brynn."

"You want to come with me to Brightside Bakery after this?" I ask impulsively. She raises her eyebrows, mildly curious, and I add, "My boss has it semi-closed for now, to keep reporters out. She's only letting her regulars in. So there are a lot of baked goods that need to be eaten. Also, she has a really fluffy dog who's exceptional at being petted."

"I see." Ellie nods. "Yes. I would like that."

"Great. I'll get you when I'm done. Maybe Brynn will want to come too." I don't have a lot of hope for that, but you never know.

"Okay," Ellie says, sounding a little more cheerful. "Oh!" she adds before I can turn away. "Guess who sent me those flowers?"

She gestures to a huge, gaudy bouquet on her dresser. Whoever it was, they were trying to make an impression. "Paige?" I ask.

"No. Mikhail Powers."

"Who?"

"Hello?" Ellie cocks her head. "*Mikhail Powers Investigates? The Bayview Four? I could be the next Maeve Rojas.*"

"I don't know what half those words mean."

She rolls her eyes. "You need to watch more true crime, Tripp."

"I'll take that under advisement," I say, even though I can't think of anything I'd like to do less.

I cross the hall and knock lightly on Brynn's door. "Come in," she says in a barely audible voice. She's in bed, propped up with a half dozen pillows, wearing a Saint Ambrose T-shirt. Her hair is loose and lifeless around her shoulders, and her face is expressionless.

"Hey," I say, closing the door behind me. "How are you?"

"Okay," she says. Her eyes are less glazed than they were the night Dexter died, but she still looks—What did the nurse say? *Profoundly sad.*

"Can I sit?" I ask. She nods, and I perch at the edge of her bed. I told myself on the way over that the right words would come once I was here. I hope they do.

"Are you feeling any better?" I ask. *Great start, Tripp.* She just shrugs. "You gonna go back to school anytime soon?"

She chews her bottom lip. "Eventually."

I could punch myself for that question. It's not like I care, and even if I did, I'm hardly the poster boy for showing up at Saint Ambrose after a crisis. I don't know why I asked, except that it suddenly feels impossible to talk to Brynn the way I used to. I'm too afraid of saying the wrong thing and making her feel even worse.

"I'm still pretty tired," Brynn says. "I don't know how long I can talk."

"Yeah, sure. I won't keep you," I say, like her next nap is a vitally important engagement she can't possibly miss. Then we both stare at her comforter. This is already excruciating, and I've been here less than a minute. I'm not sure why she agreed to see me, when she clearly doesn't want me here. Maybe I should leave.

The idea fills me with momentary relief until I think, *Coward. She didn't run away when you needed help.*

"Do you remember what you told me in Charlotte's guesthouse?" I ask.

Brynn blinks. "No? I mean, I said a lot of things. Which one?"

"You said, 'I want you to know you can trust me.' Right after you quit your internship." I pause, but she doesn't respond. Not even another blink. "I don't know if me quitting Brightside Bakery would have the same effect, exactly, but I'd do anything to let you know that you can trust me. You can tell me whatever you're thinking, no matter how dark it is, because chances are, I've thought it too. Recently."

Her eyes fill, but the tears don't spill over. For a few agonizing seconds I think she's not going to answer me, or even worse, she's going to turn away. Then she shifts to her left, as if to make more space on the bed. "Could you . . . sit closer?" she chokes out, pushing her covers aside.

I move next to her, my legs stretched the length of her bed, and gingerly put an arm around her shoulders. She grabs tightly on to my T-shirt and burrows into my chest. For a few minutes, we stay like that without speaking, and then she says, voice muffled, "I wish I'd never come back to Sturgis."

"I get it," I say.

"I wish I hadn't taken the job at *Motive*. Or gone to Mr. Solomon's, or Mad Dog Tavern, or the Winter Dance. Then none of this would have happened." Her breathing gets uneven. "Sometimes I even wish I hadn't met you. Or not *met*, obviously, because I already knew you, but—I wish we'd never started speaking again."

"That makes sense," I say, and I mean it. After Mr. Solomon died, I thought my own version of the same thing about Brynn.

"I'm so scared for Uncle Nick," Brynn says, her voice breaking. "And so sad for him too, because even if he wakes up . . . he killed Dexter. He's going to have to live with that, and he . . . he can't even stand to kill spiders. He puts them outside, every time."

"He was protecting Ellie," I say.

"That's my fault too. I got my sister kidnapped for a *story*. Because I couldn't let it go, even when everybody told me I should."

"I told you *not* to," I remind her.

"Not when it came to Dexter. You tried to warn me off."

"You didn't mean for any of this to happen," I say.

"But it did." She's crying now, full-body sobs that feel too big to fit into her small frame, and I wish there were a way to absorb them into mine. I hold her for what feels like an hour, even though it's probably less than ten minutes. I hear someone come up the stairs—her mother, maybe, with the flowers I brought—and go back down without knocking. Eventually Brynn's sobs taper off, changing to the occasional quiet gasp, and one of the hands grasping my T-shirt flattens over my heart. She sighs, like the steady beat is comforting.

"Can I tell you something?" I ask.

Her head moves against my chest. "Okay."

"I don't know much," I say, "but here's what I do know. I know that you weren't just chasing a story, you were trying to help people who were hurting find peace. I know that secrets can eat you alive, and the truth can break your heart, and sometimes it's hard to know which is worse." I can feel my T-shirt getting wetter, but Brynn is crying quietly this time. "I know that you can have the best intentions and still get the worst results. And I know"—I pull her closer and rest my chin on the top of her head—"that you won't always feel like this."

"I deserve to feel like this," she says.

"You don't. I promise you don't."

Brynn is quiet for such a long time that I'd think she'd fallen asleep if there were anything even remotely relaxed about her. But her posture is so stiff, and her breathing so shallow, that all I can think is that nothing I've said has made a difference. She's determined to punish herself, and who am I to say she shouldn't? I understand the compulsion; I did the same thing for four years. Maybe we're trapped in the kind of cycle you just can't break.

Then Brynn exhales a deep, shuddering breath and says, "Okay." After another long pause, she lifts her head and wipes her eyes before staring directly into mine. "I didn't mean what I said. I'm not sorry we started talking again."

Relief balloons in my chest, but I try not to show it. "It's fine if you—"

"I'm trying to have a moment, Tripp," Brynn says.

Even though I instantly recognize the call back to when I was in Charlotte's yard, drunkenly thanking Brynn for pulling the truth out of me about the day Mr. Larkin died, I'm not sure she meant to do it, until she offers a trace of her usual smile. It's the best thing I've seen all week. "I'm not sorry," she repeats. "I'm grateful."

I probably shouldn't, but—"Grateful enough to kiss me?" I ask, so she knows that I caught the reference. Then I pull a face so she doesn't think I'm actually trying to make that happen after she just finished crying on my shoulder.

"Not yet," Brynn says, dropping her head back to my chest. She keeps her hand over my heart, which starts beating faster when she adds, "But soon."

CHAPTER FORTY-FOUR

BRYNN

"So, call me when you get this," I tell Tripp's voicemail.

There's nothing I have to say to him that I couldn't text—just an update from my visit to the *Motive* office—but sometimes I really want to hear his voice.

It's only been a week since he came to see me in my bedroom, but the world already looks different. Later that night, we learned that Uncle Nick had improved enough that his doctors were going to start tapering off his medication. He woke up a few days ago, and even though he has a lot of recovery ahead of him, he was so much himself when I visited him in the hospital that I couldn't stop bawling.

"You're getting my blanket wet, cherished niece," he rasped.

"I'm so sorry," I sobbed, and he weakly patted my hand.

"Don't. I'm okay. You're okay. Ellie's okay. Everything else . . ."

He fell asleep before he could finish, but *everything else* is being handled by my dad. He's on a one-man mission to make sure that once Uncle Nick fully recovers, he has all the legal help he needs to handle what happened with Dexter and Mr. Larkin.

It's Dad's way of saying sorry for always giving Uncle Nick a hard time. I think we all realize now why Uncle Nick never moved on with his life after college. He and Tripp were trapped in the same purgatory over the past four years, afraid to tell the truth, and always wondering if they could have done something differently to save Mr. Larkin.

I've been keeping up with schoolwork at home, with Nadia and Mason taking turns stopping by with assignments. The first time I saw Mason, I couldn't stop apologizing, until he told me, not unkindly, to shut up. "You didn't mean for any of this to happen," he said, and even though Tripp had been hammering the same words into my head nonstop, it was still a relief to hear it from Mason. "And you'd never have figured out who I was if I hadn't gone full petty vandal, so . . . glass houses, is what I'm saying."

Then he gave me back mini-Mason "for company," which made me cry, like pretty much everything does lately.

This afternoon—when Mom took me to Back Bay so I could meet with Carly—was the longest time I've been away from my house since everything imploded at the Winter Dance. I wasn't sure what to expect at the *Motive* office, but it was actually pretty great. Carly had a catered lunch brought into Scarlet, and almost everyone came by to say hello. Including Andy, whose gift of a flowering cactus plant made me ashamed that I'd ever thought of him as "Blandy."

Afterward I sat with Carly and Lindzi alone so I could

apologize for stealing their files. "I know I should be mad at you," Carly said. "But I'm kind of impressed. Any chance you'd ever want to come back?"

"No," I said, so quickly that Lindzi snort-laughed.

"Text me if you change your mind," Carly said.

I almost did as soon as I reached the elevator. It's driving me more than a little crazy that after everything that's happened—all the lies and trauma and injury and death—we still don't know what happened to Mr. Larkin. Something keeps poking at the corners of my brain, a loose thread begging me to grasp it, but as soon as I try, the thought disappears.

I'm in my bedroom doing homework when my phone rings, and my heart skips when I see Tripp's name. I swipe and say, "Hi."

"Hey," he says. "How was Carly?"

"Good. She offered me my job back."

"Of course she did." He never had a doubt. "Did you take it?"

"What do you think?"

"I think you didn't, but you should."

"Right," I say, before adding, "Wait, really? Why?"

"Because you're a born reporter," he says. "And you miss it."

He's right, but I'm not ready to admit that. "What are you up to?" I ask instead.

"Deleting my email," he says. "I didn't get the Kendrick Scholarship."

"Oh no, I'm sorry," I say, my heart sinking for him.

"Eh, it's okay." He sounds surprisingly fine, maybe because he's not nearly as desperate to cut ties with his father as he was a month ago. "Martina deserved it more."

"Do you want to do something later?" I ask.

He takes so long to answer that I almost repeat the question. "I'm kind of already doing something," he finally says. "Something difficult."

"Oh?" I ask, and I straighten in my chair. His tone has gone serious. "What?" There's another lengthy pause, until I add, "Would it be easier with company?"

Tripp releases a long sigh. "Maybe?"

"Do you want me to come over?"

"I'm not at home," he says, before texting me an address.

At first I don't see Tripp when I get to the small, bright blue house at the edge of Sturgis Cemetery. Then I catch sight of my coatless boyfriend waving from the cemetery's nearest path. He's still in his Saint Ambrose blazer, his blond hair gleaming in the pale February sun and his cheeks red from the cold.

"Hey," I call over the short stone wall that separates the cemetery from whoever's property the blue house is on. "Taking a walk?"

"I like it here," Tripp calls back. "It's peaceful." When he reaches the stone wall, he leans over, cups my face in both hands, and kisses me until I forget we're supposed to be doing something difficult.

"I like it here too," I say breathlessly when he releases me. He grins and vaults over the wall as I add, "I parked in somebody's driveway, though."

"I know. That's where we're going," Tripp says, turning toward the front door. "This is where Lisa Marie has been staying. It's her friend Valerie's place."

I force myself to keep step with him, even though my first instinct is to stop in my tracks. "You're visiting your mom?" I ask.

"No." Tripp's features settle into a stoic expression, like he's steeling himself for bad news. "She's not here. And neither is Valerie. They're out for one last happy hour before Lisa Marie heads back to Vegas tomorrow." He jogs up the steps and then, to my surprise, reaches into the mailbox. "But Valerie left a key for me."

I blink as Tripp unlocks the door and holds it open. "Why?" I ask, crossing the threshold.

He shuts the door behind us. "So I could look for something."

We're in a neat-as-a-pin living room, the kind where you can tell everything has been carefully chosen to coordinate. The blue sky in a framed Thomas Kinkade print perfectly matches the rug, and the curtains and accent cushions look as though they were made from the exact same fabric. Tripp pulls his boots off and drops them onto a black rubber tray beside the door, and I do the same. "Valerie said Lisa Marie's room is at the end of the hall," Tripp says, turning to our right.

I'm dying to ask what he's looking for, but I'm pretty sure he'd tell me if he was ready to talk about it. So I just pad silently behind him until he opens the last door. "Yeah, definitely looks like Lisa Marie lives here," Tripp says, stepping into the room.

Compared to the rest of the house, it's a disaster area— unmade bed, clothes strewn everywhere, dishes piled on the desk and dressers, and a heap of wet towels directly in front of us. Tripp skirts past them and heads for a large suitcase in the corner, open and overflowing with more clothes. Then he pauses, reaches into his pocket, and pulls out a pair of plastic gloves.

I can't keep quiet any longer. "What are those for?"

"I don't want to leave fingerprints," he says.

My stomach twists with unease as he crouches beside the suitcase. "I thought Valerie said it was okay for you to be here?"

"She did," he says, unzipping a compartment inside the suitcase. He feels around, then repeats the process with another compartment.

"Can I do anything?" I ask, feeling equal parts useless and confused.

He turns and gives me a brief smile. "You're helping. Believe me," he says before returning to the suitcase. After sorting through all the clothes, he shuts the suitcase and unzips the front pocket. This time he reaches in and pulls out a bunch of crumpled bills. He stares at them for so long that I figure they must be what he was looking for, but then he shoves them back inside and swivels to face the bed.

"I'm gonna check under here," he mutters, lifting the bedspread.

I watch in silence as he methodically searches the rest of Lisa Marie's room—the bed, the dresser, the piles of clothes—before turning his attention to the closet. He starts with the top shelf, moving around a stack of blankets, and just when I'm about to burst with unasked questions, he goes suddenly, completely still.

"What's wrong?" I ask.

"I was hoping . . ." He swallows hard. "I was really hoping not to find this."

He pulls something off the shelf before turning to face me, and I let out an involuntary gasp when I see what's in his hands.

It's a fishing tackle box made of faded red plastic, its rusty latch unfastened, the letters *R.S.* written in black marker across the front. "Is that—"

"Mr. Solomon's?" Tripp holds it gingerly with both hands, as though he's afraid it might shatter. "Yeah, it is."

"How did you know . . ." I trail off, not sure how to best finish the question, but he doesn't need me to.

"I still haven't told Officer Patz that Lisa Marie took the class-trip money," Tripp says in a low, musing voice. "Dad keeps bugging me to do it, now that everything else has come out, and I started thinking how weird it is that money always goes missing when Lisa Marie is in town. I stopped by Mo's Barber Shop to talk with Valerie—she works there, and she's pretty cool, actually. Sick of my mother's shit, so we bonded over that." He huffs out a humorless laugh. "I asked her if Lisa Marie knew that Mr. Solomon used his tackle box as a bank, and she said yeah. Valerie had mentioned it to Lisa Marie, because that's how he paid when he got his hair cut."

"Oh," I say softly. *Oh no.*

"Yeah," Tripp says. "And Valerie said Lisa Marie hasn't been hitting her up for money lately, which we agreed isn't like her, especially since she's allegedly broke. So—long story short, Valerie offered to look through Lisa Marie's stuff. I asked if I could do it, because I needed . . . I don't know. I think I needed to see for myself." He sets the box down carefully on the unmade bed. "What did the police say, again? That Mr. Solomon might've fallen, or he might've . . . been pushed."

I don't know what to say, so I just reach for his hand.

"My mother could have killed him," Tripp says, staring at the box. "Maybe accidentally, but maybe not." His voice takes on a strangled tone as he adds, "So then I started thinking . . . what if she did something to Mr. Larkin too? She's the one who took the class-trip money. She was in town, but she lied about it until she thought Gunnar Fox was going to make her a star. And she . . ."

"Tripp, stop," I say, squeezing his hand. The reporter in me has a few immediate theories about that—number one being that Lisa Marie is too smart to partner with a true-crime show that's investigating a murder she committed. But the last thing I want, or that Tripp needs, is for him to spend another four years obsessing over a parent's potential guilt in a murder. I cup my palm against his face and turn it toward mine, forcing his eyes away from Mr. Solomon's fishing tackle box. "You don't know if any of that is true, and it's not your job to find out."

"Yeah, I know. Been there, done that," Tripp says, pulling his phone from his pocket. "I just needed to talk it through for a minute. Remind myself why I'm doing a difficult thing."

He holds my gaze for another beat, then takes a deep breath and presses his keypad. My heart swells, and the words *I love you* rush into my brain with so much force that I almost blurt them out. But I manage to stop myself, because I don't want this to be the first time he hears me say it. Instead I stand quietly by his side as he puts the phone to his ear and says, "Hey, Officer Patz, it's Tripp Talbot. I need to report a theft."

EPILOGUE

BRYNN

Almost there, the text reads.

Good. I've been standing near the Saint Ambrose green-house for fifteen minutes, shivering in the late February cold and wondering if I'm being stood up. Not by Tripp, but by someone I haven't seen much of in the past few weeks.

I pull my hat down lower over my ears and scroll through the rest of my texts, then linger on one from Tripp. It's a picture of Al sound asleep in the storage room at Brightside Bakery, and it's so cute that it makes me smile every time I see it. But that's not why I keep pulling it up; it's because I like to see the *Love you* he sent afterward.

We've said it in person now, but this is the first text version, and I'm a big enough nerd that I screenshotted it.

Then I reply with a heart to a picture of Uncle Nick giving a thumbs-up after physical therapy. His lawyer stopped by yesterday, letting us know that there wouldn't be any criminal charges in Dexter's death, and that the Sturgis Police don't consider Uncle Nick a suspect in Mr. Larkin's murder. "Maybe it really was a drifter after all," the lawyer said before she left.

But I know better. At least, I think I do.

The wind stings my eyes and blurs my vision as I hunch my shoulders and squint at the horizon. Is that—yes. *Finally.* I hold up a hand, and get a languid wave in return.

"Sorry I'm late," Charlotte says, stopping a few feet away. She's wearing a stylish black coat and no hat, and she pushes back her chestnut hair with one hand as she gazes around us. "To . . . whatever this is. Why are we here?"

I don't have a great answer, except for the fact that in some ways, this is where it all started—the committee meeting that paired me up with Tripp. "I like it here," I say. "And I wanted to talk privately." There's a loud whistle then, as the baseball team takes the field below us for what they're optimistically calling *spring training.* "But not too privately."

Charlotte arches a brow. "What an interesting beginning."

"Here's the thing," I say. "I can't stop thinking about Mr. Larkin—"

"That's your first mistake," Charlotte interrupts.

"You told me in the auditorium during the Winter Dance that it might be dangerous to keep poking around, which turned out to be true. But you also said I might not like what I found, and I'm wondering . . . Why did you say that?"

Charlotte's cool gaze roves over me for a few seconds before she replies, "Your uncle, of course. The argument in the woods with Mr. Larkin. I'm surprised the police aren't more concerned, to be honest."

"But Shane was alone when he heard that," I say. That came out during Shane's recent interviews with the police; he'd been by himself, separated from Tripp and on his way to meet Charlotte, when he came across Mr. Larkin's body. A few minutes later, he said, Charlotte emerged through the trees and started screaming. I assume the police interviewed Charlotte again too, but if so, she's been tight-lipped about it. "You weren't with him."

Charlotte blinks before offering a polite smile. "I heard it too."

"Yeah," I say. "That's what I thought." Her brow knits, and I add, "It doesn't make sense, you know. All this drama swirling around Mr. Larkin—the abusive dad, the brother in hiding, the stolen money, the argument with Uncle Nick—it just doesn't make sense that *none* of that would be related to his murder. So I started thinking: What if *all* of it is?"

"Oh good." Charlotte's lips curl into a smirk. "You're sharing theories. Why am I the lucky Watson to your Holmes, exactly?"

"Because of what you said in the auditorium."

"Look, Brynn, I was having a bad night," Charlotte says with her first touch of impatience. "I don't even remember telling you to stop poking around, but—"

"It's not that," I interrupt her. "You said, '*Mason* is Mr. Larkin's brother?'"

She shrugs. "So? I'd just heard the two of you talking."

"Yeah, but it wasn't your question that's been nagging at me. It's the emphasis you put on Mason's name. '*Mason* is Mr. Larkin's brother?'" I repeat. "If that were the first you'd ever

351

heard of Mr. Larkin having a brother at Saint Ambrose, you wouldn't have said it like that. You would have emphasized a different word. You would have said, 'Mason is Mr. Larkin's *brother?*'"

Charlotte's not wearing a scarf, so I can see her nervous swallow, and goose bumps erupt on my arms that have nothing to do with the cold. But her voice is as calm as ever when she says. "Sorry, but I don't see why that matters. You probably heard wrong, anyway. You were pretty stressed."

"I heard you fine. Here's what I think: I think you said it that way because you already knew that Mr. Larkin had a brother at Saint Ambrose—but until right then, in the auditorium, you thought it was Shane." I feel a spark of triumph when Charlotte swallows again. "You used to follow Shane around all the time in eighth grade, and his locker is right next to where Mr. Larkin's classroom was. I think you went looking for him the day Mr. Larkin told Mason who he was, and you stopped outside the classroom while they were talking. Or rather, while Mr. Larkin was talking, because Mason didn't say a word. I think you listened, saw Mr. Larkin leave, and then saw Shane come out of the classroom. He'd been asleep in the coatroom, but you didn't know that. And you didn't know that Mason was still sitting where Mr. Larkin had left him, totally shell-shocked and silent. All you saw was Shane, so you thought he'd just learned about a half brother who wanted to send him back to a dangerous father."

Charlotte, composed again, lets out a light, dismissive laugh. "Your imagination is something else, Brynn. Forget reporting. It's a waste of your talents. You should be a novelist."

"I think you wanted to help Shane," I continue. "You'd do anything for him, right? So first you wrote an anonymous letter to Mr. Griswell, accusing Mr. Larkin of stealing the class-trip money. That's the kind of thing kids our age would do—take care of the problem by getting rid of the source. But my uncle got the letter by mistake and talked to Mr. Larkin in the woods near Shelton Park—right when you were there, about to meet up with Shane. So, yeah, you heard that conversation."

I advance a few steps, keeping my eyes locked on Charlotte's. "After that, you knew what you were up against with Mr. Larkin. He wasn't the kind of guy who would back off because of an anonymous letter, or who'd be intimidated by your family. He *liked* a fight. What did you say in the library?" I move closer still, not waiting for a response. " 'There's more than one way to be awful.' Mr. Larkin must have seemed pretty awful to you then. I think you were angry, and—you struck out. Before Mr. Larkin even realized you were there." I drop my eyes to her hands, encased in soft leather gloves. "And you didn't leave fingerprints, because you were wearing those. Or something like them."

"Wow," Charlotte says as the wind artfully tosses her hair like it was hired for that exact purpose. "You're really going all in on this."

"I don't think you meant to kill him," I say. I can picture eighth-grade Charlotte vividly in my mind's eye, unable to believe what she'd done. She probably stood frozen beside Mr. Larkin's body until she heard Shane approaching, then hid—hoping, maybe, that Shane would pass a different way and not notice Mr. Larkin. But he did, and Charlotte had to make a choice: keep hiding and tell people that she'd decided not to meet Shane in the woods after all, or join him and pretend to be shocked.

As always, Charlotte picked the option that brought her closer to Shane.

"It was an unlucky blow," I continue. "But you weren't willing to take the blame—and Tripp gave you an out. You didn't know why, but you were happy to take it. And you've been keeping him close ever since."

Charlotte can't help herself. "Not lately," she points out.

"Not by choice," I counter.

When I first shared this theory with Tripp, he resisted it, and I can't blame him. In a lot of ways, Charlotte was a good friend to him. But the more we talked about it, the more he started to come around—and even though he won't say it, I think part of him is relieved that Charlotte as Mr. Larkin's killer makes more sense than Lisa Marie. He wanted to come with me today, but I didn't think it was a good idea. I didn't think Charlotte would let anything slip if he were here.

We stare at each other in silence, until Charlotte finally asks, "Are you done?"

"Yes," I say, straightening my shoulders against my body's sudden, almost irresistible desire to go limp.

"Good," she says. "This was an interesting little delusion of yours, but that's all it is, and you don't have a shred of proof that says otherwise." Her crystal-blue eyes bore into mine. "I wouldn't recommend you go around repeating this. Not everybody has my patience."

I nod, unfazed by the polite threat. I'm only surprised it

took her this long. She turns to walk away, and I say, "Bye, Charlotte."

"Get help," she calls without looking back.

Maybe I shouldn't have confronted her, but the thing about Charlotte is—I'm pretty sure it's better to see her coming. And she's not entirely right; I have a *little* proof.

Last night I took my photocopy of the anonymous letter Uncle Nick had received—he'd kept it all these years and had managed to dig it up. I brought it to the attic and rooted through my box of Saint Ambrose middle-school mementos until I found what I was looking for: the binder containing the leaf project I'd done with Charlotte back in eighth grade. After everything that had happened with Mr. Larkin, we were late turning it in, and I did almost all the work. Charlotte's only contribution was a neatly written cover page with our names.

The anonymous letter accusing Mr. Larkin was typed, but the envelope it came in was handwritten—and the writing matched our leaf project cover page. In particular, the *G* in *Griswell* looked identical to the *G* in *Gallagher*—more like the number six than a letter.

It's not much, I know. And I'm not sure, honestly, whether I hope Charlotte ultimately gets punished for what she did. I meant it when I said that I don't think she intended to kill Mr. Larkin. But she did, and a lot of people suffered because she wouldn't own up to it. I don't want Charlotte to spend the rest of her life doing whatever she wants, to whoever she wants, without ever having to answer for it. Because when that happens, you end up with a Lisa Marie.

Those matching *G*s aren't proof that Charlotte killed Mr.

Larkin, but they're a start. Step one, if you will. I watch Charlotte walk away until she's just a dot in the distance, and then unlock my phone and search out yesterday's text from Carly.

We still miss you at Motive. Can I convince you to come back?

Step two, I think, before replying: *Yes. How about tomorrow?*

ACKNOWLEDGMENTS

Nothing More to Tell is my pandemic book; a story I started writing in the spring of 2020, building off a mystery idea that I'd had years before. I struggled to get it off the ground for months, blaming the chaos of the world around me, before realizing I'd centered the story on the wrong characters. Once I reimagined my two protagonists from the ground up, the book took off and was pure joy to write.

I dedicated *Nothing More to Tell* to my agents Rosemary Stimola and Allison Remcheck not only because I wouldn't have a career without these two amazing women, but because their early insight into this book was invaluable. The entire team at Stimola Literary Studio is incredible, and I'm especially thankful to Alli Hellegers for her work on the international side, and to Pete Ryan and Nick Croce for their help in managing operations.

This is my sixth book with Delacorte Press, and I'm a much better writer now than I was at the beginning thanks to my brilliant editor, Krista Marino, who always takes my stories to levels that I wasn't sure they could reach. Thank you to my publishers, Beverly Horowitz, Judith Haut, and Barbara

Marcus, for all your support, and to the terrific team at Delacorte Press and Random House Children's Books, including Kathy Dunn, Lydia Gregovic, Dominique Cimina, Kate Keating, Elizabeth Ward, Jules Kelly, Kelly McGauley, Jenn Inzetta, Emma Benshoff, Adrienne Weintraub, Felicia Frazier, Becky Green, Enid Chaban, Kimberly Langus, Kerry Milliron, Colleen Fellingham, Alison Impey, Kenneth Crossland, Martha Rago, Tracy Heydweiller, Tamar Schwartz, Linda Palladino, and Denise DeGennaro.

Thank you to my stellar international rights colleagues at Intercontinental Literary Agency, Thomas Schlueck Agency, and Rights People for finding homes around the world for *Nothing More to Tell*. I'm grateful to my international editors and publishers for their support of this title, and my career overall.

Thanks to Kit Frick for your thoughtful feedback on this manuscript, to Mom and Dad for your support, and to my sister Lynne for being my first reader (thanks also to Lynne and Luis Fernando for letting me borrow your dog, Al, for a small but critical role in *Nothing More to Tell*). Thanks to my son, Jack; my nieces, Gabriela and Carolina; and my nephew, Erik, who are suddenly my target audience and occasionally my unpaid social media consultants. I'm the most grateful to my niece, Shalyn, for her beautiful illustrations of my characters. Thanks also to my two book clubs, my EC neighbors, and the Holden crew, all of whom helped me celebrate some big moments this year. And finally, a huge thank-you to readers, who continue to show up for my books in a way that makes me deeply grateful and reminds me of the importance of telling stories.

ABOUT THE AUTHOR

Karen M. McManus is a #1 *New York Times* and internationally bestselling author of young adult thrillers. Her books include the One of Us Is Lying series, which has been turned into a television show on Peacock, as well as the standalone novels *Two Can Keep a Secret, The Cousins, You'll Be the Death of Me,* and *Nothing More to Tell.* Karen's critically acclaimed, award-winning work has been translated into more than forty languages. To learn more about Karen and her books, visit karenmcmanus.com or follow @writerkmc on Twitter and Instagram.